$2-01$

PRAISE FOR ANITA MILLS
AND HER NOVELS

DANGEROUS
"A gem of a book from this versatile storyteller."
—*Romantic Times*

COMANCHE ROSE
"An emotional and authentic Western tale that
will pull at your heartstrings. . . . A gripping
story about the healing power of love."
—Joan Johnston

"A Texas-size love story . . . with a
tough yet tender hero."
—Georgina Gentry

COMANCHE MOON
"A perfect blend of wild west adventure and romance. I really enjoyed this story. A must read
for anyone who loves a good western romance."
—Rosanne Bittner

"A superb western romance that grabs you by the
throat and won't let go. . . . I loved it!"
—Joan Johnston

SECRET NIGHTS
"Tautly written and packed with suspense . . .
a moving story."
—*Publishers Weekly*

FALLING STARS
"A superlative love story of remarkable
depth and power."
—*Romantic Times*

Bittersweet

by
Anita Mills

A TOPAZ BOOK

TOPAZ
Published by the Penguin Group
Penguin Putnam Inc., 375 Hudson Street,
New York, New York 10014, U.S.A.
Penguin Books Ltd, 27 Wrights Lane,
London W8 5TZ, England
Penguin Books Australia Ltd, Ringwood,
Victoria, Australia
Penguin Books Canada Ltd, 10 Alcorn Avenue,
Toronto, Ontario, Canada M4V 3B2
Penguin Books (N.Z.) Ltd, 182–190 Wairau Road,
Auckland 10, New Zealand

Penguin Books Ltd, Registered Offices:
Harmondsworth, Middlesex, England

First published by Topaz, an imprint of Dutton Signet,
a member of Penguin Putnam Inc.

First Printing, November, 1997
10 9 8 7 6 5 4 3 2 1

 REGISTERED TRADEMARK—MARCA REGISTRADA

Printed in the United States of America

This book is dedicated to the memory of my grandmother, Laura Springs Tracy, who left the relative comfort of St. Joseph, Missouri, to begin her grand adventure as a bride, following her railroader husband west through Nebraska to the Wyoming wilderness. Her grit and her resourcefulness served as an example and an inspiration to her six children and to me, the granddaughter whom circumstance made the cherished child of her old age.

Many were the nights when I crawled under the quilts with her to listen to stories of how life had been when she was young. She's been gone from this earth a long time now, but I still marvel at all she accomplished and the many, many things she saw change in her ninety years. She was my grandmother, mother, confidante, and cherished friend, compactly wrapped together in that one short, rotund body, and I will miss her always.

Exhausted, Spencer Hardin leaned against the crude table and closed his eyes, seeking a moment of respite before another wounded soldier came in. For nearly twenty hours straight, he'd dissected muscle and sawed bone at a frantic pace, while his surgical assistants had held one hundred and twenty-three struggling men down. With no ether, chloroform, or opiate to ease the suffering, he'd had to shut his ears to the desperate pleas, screams, and whimpers of those losing limbs. It was a cacophony of hell without end.

Carried on the lips of the wounded, the bad news of a battle lost had grown steadily worse throughout the night. By daylight, the body count had begun, confirming the enormity of Hood's defeat. Twelve Confederate generals lost in two hours. More than fifty regimental commanders killed. The casualty lists went on and on, numbering not in hundreds, but in thousands.

"You're done in, Hardin."

He felt the weight of Ben Morton's hand on his shoulder. "I'm all right," Spence responded wearily. "I was just resting my eyes, that's all."

"You're fagged to death—that's what you are," the senior staff surgeon insisted. "You're the best leg man around, and I can't afford for you to get yourself down. Go get some sleep, and don't come back until six-thirty—I wish it was more, but that's all the time I can spare you."

"Thanks."

He didn't think he could sleep, but Spence was in no shape to argue. Plunging his hands in the wash bucket, he looked down at his blood-caked arms, at his soaked surgical apron, and he saw the young soldier being lifted to his table. The boy was going to lose an arm and a leg, and there was nothing he could do about it. He just felt helpless and defeated by the overwhelming number of wounded. And he knew he had to get away from the stifling stench of blood.

Outside, as the chill air hit him, he leaned his head against the nearest tree and wept. He'd trained as a surgeon, but he'd become a butcher.

"You all right, Doc?"

Caught, Spence straightened his shoulders. "I'm just tired."

"Gets to a body, don't it?" the soldier observed. "I been bringin' 'em in since midnight, and we still got men lying ten feet deep where they fell," he added, shaking his head. "sometimes I hear 'em crying, but by the time I can get to 'em, they're gone." He looked away for a moment, then his haunted eyes met Spence's again. "Those I know won't survive the ride in, I'm having to leave 'em out there. I feel like I'm playing God, but I know I got to do it."

"You do the best with what you've got—that's all anybody can ask of you," Spence consoled him.

"Guess I got it better'n you, don't I? Least I'm not cuttin' off pieces of 'em."

"You probably save as many lives as I do."

"You can't think that, Doc. You got a gift for what you do, and ever'body knows it. If I had to lose m' leg to live, you'd be the one I'd want taking it."

"Thanks."

"Well, I got to go back now, but I just wanted you to know you're the best, Doc."

"Thanks. Between the both of us, maybe we'll do some good."

"I got no doubts about that, Doc."

Passing the hospital tents, Spence stopped, then retraced his steps to the tent marked "Ward A," thinking to tell Mrs. Barnes to soak bandaged stumps in turpentine if she ran out of everything else.

He'd barely ducked through the flap door before she grabbed his arm, pleading, "You've got to help me, Dr. Hardin! The wounded are packed so tightly in here that they are lying upon one another, and yet they keep sending me more. I don't even have blankets to cover what I've got, and I'm at my wit's end, sir, my wit's end!"

"I know."

"We've got to have blankets. If I cannot keep these men warm, they'll perish from shock, sir—don't we owe our men more than this?"

"You'll have to take what you can from the dead," he decided. "At least they're past knowing."

"We've done that. Blankets, clothing, everything— even the bandages—and there's still not enough!"

she cried. "I'm just a nurse, but you are a doctor—they'll listen to you! Tell them I cannot keep this ward running with nothing!"

"Mrs. Barnes," he said wearily, "I'm amputating limbs with nothing—not even a drop of whiskey—to kill the pain of a capital saw biting through bone."

"But they've lost so much blood, it makes them cold. Most of them are without beds or pallets even, and the ground's too damp for them."

"I know." He fumbled with the brass buttons, working them through the buttonholes. "Here," he told her wearily, handing her his coat. "Wrap this around somebody."

"Oh, I couldn't . . . I didn't mean . . ."

"I've got another one."

"Hardin! Spence Hardin!" someone called out. "Over here!"

Sarah Barnes sighed. "It's Captain Donnelly again," she said, betraying disgust. "If I could, I'd wish him out of here, and I truly mean it. He thinks I have naught to do but wait on him."

"I'll take care of it." Turning around, he scanned shivering men packed side to side and end to end so closely that anywhere he went in the tent, he'd be stepping over someone. He spied Ross Donnelly lying on one of the few cots, covered with a heavy blanket, and he waded over bodies getting to him. "Damned if it didn't take you long enough to get here," the Georgian told him sourly. "I've been hollerin' for whiskey for hours, and all I get is water."

"It's all she's got."

"But you can get me some, can't you? Dammit,

"Yeah."

"I want that medical discharge, Spence," Ross said, returning to the matter at hand. "I'll be damned before I'll die for nothing. All we've got left now is Bobby Lee, and while he's the best of 'em all, North and South, he's not God Almighty."

"There's bound to be somebody around Macon who'd take you in."

"Maybe so. You know, the Jamisons and Donnellys have been friendly all my life. Why, I've known Lydia ever since she was born, bein' as Blackwood's right up the river from Jamison's Landing.There was even some talk between Cullen and my daddy about puttin' 'em together, but Lydia never had any particularity for me, so it never worked out. I always thought she was too stuck on herself just because Cullen had all that money, and she told Phoebe the earth'd have to run out of men before she'd look at me."

"Yeah?"

"I know it'd be a lot to ask . . ." Ross hesitated for a moment, waiting for encouragement, but when Spence didn't say anything, he came to the point. "Do you think Lydia'd mind if I was to stay at Jamison's Landing? I'd do anything I could for her until you can get home yourself, and I don't mind Sally— hell, the woman's like a mother to me, Spence. She's more'n a little flighty, but there's not a mean bone in her body. I reckon I could try to keep her out of Lydia's hair some."

For a moment, Spence wondered what Liddy would think of the idea, considering she'd expressed a real disdain for Ross's wild ways. "I'd have to tell her you've changed, and you'll have to make her believe it," he said finally.

"Would you? You tell her I'd be mighty obliged if she'd take me in, and I won't be making any trouble for her. I won't forget this, Spence, I swear it. Anything you ever need from me, you've got it. But I've got to get away from this war before I get my head blown off."

"Dr. Hardin! Colonel Henry's convulsing!" Mrs. Barnes called out.

"I've got to go, but I'll see what I can do," Spence promised. "It might work out for both of us."

He reached Matthew Henry as the colonel gave one last gasp. "He's gone," he said simply, looking to Mrs. Barnes. As he closed Henry's eyes, Spence heard her say softly, "It's a blessing, isn't it? He didn't know how he'd manage without his arms."

As Spence emerged from the tent, he felt a profound relief for Matt Henry, a lesser one for himself. Self-centered or not, Ross Donnelly could sure lift a burden from his shoulders. With somebody there, maybe Lydia's anxiety wouldn't turn into a full-blown hysteria. It was worth a try, anyway.

"Doc! Doc, it's me—Danny Lane!" a kid said breathlessly.

"What is it?"

Lane shifted his weight from one foot to the other, hesitating before he blurted out, "It's Jesse Taylor—my sister's husband, Doc." Swallowing hard, he explained, "He's took a ball in his leg—went plumb through it. I know it's against regulations, sir, but the regulations is wrong. If maybe you'd just give it a look, sir, 'cause he says he ain't giving it up."

"I was headed to bed, but Winters is taking my place."

On the verge of tears, the young ambulance driver caught Spence's coat. "But Winters'll saw it off, Doc! All the way in here, I been tellin' Jesse you're a real decent sort, that if anybody'd make a try at saving it, you would, and . . ." His voice broke, then he mastered it. "It'd be real hard on Laurie if he wasn't to come home, Doc—it'd kill her."

"I see."

"Please—he's all she's got."

Attempts to save a limb which in civil life could be saved cannot be made. Gunshot fractures of the thigh, bullet wounds to the knee, and similar injuries to the leg, which at first sight may make amputation seem unnecessary, must always in the field require the sacrifice of the limb. Primary amputation done within the first twenty-four hours is critical, reducing the high rate of infection and ultimately saving more lives. The directive wasn't open to interpretation, and Spence knew it.

"I'm not in any shape to do anybody any good right now. I'm sorry."

"She never had anything, you know. Our folks both died while we was little. Laurie wasn't even twelve yet, but she raised me. I can't let her down, Doc."

He liked Danny. The kid had never shirked his gruesome duty of picking through the dead to find the living, which was more than could be said of men older than he was. "All right," he decided. "I'll take a look, but—"

"You hear that, Jess? He's gonna fix it!" the kid crowed as he climbed into the ambulance wagon.

Holding the canvas for Spence, he said low, "Jesse's a mite tetchy now. I kinda had to land him one upside his head to get him in."

The smells of straw, sweat, and blood hit Spence as he crawled inside. Before his eyes adjusted to the dimness, he heard the unmistakable click of a gun hammer being cocked, and he felt the cold steel barrel against his neck.

"Don't move, mister," Taylor warned him.

"Don't, Jess—it's the doc!"

"Nobody's touching my leg, Danny. I came into this world with two of 'em, and I'll be leaving it the same way."

"Jess, he ain't like most of 'em, I swear to God he ain't. Just let him have a look, that's all I'm asking," Danny pleaded.

"He touches it, I pull this trigger."

Not giving up, Danny looked to Spence. "Tell 'im, Doc—tell 'im he don't want blood poisonin'. Jess, look—he don't even have a saw with him."

"If he knows what's good for him, he'll back out real easy."

"He ain't armed, Jess. It'd be murder—just plain murder. You ain't no murderer, and you know it," the kid argued. "You wouldn't hurt a fly less'n it was a Yankee. All I'm asking is for you to let him look."

"I'm not on duty," Spence said quietly. "If there's any cutting, it'd be Winters doing it."

"I've got no faith in an army quack," the man growled.

"I was trained at the Medical College of South Carolina as a surgeon," Spence told him evenly. "And if you don't put the gun down now, you can take your leg to hell for all I care."

There was a strained pause, then Jesse Taylor slowly uncocked the revolver and lay back, closing his eyes. "Well, you're either a brave man or a damned fool, so look it over, tell him there's nothing to do but cut it off, then get the hell out of here."

"I can't tell until I see it. Danny, my field kit's in my tent, under my cot. And just in case, maybe you'd better round up a pair of leg splints. Tell Winters I've got a broken leg to treat."

"Yessir!"

Spence went to work, carefully loosening the blood-soaked cloth around the wound. "I'll have to probe it first."

"Bone's broke," Taylor managed through clenched teeth. "Bullet went clean through it, taking a hunk of the leg in back."

"I see that. If the lead and bone fragments aren't cleaned out, there's a risk of gangrene."

"Just don't get out the saw—I'll stand damned near anything but that."

"I got the kit, and the splints is coming," Danny declared over Spence's shoulder. "It's gonna be all right, ain't it?"

"I don't know yet."

Forgetting his fatigue, Spence cut the pant leg, exposing the wound. Feeling underneath, he could tell there was considerable damage. Nonetheless, he probed the entry hole, finding bits of bone embedded in the soft tissue. He'd have to section the muscle to see how much of the femur had been lost. "You'd better hold on," he warned Jesse Taylor. Nodding to

Danny, he added, "Light that lantern and hold it close—off to the right a little, but close."

As he cut, probed, and picked around the broken femur, the man never made a sound. Spence worked meticulously, finding each sliver, exchanging the probe for needle-nosed forceps, retrieving every bit he could. The air was chilly, but he was sweating when he sat back and reached for the stoppered bottle.

"Soon as I get a little of this in there, I'll force the bone together, and splint it. You'd better sit on his shins, Danny."

"Jesus God!" Taylor gasped, bucking when the permanganate hit the open wound.

As he left the ambulance, Spence felt pretty good about Taylor's chances. Barring infection, the man would be limping home with both legs, but one was going to be a little shorter than the other.

In his tent, he hung his coat over the chair, washed his hands in the water bucket, then sat to remove his boots. His gaze strayed to Lydia's picture, taking in the incredibly beautiful woman and the small boy on her lap. God, it had been so long since he'd been home to see them. Every time he looked at that picture, the yearning he felt was nearly unbearable.

Poor Liddy. Nothing in her twenty-two years had prepared her for this. Born rich and beautiful, she'd been Cullen Jamison's little princess, and he'd brought her up to believe she could have anything she wanted. Incredibly, she'd wanted a young doctor barely out of medical college.

Reaching behind the photograph, he retrieved her last letter. Sighing, he lit the kerosene lantern, pulled it closer, and forced himself to read the painful words again.

Dearest Spencer,

Since last I wrote, Papa's health has worsened. Now he cannot speak or feed himself at all, and Dr. Kelso does not expect any improvement. It would be far better for all of us had he died. It breaks my heart to see him this way. And Mama is quite useless, of course. If there were a market for her tears, we should all be prosperous.

You write that you understand how it is here, but you cannot begin to know. Mama and I went to a party last Friday, but it was a sad affair. The only man there was Mr. Porter, who's too deaf to hear Gabriel's horn on Judgment Day. My throat was sore from shouting at him.

There is no social circle anymore. All discourse has sunk to an exchange of patriotic recipes, which are for the most part revolting. President Davis may say rats are edible, and meat markets may sell them at twenty dollars a pound, but I will not eat one. With not a single horse, mule, dog, cat, rabbit, squirrel, coon, or possum left in the whole of Crawford County, and flour costing one thousand dollars a barrel, and no sugar, rice, soda, butter, eggs, or lard anywhere, life here has become impossible.

You have no notion how hungry everyone is, or how low we will sink for food. Last week there was a riot at Rowley's Store over four shriveled apples, which went for twenty dollars apiece before slaves armed with pitchforks pushed the crowd out and chained the door. That night, someone burned the place down.

With every able-bodied white man off to war, the Negroes have become a lazy, insolent lot, and I am afraid of them. I keep Papa's hunting gun next to my bed at night.

In every letter to me, you ask me to be strong, but I cannot. I hate this war, I hate sacrificing everything for a doomed cause, and I hate this burden that your absence has thrust upon me. I tell you I am frightened, and you tell me to be patient. I ask you to come home, and you say you cannot get a leave. Spencer, I don't want a day or a week of your life; I want all of it. You speak of your loyalty to your country, but what of your loyalty to me? If you cannot get yourself discharged, then you must desert. For my sake, and for that of your son, *you must desert*.

Refolding the pages, he sighed. Why couldn't she understand what she was putting him through with letters like these? No matter how much he wanted to go home, he couldn't. As long as men still fought and died for the Confederacy, he had to stay. But, whether she liked him or not, Ross Donnelly just might be the answer to his dilemma.

Taking out pen, ink, and paper from the box beneath his bed, he thought for a long moment, then he began to write.

Dearest Liddy,

We engaged the enemy again yesterday, this time along the road to Franklin, Tennessee, and we have suffered a terrible loss. I expect Hood will be relieved of command for it, but that does not ease the pain I feel when I look into the eyes of dying men. I cannot even begin to tell you how it hard it is to saw through living flesh and bone.

I know how alone you feel in these trying times, and I wish I could be there with you. But with casualties here counted in the thousands, I cannot ask to leave. If you saw the misery, the suffering in the faces of our wounded, I do not believe you could ask me to abandon them. But I can offer you some company.

Our friend Ross Donnelly broke his shoulder during the battle and will be discharged for it. Since his family is out of the country, I am hoping you will welcome him into our home. As you know, he is quite the card, and I have hopes his presence will brighten your spirits and lighten the heavy burdens you bear until this awful war ends and I can be there with you.

You say I cannot know how miserable you are, but you cannot know how I long to see you and Joshua. Both of you are in my every prayer. It is your love that sustains me.

Always your devoted husband,
Spence

He reread his letter, feeling it lacked something, but he just couldn't think anymore. Setting it aside, he lay down and pulled the blanket up over his clothes. As his eyes closed, he whispered the Lord's Prayer, drifting off to sleep before he could finish it.

Near Salisbury, North Carolina:
April 12, 1865

Smelling smoke and hearing gunshots, Laura Taylor ran to her door, where she could see the dark column rising to meet lighter clouds in the sky. As nearly as she could tell, the Baker place three miles to the north was on fire. Yankee raiders were moving south along the railroad line toward Charlotte.

Her heart seemed to pause, and for a moment, she felt an awful hollow beneath her breastbone, then dread rushed to fill the void. When they'd stolen what they could and destroyed everything the Bakers owned, the blue-bellied locusts would be descending on her.

At least Jesse wasn't home, and surely the smoke would warn him to stay away until they passed. With that comfort came the realization that keeping what little they had depended on her. Her mind raced as she considered the only home she'd ever known. Those weathered walls would burn like tinder at the touch of a torch. And she knew better than to expect any mercy—the Yankee devils had been burning out wives, widows, and children as they cut a path of destruction through the heart of the South.

Scorched earth, it was called, this war they waged on women, children, and old men.

Well, they weren't getting her house, not while she still had any breath left in her body. She might not be able to save the old barn or the chicken coop, and they'd probably set fire to the roof of the stone smokehouse out back, but she wasn't leaving this house. They'd have to burn her with it.

Dry as a tinderbox, she decided, looking around at things most people wouldn't think worth fighting for. But between that leaky ceiling and the worn planks of a sagging floor, she'd spent all twenty-three years of her life here. All the memories, good and bad, echoed off these veined plaster walls. The doors had to be secured first, or they'd just come in after her, and there wasn't much time. Working feverishly, she dragged the faded sofa her mother had so insistently called a davenport across the front room to block the door, then she piled books, cast iron pots, every heavy thing she could lift, onto it. Standing back, she realized it wasn't enough to keep them out. She had to have more. Tugging and pushing and walking battered chests, both bedsteads, and the oak table and chairs, she reinforced that sofa with the rest of her furniture.

Stopping to mop the sweat from her face, she looked around her, thinking if the Yankees tried to get in that way, they'd have a job of it. But there was still the back door, and she'd run out of everything that might stop them. Walking through the four small, bare rooms, she realized she'd have to make her stand in the kitchen.

Taking Jesse's heavy Sharps rifle down from the

rack on the wall, she loaded it. One shot could drop a charging buffalo, he'd said, but once it was fired, the gun was empty. The double-barreled shotgun held two loads, but when either trigger was pulled, it kicked hard enough to send her sprawling. Her father's old cap-lock Colt was hard to load, but at least it held six shots, and she knew how to use it. As she took the pouch of powder from its place on the rack, the big black stove caught her eye, and she knew if she could move it, it was heavy enough to slow them down, giving her time to pick them off before they could get through that door.

She pulled a chair from the pile, and using a ramrod and carpenter's hammer, she knocked the flue loose, widening the crack in the plaster wall. It had taken two men to carry the stove in, she realized, but two men weren't here right now. Using a crowbar and a slat from the bedstead for levers, she managed to budge it a couple of inches. Moving from corner to corner, she worked the stove over the uneven floor all the way to the kitchen door. Her arms and legs felt like jelly, and sweat soaked her dress and her hair, but they weren't getting in there without a fight now.

She heard them coming down the hard clay road, and with her heart pounding in her ears, she loaded all six chambers of the Colt, getting powder, balls, caps, and sealing grease into them. Looking out the window, she saw half a dozen mounted Union soldiers in her yard, and she heard one of them yell, "Whoever's in there, come out! We've orders to torch the house!" And the acrid smell of burning pitch reinforced his words.

With the shotgun tucked under one arm, the revolver in her other hand, she edged to her front-room window and broke out the glass with the Colt's barrel. "You all get off my property, or I'll shoot!" she shouted.

"We won't hurt you if you come out!" he answered, banging on the door.

"Go away!"

"Either you come out, or we drag you out!"

"I've got a double load of buckshot waiting for anybody fool enough to try it!"

"Stoneman's orders, ma'am—you gotta get out before we set fire to the house!"

Sweat was pouring from her forehead, dripping from her hair. Blowing a wet strand out of her eyes, she gripped the shotgun more tightly. "You're all a bunch of blue-bellied cowards making war on women and children!"

She saw the doorknob turn and heard shoulders hitting the solid oak door. The facing splintered from the force, but the pile of furniture in front of it didn't budge. Amid a flurry of curses, somebody shouted the other way, "Door's blocked—it ain't opening!"

"Break it down!"

She couldn't tell whether it was the men or her temples pounding as they threw themselves at her door. Leveling the Colt, she cocked the hammer and pulled the trigger. As the bullet tore through the wood, a man yelped, and a cloud of gun smoke filled the room.

"She shot me!"

"Go round back! Go in and drag her out by her hair if you have to!"

Out of the corner of her eye, she saw a bluecoat coming by the window, and she fired again. He dropped down and crawled back to the riders out front.

The tone turned conciliatory. "Ma'am, we don't like hurtin' women, but we got orders to get everybody out of here. You come on out, and we'll see you get into town."

"Get off my property!" she yelled again, cocking the Colt's hammer. "If anybody leaves, it's going to be you!"

"Ma'am, we've got no choice. Just do what you're told, and nobody'll hurt you. You've got the word of an officer and a gentleman."

"You'll have to burn me with my house, 'cause I'm not leaving! That ought to make you real proud of yourselves!"

"Go round back!" she heard somebody shout again. "She can't get all of us!"

Her heart thudded painfully beneath her breastbone, but she managed to keep the bravado in her voice. "Come on in!" she challenged them. "There's enough guns in here for an army, and every one of 'em is loaded! So which one of you Yankee cowards wants the first bellyful of buckshot? You come through that door, and I'm cutting you in half with it!"

"She's bluffing! Go get her!"

She caught a glimpse of blue creeping low, trying to get around the other side of the house. She got to Danny's window in time to get a good look at his blue-covered rump. Taking aim at it, she pulled one trigger of the shotgun. It sounded like an explosion, and the recoil threw her into the wall as the shot shattered the window. Clutching her shoulder, she wasn't sure the scream she'd heard was hers or his, but when she dared to look through the jagged glass, she saw the soldier jerking and writhing on the ground. The buckshot had torn through the back of his pants, and his backside looked like raw meat.

"Dear God, forgive me, but I had no choice," she whispered, stunned by what she'd done. Recovering, she called out, "Anybody fool enough to try that again?"

"Throw the torch! Burn the bitch in it!"

Moving just out of Danny's door and into the front room, she listened intently, trying to guess which way it'd be coming, and she saw the rider raise the burning brand. "Please, God, don't let me miss," she prayed fervently as she leveled the Colt and fired.

The horse reared, then went down. As the torch hit the ground, the flames shot up, frightening the animal further. It fought to regain its legs, then bolted. The rider picked himself up and limped after it, cursing loudly.

Regrouping at a safe distance, the raiders disputed among themselves, but she couldn't make out what they were saying. Taking aim at a branch of the old oak tree above them, she fired the Sharps, hitting it, and they scattered. Wheeling their horses, they charged, giving the house itself a wide berth, going around the other side of the barn to torch the pile of hay there. As flames shot up above the roof, they circled to set fire to the coop and smokehouse, then came back to retrieve their wounded before they rode off.

She tried to open the kitchen window, but the rope stuck. With thick, choking smoke filling the air, and dry wood popping and crackling, she had to watch helplessly while flames consumed the barn. Then the chicken coop caved in.

The realization that the soldiers were gone, that she'd survived sank in slowly, followed by an awareness of her aching fingers. When she looked down, she had the Colt clutched so tightly that she couldn't turn it loose. Still holding it, she leaned her head against the wall and let the tears flow.

When she finally regained her composure, she wiped her streaming eyes with the sleeve of her faded dress, then she looked outside again. A raw spring wind was carrying live coals out toward the thicket of wild plums and bittersweet.

It could have been worse, she told herself. If Jesse'd been there, he would have put up a fight, and they'd probably have killed him and taken Old Dolly. While she'd lost the outbuildings, she still had her husband, her house, and a plow horse.

North Carolina: May 14, 1865

The rain poured over the brim of Spence's hat, soaking through his coat and shirt, chilling his weary body all the way to the bone. Beneath him, the roan horse plodded slowly, its hooves sucking at the mire with every step. The muddy road was deeply rutted, still scarred by the passage of Sherman's heavy artillery wagons two months ago. Now the ragged remnants of a beaten army were walking it home.

As they'd passed the skeletal remains of charred chimneys and burnt farmhouses, seeing endless miles of fire-blackened fields, the relief most had felt at war's end was gone, replaced by angry bitterness. Exhausted, footsore, and hungry, former butternut soldiers had themselves become foragers in their own land, fighting each other for food, horses, or enough money to get them to their own devastated farms and towns farther on.

Straightening in the saddle, Spence shrugged aching shoulders and fought to stay awake. He'd hoped to be in Georgia by now, but he knew it was still a long way to the state line. Between bad roads and worse weather, he'd be damned lucky if he made it to Charlotte tonight. If he could get there, he had enough money in his boot to pay for a place to sleep. If he couldn't, he'd have to stay awake. He'd already witnessed barefooted infantrymen pulling a careless cavalry officer from his saddle, taking his horse, his money, and most of his clothes. The fellow had been damned lucky to escape with his life.

But as bad as things were, the war was over. Dispersing the wounded from field hospitals to other facilities had taken precious time from Spence, but with the last transfers done, he was finally going home to the wife and son he hadn't seen in more than eighteen months.

He had a lot of time to make up, and maybe things would be awkward at first, but he couldn't wait to see Liddy. In his mind's eye, he'd pictured his homecoming a thousand times. She'd be waiting for him on the columned porch, smiling through her tears, and they'd just hold each other. Josh would be hanging back until Spence held out some of the horehound candy he'd stashed in his coat pocket, then he'd be glad to see his daddy. Now he could spend the summer getting acquainted with his boy. He'd take him fishing, teach him to ride, play games with him on the wide, lush lawn at Jamison's Landing.

He'd finally be the husband Liddy wanted. He wouldn't have to lie on a hard army cot, burning for her, anymore. Now he could give free rein to his memories of her whispered words, of the intoxicating scent of her skin, of the ecstasy of fulfilled desire. After four years of hell, he was going home to heaven on earth.

But right now, the spectre of violence still hovered,

fed by despair, humiliation, and a desire for revenge on the gloating, swaggering Yankees who'd plundered and burned the heart of the South. Just yesterday, a drunken bunch of bluecoats had blocked the road, telling butternuts they had to salute the Stars and Stripes before they could pass. Provoked, the former rebels had linked arms and sang "Dixie" at the top of their lungs, and forced their way through the jeering Yankees. When the ensuing fight was over, two Union soldiers lay dead in the road, and a dozen others were running for their lives.

He kept trying to think of the good things, but his mind was wandering, scattering his thoughts like buckshot. He was so tired, but he couldn't stop. At Charlotte, he'd write Liddy, letting her know he was on his way home, then he'd sleep as long as he could.

As unsettled as everything had been in those last weeks before Johnston surrendered to Sheridan, mail delivery had been pretty spotty, with little getting through. The last word he'd heard from her had been more than two months ago, but the tone of it had been better. Ross's presence had been a big help.

"Get his gun!" somebody yelled.

Before he realized what was happening, a figure darted out from a copse of trees to grasp his horse's bridle, and suddenly he was surrounded. As his hand sought his own revolver, he felt the cold steel of a gun barrel against his neck. Jerking away, he kicked at the bearded man reaching for his coat.

"Hold your fire, or I'll shoot!" Spence shouted, reaching for his gun.

"Grab his arm! Don't let him get it!"

His horse reared, nearly unseating him. As two

men rolled away from flailing hooves, he pulled the trigger. His first shot missed, then the gun jammed. Unable to fire again, he clubbed an attacker with the barrel, and kicked his horse's flank hard. As the animal lunged forward, he was pulled from the saddle and struck from behind. The world went black before his face hit the mud, and he floated in a downward spiral toward oblivion.

"You all right, mister?"

A distant voice penetrated the fog in Spence's brain. For a moment, he was on the battlefield, and the ground beneath him was cold and wet. He must've been thrown from the ambulance wagon when a cannonball hit it. But the guns had gone silent, the only sound now that of rain pelting the earth next to his ear. The wagons had gone on, leaving him for dead.

"He ain't moving."

"Wonder where he's from—looks like they took his coat, but he's got butternut pants on. Put that gun away, Will—he ain't a Yankee."

"He ain't no soldier neither, Jack—he ain't barefooted."

"Come on—we gotta get goin'—ain't no way we'll be home iff'n we don't get goin'."

"Just wonder who he is, that's all."

"It don't matter, I'm tellin' you. I got a ma and pa to worry over, Will—I ain't got no time to be carryin' nobody anywheres."

"It don't seem right to be leavin' 'im like that."

"We gotta. We ain't got no horse, and he cain't walk anywhere like that."

The voices floated off, leaving him in a fog of pain.

His fingers dug into the mud, hanging on. He'd fallen into a hole somewhere, and when he felt better, he'd crawl out.

It was either night out, or he'd gone blind, Spence decided, opening his eyes into the rain. He couldn't place where he was, and he wasn't sure how he'd gotten here, but he vaguely realized he had to get up.

His head throbbed to the beat of his heart, and the rest of his body felt as though he'd been thrown and kicked by a mule. With an effort, he rolled to sit, trying to figure out what had happened to him. The last thing he remembered was falling. Holding his chin up with his palm, he reached up to touch the back of his head. When he drew his fingers back, they were wet with something other than rain. He knew that feeling—it was congealed blood.

"Hey! What're you doing sitting in the middle of the road, mister? As dark as it is, somebody's liable to ride right over you."

Looking up through his wet, dripping hair, Spence saw the halo of a lantern moving toward him. Then he could make out a tall, gaunt plow horse as gray as the fog itself. A man swung down to take a closer look at him. Behind the lantern, a wide-brimmed hat and an oiled canvas coat materialized.

"I'd say you're in a heap of trouble, or you wouldn't be out here like this," the fellow said, dropping to his knees beside Spence. Holding the lantern closer, he said softly, "Well, I'll be damned."

"I already am. My head feels big as a pumpkin, and I could swear something kicked it."

"You don't recognize me, do you?"

"I can barely see."

"Name Taylor mean anything to you? Jesse Taylor?"

"I don't know."

"Army of Tennessee," the man prompted. "It was after the battle at Franklin that you saved my leg." When Spence didn't respond, he asked, "You remember Danny Lane, don't you?"

"Yeah."

"He was my wife's brother. He was hell and be-damned to bring me in, but I knew if I did, I'd be losing m' leg for sure. Whether you remember it or not, you cleaned out the hole and set it—it healed up real nice, Doc. I always felt sorry about holding that gun to your head, but I figured if I didn't, you'd start sawing."

"Yeah, I remember. If I hadn't set it, you were going to hell with it."

"That's right. Looks like somebody bushwhacked you, Doc."

"They wanted my horse—that's all I remember. I was riding home, and they surprised me, then the damned gun jammed."

"How long have you been out in this rain?"

"I don't know—long enough for it to turn dark."

"The bastards took your coat."

"It was butternuts."

"Hell of a thing to do to somebody that's served with you, but there's some like that."

"Too many."

"Well, I'm not about to leave you here like this. Come on," Taylor said, catching Spence under his arm. "That's it—you just come up real easy." As the light illuminated Spence's black hair, the man observed, "I'd say you took a real whack on that head of yours. When I get you home, I'm going to have my wife take a look at it. If it's as bad as I think it is, she'll have to stitch it up for you."

"It'll be all right."

"It's a good thing you don't have eyes back there—that's all I can say. If we were still fighting the war, one of those army docs would be wanting to trepine that for you."

"You don't have much faith in us, do you?"

"Just you—the rest of 'em weren't worth a hill of beans between 'em." Steadying Spence, Jesse Taylor held the lamp to his face. "You've got a black eye, too. Queasy?"

"Yeah."

"You took a hard hit, Doc. But I'm not doing you any good standing out here in the rain." Casting a sidewise glance at the bony horse, he admitted, "I don't know if Old Dolly'll carry both of us, but if she won't, I'll be the one to walk."

"I'm all right." But even as he said it, Spence knew he wasn't. He'd be real lucky if he didn't have a concussion the way his head hurt.

"Here," Taylor said, shrugging out of the canvas coat. "At least I've got more than a shirt on under this. You'll catch your death soaked like that. It may be the middle of May, but this rain's downright cold." He thrust Spence's arms into the sleeves and pulled it closed around him. "You may be wet, but this'll at least help you get warm."

"Thanks."

"They take anything but your coat and horse?"

"Yeah."

"If they got your money, Laurie's got a little put aside that we can spare. Maybe it'd be enough to get you home."

Spence shook his head and wished he hadn't. "I had my money in my boots—I didn't want anybody seeing it."

"Well, it'd better be hard cash instead of Confederate scrip, that's all I can say."

"Yeah, I know. I've got fifty dollars in Union money under my foot."

"Whooeee—and I was offering *you* money," Taylor said, grinning. "Around here, that'd make you a rich man."

"The hell of it is they got my bag, and my wife's picture. I kept it in a book so I wouldn't lose it, and it's gone."

"Only hope you've got of seeing that again, Doc, is if they trade your clothes for money."

"It was in my bag—in my field kit. They stole my field kit. I had the damned thing through the whole war, and now it's gone, too. There's no way I can replace it or my wife's picture."

"I'll ask around tomorrow, but first I've got to get you home. Can you mount up by yourself, do you think?"

"Yeah."

"Then you take the saddle, and if Dolly'll hold us, I'll get up behind you. That way if you get to falling, I've got my arms to stop you. But we'd better get going, or Laurie'll be worried something's happened to me. You'd think she'd know if I made it home from the war, she can count on me being around, but I guess Danny's death changed her some—she's afraid to take anything for granted."

"He said she raised him," Spence remembered.

"Yeah. If you can get your foot in the stirrup, I can boost you up," Jesse said. "Dolly won't move until you're up there."

Grasping the saddle horn, Spence pulled his aching body into the saddle. He'd made it without help.

"Your wife won't mind having unexpected company?"

"No. Laurie's not exactly your ordinary woman, Doc. Little inconveniences don't bother her. If they did, she wouldn't have made it with the life she's had. When her ma died, she was just shy of twelve, and Danny was only five. There was a notion afoot about splitting them up to raise 'em, but she wouldn't hear of it. She'd promised her ma she'd look after him, and by God, she did it. She did more than a grown woman would have—cooking, cleaning, sewing, teaching him to read like you would expect, but that was only half of it. She either raised or hunted everything they ate, and she got an egg business going, too. She's a hard worker, and she knows what she's doing. I think you'll like her, Doc."

"I look pretty rough right now," Spence murmured.

"She won't care. Danny wrote her about you, and I came home with both legs because of you. That's enough for her. You might find her a little different from most women, though."

"How's that?"

"She likes to read—no, it's more than that—she's got a *passion* for it. First Christmas we were married,

I wanted to buy her a Sunday dress, but she wanted books instead."

"Lydia isn't much for books of any kind," Spence conceded.

"Not too many of 'em are. I don't mean to say Laurie lets herself go, or anything like that, Doc. She's a pretty woman, no matter what she wears." Realizing he'd been running on about someone Hardin had never seen, Jesse forced himself to change the subject. "Looks like Dolly'll carry double just fine."

"Yeah."

"Riding all right?"

"Yeah."

"The way you're wobbling in that saddle, I'd be surprised if that was the truth."

"I'm dizzy, that's all."

"If you think you're going to fall, we'll stop."

"No."

"She's going to ask you about Danny, you know. I'm not asking you to lie, but I'm hoping you won't tell her anything that'll upset her. Cholera's a hard way to go, and I'd just as soon she doesn't know everything about how he went. You were down in Mississippi with him when it happened, weren't you?"

"Yeah."

"She's got a lot worrying her right now, Doc. If nothing goes wrong this time, we'll be having a baby before Christmas. She had a hard time of it when we lost a stillborn son right before the war. She doesn't say much about it, but I know she's scared it'll happen again."

"What went wrong?"

"Since you're a doctor, maybe you can tell me. All I know is the doc we had wasn't fit to be calling himself one. Now, nobody's ever called me a coward, but honest to God, I couldn't have stood what she did."

"None of us could. If it was up to men to have babies, the species would have died out in the first generation. It's a lot of pain and hard work."

"It was more than that for Laurie, I can tell you," Taylor declared flatly. "Doc Burton let her suffer until she was about dead herself before he decided to do anything about it. Four days, Doc—that's how long she had those pains—and he kept telling her it'd come when it was time, when he should've known something was wrong. There wasn't any way that baby could have come out—it was lying almost crosswise, and all those pains couldn't push it out."

"He should have tried to turn it before things got that far."

"It wasn't until she started losing a lot of blood that he did anything, and then the bastard made a botch of that, too. He got it to coming feet first, but by then she was too tired to push, and I was sure I was going to lose her. He said it was dead before it was born, and I reckon that was about the only thing he had the right of. But let me tell you, Doc—that baby was fighting to live for most of those four days. You could see it move, and she could feel it kicking. Hell, you want to know why I don't have any faith in doctors? I could've got it out myself better than he did. He lost my son, and he nearly killed my wife. No, sir, I'm not about to forgive or forget that."

"I'm sorry."

"It wasn't your fault—it was his. When it was over, I wanted to kill him. If Laurie had died, he wouldn't have got out of my house alive."

"I don't blame you."

"And the hell of it was she insisted on paying him, like it was her fault, not his. It was blood money he took, Doc. It wasn't right."

"It'd be pretty hard to charge for something like that," Spence admitted. "I don't know that I would, anyway."

"Of course you wouldn't! You're not like the rest of 'em, and you know what? If it'd been you there, it wouldn't have happened. You wouldn't have let it go on like that."

"I don't know what I would have done under those circumstances. I'd have been pretty green myself. The only births I attended were during medical school, and it didn't take many of them for me to decide I'd rather be a surgeon. I thought I'd be going out into the world doing something useful, but I don't know that it worked out that way. Long before the war ended, I realized I was practicing butchery, not medicine."

"You're too hard on yourself, Doc. Danny saw all of you work, and he said you were the best the Army of Tennessee had. He said the other surgeons working with you knew it."

"If success were measured like cordwood, I probably was. I maimed with the best of them. If the experience taught me anything, it was that whatever gift I had, I didn't want it."

"You can't look at it like that. All anybody, even

God, has a right to ask of you is that you do what you can. Instead of looking at those legs and arms stacked up outside the surgery tents, look at how many men went home."

"Thanks."

"Hungry?" Jesse asked, changing the subject again.

"Right now, I could eat grass, but I know I'm not alone in that at least."

"It's been pretty bad around here," Jesse conceded, "but we've got beans and cornmeal, so we're not starving yet."

"I don't mind beans."

"That's good, because we've got a lot of them."

Both fell silent then, and the night was broken only by the steady sounds of rain hitting mud and Old Dolly's hooves pulling out of it. Hunched miserably over the saddle horn, he didn't even know where he was, only that he was still somewhere north of Charlotte, North Carolina, and at the rate he was going, he could've crawled home faster.

"Where are we?"

"Almost to Salisbury," Taylor responded.

"Where's that from Charlotte?"

"About forty—maybe a little more—miles."

Spence wished he hadn't asked. On a good day that'd be another four hours. In this mud, it'd be seven or eight. "How far to Salisbury?" he asked wearily.

"About a mile. Next road to the right goes to my front yard. If you can hang on about another five minutes, we've made it home."

"What day is it?"

"The fourteenth for about four more hours."

If he could get a horse anywhere, Spence still had from two to four days of travel ahead of him. And he might as well forget about writing Liddy from Salisbury. The place probably wouldn't even have a post office.

"Yeah, there's a lantern on the porch," Jesse murmured. "Soon as we get inside, we'll get those wet clothes off you, and Laura will clean up that head. When that's done, we'll eat the beans, and then you can sleep in Danny's bed."

The horse sensed food and broke into a hard trot right up to the door. Jesse dismounted by leaning far enough to catch a tree branch, then easing his body to the ground. "If you can get out of the saddle, you might want to do it real fast. Otherwise, you'll be getting down in the smokehouse. The old girl puts herself up at night."

"Jesse?" A woman peered out the door.

"Yeah!" he yelled. "We've got company—I found Doc Hardin on the road. You'd better get out the turpentine and a good needle, because he's needing his head sewed up!"

She came outside at that. "What happened?"

"Butternuts waylaid him for his horse. He'll need dry clothes, too."

"Yes, of course." Forcing a smile she held out her hand to Spence. "Danny wrote of you often, Dr. Hardin. He admired you very much."

"He was a fine young man." Rather than shake her hand, he let her see his. "I'd just get you all muddy."

As soon as he was in the house, she took down the porch lantern and held it up to look at the back of his head. Her fingers separated his hair until she found the place. "I think we'd better take care of this first. When I get the clot washed away, you may bleed all over the place."

"What does it look like?" he wanted to know.

"About like someone took a butcher knife to the back of your head. I don't know what would've done something like this."

"I don't know—I don't remember much of anything, except I was riding home, then the next thing I knew, your husband was picking me up out of the mud. I don't even know how long I was out."

"No, I don't expect so. If you can sit at the table, I can sew the wound up. It won't be the way somebody who knew what he was doing might do it, but maybe it'll hold the scalp together long enough for it to heal."

"I'd be grateful, ma'am. I just hate asking you to do it."

"I don't mind. Truth to tell, I owe you a whole lot more than that for what you did for Jess. Anything you need, you just ask, and we'll sure try to get it."

"No, I just want to get home. I've been gone too long already, and I've got a wife and son waiting for me."

"I remember how that was," she murmured, holding a ladderback chair for him. "When Jess came through that door, I was so happy I cried my eyes out, knowing he'd made it home."

"Yeah." Exhausted, he dropped into the chair and held his head in his hands, fighting sleep. It seemed like seconds before he felt the rag touch his head, and he smelled homemade lye soap. He sat still while she trimmed his hair away from the gash, then washed the area again. It wasn't until he smelled the turpentine that he had to brace his elbows against the table.

"Danny always said this hurt," she said, soaking another rag with it. "I thought I'd better warn you, because I'm putting it right into the raw place." As she said it, she pressed the wet cloth against his scalp and squeezed it, flooding the wound. She felt him flinch. "I'm sorry to do this, but it's all I know. My mother used to put turpentine on anything that bled."

"That's all right—it works. I used it myself when I had to."

"I don't think I could've done what you did, Dr. Hardin. I don't know how you stood it."

"Sometimes I couldn't."

"But you had to do it, anyway—that was the hard part, I expect."

"Yes."

"There's more than one kind of hero, you know," she observed quietly. "One kind throws himself into enemy fire for a cause, but your kind puts him back together so he can go home."

"They went home on crutches, Mrs. Taylor—if they went at all."

"But that's something, isn't it?" Returning to the matter at hand, she said, "This cut's about three inches wide, maybe a bit more. Is there any particular way you want it stitched?"

"No. Just pull it together and sew it like cloth. If it won't match, you can leave little places like buttonholes up to half an inch, and if all the debris is out, it'll fill in with scar tissue."

"I expect this is going to hurt."

He felt the needle jab through his skin, tugging it into place as she sewed. Judging by the number of times she stuck him, she was taking small stitches.

"Do you do this often?" he found himself asking.

"No. Just when Danny fell over the plow, and when the axe slipped and cut into Jesse's foot. He wouldn't have a doctor, so I soaked it in turpentine, then I just started putting everything back together as best I could."

"That's quite an accomplishment."

"It was luck, Dr. Hardin. I was afraid it'd turn black and gangrene would set in, but it didn't. I made sure he wore a double pair of wool socks to keep that foot warm."

"Warmth improves circulation," he acknowledged, impressed.

"He was just lucky," she insisted. Tying off the last stitch, she cut the thread, then laid the needle aside. "Mud's going to get onto your pillow, and when you turn your head, it'll get into the wound again. I'd better wash your hair."

"You don't have to."

"Is that a doctor or a tired man talking?"

"It'll be all right."

"You're about to drop, that's what you are. If you can lean your head over a bucket, it won't take me long to get it clean. Then I'll give you a pitcher and soap to take into Danny's room, and I'll get supper. You can either put on the clean clothes on the bottom of the bed, or there's a nightshirt in the wardrobe. I don't mind you sitting down at the table in anything, as long as you've got yourself decently covered."

When she came back, he leaned over the bucket she put on the floor and endured a thorough head washing, the kind his mother had given him as a boy. Laurie rubbed that lye soap through his hair with her fingertips, working up a lather, then she rinsed it. When she finished, she dropped a towel over his head and dried his hair vigorously.

"Thanks."

"If it wouldn't take half the night to heat the water, I'd fill the washtub and you could soak in it. But right now you probably need sleep worse."

"I fell like I could sleep a week, but I know I've got to get back on the road in the morning."

"Well, you'll be going with clean hair," she said, stepping back. "When you come out, bring what you're wearing now with you, and I'll wash them first thing in the morning." Lifting the bucket of rinse water, she headed for the back door to empty it.

He had to get up from the table, Spence told himself, but he was so damned tired that his body rebelled. She came back, bringing a lighted lantern with her.

"You'll need this if you're to see anything in there."

With an effort, he looked up, and for a moment, he forgot his fatigue. The lantern flame reflected in her brown eyes made them seem almost gold. As callused as her hands were, as faded as her dress was, there was a quality in her eyes that pushed those thoughts from his mind. For a second suspended in time, he thought her husband had erred in describing her as pretty. Laura Taylor was beautiful.

When Spence woke up, the sun was streaming through the small window, and the tatted edge of the muslin curtain cast a lacy shadow on the wall across from it. For a moment, he wondered where he was, then he remembered. He'd been ambushed and left for dead, but Jesse Taylor had found him and brought him here.

He turned over and realized every muscle in his body was sore. But he was alive, he reminded himself, and for that alone he ought to be damned grateful. His head still hurt, but not with the pounding, throbbing pain of last night. Touching the back of it, he could feel the short place where his hair had been sheared, then he checked the stitches. They were surprisingly good, considering the fact someone with no training had done them.

There wasn't much in the room—a bedstead, a chest, and a narrow wardrobe. Danny's room, they'd called it. If it was painful for him to remember the kid, it had to be unbearable for the Taylors. Things like that were hard to get over.

He smelled coffee. She was fixing breakfast, and he'd better get up if he wanted any. Then he'd ask

Taylor to take him into Charlotte, where he'd have to buy himself a horse. And a gun. From here on out, until he got home, he'd be a lot more aware of what went on around him. He couldn't afford any more daydreams.

Clean clothes lay on the bottom of the bed, folded next to his feet. The shirt might be his, but the pants weren't, and neither were the socks. But they were clean. If Jesse would let him borrow them, he'd see they got back.

"Dr. Hardin, are you awake?" Laura Taylor's voice carried through the closed door.

"Yeah!"

"I've got salt pork fried and mush made."

"I'll be right out!"

"There's no hurry—it's hot enough it can wait for you."

It didn't take him long to throw on the clothes and pull on his boots. The pants were about an inch short, but other than that, they were a surprisingly good fit. His fifty dollars was right where he'd left it—in plain sight on the chest. He stuffed it into the pants.

She looked up from the table when he came out. "Well, you look a lot better this morning than you did last night," she observed, smiling.

"I feel better, that's for sure." Taking the chair in front of the empty plate, he glanced around. "Where's your husband?"

"He went into Salisbury, but he'll be back before long. He said he needed to see about something."

"Oh?"

"You drink coffee, don't you?"

"Yes."

"This might not taste very good to you, but it's all we've got. The way things are around here, we're lucky to have any, so we have to stretch it a little. If you don't like it, you can pour it out. The pump squawks and squeals, but it works, so there's plenty of water."

"It'll be all right."

"You might want to withhold that judgment until you taste it," she warned him. "I do have a little raw sugar, if you want to cover the taste a little. I asked Jesse to see if anybody has cream in Salisbury, but I don't expect him to find any. There aren't many cows around, and what milk there is goes to the children," she explained. "Sometimes, somebody will skim a little cream off to sell. And sometimes, that's just wasted, because nobody's got any money to buy it."

"Time's are pretty hard, all right. We'll be years getting over the war."

"Yes. But we're better off than a lot of folks right now. Last month, Jesse helped Silas Hawkins bury his wife—he made the box and dug the hole for him. When he was leaving, that old man gave Jess five dollars, saying he had more where that came from. I shouldn't be telling that, but I don't think you'll be trying to rob Mr. Hawkins, anyway. We've kept quiet about it around here, though."

"Five dollars isn't much for that."

"It is if nobody's got any money," she countered.

"I suppose so. It's just hard to get to think that way when there used to be plenty of it. My wife spent more than five dollars on a pair of stockings."

"Really? You've got rich folks, then. Even before

the war, I would never have asked for anything like that. Books maybe—but not stockings."

The way she said it, he felt almost ashamed. "Well, it wasn't my money," he conceded. "Her daddy owned half the county."

"Oh. I guess that explains it, then. Still, he must've been pretty wasteful."

She didn't know the half of it, he thought. Five dollars wasn't much more than a cigar to Cullen Jamison. Or it hadn't been, anyway. Thinking to shift the conversation to a more common ground, he took a sip of the coffee and he almost couldn't swallow it. When he looked up, she was watching him expectantly, and he felt compelled to say something.

"It's got an unusual flavor to it." Setting the cup down, he dared to ask, "What's in it?—besides coffee, I mean."

"I thought you might ask that," she murmured wryly. "There is *some* coffee, but it's mostly roasted cottonseed, a little parched corn, and some chicory. I had to grind all of that with the coffee or we'd be drinking plain water. It takes getting used to," she admitted. "I guess you'd probably have the water, wouldn't you?"

"No, it's fine," he lied. "It just had a different whang to it, that's all, and I wondered where that came from."

"You're being polite, Dr. Hardin. The first time I fixed some for Jesse when he came home, he told me it wasn't fit for hog swill, but when he found out there wasn't anything else, he started drinking it. We've tried a lot of things around here, but none of them taste much like coffee." She started to rise. "It won't take me any time to pump the water."

"It's not necessary, Mrs. Taylor. I'll do just fine with this, but I will take some of that sugar."

She sat back down. "How much?"

"How much have you got?"

"Some," she replied, passing him the half-empty bowl. "I was just going to put it into your coffee for you. It looks better after it dissolves."

Digging a spoon into it, he noticed whoever had broken it up had left some rather large grayish brown chunks. He felt guilty for taking so much, but he put two heaping spoonfuls of it into the misnamed coffee. As he stirred it, small black specks floated to the top.

"I'll get you the water," she said again.

"Sit down."

"Those aren't bugs, you know," she offered. "I cooked it down in a cast-iron pan, and some of the seasoning came off into it. It didn't look so bad until after it evaporated."

He took another sip. Now there was a greasy sweetness to the stuff. "Much better," he managed.

"You're sure?"

"Positive."

She pushed the platter of mush slices toward him. "There's no syrup, but I have some preserves in that little white jam pot. It's chokecherry."

"I'll eat anything."

"There you go again—deciding before you try it."

"I'm not a hard man to please."

"That, Dr. Hardin, remains to be seen. The war

may be over, but we're still living on secessionist recipes."

"This looks good to me," he assured her. "Last winter, my wife wrote me that butchers down home were selling dressed rats for meat."

"I don't doubt it. Yankee thieves picked us pretty clean, too, and people were eating their horses and mules for meat, but I was one of the lucky ones. Old Dolly got pretty skinny, but both of us managed to stay alive until Jesse came home. We've just about got the only garden in the neighborhood because he was here to plow it." Her expression clouded for a moment, then she managed to smile. "I don't know that we'll get to eat most of it, but if we stay, we'll have plenty."

A bite-sized piece of mush was headed to his mouth. "You're thinking about leaving?"

"Jesse is. I try not to, but the question isn't whether we go anymore—it's when. He says we're poorer now than we were before the war, and it's only going to get worse. He says the Yankee politicians are going to be even worse than the soldiers. He thinks North Carolina is going to be like an occupied country."

"He's probably right about that."

She closed her eyes to compose herself, then looked across to Spence. "The war changed everything, Dr. Hardin—it took Danny's life as surely as if he'd been shot on the battlefield, and it sent home a different Jesse. He used to dream of making this place prosper, and now he just thinks it's downright worthless. He's got it into his head that his only chance of amounting to anything is with the railroad. He wants us to go out west and start over."

"And you don't want to go."

It was a statement, not a question, but she answered it, anyway. "It isn't so much that I don't want to go. It's that I don't want to leave. I was born in this house. Danny was born in this house. Mama died here, and so did Daddy. I've never lived anywhere else in my life, Dr. Hardin." As his gaze took in the cracked walls, the rain-stained ceiling, she sighed. "I know it's not much—but it's home to me."

"Maybe you should tell him that."

"I did. He says I'll get over it, that there's a whole world out there, and when I see it, I'll be glad we left North Carolina."

"You could put your foot down, I guess."

"I'm not sure it would do much good. Do you ever read any military history?" she asked suddenly.

Momentarily baffled, he responded, "Like what?"

"About the great generals."

"Not much, anyway. Why?"

"Well, I've read about some of them—Alexander the Great, Hannibal, William the Conqueror, Marlborough, Napoleon, Wellington—any I could get my hands on, anyway."

"Oh?"

"Yes, and there's two things I've noticed about the winners—they chose where they fought their battles, and they saw each one of those battles as part of the whole war. That's where Hood went wrong at Franklin, you know. Once the Yankee army got past him, he should've let it go instead of risking everything right there. His objective was Nashville, but by the time Franklin was over, it was the Army of Tennessee that was gutted.''

"Yeah.''

"I can't fight to keep this place if it means losing Jesse," she went on. "If I put my foot down and say I won't go, Jesse'll stay here, and he'll be miserable. Maybe I can win the battle, but I'll lose the war. This place isn't good enough for him, and if I make him stay, maybe I won't be either.''

"I don't see that happening, Mrs. Taylor. He brags about the way you survived without him and Danny, about how you stood off Stoneman's cavalry by yourself. I don't see him walking out of here without you.''

"I know. But his dreams aren't here anymore. Jesse's the kind of man who's got to have his dreams. If I take them away from him, he'll just give up hope, and I can't let that happen. I won't let that happen.''

"Everybody's got dreams, but sometimes we don't understand what they cost.''

"But I don't *need* a big, fancy house, or silk dresses, or anything like that. He wants things for me that I don't really want for myself. But," she added, sighing, "he's going to give them to me, come hell or high water, or else he'll die trying.''

"I see.''

"I don't know why I'm telling you this—I don't even know you," she mused. "I just guess I've got to say it to somebody, because Jesse's not listening. This place is like the Ancient Mariner's albatross to him. I'm going to have to go with him, Dr. Hardin.''

"Maybe if you just sat down and talked, you could make him understand," he offered sympathetically.

"Maybe you could ask him to give you a little time to get used to the notion."

"You're very kind, sir, but I'm not going to fight him over this. If I have to leave, I suppose now is as good a time as any. It'll be harder to move next year with the baby. He's got his heart set on it, and I'll have to go. I promised to love, honor, and obey him, and he's done his part. He's the one that earns the living, you know." Straightening up in her chair, she managed a smile. "I'm being silly, that's all there is to it. I don't feel right about it, but maybe it's just the baby making me moody."

"I was going to send Jesse his pants back when I got home."

"Well, you'd better send them quick, or else you'll have to put them in care of the Union Pacific railroad."

"They might not hire him with that limp."

"They'll hire him. They'd be fools not to. I mean, he's a hard worker, he's as honest as they come, and his word is his bond. He says with the war over, they'll be building tracks across the mountains to California. He says they're hiring men who can't even speak English, and the pay's more than good. If that's so, they ought to leap at the chance to get someone like Jesse. He's the kind of man who'd give his life for you if you needed it."

"I see."

"And I'm just being silly," she said again. "I know everything he's saying is right, but for some reason I'm scared."

"He told me about losing the first baby."

"If that happens again, I don't know what I'll do.

If after all that labor, I don't have a child to show for it, I don't think I'll want to do it again."

"It probably won't. Most babies manage to get themselves headed the right way."

"I know."

"That's what's got you worried, isn't it?"

"That's only part of it. The other part is leaving all these memories behind."

"That's the good thing about memories, Mrs. Taylor. They're with you all your life."

"You're a kind man, Dr. Hardin, and your wife is a lucky woman. She may have money, but there's more worth in a good heart than in gold. You've got that good heart—I can just tell it in the way you've let me run on about my worries, when you're bound to have worries of your own."

"Thank you. If I had my bag, I'd show you her picture, and you might change your mind. I'm still surprised she wanted to marry me. I didn't have much to recommend me at the time—just a brand-new diploma from the Medical College of South Carolina."

"That's in Charleston, isn't it?"

"Yes."

She looked over the rim of her cup at him. "Well, at least that explains something."

"I don't follow you."

"The new diploma. The way Danny and Jesse talked about you, I figured you were a whole lot older."

"I'm twenty-eight, Mrs. Taylor—I'll be twenty-nine in December. I'm not exactly wet behind my years, you know."

"I'll be twenty-four in September."

"Now who's the young chicken?"

"When I think of packing all my belongings up, I don't feel all that young."

"I came out of the army feeling a hundred years old," he admitted. "It'll be a relief to practice real medicine. I don't care if I ever amputate anything again as long as I live."

"But you're a surgeon," she reminded him.

"I spent an extra year at that, but I was trained in general medicine first. I used to think I'd be bored beyond endurance looking at sore throats and prescribing liniment for rheumatism. I don't feel that way anymore. The way I feel now, I could go the rest of my life without cutting on anybody."

"That'll change. If you've got a gift for something, you can't turn your back on it any more than you can stop breathing. But pretty soon you'll be taking the temperature of that mush."

"Huh?"

"It's getting cold."

"Oh, yeah." Cutting off another bite of fried mush, he forked it into his mouth.

"Jesse's home," she announced, folding her napkin and laying it across her plate. As if by a theater cue, he threw open the back door and came in grinning. "You must've found it," she decided.

"Last place I went," her husband responded smugly. "They sold it to the Sprague woman for two loaves of bread and some honey. She said she bought it just to get them out of her yard." Holding the leather bag up in his hand, Jesse looked to Spence. "This better be yours, Doc, 'cause it's got your name on it. I don't think they took much of anything out of it, because it's pretty heavy. Feels like there's a load of bricks in here."

"They probably thought medical books made for dry reading," Spence answered, reaching for it. Releasing the brass hasps, he looked inside. "They rummaged through it, but I don't guess they knew what to do with most of it."

"Now you can show me that picture," Laura reminded him. "When you're done eating, I mean."

"What picture?" Jesse asked.

"His wife."

"And my little boy," Spence added, washing the mush down with the strange coffee. "We've got a son, and he's in the photograph with her."

"Jess, did you find any cream?" she remembered suddenly.

"There wasn't any." Dropping into a chair across from Spence, Jesse eyed the black bag again. "Good thing you had that brass nameplate on it, or I'd never have gotten it back. Mrs. Sprague was planning to put her sewing in it until I told her how you came to lose it." Looking to Laura, he remembered, "We owe her bread, but she said she didn't need the honey right now."

"That's good, since we don't have any."

"That's going to change. According to a flyer in the post office, the Union Pacific Railroad is paying five dollars a day to anybody willing to go up to the Nebraska Territory. That's just for laying track, and there's even more money in repairing what's already been laid. I don't know why that is, but that's what the paper said."

She sat very still for a moment, and Spence could almost feel the tension in the air. To divert her, he opened the cover of *Universal Formulary* to retrieve the picture. Handing it to her, he said proudly, "Here's Lydia—and Joshua's on her lap. He'll be four next February."

Both of the Taylors stared at the photograph, and then Laura said, gasping, "Why, she's beautiful! Jess, isn't Mrs. Hardin beautiful?"

"Yes, but she's not one bit prettier than you, Laurie."

"Oh, for heaven's sake, Jess! She's got a face like an angel—and you could just about get your hands around that waist." Peering more closely at the boy on the woman's lap, she observed, "He's sure the spitting image of her, isn't he?"

"They've both got Cullen Jamison's eyes—Cullen's Liddy's father."

"How you must miss them," she murmured sympathetically. "It had to be hard to go off and leave her."

"The hardest thing I've ever had to do. We'd just been married two weeks when I left. Then two months later, she wrote me that Josh was on the way, and I realized we should've waited. It wasn't fair of me to leave her like that, but I'd already been signed up to go."

"War's a terrible business," she said softly. "A terrible, terrible business."

"I wasn't even there when he was born. In the three and one-half years he's been alive, I've seen him twice."

"That's a shame. He looks like such a sweet child."

"He's been a handful for Liddy, I'm afraid."

"He won't be now. You're on your way home, and they'll both be glad to see you," she predicted.

"Not half as glad as I'll be to see them. I've waited a long time to hold her and the boy." Pushing away from the table, he told Jesse, "If you can spare the pants I'm wearing, I'll send them back clean—or you can keep mine and call it even."

"Yours are a lot better than mine, Doc."

"By the time Mrs. Taylor gets them cleaned up, she's more than earned the difference."

"You're sure?"

"Yeah. I've got to get on down the road. I know you don't have a horse to spare, but if you can get me into Salisbury, I'll try to buy one."

"I've already taken care of that, Doc," Jesse said. "I asked around, and I got lucky—Webb Hulett said he had one he'd part with, so I took him up on it."

"Jesse, what did you use for money? You didn't take but five dollars in with you."

"Didn't need any. I told him he could have the mattress, bedstead, and chest out of Danny's room when we leave. He said that was fine with him—and that's how we left it."

"Danny's bedstead?" she echoed in disbelief. "You gave him Danny's things?"

"Laurie, I'll buy you another one when we need it. Right now, we don't need it. I don't aim to take anything I don't have to with us." Not daring to meet her eyes, he added, "I wrote the railroad, telling 'em I'll be taking the job. I said we could be in Omaha by the middle of June."

It was as though the news knocked the wind out

of her. She sank back into her chair, saying nothing. But her eyes did the talking for her. The gold flecks all but disappeared, leaving them a bleak brown. As much as he felt her distress, Spence knew he couldn't help her, that the matter was between them. He pushed away from the table.

"I'm obliged to both of you," he said, rising. "Jesse, if you'll write me—just put it in care of Jamison's Landing in Crawford County, Georgia—I'll see you're paid for the horse. Just tell me how much and where to send it, and I'll see you get the money."

"The hell you will, Doc. No, sir, I wouldn't take your money if I was broke, which I'm not," Jesse declared flatly. "I owe you a lot more than a horse, anyway. That chestnut tied to the tree out front answers to Trader, and he's all saddled up and ready to go. Webb said he's a little skittish, but once he gets used to you, he'll settle down. So go on—I don't want to hear about any money."

"You're sure I can't pay you something? It's a long way from here to Omaha."

"Not a cent. I'd be real insulted if you tried."

"Thanks."

As Spence headed for the small bedroom, he heard Laura Taylor ask, "Jesse, how could you sell Danny's things?"

"I did it for you, Laurie," the man answered. "You've got to let go of the ghosts in this house. If I don't get you out of here, this is all we'll ever have. And we can't take much with us—it'll be about all we can do to get out there in thirty days."

"You might've said something to me before you told them we'd be there then."

"I know, but I knew if I gave you a lot of time to think about it, you'd think of a dozen reasons why we ought to stay here."

"But what about the house? We can't just leave it empty, Jess."

"It's not worth much, but I've got a notion where I can find a buyer. I know you don't see it this way, Laurie, and I'm sorry."

"But—"

"I'm willing to work hard for you, and I'm promising you right now that if you don't kick up a fit about going, I'll build you that house Danny and I drew up the plans for. Only I'm going to make it a lot better. You won't be living in four little rooms, Laurie. You're going to have polished floors and papered walls, fancy rugs, and anything else you want. I'm giving you my word on it."

"Jess, I—"

"And don't you go telling me you don't need those things. If a man can't take care of his wife and kid better than this, he doesn't deserve to have 'em."

Spence couldn't hear her reply, but he could see both sides. She had roots halfway to China, and Taylor had dreams of being somebody. He pulled the wrinkled bedclothes up and laid the pillow on them, looked around to see if he'd forgotten anything, then realized he didn't have anything to leave. He dug into his pocket and brought out his money.

As he came back out to say his good-byes, he discovered why he hadn't heard her. She had her head down on the table, and while he couldn't see her face, he was pretty sure she wept. He looked at Jesse, a silent question on his lips, and the man nodded.

"Well, I'll be going," Spence said awkwardly. "I just want both of you to know if there's ever anything I can do for either of you, just let me know."

She looked up at that. "I guess we'll be somewhere west of Omaha, Dr. Hardin. If you get out that way, be sure to ask around, and somebody will probably know where to find us. If we've got another bed by then, we'll put you up; if not, we'll at least feed you."

"Thanks."

"She means it, Doc—so do I."

The chestnut tried to back away as Spence stepped into the stirrup and pulled himself into the saddle. "Trader, huh?" Spence said softly, leaning forward to smooth the glossy mane against the long neck. "Well, boy, we're on our way home." As he turned the animal toward the road, he wondered what Laura Taylor would say when she found the five dollars he'd left her. Looking over his shoulder at the dilapidated farmhouse, he shook his head. He didn't know why he felt so sorry for her, when reason told him that she'd be better off almost anywhere else.

Central Georgia: May 18, 1865

The chestnut had made good time, covering more than two hundred miles in a little more than two days, and for the first time in well over a year, Spence was almost home. As his eyes took in the Georgia countryside, his heart raced in anticipation of seeing Lydia and the boy. He promised himself it'd be a long time, if ever, before he'd leave Crawford County again.

Jamison's Landing was less than a mile down the Flint River now, just around the next big bend. Closing his eyes briefly, he could envision the big white house, the wide veranda that stretched across the front, the green-shuttered windows that seemed to blend into the trees dotting a sweeping expanse of lush lawn. He'd never been particularly fond of Cullen Jamison's magnificent mansion, but now it was like the Promised Land, beckoning him home.

Yeah, there it was up ahead. Sitting on a tree-covered knoll, it rose from that red Georgia dirt to preside like a queen over the languorous countryside. Even on days when the landing itself was filled with bales of raw cotton ready to be loaded, there had been a somnolent quality to the place, as though life had slowed to a sleepy pace, and the low, rumbling songs sung by Cullen's slaves were its lullabies.

But the river landing was bare now, bereft of bales and slaves, and the only sounds cutting through heavy, humid air were the lapping of water against wood and the strident cawing of two crows. There was an otherworldliness to the place.

Spence's gaze traveled up the worn pathway to the fork in it, one to the main plantation house, the other to the buildings beyond. His eyes sought the house, and he suddenly realized something was terribly wrong.

What had appeared so majestic at a distance was anything but that up close. A derelict shell of its former self, its broken windowpanes, fractured lattices, and dangling shutters no longer hidden by the curtain of trees, it loomed silent and forbidding over an empty world. The almost decadent opulence of Cullen Jamison's grand home had given way to a pervasive decay in months, not years. Spence stared in disbelief, his mind denying the scene before his eyes. It couldn't be, but it was. As numbness faded, his thoughts raced, seeking some explanation.

Lydia and her family had been forced from the house, either by Yankee soldiers or by rebellious slaves, the latter thought the more unbearable. Whatever had happened, it had been cataclysmic enough to scatter nearly a hundred inhabitants, leaving none to tell the tale. He didn't even sense another soul.

Union soldiers would have burned the place down, but there was no sign of fire. And if the Landing's slaves had ransacked it, where was everything? French-made carpets, Austrian crystal chandeliers,

Venetian wallpapers—none of those things would have meant anything to them. Even if they'd killed every white and all the house Negroes, too, they'd still be here, if for no other reason than they had nowhere else to go.

And yet he couldn't quite discount what Lydia had written him more than six months ago. *With every able-bodied white man off to the war, the Negroes have become a lazy, insolent lot. The way some of them look at me chills my blood to the bone. Josh and I sleep behind a locked door, and I keep Papa's hunting gun with me at night.*

He'd sent Ross Donnelly to her for that very reason. But with the war over, had Ross left for England? While that seemed plausible enough, what about the rest of them? Maybe Lydia and Joshua had fled to Macon, but surely she would have written Spence from there. And what about the old Negro woman who'd raised her? Auntie Fan, Liddy'd called her.

As far as he knew, the Jamisons didn't have much family anywhere. Cullen had come from Arkansas by himself years before, and by virtue of being an only child, Sally Winslowe Jamison had been an heiress. Lydia had been their only issue. Not much to choose from there. Except he'd heard Liddy say her mother had a cousin, a distant cousin actually, in Macon. Was it Stevens? Stephenson? Eliza Stephenson maybe. He was pretty sure Liddy had said the woman's name was Stephenson. If he went into Macon, he could find that out. All of Cullen's family had died off, except for some distant relations in Arkansas.

Spence reined in just short of the porte cochere at the west side of the house and dismounted. He crossed the deserted porch to press the latch on the unlocked doors. The heavy panels creaked inward, sending a wedge of sunlight across the empty foyer floor, casting his shadow almost to the ceiling. As he walked, the echo of his boots reverberated off the high white walls. Above him, an ornate plaster circle surrounded the bare spot where the elaborate hundred-candle chandelier had hung.

The curved staircase was gone, but the wall still bore the outline of the boards that had once attached it there. Even the second-story banister and the balustrades had been removed, giving the impression that the hallway above was suspended in thin air. The staircase had been wide enough for three hoop-skirted women to share its steps on either side. The first time he'd seen Liddy, she'd been watching from that banister above, then at her father's bidding, she'd glided gracefully, her skirts billowing, down those stairs.

As he opened interior doors, he found the whole place was empty, utterly devoid of its former grandeur. Every piece of elegant furniture, every French-made carpet, the carved marble fireplace surrounds, all the portraits and mirrors—everything of value had been removed. The place was more than abandoned. It was gutted.

He had to go outside to use the fire stairs to Cullen's second-floor bedroom window. Again, the panes were gone, their lattice frames splintered. Easing his body through the hole, he walked through the empty room to Sally Jamison's bedchamber, where a water-stained brocade chaise with one leg missing lay on its side next to one kidskin slipper.

Liddy's room was as bare as the rest. No furniture. No rug. No draperies. Nothing but a broken glass perfume bottle without its stopper. It looked like the one he'd sent her from Atlanta, but he couldn't be sure. Picking it up, he sniffed the neck. It smelled like dust.

Moving to the window, he looked out toward the stables. Cullen had loved his horses more than his wife, everybody said, and the old man hadn't denied it. Like Midnight Folly, they'd all been purebred Arabians. Under pressure from the Confederate government, the old man had sold most of them for cavalry mounts, and two weeks later, he'd had his first stroke.

As he started to turn away, Spence thought he saw movement near the corner of the stable. He looked down again just as a barefooted Negro boy disappeared inside.

"Halt! Stay right there!" he shouted, racing down the fire stairs. Drawing his revolver, he kicked open the stable door, and the force stirred up a cloud of moldy hay dust. "Don't move, or I'll shoot!" he shouted, edging inside.

Two dark, skinny arms came up from behind a pile of tack, followed by a head. "I ain't done nuthin'—I ain't!" The whites of the kid's eyes were round in an almost black face. "I's sleep here, massa!"

Spence didn't recognize the boy. "Where's Jamison?" he demanded tersely. "Where's the master?" When the kid didn't answer, he leveled the gun. "Where is Cullen Jamison?"

"He be gone."

"Where?"

"Prob'ly hell." The boy rolled his eyes. "He daid." Dropping one hand, he scratched his distended belly. "He mean old man, but the devil he be burnin' 'im up now."

"What about the others? Where are the others?" Spence asked urgently.

The kid shrugged. "They gone—ain't nobody here 'ceptin' darkies like me." Shuffling his bare feet on the dirt floor, he came close, jutting his chin out. "We be free—I don't got to do nuthin' white folks axe me—ole Abe Likken, he done saw to that," he added, grinning.

"Miz Sally—what about Miz Sally?" Spence prompted. "Where is she?"

The boy giggled, then thumped his head, and a couple of flies took off. "Ain't right no mo. Miz Sally, she doan know nuthin' no mo."

"She's dead?"

He shook his head and grinned again, showing off white teeth. "Miz Sally ain't daid—uh-uh, she ain't. She jes doan know nuthin', 'cause she be real sick. Miz Liddy, she be mighty mean, fussin' at Miz Sally like that."

"Where's Miz Liddy?"

The thin shoulders went up and down again. "Doan rightly know. She gone, too."

"There was a man here—Ross Donnelly—what do you know about him?"

"He gone, jes' like the rest of 'em."

Relief washed over Spence. Ross had probably taken her somewhere safe, and someone was supposed to tell him. "I don't suppose you know where they went, do you?"

"Uh-uh."

Pulling the horehound drops from his pocket, Spence unwrapped the package, then held out a piece, keeping it just out of the boy's reach. "Look—tell me straight, and you can have this. Where's Miz Liddy?"

The boy hung back. "Thas fo' me?"

"If you tell me what you know. I've got to find Miz Liddy and the young master—her little boy. Can you help me?"

"They's ain't here—they's ain't. They be gone long time now. They's jes' darkies like me here."

"How many?" he asked quickly, hoping he could find one who'd tell him more than the kid.

"Some," the boy responded evasively, reaching for the candy. "Ain't no cotton no mo—cain't do nuthin'. Folk's be hongry, and they ain't nuthin' t' eat."

"How many freed slaves are here?"

"Doan know—cain't count." He appeared to consider the matter for a moment, then shook his head. "Mos' jes' run off, but they's nowheres t' go."

"What about Auntie Fan?"

"Miz Liddy, she be makin' Fan go. Fan, she say that girl jes' be evil."

He couldn't remember the name of the old mammy's husband. "Auntie Fan's man—where is he?"

"Daid. Buck be dyin' same time he be diggin' Mistuh Cullen's hole."

He'd probably gotten all he could from the kid, but he tried one more time. "When did they go? Miz

Liddy—Miz Sally—Auntie Fan—when did they leave?''

"They be gone long time ago. Befo' th' trees be comin' out."

"And they took Miz Sally with them?"

"No suh—Miz Sally, she be—"

"Sick," Spence finished for him. "All right—if Miz Liddy didn't take Miz Sally, but she did take Auntie Fan—then where is Miz Sally now?"

The kid twisted from side to side, swinging his arms, then looked up. "Got mo' candy?"

"Yes." Fishing out another piece of horehound, Spence held it out. "You little dickens—you know where Miz Sally is, don't you?" Keeping a tight grip on the candy, he said, "You don't get it until you tell me."

"Miz Sally, she be in town." In a flash of black, skinny arm, he grabbed the horehound and ran.

There wasn't any sense going after the kid, Spence decided. He'd gotten about all he could there. The only town of any size around here was Macon.

As he climbed the few steps to the gray porch, Spence hoped he had the right house. When he'd asked around for an Eliza Stephenson, he'd been directed to the "Widder Stephenson," but nobody seemed to be able to connect her to the Jamisons. And judging by the modest clapboard structure, things didn't look promising.

At the door, Spence smoothed his hair before he rapped on the door. Unless the widow proved to be Sally's cousin, he'd reached dead end. Pasting a smile on his face, he waited.

It seemed like an eternity before anyone answered, but the door finally opened, and a young Negro boy peered out. Looking Spence over, he said, "Yassuh?"

"Is Mrs. Stephenson in?"

"Whut yuh be wantin' with her?"

"I'm a relative of sorts."

"Oh, for heaven's sake, Willie—who is it?"

"Doan know." He opened the door wider. "Says he be kin t' yuhs, Miz Liza."

"Well, let him in," an elderly woman ordered impatiently. Coming to the door herself, she murmured apologetically, "Don't mind Willie—he's still learning. Now go on with you," she told the boy. "We'll practice this later." Her dark bird's eyes took in Spence's face, trying to place it. "I'm afraid you have the advantage of me, Mr. . . . ?"

"Hardin—Spencer Hardin, ma'am. We haven't met, but I'm Lydia's husband. I believe you're related to Sally Jamison, aren't you?"

"Yes, but . . ." Her eyes widened, betraying dismay. "Oh, dear . . . you're the doctor, aren't you?" Before he could answer that question, she answered his. "Yes, my mother and Sally's were cousins, sir. But Lydia—"

"Is she here?"

"Certainly not."

"Do you know where she is?"

"I have no idea—none at all." Seeing the disappointment in his face, she stepped back. "Perhaps you'd best come in and sit down, Dr. Hardin." Turning away, she admitted, "I just hate this, truly I do. How that wretched girl—well, it's just beyond me—it just is."

"Nothing's happened to her—she's not ill, or anything like that, is she?"

Instead of answering him, she walked through a doorway into a shabby genteel parlor, then gestured to a pair of chairs. "Do sit down, sir, and I'll have Willie bring you some coffee. It's certainly not the best, by any means, but I'm fortunate to have any at all. With a little sugar and some cream, it's almost passable. Willie!"

"Yassum, Miz Liza?"

"Coffee for Dr. Hardin, if you please. And do bring the cream pot and sugar bowl, too." As the boy left, she turned her pale eyes to Spence before she sighed. "If Sally were herself at all, I'd certainly let her be the one to tell you, but she's in a dreadful fix, Dr. Hardin."

"I'm afraid I don't understand, ma'am."

"Well, she never was the strong sort, of course, and cousin or not, she has to be the flightiest woman I ever met—even as a girl, she had more looks than brains, you know."

"Yes, I know," he murmured dryly, wondering how long she meant to meander on. "And I expect the war made her worse."

"It wasn't just the war, Dr. Hardin. With Cullen passing on, and the girl misbehaving like that, it'd be a wonder if she *had* kept her sanity, I suppose."

"She's had a nervous collapse?"

"She certainly has—mad as Ophelia, I'm afraid. Not that Lydia cared for that, though. She's got no thought for anyone but herself." She caught herself and looked up at him. "I'm sorry, Dr. Hardin, but

I've never been one to mince words, and I don't mean to start now."

"Mrs. Stephenson—"

"Sally doesn't even know where she is or how she came to be here, I'm afraid. I'm not even certain she knows who I am, either."

"I'm sorry."

"You weren't here, so I don't fault you, but Lydia is quite another matter," the woman declared, her lips thinning in disapproval. "She knew exactly what she was doing, sir."

"Mrs. Stephenson, Lydia is my wife," he reminded her. "All I want to do is find her and my son. I'm worried something is wrong."

"Wrong? I'll say it is. The hussy just brought Sally here—for a visit she said—and while I was cutting lemon cake to go with the coffee, she just took herself off. We all thought she'd be right back, and Sally waited up all night like a dog for its master, but they'd just gone on without her."

"That can't be."

"Well, it is. And it has been a struggle keeping body and soul together. I couldn't afford food for myself before, and now I've got to feed Sally. If I didn't have Willie, I don't know what I'd do. I give him a quarter a week, and it's a strain on the pocketbook to do that."

"There's got to be some mistake."

"Mistake? I hardly think so. Lydia knew what she was about, sir. They didn't want to be bothered with Sally, and to tell the truth, I'm surprised they took the little boy."

"What in *hell* are you talking about?" he demanded. "Can't you just answer me?"

"Really, sir, but there is no need for vulgarity, is there?" she responded stiffly.

The woman was driving him mad with a piecemeal tale. Running his hand through his hair distractedly, he tried to placate her. "Look, I'm sorry. But surely you can understand my concern. I've had no word from her in months, and now I've come home to find her gone. I'm just asking you what happened, Mrs. Stephenson, and that's *all* I want to know."

"There's no need for temper, is there?"

"I don't know."

"Well, I suppose you have a right to be angry," she decided. "Willie, have you gotten yourself lost? Dr. Hardin wishes his coffee!" As the child appeared, carrying a large tray, she smiled thinly. "Just set it on this table and run along, will you? That's a good boy." Pausing long enough for him to leave the room, she filled two cups from the pot, added two hard chunks of raw sugar and a dollop of thick cream to each, then pushed one cup toward Spence. "There was a time when I had more to offer than this, but I don't guess anything will ever be the same anymore. I just wish she would have left something for the care of her mother, but she didn't. All that money and not one cent to spare for Sally."

He was ready to strangle her, but he reached for the cup instead. Taking a polite sip, he found the stuff too bitter to drink, even worse than that concoction of Laura Taylor's.

"It's not very good, is it?" she asked, sighing.

"No, it's all right," he lied. "You were about to tell

me what you knew of Liddy," he added, pointedly reminding her.

"What is there to tell? She's just gone."

"Where?" he managed through gritted teeth.

"They certainly didn't tell me where they were going."

"Who is *they*, Mrs. Stephenson?"

"Why, she and that man. One of the Donnellys, I believe—yes, I'm sure it was."

"Oh." Somewhat relieved, he sat back. "I expect if I asked around, she's somewhere here in town, then."

A thin eyebrow shot up. "I hardly think so, sir," she said stiffly. "Macon is not that sort of place. We don't welcome jezebels here."

"It's not what you think, ma'am. I knew he was here—I sent him to Jamison's Landing myself."

For a long moment, she regarded him as though he were an utter fool. "Then you set the fox in the henhouse, Dr. Hardin. And you needn't take my word for that, because there are plenty of others who can tell you what went on out there." Taking in his thunderstruck expression, she nodded. "There's no pleasant way to say this, but she's run off with him."

"*What?* I don't believe you!"

"Shouting won't alter the truth, I'm afraid." Feeling genuinely sorry for him, she looked away. "I didn't want to believe it either, but the morning after she left Sally here, I walked downtown, which wasn't an easy thing to do on these old legs, believe me. You cannot imagine my shock when I discovered Lydia and young Donnelly been living together as husband and wife for a good month before they left.

Leaving like that wasn't any spur-of-the-moment thing, sir—they'd planned the whole thing."

"No," he said hoarsely.

She nodded. "After Cullen died in January, Lydia put everything up for sale with absolutely no regard to the fact that it was Sally's, not hers. When she couldn't find anyone with enough hard money to buy the Landing itself, she sold things piecemeal, according to the banker. She made a tidy sum for herself—close to twenty thousand dollars in these hard times—and that wasn't the whole of it. The conniving little thief found where Cullen had buried his strongbox, and she brought four thousand dollars in gold to the bank two days after his death. When Mr. Davidson said she had to put the money in her mother's name, she caused quite a scene, insisting Sally was too incompetent to be trusted with it."

"My God."

"He refused to let her take it back, or it'd be gone, too. As it is, Sally sits here starving with me, because she can't touch that four thousand dollars until it goes through probate, and as far as I know, there hasn't even been an executor appointed. She's not going to live long enough to see a penny of it, and then it will go to Lydia anyway."

"Liddy wouldn't—she couldn't leave her mother destitute."

"Oh, you don't have to believe me, sir—you can ask the banker or Cullen's lawyer or anyone else, for that matter. With no regard for decency or the law, she cleaned out everything that should have gone to Sally. Then she and Mr. Donnelly packed up what they wanted and left town. I worry about that little boy, sir—anybody as indifferent as Lydia was to the woman who bore her cannot be much of a mother herself."

He was too numb to respond. It couldn't be, he told himself. Liddy didn't even really like Ross. "Handsome enough, but exceedingly shallow," she'd pronounced him once.

"When they were driving out of town, she had her head on his shoulder, and he had his arm around her, according to those who saw her. The way they were acting, Mrs. Henderson said she thought the man was Lydia's husband. Now if that isn't a jezebel, I don't know what is."

He had to get out of there before he exploded. He couldn't think. He couldn't even breathe. Pushing the coffee cup out of the way, he stumbled to his feet and bolted for the front door. In the front yard, he leaned against a huge oak tree and closed his eyes, waiting for the rage to pass. The woman had to be lying about Liddy. But that didn't make any sense either.

"Don't you want to see Sally?" the old woman asked from the porch.

Straightening up, he managed to answer, "Later—not today."

Once out of Macon, Spence rode hell-for-leather to nowhere in particular, with no regard for anything until his exhausted horse slowed to a walk, then finally stopped, too winded to go any farther. Dropping from the saddle, Spence lay facedown in the steamy grass, cursing Liddy, Ross, and the whole damned world.

The witch had left him. While he'd been away in

the hell called war, she'd betrayed him with a man he'd counted a friend, and then she'd left before he could even get home, stealing his son. Jezebel wasn't a strong enough word for what she was.

He didn't care who had seduced whom. They'd both betrayed him. And they'd pay for it, he promised himself. No matter how long it took, no matter how hard they tried to hide, he'd track them down, and he'd kill them. And by God, they were going to look down the barrel of his gun and beg his forgiveness before he sent them both to hell.

Near Fort Kearny, Nebraska Territory: July 31, 1865

Flies buzzed, playing cat and mouse with the rolled newspaper in Laura Taylor's hand. Drawn by food, they swarmed over the camp, and a closed tent flap was no match for the winged beasts, she realized wearily. By day, they held sway, feasting on everything from bread dough to meat cooking on a spit over fire, drowning themselves indiscriminately in coffee, milk, and gravy. Then at night, the mosquitoes from the Platte River took over, attacking any exposed inch of human skin in an insatiable quest for blood.

Today, the supposedly dry heat was anything but, and within the confines of the tent, the humid air was stifling. Between swats, she had to stop to mop the sweat from her face. Telling herself she had an easier life than Jesse, she uncovered the bucket long enough to fill the dipper and wet a rag with the tepid water. After wiping her face, arms, neck, and the crevice between her breasts, she felt a little better, but as she reached to put the piece of wood back, she realized she was too late. Two flies were already swimming in the bucket.

People who thought hell was a fiery pit deep in the earth hadn't been to Nebraska in July, she decided as she secured the towel covering the bowl of bread dough. Sighing, she picked up the almost full bucket and carried it outside, where she tossed the flies out with the water. She supposed if she'd been like the men, she'd have just strained out the flies and drunk what was left, saving herself a lot of trouble. Bucket in hand, she headed to the river for water she'd have to strain and boil before she used it.

While Jesse had it hard, too, she couldn't help resenting how much of himself he was willing to trade to the railroad for that good pay. All William Russell had to do was dangle a little more money in front of him, and Jesse'd volunteer to do anything, work anywhere, even if it meant he had to work six and one-half days a week so far away that he only got back to camp twice a month, and then for just long enough to spend the night and pick up a clean change of clothes before he left again.

He was doing it for her, he said, but she knew better. She hadn't asked him to, she didn't want him to, and no matter how much money he made, no dream was worth what he was doing to himself. She'd been alone through years of war, waiting for him to come home, and she was alone again, only this time she was fifteen hundred miles from home, living in a tent smack dab in the middle of a camp of the roughest, dirtiest men she'd ever laid eyes on. It was hard to dream in a place like this.

But perhaps the worst aspect of the situation was that for the first time in her life, she found herself regarded as a liability. Jesse's foreman had made it

more than clear that he preferred hiring bachelors. In
his opinion, a man's having a wife gave him divided
loyalties and kept him from giving his all to the railroad. There wasn't any place for a decent woman
here, he'd told Jesse. And when he'd seen her, he'd
suggested she ought to go back to North Carolina,
which was impossible.

She and Jesse had sold her homeplace for just
enough money to get them out there, so they'd have
to make the best of things, she told herself resolutely.
Her only other choice right now would be to go back
to Omaha and stay there until fall, when the Union
Pacific would be setting up winter quarters farther
west. But she didn't have anyone in Omaha, either.

The one thing that Mr. Russell had been right
about was that there weren't any decent women out
here, or if there were, she hadn't seen them. But there
sure wasn't any dearth of the other kind, the hard-
eyed hussies who plied their unfathomable trade in
tents a few hundred yards beyond the camp. Hog
ranches, those places were called. After pay envelopes were handed out, the unwashed, unkempt men
streamed across the staked rail beds to stand in line,
money in hand, for a ten-minute turn with a girl
dozens of men had already been with that day. And
when they came back, drunk and loud, they'd brag
about how such and such a girl wouldn't be able to
sit for a week.

No, she'd just have to get by alone until fall, she
told herself. Russell had told Jesse if they got far
enough west before they made winter camp, there
was an abandoned trapper's cabin on the railroad
right-of-way out beyond Fort McPherson she and

Jesse could use until it was time to move on in the spring. Jess didn't know much about the place, but he said even if it was a shack, he'd make it habitable for her and the baby.

"Well, ain't you something?" somebody said behind her. "Umm-umm—if you don't look good enough to eat, honey."

Whirling, she faced a leering stranger, and his manner frightened her. Running the tip of her tongue over dry lips, she considered her escape while she stayed outwardly calm.

"Whatsamatter? Cat got your tongue?"

"No," she responded coldly. "I don't like being startled."

His gaze dropped lower, taking in the gentle round of her stomach. "Since you already got yourself a bun in the oven, I reckon you know how to show a man a real fine time, don't you?"

"You made a wrong turn, mister—the hog ranch is on the other side of those tents," she told him tartly. "I'm told you can get whatever you want for a couple of dollars over there."

"I got no interest in some tired ole whore, honey. I got myself a real hankerin' for fresher meat, and I don't see anybody out here but you," he said, lunging for her.

Dodging him, she flung the empty bucket at his face and ran back toward camp. He was so close behind her that she could feel his hot, reeking breath, and smell the ripe stench of his sweat-soaked clothes. His dirty hand caught her sleeve, ripping it from the shoulder of her dress as she jerked free. Gulping air, her heart pounding in her ears, she managed a desperate burst of speed.

"Damned bitch—I'm gonna hurt you for this—ain't nobody ever gonna see that purty face again," he threatened her.

As her foot gained the road, the heel of her shoe broke, sending her sprawling face first while white-hot pain gripped her ankle. She tried to scramble to her feet, but the ankle wouldn't hold her. Feigning capitulation, she lay still.

"Yeah, you and me's gonna have some fun, all right," he said, bending over her. His hand grasped her damp hair roughly, jerking her down into a shallow ditch, as she tried to claw her way free. He hit her, snapping her head back, then crouched over her, unbuttoning dirty trousers. "Now you buck real good, you hear?" he said as his other hand pushed up her skirt.

A gunshot split the heavy, humid air, and her attacker jumped back, tripping over his sagging pants. "What the hell—? Tommy!"

"Leave her alone! You don't, and I'm pulling this trigger again! I won't miss twice neither!" a younger voice shouted. "I mean it, Jake! You back off her or I'll plug you right there!"

"Hell I will! You damned little bastard—"

While her attacker was distracted, Laura scrambled on all fours for the stranger with the gun. "He was . . . he was trying to force himself on me," she managed as he stepped between her and the man he'd called Jake.

"It's all right, ma'am," the red-headed kid reassured her. "He ain't touchin' you again." Facing the glowering man, he declared, "You're a no-count son-ofabitch, Jake Eldred, and I aim to see you get what's comin' to you. I don't reckon you're gonna be hurtin' Maggie or any other woman like this again."

"You sniveling, lily-livered little—you ain't got the guts to shoot again, and you know it. You're as spineless as that puling sister of yours."

"Ain't nobody on earth deserves a beating like that. She lost the baby, but seein' as it was yours, maybe that part of it was a blessing," the kid told him. "You ain't gonna be gettin' no more babies on her or anybody else, Jake."

"Go to hell, Tommy. I ain't afraid of you." Rising cautiously, Jake measured the distance between them with his eyes.

"Watch out!" Laura screamed as he jumped for the kid's gun.

Tommy pulled the trigger, and Eldred pitched to the ground again, holding his elbow, as blood soaked his sleeve.

"My arm—you broke my arm! You little bastard, you broke my arm! My elbow's gone!"

Cocking the hammer, Tommy moved closer. "Let's see you hit a woman now, Jake," he gibed. "Let's see you swing on somebody now. I took care of one thing, and I'm about to take care of another."

"Don't kill him—you'll just ruin your life, too," Laura argued. "Let the law take care of him."

"Not much law out here, ma'am," the kid said, leveling his sights on the wounded man. "But killin's too good for him, so I'm just gonna fix him."

Realizing what the boy meant to do, Jake Eldred cringed. "No, Tommy . . . don't . . . don't do this,

Tom. I didn't mean to hit Maggie like that, but she riled me—dammit, a man's got a right to do what he wants to his wife, Tom, and it ain't like she . . . No . . . don't shoot . . . No! *No!*"

As the gun fired, the man on the ground gave an unearthly shriek, then he doubled up, jerking and quivering. When Laura dared to look down, he was babbling incoherently, holding what was left of his bloody crotch.

"Don't guess you'll be puttin' that where it ain't wanted no more," the kid said coolly.

"Oh, God . . . oh, my God . . . Jesus . . . ohhh . . ."

Turning to Laura, the boy shook his head. "I shoulda done that the first time he beat up on my sister. He'd change after the baby came, she said. He was upset. She made everything out to be her fault. But it didn't make any difference whether she crossed him or not. He was always upset about something, and he was always hittin' her. Now they got two little kids, not countin' the one she just lost." Squinting up at the sky for a moment, he added, "A man don't change his nature—if he's born mean, he stays mean until somebody takes it out of him. I shoulda done that a long time ago."

"Thank you," she managed. "If you hadn't shown up when you did, I don't know what I would have done."

"I heard you hollerin', so I figured I'd find him. You're lucky he didn't cut you up some first, 'cause he likes to do that, too. Jake don't enjoy a woman 'less he hurts her."

"He's done this before?"

"Yeah. There's been two others I know of, but the

law wouldn't do anything about it, 'cause the women wouldn't say it was him. I guess they figured if he wasn't hanged for it, he'd be back to kill 'em, and they was beat up pretty bad the first time, you know. And Maggie woulda sworn he was at home when it happened, anyways, 'cause she'd be afraid to tell on him."

"I see."

"No, you don't. Nobody can. Three days ago he beat her until she spit up blood, and like I said, she lost the baby. She's twenty years old, and she looks forty."

"I'm sorry."

"But I got even for her," he went on. "To somebody like Jake, his life ain't worth much without his tallywhacker."

"Aren't you afraid he'll come after you?"

He looked to his brother-in-law, who was still flopping on the ground like a fish out of water, crying and moaning in agony. "By the time he can get on a horse and ride, me and Maggie and the kids'll be somewhere he can't find us." Walking to his horse, he swung up into the saddle. "You tell 'em what you have to, ma'am, 'cause the law ain't findin' us neither."

"She's lucky to have a brother like you," Laura said softly.

"I'm just sorry it took me so long to grow up enough to help her, that's all." Adjusting the brim of his hat to shade his face, the kid kneed the animal. "Tell 'em it was Tommy Hale that shot him." Turning his horse, he went east on the Platte Road toward Omaha.

"Jesus . . . you gotta help me," Jake Eldred gasped. "My privates is gone."

Instead, she walked away. Her pity had left with the boy. "Hey, you!—I gotta have a doc—I gotta!" Eldred called after her.

When she reached the cluster of tents, she hesitated for a moment before she ducked beneath an open canvas flap. "Mrs. Taylor," Dr. Warren murmured, looking up from a battered campaign chair. Refolding the newspaper on his lap, he exhaled. "Is there anything I can do for you?"

"There's a wounded man across the road—over by the river," she said, coming to the point quickly. "He accosted me when I went for water."

"I can't say it wasn't bound to happen," he observed dryly. "This is hardly the place for a decent female, and so I told your husband when he brought you out here." Realizing how unsympathetic that sounded, he unbent enough to ask, "You aren't hurt, are you?"

"Just my dress, and I can fix that."

"I told your husband your condition wouldn't protect you—there are men in these camps so woman-hungry that a wart-covered crone isn't safe around them."

"He wasn't from camp—he'd apparently just stopped for water when he saw me."

He heaved himself up from the folding chair and reached for his hat. "I'll see if I can round up some fellows to look for him, but if you're going to stay out here, things like this are bound to happen. It'll be different in another year or so, but right now, it's no place for a lady."

"I'm not the only female out here," she pointed out.

"Oh, we got hog ranches popping up like dandelions after a rain, all right, but women like that know what they're getting into."

"There's no need to send anybody out to look for the man who accosted me, anyway, Dr. Warren," she said tiredly. "He's been shot twice, so he's not going anywhere."

"No need to get uppity with me, Mrs. Taylor. The truth's the truth, regardless of the messenger. But you've come to the right person, anyway. Who shot him?"

"I don't know—somebody who just happened to see what was happening. I didn't even get a chance to thank him before he rode off."

"Probably running from the law, and he didn't want any notice."

"I don't know."

"Well, there's no need to bring you into it at all, then. I'll just report finding a wounded man, and if he dies, that'll be the end of it. If he doesn't, he'll be too afraid of hanging to mention his part in the business."

"Thank you," she said dryly.

"Doc! Doc Warren!"

"Excuse me, ma'am. Yeah?" Warren answered loudly.

A breathless fellow burst through the open tent flaps. "There's been an accident 'bout thirty miles up ahead! You gotta come real quick!"

"How bad is it?"

"Real bad, Doc—I guess they got a man about cut

in half up there. They ain't moving the car off 'im till you get there to say he's dead."

"I'll get my bag just in case," Warren decided. Noticing Laura again, he said brusquely, "Your little matter will have to wait, I'm afraid."

"But—"

"Mrs. Taylor, I'm in a hurry. If that fellow across the road dies before I get back, it's not much of a loss, anyway." Having said that, he picked up a large canvas bag and pushed past her.

Not wanting to go back to face Jake Eldred by herself again, she went to her own tent, where she sank into a scarred kitchen chair, laid her head on the table, and wept. She didn't know what she'd expected of Warren when she'd gone to see him, but what she'd gotten was little more than censure, she reflected bitterly. If she'd gone in there shaking and crying, vowing to go back to North Carolina, the railroad doctor would probably have rushed over to pin a medal on the man on his way out of camp.

She hated it here. She hated everything about the place—the isolation, the heat, the hostility, the endless days of waiting for a husband too tired to talk when he came in. The war had taken more than Danny from her. It had changed Jesse to a driven man.

The stinging tears of self-pity subsided, and she sat up. Things would get better. She'd be all right. She was a strong woman. Instead of feeling sorry for herself, she ought to be praying for the man trapped under that train thirty miles up the track.

Feeling better, she washed her hands, then turned her attention back to the bread dough. Punching it down again, she separated it into three parts, flattened them on a wet cloth, then rolled each piece, pinching the ends together before she put them into the loaf pans. As hot as the weather was, it wouldn't take them long to rise this last time.

Determined to keep busy the rest of the day, she baked, mended, and sewed on the fancy lawn christening dress she was making for the baby. The whole front was delicately pleated with tiny stitches, while the yoke above them was intricately embroidered with white silk roses on white lawn. The work was so tedious and so time consuming, it'd take another month to finish the gown the way she wanted it to look.

That night, she read in bed, all but oblivious to the storm outside, finding company in the mythic heroes of the Trojan War. Too sleepy to finish the story, she trimmed down the lantern wick, then blew out the flame. As the thin line of smoke curled into the darkness, she closed her eyes.

"Mrs. Taylor! Mrs. Taylor!"

At first, she thought she'd been dreaming, then she realized someone was outside, shouting to waken her. Rolling over, she groped for the lantern. The wind had died down, and the rain had stopped, but the sun wasn't up yet.

"Mrs. Taylor, can you hear me?"

"Yes," she mumbled sleepily. "Yes!" she answered more loudly. "Who is it?"

"Russell—Bill Russell! Are you decent?"

"Yes!"

Leaning over the side of the bed to reach the lantern, she searched for the box of sulphur matches.

She could hear Russell fumbling to unfasten the tent opening.

"I'll get it!" she called out.

She struck a match and lit the wick, watching the flame grow until it cast grotesque, flickering shadows up the pale canvas walls. Padding on barefeet to the front of the tent, she managed to unlace the heavy flaps. The yellow light illuminated the man's haggard face and reflected in his red-rimmed eyes.

"Whatever—?" She could feel the ground sway beneath her feet, and she knew. "It's Jesse, isn't it?"

"I wish I could say it wasn't," he answered. "I'm sorry, Mrs. Taylor—there wasn't anything anybody could do."

The ground gave way, and the world tumbled like a brick wall collapsing around her before everything went mercifully black.

Nebraska Territory: September 11, 1865

Spence reined in and leaned forward to ease his tired shoulders as he stared at the muddy Missouri, thinking it was still a long way to California, and he had to keep going or he'd never make it across the Rockies and the Sierras before winter hit. He'd probably made a mistake by taking the Platte Road west, but he'd wanted to avoid the Comanches and the desert heat in Texas, and any way he chose, he couldn't miss hitting mountains. Besides, Ross and Liddy had been down this road six months earlier.

It had cost Spence more than five hundred dollars and a lot of wasted time before Allan Pinkerton's agency in Chicago had gotten back to him with information gleaned from Ross's sister Phoebe in England. By telling her Sally Jamison's will had been probated, leaving Lydia a sizable amount of money, Pinkerton's man had managed to get the address of Ross's maternal uncle in San Francisco.

While expressing horror at her brother's scandalous behavior, she'd confided that he'd written his family, saying the blockade had made it impossible for him to join them, and he and Lydia were heading west instead, where he'd been promised a position

in their uncle's banking business. Assuring them of
his noble intent, Ross had also said Lydia had opened
his eyes to her husband's true character, implying
that Spence had married her for her money. Once
they were settled in, he also indicated she'd get a
divorce, and they'd legalize their "irregular union."

Irregular union, hell. It was adultery, no matter
what they wanted to call it. And Spence would see
both of them dead before he'd agree to any divorce.
They'd dashed his dreams, stolen his child, and made
him the laughingstock of Crawford County, and
there was no way on earth he'd forgive them for it.

He just wished he'd found out where they'd gone
earlier, before he'd had to spend months enduring
the whispers, the knowing looks that told him the
whole damned neighborhood knew his wife had
cuckolded him. And it hadn't helped one damned
bit to know that most of them pitied him. If he hadn't
been waiting to hear from Pinkerton, he would have
gotten out of there a long time ago.

But so far, the information he'd paid for was prov-
ing out, he conceded. There'd been a Mr. and Mrs.
Ross Donnelly and son registered at the finest hotels
in St. Louis and Kansas City last March. Now, if he
found they'd stayed in Omaha also, he'd know he
wasn't on a wild-goose chase.

When he reached town, he wanted to find a hotel
where he could get a bath and a decent meal for a
change. Not knowing what he'd get into in California, and not wanting to carry a lot of money on him,
he'd been sleeping under the stars, making himself
skillet biscuits and strong coffee, and fishing in the

river whenever he could. By now, he was pretty sure he smelled worse than a billy goat.

The bay sidestepped suddenly, and Spence jerked to attention. He heard the heart-pausing buzz before he saw the coiled rattlesnake, and he pulled the reins taut with one hand while he went for the Navy Colt with the other. He pulled the trigger, and the headless coil unraveled to writhe a couple of times before it lay still, looking like a dirty piece of rope in the dusty road. As the gun smoke dissipated, he shoved the revolver back into its holster.

Four months ago, he probably couldn't have killed the snake with one shot. It had taken him hundreds of hours of practice, but now he could cock and fire five times and hit his mark with every bullet. And he'd made himself quick enough that he could draw and shatter a dropped shot glass before it hit the ground. Ross wouldn't have any more of a chance than that rattlesnake.

"Come on, Clyde," he murmured, nudging the horse. "We're not getting anywhere just standing here."

Clyde. It was a helluva name for a good animal, Spence reflected wryly. But when Trader had gone lame outside Boonville, Missouri, he'd been damned lucky to find the chestnut gelding that he hadn't cared what they called it. "Clyde's a mite fidgety, and that scares some folks off, you know," the fellow had warned him as he took Spence's hundred dollars. Fidgety had turned out to mean if the animal was given its head, it ran like an Arabian. What Clyde had lacked, Spence decided, was exercise.

A steam whistle sounded behind him. Half turning

in the saddle, he could see the train coming down tracks parallel to the road. Suddenly, the air brakes squealed, and the black iron locomotive shuddered before it slowed. The cars passing him proclaimed UNION PACIFIC R. R. in bold, gaudy letters. Mustachioed men and bonneted women stared out of windows rolling by. In one of the cars, a tow-headed little boy had his nose pressed against the glass while he waved at Spence.

As the track cleared, a wide sign peered across the rails, welcoming strangers. OMAHA. THE GATE CITY OF THE WEST. The train's clattering wheels ground against the steel tracks as the air brakes grabbed again, venting a burst of steam and smoke into the air. Mastered now, the cars rolled docilely into the whitewashed depot marked simply, OMAHA.

While porters pulled iron steps down and a heavy door swung open, Spence scanned the street ahead, looking for a place to stay. Two signs stood out, one calling attention to a boardinghouse, the other announcing a hotel. In about five minutes the street would fill with people leaving those railroad cars.

Giving Clyde another nudge, he guided the horse up to the hitching post just as a huge man with beefy arms and enough hair on him to keep a buffalo warm threw a decidedly scruffy cowboy outside. The fellow pulled himself up by the crosspost, tucked his shirt in, and ambled off down the dusty street.

"Come back, and I'll set the bedbugs onto you!" the big man called after him.

Spence dismounted and pushed the broad brim of his hat back for a better look at him. "How much without the bedbugs?" he asked.

The behemoth looked him over before answering, "Three dollars, if I had a room, but I don't. Railroad keeps me full up."

He decided to try the hotel. Crossing the street, he stepped up onto the wooden porch that ran the length of the establishment. It looked respectable, but that was about all. A sign posted outside listed the menu, featuring fried bullhead, buffalo stew, and something called slugbelly, each costing fifty cents. Bold letters at the bottom, NO WHISKEY ON PREMISES, leapt out at him.

The clerk looked up, took in the gun and holster tied down to his leg, then shook his head. "No firearms in the parlor, mister. I know," he added, waving his hand as though he'd heard more than his share of complaints. "But if we let you carry a gun, then we got to let the cowboys, and they'll shoot up the place. And no spitting on the floor either. If you chew, use the spittoons."

"I don't chew," Spence murmured, unbuckling his gun belt.

"The maid'll be glad to hear it." The clerk opened a big black book and turned it around. "Name, where you're from, and where you're going."

"You don't want to know much, do you?"

"If you don't pay up, we send the law after you. And don't put down John Smith either," the man told him dryly. "He's already been here three times this week."

Taking the pen, Spence wrote "Spencer D. Hardin, Crawford County, Georgia." Following the line across, he added, "San Francisco, California."

The clerk turned the register around, then noted, "I reckon you're a Reb, ain'tcha?"

"Was. The war's over, and we're all just one big, happy family of Americans now."

"Georgia, huh?"

"Yeah."

"I been seein' a lot of you folks coming this way. I guess since you lost, not too many of you got much stomach for staying put." To demonstrate, he pushed the book back to Spence. "Lookee here—any page you want to open, I reckon there's half a dozen Rebs on it."

Thumbing through it, Spence scanned the names until the entry he was looking for caught his eye. *Mr. and Mrs. Ross Donnelly, Macon, Georgia. Headed to San Francisco.*

Apparently, his expression gave him away. The clerk looked at him, then to the page. "Guess you seen somebody you know, huh?"

"Yeah. I don't suppose you remember the Donnellys, do you?" he asked casually. "He's a tall blond fellow—about my height, I'd say—and she's a very pretty woman with dark hair and eyes. They had a little boy with them," he added, trying to jog the man's memory.

The clerk followed the line with his finger, noting the date. "That'd be quite a while back, but seems to me . . . yeah, the Donnellys. Be hard to forget that pair, that's for sure. They was here quite a spell—didn't check out for a couple of weeks."

"Oh?"

"She was more'n pretty, mister—she was the kind that'd make a man sit up when she walked by. And

that little kid was the spittin' image of 'er, too—
didn't look anything like his pa."

"That'd be them, all right."

" 'Course when I got to know 'em, I wouldn't have
that woman for all the tea in China," the man declared flatly. "Got a nasty temper if things don't go
her way, if you know what I mean."

"Yes," Spence agreed dryly. "High-strung."

"Exactly. She didn't like it none that we wouldn't
take coloreds, but I'd like to see a place that does,"
the clerk recalled with feeling. "I had to send the old
woman over to the undertaker, and the missus was
wanting her to take the boy with her. Said she was
too tired to fuss with him, you know. Them was a
long two weeks for everybody, I can tell you. By the
time they left, I was feeling sorry for the mister, even
if he was a mite uppity himself."

"Two weeks seems a long time to stay in Omaha,"
Spence murmured.

"Ain't it? But he said they'd been told they
couldn't get through the mountains afore May, and
he didn't see no sense in sitting around with no creature comforts at Fort Laramie while they was waiting
for the road to open. Then the old woman takin' sick
didn't help things either, I guess."

"I thought you said she stayed at the
undertaker's."

"Yeah, and Joe Black told me all about it after they
finally left. By then, Mrs. Donnelly wasn't feeling too
well herself. Donnelly said he thought it was something she ate, but it wasn't."

"How's that?"

"She took her meals here, but nobody else came

down sick that week. No, sir, if it was anything, it was all that bile boiling up in her—that woman was downright peevish about everything. Now I ain't for hittin' no woman, you understand, but if she'd been mine, I believe I'da made an exception. When she wasn't screeching about something, she was crying over it. Nothing the husband or kid did suited her."

"Traveling was probably hard on her," Spence murmured. "I don't think she'd been out of Georgia in her life before then. But you were telling me the old woman was sick, too."

"That's right. Joe was complaining about what she'd cost him for a month afterwards."

"Joe?"

"Joe Black's the undertaker. He's got a place in his shed for coloreds and Chinamen, 'cause we can't have 'em stayin' here."

"Where would I find him?"

"Go right outside, take a right to the corner, then another right at it. Two blocks after you turn, you're standing in front of the place. If Black's not in, he'll be at the cemetery, which is straight down the same road."

"Thanks."

So Ross had seen the other side of Liddy. As he took his gun back and slipped the room key into his pocket, Spence enjoyed a grim satisfaction. He hoped she'd given the bastard hell all the way to California.

Following the man's directions, he made the second turn, then walked two blocks down the dusty street. Directly ahead of him a black-lacquered coffin had been placed on two sawhorses. On the side facing him, red letters traced with gold advertised the place.

FUNERAL PARLOR AND EMPORIUM
Joseph W. Black, Proprietor
Dignified Services Reasonable
In Omaha Since 1856

"Anybody here named Black?" he asked of a man standing outside.

"Might be." The fellow flicked ashes off the end of his cheroot as he gave Spence the once-over, then shrugged. "I reckon you'd find 'im inside if you was to look for 'im. Ain't seen 'im come out, leastwise. Been kind of a slow day so far. Guess you could say Omaha's gettin' to be downright respectable. Ain't that always what happens? Once the tracks is built, the wives start coming, then the churches go up, and pretty soon the damned place ain't no fun anymore," he lamented.

"They call that civilization," Spence observed.

A fat, balding man with spectacles looked up from the newspaper spread over a long, scarred table as Spence came through the doorway. "Help you, son?"

"I'm looking for somebody."

"Alive or dead?"

"A colored woman. Fellow over at the hotel says you put her up overnight last March."

"Could be. March is long gone, son, and I don't pay much mind to who stays here as long as they pay up."

"This one's a big colored woman—about as round

as she is tall. Waddles when she walks, too. She probably weighs a good two hundred pounds."

"Nah—that don't help me. Like I said, I don't pay much attention."

Spence decided the undertaker wasn't nearly as garrulous as the desk clerk. "She might have had some folks with her—a blond fellow in his late twenties—a little dark-headed kid—maybe even a very pretty dark-headed woman."

"They all sound like you?"

"Pretty much."

"Maybe," Black said, going back to his paper.

"It's him I'm looking for, not her. Him and the boy." Reaching into his pocket, Spence took out a silver dollar and laid it on the open newspaper. "This help any?"

The man studied the coin for a moment before he looked up, his eyes narrowing. "Not a bounty hunter, are you?"

"No." Spence almost couldn't get the words out, but he managed to say, "He and I were friends in the war, and I've got something I want to give him."

"Well, I didn't see much of the white folks, but the old mammy stayed in the shed out back for a week or two. She took sick a couple of days before they came to get her—stunk up the whole place with the runs. Had 'em so bad I had to get rid of the mattress and lime the privy pit after she left."

"She was that sick?"

"Mister, I've been in the undertaking business a long time," Black told him, "and I've buried a lot of folks. I don't know where that old colored woman was headed, but I'd be surprised if she got there."

"What do you think ailed her?"

"Well, I wouldn't say it to anybody around here, but there's a couple of things it could've been, both of 'em bad." When Spence said nothing, he went on, "If I had to guess, I'd say it was cholera."

Feeling as though the wind had been knocked out of him, Spence managed to ask, "What makes you think that?"

Black looked at him as if he were an imbecile before he answered, "I could smell it. I'd seen whole families wiped out with it before—young folks, old folks, and everything in between. Been two epidemics I know of just since I came out here, and a lot of folks died. I didn't take any chances, mister—I burned that mattress as soon as she was gone."

Spence had seen enough cholera firsthand to haunt him a lifetime. He'd watched Danny Lane and a hundred others die from it in the last four years. Diarrhea. Vomiting. Dehydration. Death. It took about two weeks from exposure to come down with the damned stuff, and another week and a half to die from it. If Black was right and it had been cholera, then there was a good chance they'd all gotten it.

It wasn't universally fatal, Spence reminded himself. Beef tea, rice, and a lot of boiled water kept some cholera victims alive long enough to outlast the lethal effects of diarrhea. But once a patient became too dehydrated, his fever shot up, causing delirium, and he didn't want to put anything in his stomach, quickening the fatal end. He thought of Joshua, and he knew small children rarely survived.

Across the table, the undertaker drew a deep breath, then looked at Spence soberly. "I expect she's dead by now, probably buried somewhere between here and Fort Kearny. Last I saw of her, your friend was making her carry that little boy. Said he hadn't gotten much sleep himself—that he'd been up more'n half the night taking care of his wife.''

Unable to stand hearing any more, Spence turned away to walk blindly past the door. He hadn't come all this way to find his son dead of cholera. Now it was more than the need to get across the mountains before winter that drove him.

He'd have to travel by daylight and go slow enough so he wouldn't miss a grave along the road. It'd be like looking for the needle in the haystack, but he had to do it. He had to know if Liddy and the boy were alive.

He'd looked at every grave along the way, dismounting to read the crude, misspelled markers. *Ellen Davis, Biluved wif, sadly mist. Billy Tompkins, aged six. Tansy Wilson, dyed of milk fevver. She wer onlie twenny. Grampa Hayes, he dint mak it. Eliza Campbell, age 19, and babby gril. Babby Willy. Tess Carpenter, age 11. Mother Lillie, Son Jonny, Dotter Mary, all ded of fever. Macy Harris, gone to her maker, July, 1865. Thad Hayes, cot colera.*

They went on, seeming to dog every mile telling their tragic stories.

Reading the boards and rocks set over those final resting places, he noticed a common thread—the road west was hardest on women, kids, and old folks. But Liddy and her Auntie Fan had apparently made it this far. Either that, or Ross and Josh had perished, too, and there'd been nobody left to bury them. He'd seen the bare human bones along the road, and most of them had been gnawed on by wolves and coyotes.

But it was getting too dark to look for anything, and it was about to storm. Flashes of lightning intermittently lit the bank of thick, roiling clouds overhead, and the air was heavy with dust and the smell of a coming rain. Somewhere in the distance, coyotes conversed with the hidden moon, their howls piercing the night, while nearby owls questioned his presence, calling out, "Who?" and answering with the same.

Those owls bothered him. For the last several miles, he'd been hearing them, each time sounding closer than the last. He'd never known owls to congregate in groups like that. The thought that ran through his mind sent a shiver up his spine. *Indians.* It could be his imagination, but if it was, Clyde seemed to share it. The horse's ears pricked up with every call.

Indians couldn't see him any better than he could see them, he told himself. But they knew the area, and he didn't, his mind argued. There it was again, that sound. Sitting so still in the saddle that he could almost hear his own heart beat, he listened hard. But it was his nose that told him he wasn't alone.

He smelled smoke. Lightning had either struck somewhere, or somebody had a fire going. Standing in his stirrups, he strained to see nothing. The telltale glow of a prairie fire wasn't there. He was just spooked, that was all. The smoke probably came from a lone campfire. A railroad crew. Or a war party. His hand found the butt of the Colt, seeking reassurance there.

As thunder rumbled overhead, he thought he saw tiny points of orange light along the horizon ahead. Every muscle in his body tensed as he drew the gun and his finger crooked around the trigger. He might be green when it came to Indians, but he wasn't a fool.

The owl hooted again, closer still. Holding his breath, he listened, hearing the pounding of hoof-beats against the hard earth behind him. He hadn't imagined any of it. He was being followed. And by more than one rider.

Glancing over his shoulder, he saw the shadowy shapes of at least a dozen pursuers, and he knew he was in for the run of his life. Digging his spurs into Clyde's sides, he loosened the reins, and the big bay stretched long legs, heading toward the smoke. Shouting, "Come on, boy—run!" Spence urged the horse on, hoping it was a railroad camp instead of an Indian village. If he guessed wrong, he'd be a dead man. Behind him, a war party whooped and hollered now, and bullets whistled past him.

Lightning flickered, illuminating roiling black clouds hanging low over the road ahead. He couldn't tell now whether it was thunder he heard or the roar of blood pounding in his head. Beneath him, Clyde ran hard, and wet, foamy lather soaked the animal's neck and shoulders, spattering Spence's face and coat.

The damned Indian ponies were closing in on him. Turning in the saddle, he fired a shot, missing his mark. They weren't tin cans and bottles, but living, moving men, and with four shots left, he couldn't afford to miss again. Some sense warned him there was a rider almost even on the other side. This time when he twisted to face a painted warrior, he pulled the trigger at close range. The Colt belched acrid smoke again, and the Indian jerked before he pitched from the pony's back.

Another shot spun a rider halfway around in the saddle before he fell beneath his mount. Spence had exactly two shots left and no time to reload. Glancing ahead, he saw the lights of a campfire glowing red-orange in the night, and behind them, white canvas tents billowed in the wind, beckoning him in. The camp was Mecca and the Promised Land rolled into one.

Before he could see them, he heard men shout, "Indians! Get the Gatling! Secure the horses!" The loud boom of a Sharps shattered the heavy air, punctuating a volley from smaller rifles. A dark, hideously painted warrior dropped over the side of his pony to reach for Clyde's bridle, but a bullet from the Sharps slammed into the buck's shoulder with such force that he seemed to stand before he fell.

The war party behind Spence lagged back, and the shrieking lost its bravado as the buffalo gun found its mark again. With a range of a thousand yards, it had Spence covered, but he wasn't taking any chances.

"Hold your fire!" he shouted, waving his hat. "I'm coming in!"

But even as he yelled, a shot from the Sharps found another mark. As Spence looked over his shoulder, an Indian pony let out a squeal, stumbled, and went down on its front legs. Its rider scrambled on all fours toward the war party, but as one of them leaned down to help him, Spence shot him. Faced with his Colt and the Sharps, they wheeled and retreated out of range, waving muskets and taunting him from a safe distance.

Given his head, Clyde raced the last hundred yards to jump over a wall of full flour sacks stacked along the camp perimeter. As the railroad crew scattered to give the horse room, Spence reined in. His heart was pounding and his face was dripping sweat, but he'd made it in with one bullet left in his revolver.

"That was sure some shootin' with that Colt, mister," a man told him as he dismounted.

Spence's legs felt like jelly underneath him, and his heart pounded in his chest. "I liked the way you handled the Sharps, too. Thanks for the cover," he managed between breaths. "I thought they had me for sure."

"First horse I seen outrun a pack of injun ponies. Yessir, he's a good 'un," the fellow said appreciatively as he ran his hand over Clyde's lathered shoulders. "Ever race him?"

"Not till tonight."

Broad slashes of lightning silhouetted what was left of the war party against the roiling sky. As Spence stared at the crest of that low slope, thinking how lucky he was, the riders separated by twos to charge down it. Instinctively, he aimed the Colt and fired the last bullet.

"They're out of your range," the man said. "They're just coming back to pick up their dead and wounded, then they'll be going. They don't fight even, you know."

"If you'll give me that buffalo gun, I can pick another one of them off. I hate to see the bastards get away."

"By the time you get the bullet in the breech, they'll be headed the other way. They've lost their taste for fighting right now."

"I haven't—they damned near got my scalp."

Another stranger handed Spence his rifle. "It's racked and ready to go, mister. I reckon I know how you feel."

Spence drew a quick bead with the back sight and pulled the trigger, dropping the front brave. As the Indian slumped, his companion caught him, taking him onto his own pony, and they retreated up the low hill out of range. The war party spread out into a single line silhouetted against the flickering sky as they rode off. A mournful death chant floated eerily on the wind.

An almost collective sigh broke the macabre spell, and the railroad men turned to Spence. "Gets to you, don't it—the way they can ride, I mean," one of them said. "I seen it half a dozen or more times, and it still sends chills running down my back. You know there's nothing lower on this earth than an Indian, and you know if he catches you, you're in for hell, but you gotta respect 'em, anyway. They'll risk their lives to take their dead back with 'em."

"I got no respect for 'em," somebody muttered.

The man who'd covered Spence held out his hand. "Name's Russell—Bill Russell."

"Spencer Hardin."

"You're a Reb, aren't you?"

"Was. War's over."

"I didn't mean it in a bad way, Mr. Hardin. Best man I had working for me came out from North

Carolina. I'd like to have a dozen like him, 'cause if I did, we'd be to the Rockies before winter."

"Worked hisself to death, too. Man was so damned tired he couldn't see straight. If he hadn't been, he'd a got hisself out of the way of that car," somebody grumbled behind Russell. "It was the damned railroad that killed him."

"I don't want to hear that kind of talk. The man volunteered to stay on the job till it was done," Russell snapped. "I'd have taken him off it if he'd asked."

"Just the same, it weren't right to let 'im do it, not with his wife like that," another man spoke up. "What's she going to do come winter?"

"She'll find herself another man, that's what. Hell, I wouldn't think twice if there was a chance she'd take me," a fellow declared. "She's about the purtiest woman I ever laid eyes on, even if she's about to pop with that kid."

"Looking for work, mister?" Russell asked Spence, abruptly changing the subject. "As far behind as we are, we could sure use another hand."

"I'm headed for California."

"This time of year? You'll play hell making it out to the Mormon settlements before the hard snows hit."

"I know, but I have to."

"Ever been up in the mountains in winter?" Russell countered. "There's drifts a hundred feet deep, and the wind comes whipping through 'em so hard a man'll freeze in fifteen minutes. If you aren't to Laramie by now, you don't have a chance of getting past the Salt Lake. You'll be spending the winter with the damned Mormons, and I'd as soon take my chances with Indians as with them. No, sir, you sign on with the Union Pacific, and you'll have money in your pocket come spring. *Then* you can make it to California, but I sure wouldn't try it now."

"I'll keep that in mind," Spence promised. "Right now, I'm hang-dog tired. I'd just like to find a spot to lay my bedroll down."

"You'll get yourself soaked," somebody said. "If you don't mind crowdin' up and you don't have mites or fleas, you can put it down in our tent. I got me a horse ring nailed down outside, and you can tie that big fellow up with mine. That way if the Indians come back to raid the corral, they won't get your horse."

"Thanks."

The first big drop of rain splatted on the dirt at Spence's feet, then the black cloud overhead let loose with a vengeance. A burst of wind drove the rain, pounding everything in its path, and the railroad crew scattered, running for cover.

"Follow me!" Spence's host shouted over thunder, grabbing Clyde's reins and heading for a ragged tent. "All hell's gonna break loose!" He tied the horse to the iron ring, then ducked inside to hold the flap for Spence. Small hail hit the canvas overhead like a blast of buckshot, and the howling wind blew and sucked at the tattered walls.

Two other men dived inside with them, filling the damp air with a heavy odor of sweat as they closed the flap behind them. The four of them hunkered down on the dirt floor while the storm raged outside, screaming like a banshee as it tore through the camp.

The canvas billowed and bowed loudly where it was anchored to the poles.

Gradually, the wind let up and the rain settled down into a steady beat. Someone struck a match, and the welcome odor of sulphur momentarily overpowered the stench of unwashed bodies as a flame crept up the sooty lantern chimney.

"Whooeeee—I thought we was gonna blow away! This damned Nebraska weather sure ain't what I'm used to."

"Kansas ain't no better," one of his companions muttered.

The man who'd invited Spence to join them looked up from the lantern. "Six of one, half a dozen of the other—ain't no difference between either of 'em. Me, I'll take Illinois any day." His gaze shifted to Spence. "Sorry, the hail made me forget m'manners—name's Charlie McKinnon—Mac to m'friends."

"Mac."

"And those two worthless cusses next to you are Davy Yoakum and Ned Miller." As he named them, they nodded. "Well, it ain't much, but it don't leak too bad," he added, gesturing to the canvas above. If you don't mind worms and grasshoppers, then the onliest thing you got to worry about is rattlesnakes, 'cause they been known to crawl under the walls."

"Hungry?" Davy asked. "We was fixin' to eat when the whooping and hollerin' started, and we don't mind sharing. You got your choice of salt pork or buffalo jerky, and there's beans and biscuits to go with 'em. Mac's biscuits ain't too good, mind you, but if you soak 'em in your coffee, they'll soften so's you can get 'em down."

"Thanks. I haven't eaten since morning."

They sat cross-legged on the earth with tin plates balanced on their laps while they ate in near silence. Yoakum hadn't lied about the biscuits, Spence discovered. They were like rocks, and if left in the cup long enough, they absorbed enough coffee to double their size. But they were filling to a hungry man's stomach.

"Russell say where we're goin' next?" Ned asked with his mouth full.

"Yeah. They're finally moving the advance camp clear out past McPherson, where it was supposed to be last month. Looks like that might have to be where we'll spend the winter."

"Any idea what Russell's gonna do about the Taylor woman?" Ned wondered suddenly. "I heard he offered to send her back where she came from. Said the railroad would take care of the fare, but she wouldn't go."

"That's real white of him, seein's how he's to blame for what happened." Pushing his plate aside, Mac was thoughtful for a moment. "I don't know what's to become of her this winter if she don't go."

"She'll have to find herself a man, like Billy said. Woman like that can't make it alone."

"Well, she's got pretty slim pickin's around here," Mac observed.

"Hell, she can have me—or damned near anybody else, for that matter," Davy declared.

"That's just what I said. A woman like that ain't gonna want no foul-mouthed drunk, which is what half of us are—and the other half is furriners. How long's it been since you had a bath, anyway?"

"Payday."

"Yeah? Which one?"

Ned grinned. "He got you there, Davy. Iff'n a man goes courtin', he's got to clean hisself up some." Sobering some, he predicted, "Big as she is, there's gonna be a run on soap come payday."

Turning to Spence, Mac explained, " 'Bout six weeks ago, we had a man killed when a car missed hitting the siding we was building."

"So I gathered."

"Thing of it is, it was a real shame, 'cause he left his wife in one hell of a pickle. She's got a baby coming and nowhere to go. Pretty woman, too, and that makes it even harder on her—we got every hard-case and outlaw that works on the UP hankerin' for her, and not a one of 'em can measure up to Jesse. Hell, if I thought she'd go, I'd give her some money myself."

"If you're gonna tell it, tell it right, Mac," Ned insisted. "You'd be hankerin', too, but you already got yourself a wife back in Springfield, Illinois."

"That ain't stoppin' some," Davy pointed out. "Ben Henry's got his eye on her, and his wife's got a houseful of kids. He's always bragging how ever' time he gets home, he slips another one in on the poor woman. Yet here he is, lollygaggin' after Mrs. Taylor. And the man's a brute—if I was a woman, I'd sooner lie down in a pack of hungry wolves than with Ben Henry."

Only half listening, Spence somehow made the connection. "Did you say Mrs. Taylor?" he asked suddenly.

"Yeah."

"I knew a Jesse Taylor from the war. He was from North Carolina, and he was thinking of working for a railroad."

"Less'n there's two of 'em, I reckon that'd be her husband, 'cause his name was Jesse, all right," Mac told him. "And it's been hell on her. Russell said the hardest thing he ever had to do was tell her Taylor was dead. This is no place for a woman, Mr. Hardin—no place at all. And once that baby gets here, we got men that'll be treatin' her like the women at the hog ranch. They got no respect for a decent woman, 'cause they don't know any. It'll be like dogs after a bitch in heat, whether she wants it or not."

"Yeah."

"Maybe since you knew her husband, you can talk some sense into her. Tell her me and some of the boys'd be glad to send her back with a little money to help her get settled in, you know. Tell her she don't belong out here."

"I don't know." The image of Laura Taylor apologizing for that godawful coffee came to Spence's mind. "I sure hate to hear about Jesse," he murmured, shaking his head. "Yeah, I'll try to talk to her before I leave for Fort Kearny."

"Kearny ain't but five miles on up the river," Davy said. "Not much there, though, if you're lookin' for supplies."

"I want to visit the fort cemetery."

"Oh. Well, Jesse ain't buried there," Davy conceded. "Seein' as it was the last day of July and hotter'n hell, we had to get him in the ground close to where he was killed. If you've got a mind to, I can tell you where to find his grave."

"Maybe in the morning. Right now, I'd just like to get some sleep."

But later, when the lantern was doused and the men rolled up in their blankets, Spence lay awake on the hard ground, staring into the darkness. Jesse Taylor was dead, leaving behind a destitute young wife and a child he'd never see. No matter how far he got from Georgia, it was still a miserable world.

The sun shone overhead, but the camp was a mud-hole when Spence walked through it to cross the road to the Platte River. Laying his saddlebag on the riverbank, he eased down the mud-slick slope to fill his wash pan with the opaque water. Mac had said if he let it sit a few minutes, the dirt would sink to the bottom, and he wasn't going to drink any of it, anyway. He'd seen too much of what bad water could do to a man.

Squatting down, he dug in his bag for the soap he'd bought in Omaha, a thick, gray-white chunk that looked as though its maker had left some of the ashes in it. He laid it and the small towel it was wrapped in next to the pan while he retrieved his razor and shaving mirror. When he looked at the water, he couldn't see much improvement. Patience was supposed to be a virtue, he told himself, but as pressed as he was for time, he didn't feel very virtuous right now—just dirty, tired, and cranky beyond reason.

While he waited, he brushed his teeth with a little baking soda and whiskey to get the rancid taste of pork tallow out of his mouth. The fatty meat he'd had for breakfast had been swimming in the stuff, but the other three men hadn't seem to notice it. Spitting the whiskey on the ground, he screwed on the cap and replaced it in his pack.

Finally, tired of watching the water in the pan, he stripped off his sweaty shirt, then pulled off his boots, socks, and pants. He'd just have to be careful he didn't swallow any of it, he decided as he plunged into the river itself. Sinking down, he felt the water lift his hair and swirl around his body, and he realized it was damned cold. As quickly as he'd gone in, he climbed out. His wet drawers bagged with the added weight as he picked up the pan, soap, towel, and razor before heading into a stand of cottonwood trees.

He soaped everything he could reach, including his wet hair and the rough stubble on his face, then positioned the mirror in a crevice between a branch and the trunk of a tree. He'd had better lather, he decided as he drew the straight razor along his jaw to his chin. His eye caught movement in a corner of the mirror, and he spun around.

Her first instinct was to run when she saw the nearly naked man, then she recognized him. "Dr. Hardin! What on *earth* are you doing out here?"

His gaze took in her flushed face, the damp hair that clung to her neck and temples, then dropped lower to the decided swell of her abdomen beneath the faded calico dress. Whisking the little towel from a tree limb, he held it over his drawers. "You always sneak up on a man when he's shaving, Mrs. Taylor?"

"I didn't see you," she said simply. "I was just getting water."

"Well, don't drink it, or the stuff's liable to give you typhoid or cholera."

"If I use it for cooking or drinking, I boil it. But you're a long way from Georgia, sir."

"I'm headed for San Francisco."

"Oh." Surprised, she couldn't help asking, "What about your family? Are they with you?"

"No. They're already out there."

"So you're going to join them," she said, nodding.

Instead of answering, he said, "I heard about Jesse. I'm sorry."

"So am I. I want to believe I'm in a nightmare, and when I wake up, he'll be here. But I know he won't."

"Yeah."

She sucked in her breath and let it out slowly. "I'm surprised you took the northern route this time of year."

"Yeah, well, I thought it'd be easier than crossing the desert."

"So you're going to cross mountains."

"Or die trying, I guess. With Jesse gone, what are you going to do now?"

"Stay with the railroad until after the baby comes. I know they don't want me, but there's nowhere else to go."

"What about Salisbury? You could go back there, you know."

"To what, Dr. Hardin? We sold the farm to come out here."

"I know, but you need your people at a time like this," he said gently. "You can't raise that baby alone in a damned tent."

"You know, I get real tired of hearing that," she responded dryly. "I don't have any people anywhere."

"Yes, but surely—"

"Without Jesse, Danny, or my house, there's nothing back there for me, so I've got to stay whether I want to or not."

"You've got no man to take care of you," he reminded her.

"Is that what you all think I need?" she demanded, her voice rising. "Well, let me tell you something— I've been more or less alone all my life, and I've managed to survive. As long as I can keep a roof over my head, I'll make it here or anywhere else."

"How?"

"I'll do what I have to. Look, I'm sorry I interrupted your daily ablutions, but I've got to fill this bucket and get back, or I won't get done today." With that, she walked to the riverbank.

"You can't be serious, Mrs. Taylor!" he called after her. "You can't like living out here!"

She swung around to face him again. "Like it? I *hate* it! I hate everything about it, but the Almighty didn't give me a choice when He took Jesse, so I'm just stuck here."

"Look, if it's money you need—"

"I'm not a charity case, Dr. Hardin," she declared stiffly. "I'll get by on my own."

"You're too damned stubborn for your own good—you know that, don't you? Listen—let the railroad pay your way back to North Carolina. I've got a little money I can loan you, if you think you have to pay me back. Take it and go live with one of your friends until after the baby's born and you can get on your feet."

"Friends!" she spat out disgustedly. "The only one who'd have me is poor old Silas, and the last thing he needs is a woman with a baby. The rest of 'em's looked down on me as long as I can remember, and I'm not about to give 'em the satisfaction of doing it again, sir. I may be poor, but I've got my pride left. Now, if you'll excuse me again, I've got to get busy."

If her belly hadn't been so big, she'd have flounced down that riverbank, but as it was she was just awkward and ungainly as she negotiated her way to the water. Watching her, Spence sighed. "You know, Jesse wouldn't want you living like this!" he yelled.

She stopped again, but didn't look back. "Jesse's gone," she said evenly. "And if he didn't care when he was alive, why would he care now? He left me in this fix, and it's up to me to make the best of it." Bending over, she filled the bucket, then straightened her tired back. Struggling up the bank, she saw Spencer Hardin pulling on his clothes, and she felt guilty for what she'd said to him.

"I guess it's my turn to be sorry," she admitted as he turned around, buttoning his shirt. "I'm just tired of everybody telling me to do something I can't. I just have to work things out for myself."

"Yeah."

"But it's good to hear another Southerner. I get homesick for that, you know."

"I didn't mean to bully my way into your business."

"No, I expect Mr. Russell asked you to, didn't he?"

"No. I just sort of blundered into that on my own."

"He doesn't want me here. He thinks I'll be a nuisance, but I don't aim to be. All I want is a place to stay until after Jesse Daniel's born and I can get him to where I can travel. Then I don't know where I'll go, but I've got the winter to decide."

He walked over to where she stood and reached for the bucket. "You shouldn't be carrying things this heavy. There must be somebody around who'd do it for you."

"I'm not about to give the men around here any encouragement," she murmured as he took it. "And they sure don't need much, either."

"So I've heard."

"No, you haven't," she countered, falling into step beside him. "Jesse wasn't in the ground a day before they started coming around. You haven't heard anything until you've listened to somebody telling a grieving widow with a big stomach what she needs is another man in her bed to make her feel better. And he was serious enough that he slicked his hair back with grease, thinking it'd make him handsome, when he hadn't had a bath in six months."

"Good God."

"I guess he figured he could save the money he was spending at the hog ranch by marrying me. And that was just the first fellow. You'd think they'd know if a woman was crying, she wasn't interested in romance, but they didn't."

"They don't see too many good-looking women out here, I'm told."

"And then there was the fellow from the hog ranch," she went on. "He came visiting to tell me if I needed any money, he could fix me right up as soon as the baby was born. Said I could make more'n a hundred dollars on payday, and that was with him keeping half of what I brought in. He figured I could get five dollars." She looked up at him, fixing him with those golden brown eyes. "I don't understand how a woman could do that for money—I just don't."

"No."

"And he wasn't about to take no for an answer until I racked Jesse's shotgun and pointed it at him. It was like he was talking about a piece of meat instead of a person."

"That ought to tell you you can't stay here."

"That's what Mr. Russell said when I told him I couldn't go back to Salisbury. I guess he thinks I can just build myself a house on somebody else's land." She stopped in front of a wagon. "Thanks. I can take the bucket now."

"Where's your tent?"

"I took it down. Everything I own is in this wagon, Dr. Hardin, and I'm not about to give any of it up."

"You're living in here?" he asked incredulously.

"It sits off the ground, which makes it easier for me to defend myself from both kinds of varmints, be they animal or human. Anybody wanting to crawl in with me will have to climb up, and when I hear him coming, I'll have a double load of buckshot ready." She looked up at the tattered canvas cover for a moment, wrinkling her nose at it. "If Jesse'd lived, Mr. Russell had a cabin over by Fort McPherson he was going to let us have for the winter." Forcing a smile, she turned back to Spence. " 'The best-laid schemes o' mice and men gang aft agley,' " she said huskily.

"I don't guess Robert Burns had any better life than I have."

As soon as she'd climbed inside the wagon, Spence went looking for William Russell, and he found him shouting at a Chinese worker who couldn't understand him. The poor fellow just stood there, smiling and bowing, while his boss hurled epithets at him.

"Goddamn Chinks," Russell muttered, throwing up his hands. "I'd sooner have a passel of Negroes working for me. All right—get the hell out of here," he decided, waving the man away. Seeing Spence, he shook his head. "They send me any more of these yellow boys, and I'm apt to kill somebody over it."

"I'd like to speak with you about Mrs. Taylor," Spence told him.

"You and damned near every other man in camp— the woman's a curse, that's what she is. I'm supposed to be laying track clear to Laramie, and I'm too far behind for 'em to be making eyes at the Widow Taylor. So unless you've got a notion of how I can get her out of here, I don't have time to talk."

"There's nothing for her back in Carolina. They sold her place to pay for the trip out here. Besides, it's too late for her to travel that far."

"That doesn't help me, does it?" Russell retorted. "I got no room for anybody that don't work and no time to spend keeping the men from pestering her."

Spence realized he'd caught the man at a bad time, but he couldn't wait for a better one. "What about the place out by McPherson?"

"Hell, the army don't want her either. Those soldier boys'd be as bad as mine, and morale's worse there than here. At least we pay decent wages, which is more than can be said for the U.S. government."

"What about the cabin you promised Jesse?"

"I told him the place's a shack, but he said once the work slowed for winter, he could fix it up enough for 'em to get through to spring in it. It's about a quarter mile from where we'll be making winter camp."

"It'd be better than a tent, wouldn't it?" Spence persisted.

"And how the hell am I supposed to make it habitable? Taylor was going to do that, but he's dead now." Russell paused to rub a day's growth of beard while he pondered the matter, then nodded. "Least she wouldn't be underfoot. Think you could get her to take it?"

"I can try."

Warming to the idea, the foreman said, "Tell her I got a couple of Chinese fellows I can spare to nail it up some. Surely to God they know how to use a hammer."

"Thanks." As he walked away, Spence felt as if he'd settled the debt he owed to Laura and Jesse Taylor.

Near Fort Kearney: September 15, 1865

Spence leaned forward, scanning the horizon, thinking he had to be insane to involve himself in Laura Taylor's business. He hardly knew the woman, and he already had more than enough problems of his own. The obligation he'd felt he owed her husband last night had faded in the clear light of dawn. But he was committed to getting her as far as McPherson, he reminded himself, and he'd do it. After that, she was on her own.

Still, he chafed restively at the slow pace, knowing he had a thousand miles of rugged, inhospitable territory between him and San Francisco. He was just going to lose two or three days he couldn't afford, but it couldn't be helped.

Even if he could get Dolly and the old mule to run, he suspected the rickety wagon would shake itself apart and strand him out here with no help in sight. It already squeaked, creaked, groaned, and shimmied as the iron-clad wooden wheels ground into the muddy ruts of the Platte Road. The damned thing was just plain overloaded, but the stubborn woman beside him had refused to leave any of her furniture behind, he recalled resentfully. And it didn't help his temper any that most of the stuff was damned near worthless.

The way his luck was running, an axle was going to break somewhere between Forts Kearney and Mc-Pherson, anyway, and they'd be sitting ducks for any war party that happened along. And while three guns and two half-empty boxes of ammunition were plenty for a running chase, they wouldn't be enough if he had to make a stand. His gaze sought the uneven rumps of the mismatched team for a moment. The five or so miles into Fort Kearney felt like a hundred already, and they'd have another eighty or ninety miles after that before he could abandon the silent woman or her wagon.

She hadn't said much since they'd left camp almost an hour earlier. Every attempt he had made at conversation had died in short answers, until he'd given up on expecting much company out of her. She was probably still mad about that little tiff he'd had with her over the junk in back. And damned if he hadn't seen better in slave cabins.

At least Laura Taylor wasn't like Liddy, he decided charitably. Liddy wouldn't have been stoic at all about the discomforts of a journey like this. By now, Liddy would have already filled his ears with a myriad of complaints, real and imagined. Her back was tired from the constant jostling. The rain had encouraged a late batch of mosquitoes. The sun was burning her skin. Her head ached miserably. The whole of Nebraska was godforsaken and unbearable. She sure hadn't been a woman to travel much beyond Crawford County, he knew that much. It made him wonder how much grief she'd given Ross on the way to California.

Looking back now, he had to wonder if he would have married her had he had more time to get to know her—if he'd been too bedazzled by all that beauty to realize what he was getting. He didn't even know if he'd ever really loved her. One thing was for damned sure—it had been she who'd wanted to get married before he left for the war, then she'd left him before he could even get home from it.

Casting a sidewise glance at the Taylor woman, he couldn't help seeing the contrast between her and Lydia. Unlike Liddy, she wasn't always posturing, fiddling with her gloves, the tilt of her bonnet, the drape of her skirt. Lydia had always been so aware of how she looked, of how pretty she was, and she'd wanted every man she ever met to know it. She'd known how to cock her head just so, flash those dark eyes, and smile at him, until she had him making a fool of himself. And he'd sure been easy to lead, he realized now. Instead of being a treasure, the glittering beauty had turned into fool's gold at the first inconvenience.

Laura Taylor, on the other hand, seemed pretty unconscious of her looks, as if she didn't realize how pretty she was. With half the damned railroad camp hanging after her, she was sure it was because they were just plain hungry for a woman, not because they'd never seen anything like her.

She was hanging on to the board under her with no thought given to the horror of freckles on that straight little nose of hers. She had no bonnet, no gloves, no jewelry, except a narrow gold wedding

band, and certainly no fancy clothes. Her shoes were
plain black with serviceable soles and laces instead
of little jet buttons. But with the sun shining down
on it, that brown hair had red and gold in it.

His gaze dropped lower, to her rounded abdomen,
to the callused hand gripping that seat. She'd known
hardship, disappointment, and loss, but she'd clung
to her pride, and he had to admire her for it. There
weren't many women who could face what the future held for her. Widowhood. Poverty. Isolation. A
child to rear alone. God, he wouldn't want to walk
in her shoes for a minute.

He had to wonder if Jesse Taylor had even realized
what he'd had. The man sure hadn't given much
thought to her comfort when he'd brought her out
here, then left her alone for weeks without another
decent female for company. But that was the way
things went, he supposed. A man tended to take the
good things that came his way for granted, while he
cursed the bad.

For Spence, whatever joy Lydia had given him had
turned to bitter gall, and her betrayal had left him
with a festering sore that wouldn't heal. And the
more he picked at it, the worse it got. Thad Bingham
had once told him that hate feeds on its host's guts
until it kills him. He hadn't understood what his
stepfather had meant back then, but he knew now.
Only before it killed him, it was going to take Ross
and Lydia, too.

"I see something over there."

Laura Taylor had said it so calmly that he wasn't
sure he'd heard her right, but the tense hand grip-

ping his arm was real. Pulled from his morose
thoughts, he looked around.

"Where?"

"I thought I saw movement behind those trees
ahead."

"Probably leaves blowing in the wind." Nonetheless, he drew the Colt and handed it to her before
he retrieved the Sharps under the seat. As he
straightened up, he realized there was no wind, not
even a faint breeze, and he felt his skin crawl. Staring
hard, he thought he could make out a lone rider.

"You've got good eyes," he murmured, his finger
closing around the trigger. "I'm not sure I see
anything."

"Out here you have to." Turning around on the
seat, she looked back. "There's not many, but they
could be scouts for a war party. Mr. Russell says
sometimes they fool you and there'll be a whole passel of 'em over the next hill."

"Yeah. And we couldn't make a quick getaway if
we had to."

"Just don't act like you notice anything out of the
ordinary while I get the box of cartridges. How fast
do you think you can clear the breech and reload?"

"Pretty fast."

"I'd better warn you not to drop the gun when the
fire runs up the breech—it's just a flash and it's over,
but it tends to startle if you're not expecting it. Jesse
said the seal leaks, and that's why it does that. I just
know there's a flare when you shoot it." Sliding the
box onto the seat between them, she added, "It's an
1853, so Mr. Russell just gave it to us. The newer

ones cost thirty-six dollars, and Jesse didn't think we could afford it. This one's accurate enough, anyway."

"Where did you learn so much about a gun?"

"There was just Danny and me, and we had to eat. But we didn't have anything like this—we just had Daddy's old Hawkens."

"I see. I guess you must've been a real Diana back then."

"The Romans didn't have rifles, Dr. Hardin," she said dryly. "I couldn't hit the wide side of a barn with a bow and arrow."

He looked to the stand of trees again and cursed under his breath. He could see three Indians now. Trying not to frighten her, he said, "It looks like you're going to get a chance to use the Colt."

"They're still out of range." Shifting her weight on the seat, she casually rotated the cylinder. "I don't suppose you've got another bullet handy, do you? You've got an empty chamber."

"To keep from shooting myself in the leg or worse."

"Yes, I know that, but I'm holding it in my hand right now, and I'd like to start out with all I can get." Seeing that he was about to raise the Sharps, she suggested, "I'd hold my fire until I knew what they aimed to do. If three's all there are, they might just let us go by. And if there's more waiting up ahead, you might not want to start anything just yet."

"It's a hell of a place to make a stand, that's for sure," he muttered. "We can't make a run for it, and there's no place to hide."

"I'd say so."

"Are you always so calm, Mrs. Taylor?"

"No." She turned her gold-flecked brown eyes to him. "Hysterics wouldn't help much now, so I figure I'll be worth more to you if I keep my hand steady. But I can't vouch for what I might do when the fight's over." Out of the corner of her eye, she saw a horse moving. "Now's the time to show the Sharps, Dr. Hardin—they're headed this way."

He could feel the hairs stand on the back of his neck as Indians emerged from the trees. She sat very still beside him, but the only fear he saw was the stiff way she held herself now. He rested the big buffalo rifle across his knees in full view, ready to take aim at the first sign of hostility. Her finger was crooked so tight around the Colt's trigger that the knuckle was white.

A big buck separated from his two companions and rode forward. His face wasn't painted, but he didn't look friendly. Stopping about twenty yards ahead of them, he raised one hand and shouted something. Whatever it was, it wasn't polite.

"You have any notion what's going on?" he asked Laura Taylor.

"No. Just don't let him see you're scared, and keep going. If they're going to make any trouble, I'd say it's about to happen."

"Yeah." His mouth was so dry, it felt like it was full of cotton. "If all hell breaks loose, I'll take the farthest one, and you can have the fellow staring at us. If the last one doesn't run, you're the one with bullets left, and you'll have to fire while I reload."

"I understand."

The thought crossed his mind that he'd made it through four years of war without firing a shot, and it'd be a shame if after the hell he'd been through, it was a damned Indian that got him. His hand rested uneasily on the Sharps's breech, ready for his finger to take the trigger, and his heart pounded while his brain told him that whether he was ready or not, this was it.

"Hello!" Laura called out, forcing a bright smile.

"What the hell are you doing?" Spence demanded furiously. "This isn't a Sunday picnic, and they're not after fried chicken."

"I'm not showing fear. I don't know much about Indians, but I've heard they respect that." Keeping a tight grip on the revolver, she raised her other hand to wave at the scowling brave. "We're just passing through!"

"Are you insane?"

"I don't know yet. If it'd help, I probably would be. I read somewhere if they think you're more than a mite tetched, it'll spook them, but I think the article was about Comanches."

They were less than twenty yards from the rider when he raised his war lance belligerently with one hand, while the other one brandished what looked to be an old musket. The gesture brought his companions out of the trees, one of them charging, raising a war cry.

"I'd say we're in deep trouble," he muttered under his breath.

Her hand crept to the box of linen cartridges, easing the lid off so he could get at them. "Yes," she said simply. "They're in range now."

At that, she brought up the revolver and pulled the trigger, shattering the lance in the big buck's hand. He jerked as though he'd burned his fingers, then he leveled the musket on her. Before he could shoot, Spence fired the Sharps, dropping him. Laura Taylor's second shot hit one of the others, and he pitched forward, then slumped over his pony's neck. The third Indian zigzagged, trying to lessen his chances of taking a bullet. Leaning out, he scooped up the wounded man's reins, spurred his own horse, and tore out of there at a full gallop while the injured warrior flopped like a rag doll but managed to hold on.

The Indian in the road lay where he'd fallen, and as the wagon passed by him, Laura looked away. When that fifty-two caliber bullet had torn through his brow, the rest of his head had exploded. Spence heard her gag, and he felt sorry for her. It wasn't any sight for a woman to see.

"I just hope there aren't any more of 'em," he muttered.

"Yes. I don't much believe in killing anything I can't eat."

Her voice was so quiet that he turned to look at her. She had her eyes closed and her chest was heaving, but the Colt was still in her shaking hands.

"Are you all right?"

"Yes," she said, shuddering almost convulsively.

Laying the Sharps across his knees, he found her hand. It was as cold as ice beneath his fingers. "Laura—"

"I'll be all right," she managed, her voice quavering now. She swallowed visibly, then raised her eyes to his. "I've never been more frightened in my life—never ever."

He slid his arm around her shaking shoulders and held her until she calmed down. "You could've fooled me, that's for sure. I thought you were magnificent. All the women I know would've been cowering under that seat."

"I wanted to, but then you'd be standing them off by yourself, and that wouldn't be right." Squaring her shoulders, she sat back, "We'd better reload. As loud as that Sharps is, everybody within five miles had to hear it." She took a deep breath, then let it escape slowly. "I'm fine now," she announced.

"My heart's doing double time," he admitted.

"You wouldn't be human if it wasn't. It's the fools who rush in where angels fear to tread—Alexander Pope said that, or at least something very like it. If a body's not scared by that, he's a fool."

"Where did you ever get all those books, Mrs. Taylor?" he asked softly.

"I worked for most of them. When Daddy was alive, he used to read to us from the Bible and a collection of fables. When it was too cold to work in the fields, he'd get out the old lantern, and Mama and I would sit on the floor with Danny between us, and we'd just listen to the same old stories over and over. His voice and the fire in the stove made us forget that the wind was blowing across the floor, and the windows were rattling like they'd break. My daddy would've made a good preacher, but he said there wasn't much of a living in it."

"I was raised by a preacher myself," he admitted. "You know, when I was a little kid, I used to think he wasn't much of a man for hiding behind that Bible instead of earning a man's living. Now I know I was

just dead wrong. If anything, Thad Bingham was the **finest** man I've ever known, and I'd be a hell of a lot **better** off now if I'd listened to him."

"I'd say being a doctor is doing all right."

"Not if you've lost the heart for it."

"It was the war that did that, wasn't it? Once you get to where you can forget all that carnage, you'll remember the satisfaction of saving lives," she predicted.

"Which fable did you get that from?"

"If you weren't called to medicine, you wouldn't have made it through medical school."

"That was a long time ago."

The way he said it made her look up at his closed face and the tight jaw. His expression was bitter, almost hard. "You know, you weren't like this when you came through Salisbury," she said slowly. "All you could think of was getting home to your wife and little boy."

"Yeah, well, it didn't live up to my expectations."

The tone in his voice told her he didn't want to discuss it. Sighing, she sat back on the hard seat. "I guess I understand. There's things I can't bring myself to talk about either."

"Yeah."

He saw the cluster of buildings, the United States flag flying over them, and he knew they'd finally reached Fort Kearney. Squinting into the sun, Spence studied those Stars and Stripes as the slight wind unfurled them against the sky, and he couldn't help thinking of the thousands of men who'd fought and died for and against the country it stood for. His country now, he had to remind himself, but like damned near everything else, it was a bitter thought. The struggle had cost him everything but his life.

Lowering his gaze to the dry, dusty prairie, he felt like he'd reached the end of the earth. He didn't know how Laura Taylor could stay here, spending the harsh winter huddled in some hut, listening to the coyotes and wolves howling every night. Come spring, she'd be more than ready to take the first train going east, he expected—if she survived.

Looking at the row of officers' houses, the low buildings behind it, the neat parade grounds in front, he thought about trying to persuade her to stay here. At least she'd have the post doctor around when her time to deliver came, and surely some of those officers had wives living in those whitewashed houses.

He pulled up at the corner of the parade ground and tied the traces to the wagon seat before he jumped down. "Seeing as how you've got everything you own back there, maybe you'd like to wait in the wagon."

"Yes."

"I won't be long, but if you need to stretch your legs, you'd better do it here."

"I'll be fine."

"Do you want me to check if there's a privy handy?"

"No."

Pushing his hat back from his brow, he approached a group of soldiers lounging on a weathered board porch. "Know where I can find the post doctor?"

"Hospital's over back o' the bachelor officers' quarters, which is behind the officers' houses," one of them spoke up.

"You sick, mister?" another wondered. "He ain't much good for anything but physickin' a body—it don't make any difference what ails you, that's what he does—if you ain't got the runs, he'll give 'em to you."

"I'd just like to talk to him, that's all."

It didn't take him long to find the place. As he entered the building, the smell of turpentine and camphor overpowered that of diarrhea. In two rows of cots lined up along the walls, more than a dozen men lay uncovered, their bodies curled around griping guts. Dysentery. It was the bane of every military camp he'd been in. At the end of the long room, a redheaded man with a darker auburn beard turned around.

"Don't know you, do I?" he said, giving Spence the once-over.

"Hardin—Spencer Hardin."

"Benjamin King. I'm supposed to be the surgeon around here, but I do a lot more dosing than cutting." He cocked his head slightly, studying Spence's face. "Didn't waste any time signing you Rebs up to fight Indians, did they?"

Spence shook his head. "I'm through fighting for anything. I was just passing through, and I thought I'd ask about some sick folks who might've come in some months back—early to mid-April probably."

"That'd be a little early—summer's when we get travelers in. Oh, some stop in every now and then, but usually it's for snakebite . . . wagon accidents . . . things like that. Most of the time I'm just treating the men here for dysentery," King allowed, rubbing his beard. "Got enough of that around—so much I'm running out of Hope's camphor, if you want the truth. I keep putting requisitions in, and they keep sending me out the damned blue mass."

"I'd rather do nothing than give anybody blue mass," Spence agreed. "It's too corrosive on a gut that's already sore. I'd mix half a grain of opium with a quarter grain of copper sulfate and add it to two ounces of whiskey. If they can keep a tablespoon of that down every two or three hours, they usually get better."

"I'd as soon do my own dosing, if you don't mind," the surgeon snapped. "Now—I'm a busy man, so let's get down to brass. Just describe 'em, and I'll tell you if I've seen 'em."

He'd said it so often, he could rattle it off by rote. "A blond man in his late twenties, a pretty, dark-haired white woman, a heavyset Negro woman, and a little white kid that'd look about four, all Southerners."

King thought for a minute, then nodded. "If he's pretty enough to be a girl, and he thinks the whole world ought to be at his beck and call, then I've seen him."

"What about the others?"

"The kid don't look anything like him," the surgeon said, nodding again. "Wife's named Olivia or something like that, and if she wasn't sick, she'd sure be a looker."

"Lydia. She's passing herself off as his wife, but she's married to somebody else. The boy belongs to her husband, not Donnelly."

"Yeah. When they stopped here, the old woman was dying, and the young one was downright delirious herself, but they wouldn't even wait for the old woman to pass on. I think maybe they were scared, but I don't know. All I know is they left as soon as the colored one died, and he didn't even leave anything to bury her. Said her name was Fannie Jamison, but he didn't want to say much else. Like I said, he was in one hell of a hurry to get out of here, and he wasn't about to listen to anybody tryin' to tell him he'd damned well better stay."

"Did you tell him it was cholera?"

"I said it sure could be."

"What did he say to that?"

"Not much. Just that they'd stop at McPherson if they had to." King's gaze met Spence's. "I reckon they had to—if she made it that far. She couldn't hold her head up. I gave her a good dose of Hope's camphor, but I doubt it helped much. I figure if it didn't, she's long dead now."

"What about the boy?"

"Well, he wasn't showing signs of sickness, but he was exposed to it. I'm a physician, not a fortune-teller, but if I had to guess, I'd say Donnelly and the kid probably came down with it soon after they were here. Cholera's damned catchin', you know."

"Yeah. I can't believe Liddy would abandon Fan, though," Spence murmured, shaking his head. "That old colored woman raised Liddy."

"That so? Well, I couldn't tell you what she was thinking, but I don't think she had the strength to put up much of a fuss. Him I didn't care for at all. He just left me with a mess of problems and went on his way."

"Yeah?"

"There was a real hullaballoo over burying the old woman, seein' as what she was. I had to tell 'em to get her in the ground before we had an epidemic on our hands. They put her off to one side of the cemetery, but I couldn't get a marker for her. The major didn't want it known there was a colored woman in with white folks, as if anybody'd know by the name," King noted with disgust.

Reaching under his coat, Spence pulled out a wad of banknotes. As he peeled off ten dollars, he said, "Everybody knew her as Auntie Fan. You don't have to put that on it, but I'd like to know the place was marked some way—a cross maybe, or some flowers planted over her."

"Sounds like you must've owned her before the war."

"No. My wife did."

He was halfway across the parade ground before King caught up to him. "Here," the surgeon said, pressing the ten dollars into Spence's hand. "Come spring, it won't cost anything to plant a wild rose bush there. We've got 'em all over the place."

"What about the cross?"

"I don't know as I can do that, so you take your money. If I can, I will, but like I said, it's a touchy matter." The corners of Ben King's mouth turned down for a moment. "I'm real sorry about your wife, mister."

"Yeah. So am I."

As Laura watched him come back across the parade ground, she knew something was terribly wrong. And as he swung up beside her, the haunted look in his eyes confirmed it. Without thinking, she laid a hand on his arm.

"Are you all right?"

For a time, he didn't answer. He just sat still, staring across the grassy ground, seeing nothing. Finally, he untied the worn leather traces and slapped the ends across the mule's flank. "Yeah," he said heavily, "but I've got to get to McPherson."

McPherson didn't even look like a fort—it was just a cluster of wood buildings gathered together, dwarfed by endless miles of prairie stretching out from it in every direction. About the only thing setting it apart from a dozen small, dusty ranches between here and Omaha were the large corrals holding enough horses to mount a trooper company.

"It's sure not much, is it?" Laura murmured, echoing his thoughts.

"No."

He hadn't said much in the nearly three days it had taken them to travel less than a hundred miles. Whatever he'd learned at Kearny was eating at him like a cancer, turning him from haunted to haggard. She didn't think he'd gotten much sleep either—every time she'd had to take a quick trip to the bushes during the nights, his bedroll had been empty when she passed by it. And twice her lantern had caught him, leaning against a tree, staring into the darkness. She didn't know why, but she was pretty sure he was hurting as much as she was.

"If you don't mind, I'd like to walk with you," she

said quietly. "I've got a cramp in my leg from sitting."

"No," he responded shortly. "I'd as soon not have company right now. If you need to stretch that leg, you'd better stay close to the parade ground."

"Yes, of course." Rebuffed, she remained on the seat while he climbed down from the wagon. "I hope you can find what you're looking for, and it'll give you some peace."

He swung around. "What the hell's that supposed to mean?" he snapped.

"Well, you need something, or you're going to break like a spring that's wound too tight. You've barely eaten, slept, or talked since Fort Kearny."

"Maybe I don't want to."

Hunching his shoulders against an ominous wind, he looked for the post hospital. The cemetery ought to be close by it. Yeah, there it was. Pausing to suck in his breath, he let it out slowly, and he told himself he was prepared to find Ross, Liddy, and Josh lying under tombstones in there. He had to force himself to walk between the graves. The burden lightened as he read each marker, finding only strangers in the first two rows. Maybe by some miracle, it hadn't been cholera after all, and the three of them were still alive. Then, at a grassless mound on the third row, his heart paused.

The neat black letters printed on the white cross leapt out at him. *Lydia Jamison Hardin, 1841–1865.* He stared at the grave, too numb to feel anything. But he couldn't help wondering if Ross had repudiated her at the end, or if it had been her wish to rest forever under her married name.

Taking his hat off, he knelt in the dirt and tried to pray, but every eloquent word Thad Bingham had taught him was gone. Finally, he said simply, "Father in Heaven, forgive her, for I cannot." Rising, he stared at the barren ground, finding it hard to believe that anyone as young and full of life as the Liddy he'd known could be down there. Closing his eyes for one brief moment, he allowed himself to remember the night he'd seen the stars reflected in her dark eyes.

Spoiled and willful, her father had described her, Spence reflected somberly, but old Cullen had told him only half the truth. He should've added self-centered, faithless, and shameless to the warning, but it probably wouldn't have mattered back then. All Spence had seen was the glittering, mesmerizing facade of her beauty, and he'd been utterly bedazzled by what he thought she was. While that explained his folly, he didn't know what she'd ever seen in him. If she'd thrown herself at him out of pique with someone else, they'd both paid a terrible price for it.

"Oh, *no!* I'm so sorry—I had no idea—none at all," Laura Taylor whispered behind him.

Before he could respond, she backed away, white-faced, then turned and fled from the little cemetery. As he watched her walk away, he realized he was even too numb for anger.

She felt like a fool for following him, but he'd been out there so long it'd worried her. When she dared to look back from the parade ground, she saw him dusting his pants with his hands. She understood now why he'd needed to be alone, but as she took her seat in the wagon, she had to wonder what on earth had brought his wife clear out here without him. It wasn't her business, she reminded herself. Besides, she'd already discovered that grief was a solitary pain, and no matter what anybody said or did, it didn't help the hurt much. It was something that didn't let go for a long time. She knew, because after six long, miserable weeks, it still had a stranglehold on her own heart. Turning away, she wanted to cry for him.

The north wind was cold for September, but he scarcely noticed it. As much as he hated facing anyone right now, he knew he had to find someone to ask about Joshua. There had to be somebody who'd remember whether Ross or the boy had been sick when they left the fort. He needed to know whether he'd be looking for another grave.

And yet as the wind whipped his hair and coat, he stepped back from the clay mound to look at the clouding sky, and the numbness became a terrible, impotent rage. He'd befriended Ross Donnelly, and he'd pulled strings to send him home from the war, only to have the man betray him. Well, he couldn't do anything to Liddy now, but unless Ross was dead, too, he was going to pay the highest price possible for stealing Liddy and Josh. And the end wasn't going to come easy, Spence promised himself. No, Ross was going to know he was about to die, and he was going to squirm before Spence pulled the trigger and sent him to hell.

"You lost, mister?"

Pulling himself together, Spence managed to ask, "Where do I find somebody in charge around here?"

"Depends on what you want. He ain't in the graveyard, that's for sure. Not much goes on around here that I don't know about it."

"I want to know about the woman buried here," Spence told him, pointing to the grave.

"The Hardin woman?"

"Yes."

"Not much to tell about her, except that she was dead before she got here. Fella came in, said he had a body he wanted buried, that they'd been headed west when she took sick. Said she was a widow woman, that her husband was killed in the war, and he was taking her to stay with relations in California, but she didn't make it."

"Did you see a small boy with him?"

The soldier nodded. "No bigger'n a mite, probably three or four at the most. I sure felt sorry for him, too, 'cause he was missing his ma. Funny thing was, all the time he was crying, he kept calling her Fanny. They was supposed to stay around long enough for the major to make a report on the body, but while we was getting her in the ground, they took off like the devil was after them."

"It wasn't the devil—it was cholera."

"Cholera." The soldier digested that for a moment, then said, "Well, if it was, he shoulda known he couldn't outrun it. I mean, she died in that wagon, didn't she? And I guess he had to know it, 'cause he said the doc over at Kearny told 'im she was bad off. He said he tried to leave her there, but she wouldn't stay. She must've passed on right after, too, because by the time he got her here, she was pretty rank, I can tell you. I'd say that last day they was out, it must've been hell in that wagon." He paused to spit tobacco juice. "Yessir, it was a shame—just a damned shame for her to die like that. And you know, that was a pretty little boy—man said he looked just like her."

Spence exhaled heavily and looked away. "Yeah, she was pretty, all right—about as pretty a woman as you'll ever see. But the boy—he wasn't sick, too, was he?"

"No, but he was sure crying for his Fanny—Lt. Davison said he thought he was calling her his mammy, but I heard him real clear, so I know that wasn't what he was saying."

"Auntie Fan," Spence murmured, nodding. "She was the Negro woman who raised both of them— the boy and the mother. They left her to die over at Fort Kearny."

"You don't say. Last time I seen 'em, the blond fella was driving off, holding the kid on his lap. Everybody'd kinda thought they'd stick around, seein' as he was a little queasy himself."

"Ross?"

"The fella that brought her in. I thought he said the name was McDonald, or something like that."

"Donnelly. Ross Donnelly.

"Yeah. He got some soda from the doc for his stomach, but Doc said he was probably sick from the smell, you know. 'Course he didn't know about the cholera, or we'd have limed her up good before we buried her."

"King over at Kearny said that's what he thought it was, anyway."

"Probably so, then. Doc or not, King's a good man. Say—I don't believe I caught your name, did I?"

Spence took a breath, held it for several seconds, then let it out slowly. "It's Spencer Hardin."

"Oh. Then you must be kin to her husband, huh?"

"Something like that."

"Too bad you weren't here to identify the body, 'cause all we had was the man's word it was Mrs. Hardin." The fellow looked past Spence to the cross. "Yeah, it was sure a shame. Guess she wasn't but twenty-five."

"Twenty-four. She was born in December."

"Even worse." He shook his head. " 'Bout all I know, mister. Guess you could talk to Doc, but I doubt he could tell you anything more. They weren't here much longer than it took to drop the body off."

"Thanks."

"Sorry I couldn't help you more. But if you want to see Doc, he's over at the hospital."

"No. I'd like to make a few more miles today."

"Don't know as I'd want to be alone out at night," the fellow allowed. "Been some Indian trouble— stock run off, folks killed. I been here long enough to see some of it, and it ain't pretty. Had to bury a fellow once, and when they was done with 'im, I was puttin' pieces of 'im in a sack instead of a box."

"I'll watch out."

"You'd damned sure better. I'd put a bullet in myself before I'd let 'em catch me. They turn you over to the squaws, you got a hard way to go, mister. Yessir, we got Cheyenne and Sioux war parties out, and if it was me, I wouldn't be anywheres on the Platte Road come night. And if I had to be out, I'd be eating in my saddle, and I wouldn't be cooking nothing. Fire'll give you away quicker than anything, and Indians got good noses when it comes to smelling smoke."

"I'm just taking Mrs. Taylor and her wagon as far as the advance Union Pacific camp."

"Railroad man?"

"No. Just passing through."

"Headed west, are you?"

"California."

The soldier looked up at the sky for a moment, then back to Spence. "Well, you might make it, but I'd sure doubt it. Them clouds up there already came across the mountains—that's why the road's nigh to empty, you know. Snow'll be hitting in another couple of weeks, too—you got to get worried about that before the end of September, mister."

"Once I drop her off, I'll be traveling light enough to make good time."

"Yeah, but California's a fur piece from here, you know. Gettin' through the Rockies don't put you halfway there. You got the desert, then the Sierras to cross after the Rockies."

"I know."

"Do you now?" the fellow countered skeptically. "Don't guess you heard about those Donners, did you?"

"Yeah, but I've got to go."

"You get caught by a blizzard up in them passes, and you ain't never getting to California, mister. Talk to 'em over at Laramie, and they'll tell you right. Snow's twenty feet deep, wind's blowin' ten times faster'n a race horse can run, temperature's down to thirty below—once you eat your horse, you're done for. You got no food, no way out, and no place to keep from freezin'—that's what it's like up there. Won't anybody find you before summer, neither."

"I'll keep that in mind," Spence told him impatiently. "Look—"

"If you don't, you're a damned fool—that's all I got to say." The fellow spat tobacco juice again. "It ain't me that'll be burying you, anyway, so I don't know why I'm wasting my breath on you. If there's anything left by spring, Laramie'll get that job." Holding out his hand, the soldier added, "Well, whatever you do, good luck to you." As Spence shook it, the man's grip tightened briefly. "You remember to look out for Indians, you hear?"

"Yeah."

Laura Taylor looked away when Spence swung up onto the wagon seat next to her. As he took the reins, she offered, "If you want to talk about her, I won't mind, and if you don't . . . well, I won't mind that, either. I know what it is to hurt inside."

"I'm not hurting—I'm just damned mad," he lied, "and I don't want to talk about anything right now."

"All right. Would you like me to drive the wagon?"

"No," he answered tersely. "I'm just fine and dandy."

But he knew he wasn't. When he'd left Georgia, he'd never expected to find Liddy buried alone in such a godforsaken place. No, he'd spent his waking hours thinking about wringing her slender white neck, and now it wasn't going to happen. The Almighty had gotten even for him there. And the hell of it was he'd have to pray to God that Ross had made it to San Francisco with Josh, because the alternative was unthinkable. Losing Lydia had been a terrible blow to his pride, but losing Josh would mean he had nothing he loved left on this earth.

Laura sat silently, her hands gripping the seat as the wagon bounced over the rutted road, her thoughts fixed on that grave, on what he'd just said. *I'm not hurting—I'm just damned mad.* If he believed that, he was surely deluding himself.

But the whole thing didn't make any sense. What in the world could have brought the woman out here? Why had she died? And where was the little boy in the photograph? As curious as she was, she wasn't about to ask him. If he wanted to tell her, he would. If not, it was his business, not hers. But she had to wonder if he still meant to leave for California tomorrow.

Having already wasted days he couldn't spare, Spence had planned on heading out as soon as he got Laura Taylor to the camp, but he could see now it wasn't going to happen quite that way. As he drove through the crude little camp, he was furious with himself, her, and the whole damned world. The damned place was nothing but ten or twelve tents pitched beside a trackless railroad bed, with a primitive latrine ditch less than twenty feet behind them. There wasn't anything resembling a privy in sight.

And the men loitering around the few tents looked worse than the thieves and cutthroats Mississippi paroled to fight in the war. None of them looked as if they'd seen any soap in six months, and the clothes on them were so caked with dirt and grease they could stand alone. It'd take a year's supply of lye soap and a good, hard hide-scraping before anyone with a nose could get within ten feet of that crew without gagging. As miserable a bunch of hardcases as any he'd ever seen, he decided sourly. As the wagon passed by, one of them tilted a bottle of whiskey, guzzling the stuff so fast it dripped from his matted beard. When he finished it, he threw the empty bottle on the ground, then ambled off to the latrine to relieve himself in plain sight.

No matter what Laura Taylor had said about having nowhere to go, she sure didn't belong here. He didn't even see anyone in charge of the hellhole. Damning her for the inconvenience and himself for being a fool, he jerked the reins savagely to turn the wagon around. Out of time or not, he had to take her back at least as far as McPherson, maybe even all the way to Kearny, to put her on a train headed east. And unless he wanted to use up more of his time trying to find Russell, he'd have to pay for her ticket himself. She wasn't going to like it, and she'd be as balky as a damned mule, but he couldn't help that.

"As difficult as it is to imagine, by the time the crews move on, this place will be on its way to being a town," Laura murmured. "And in a couple of years, it'll look like Omaha. There'll be churches and schools and enough decent women to civilize it."

"Well, it's a long way from it now," he retorted.

"Not as long as you'd think. When the rest of the crews arrive, the camp will fill up."

"Yeah—with sots and whores. No, you don't belong here—you've got no way to support yourself— nothing. I must've been out of my mind, or I'd never have done this," he muttered.

"I'll be all right, really."

"Like hell!" he snapped. "Jesse'd turn over in his grave if he had any notion you were out here alone."

"Well, it's no worse than the last place he left me," she said mildly. "And since he was never around, I might as well have been alone."

"But you had a husband, and everybody knew it," he pointed out tersely. "Look around you—how the hell do you expect to feed yourself, let alone the kid?"

"I'll have to go into business."

"Doing what?"

"I don't know yet, but I'll think of something. I have to."

"No. I'm putting you on a train home."

"What? Oh, but you can't! I don't *have* a home anymore!"

"You can screech and squawk all you want, but you're going."

"Oh . . . now, you wait just a minute . . . it's my life, not yours. Just because you've got some fancified notion of what's proper, you've got no right to make me fit it. You turn this wagon around, you hear? I'm not going anywhere!"

"The hell you aren't."

"You sure like that word a lot."

"Huh?"

"Hell. You can't say a sentence without it, but you think you're the civilized one in this wagon, don't you? I don't know why you bothered to bring me out here, considering you don't think I've got the brains of a goose." Her chin came up defiantly as she added evenly, "But this wagon's mine, and so is everything in it, except you and that horse tied on back there. If you want, you can take it and go on—that's your right. But you can't make me leave all my belongings behind and go somewhere I don't want to go, just because *your* pea-brain tells you I ought to do it."

"Jesse'd never—"

"Jesse's dead, Dr. Hardin. I've got to look out for me and the baby myself now. I've got two guns, and I'm not afraid to use them. Maybe your wife would be, but I'm not."

"Leave Liddy out of this!" he snapped. "You don't know anything about her!"

Taken aback by the anger in his voice, she regarded him soberly for a moment. "No, I don't, but I know me. Once I find Mr. Hawthorne, you can take your horse and go on with a clear conscience."

"Yeah? And I suppose you're going to unload the damned thing by yourself?" he countered sarcastically.

"If I have to."

"Like hell."

"There you go again, using that word. Those men look worse than they are, if that's what's bothering you," she said patiently. "The railroad doesn't put up with rowdies—they have to cross the tracks to raise hell."

"A drunk man doesn't know his direction," he muttered.

"Do you?"

"Yes," he answered tersely.

"Then turn this wagon around, because you can't get to California this way."

"The privy's a damned ditch!"

"You say too many damneds, too."

"Well, what are you going to do?—squat over it?" he gibed. "Those men will be relieving themselves in front of you!"

"I don't aim to watch them. Besides, the cabin's supposed to be a little ways from camp," she reminded him. Pulling herself up to stand in the slow-moving wagon, she contemplated the ground.

"What the hell do you think you're doing now?"

"Fixin' to walk back, I guess, since you're determined to go the other way."

"Sit down before you fall out." Goaded, he turned the wagon again. She was too damned stubborn for her own good, and it'd probably cost her, but at least she was making it easy for him to leave her. Pulling up in the middle of the camp, he muttered, "Wait here," as he climbed down. "Anybody comes near you, use that whip on him," he flung over his shoulder as he stalked toward the nearest tent.

"Tell Mr. Hawthorne I want the cabin!" she called after him. Leaning back on the hard seat, she stretched her legs out over the front of the wagon, trying to ease the stiffness. Aside from the labor pains, the worst thing about having a baby was the backache, she decided. She was about to close her eyes when she realized she'd gathered a group of grimy admirers. One snaggle-toothed fellow had sidled close enough she could smell him. "Looks like I got here just in time," she told him.

"Huh?"

"I'm opening a laundry." The notion had come to her on the spur of the moment, but she warmed to it as she looked around the men. "I'll wash, dry, and iron, but it'll cost you ten cents a piece, providing I get it on Monday, which is my wash day. If you're out laying track somewhere, I'll hold your clothes two weeks; if not, you'll have to pay for them by Friday."

"That ain't what we thought you was," someone admitted.

She patted her stomach, drawing attention to it. "I don't know if any of you knew Jesse Taylor, but he was killed six weeks ago in a railroad accident over by McPherson, and I'm his widow. Since I'll be having this baby in another couple of months, I've got to work to feed it, and I'd sure appreciate if you'd bring me your laundry."

"Hear that, boys?—she's a widow woman!" the snaggle-toothed fellow announced, taking off his hat to reveal a matted mass of hair. "Name's Wiley Skinner, and I sure am glad to meet you. My clothes is holey, but you're sure welcome to wash 'em come payday."

As hats doffed around her, she saw another need. "I can barber, too—quarter a head—but you'll have to wash and delouse your hair first."

"What the hell do you think you're doing?" Spencer Hardin demanded, coming back to the wagon.

"Getting acquainted with my neighbors." Looking over his head to the others, she said, "I hope you all don't forget about Mondays."

Spence swung up beside her and took the reins, slapping them against the mule's flank. "You don't do anything you're told, do you? You could've been pulled from that seat by letting them get so close."

"Well, I wasn't."

"Most of 'em couldn't tell a decent woman from a hussy."

"I've heard more swearing from you than anybody else. Did you find out about the cabin?"

"He said it'd need a lot of work to make it livable.

Apparently the old hermit trapper didn't spend much time there, or if he did, it was a long time ago." He pulled a piece of paper from his pocket, studied it a moment, then put it back. "Unless I've mistaken the direction, it's just over that hill over there."

"I don't see any wagon tracks."

"There isn't any road," he said, cornering the wagon.

A wheel struck a rock, shifting the furniture in back, nearly unseating her. "This can't be right—I'd like to look at that map, if you don't mind."

"You don't think I can read? I just looked at it, and if the place isn't right up there, Hawthorne can't draw."

The old wagon was shaking as though it'd be going to pieces any minute. She could almost feel her teeth rattle as the rusty iron-covered wheels clattered over rocks. "Did he say anything else about the place?"

"Yeah—it's not fit for pigs."

"What? Oh, now, that can't be right. When Mr. Russell told Jesse about it, he—"

"There it is," he said, cutting her off. "Take a look for yourself."

She didn't see much of anything except grass-covered rocks and a bare board shack farther up the hill. "Oh."

He reined in, reached beneath the seat for his shotgun, then jumped down. "Wait here until I see how many rattlesnakes live in it."

Holding onto the frame of the wagon, she gingerly climbed down. "Wait up!"

Coming back to take her arm, he directed her toward the almost square structure. "Well, it's not canvas and it's got walls that won't flap in the wind, but that's about all I can say good about it," he observed. When he looked down, the expression on her face turned his irritation into sympathy. "I'll take you back," he said gently.

She wouldn't cry. She was made of sterner stuff, she told herself as she stared at it. Squaring her shoulders, she sighed audibly. "I'd better see what it looks like inside before I make up my mind between it and a tent."

She was a game one, he'd give her that. "All right, but it's only got one advantage I can think of."

"I'd like to hear it."

"Not too many drunks will be climbing up here."

"Yes, that is something, isn't it?" Feeling as though she'd had the wind knocked out of her, she began walking toward the shack. "It does look isolated."

"I guess it was like this when the government ceded the land to the railroad. Hawthorne thought maybe it'd been empty for years before that, because a receipt for pelts he found in there was dated 1848. He thought maybe the trapper died up in the mountains."

"Or Indians found him."

"Yeah." He tried the door and found it shut. "Door's swelled some."

"That's better than leaking air—it can be planed down enough to make it fit."

Throwing his shoulder against it, he forced it open and cautiously stepped over the threshold into a dark room. The sun outside cast a wedge of light from the door halfway across a dusty, uneven floor. There was a musty odor hanging in stale air. As he took another step, something loose wobbled under his boot.

"Looks like instead of using planks, he cut some tree trunks crosswise, then just laid the pieces down and filled the gaps between them with clay."

"It's a puncheon floor. A lot of poor folks have them out here to keep the snakes and digging varmints out."

She couldn't see much beyond that slice of light. He struck a match, then held it up. Particles of dust floated around the steady flame.

"I'd say you don't have to worry about the wind unless there's a storm," he observed. "But he sure wasn't much for sunlight, was he?" he added, directing her attention to the two small windows. "Looks like maybe he had paper or oilcloth there before somebody nailed boards up."

"I can order some glass. Supply wagons come out from the end of the line every other week."

As the flame burned down to his fingers, he dropped the match and stepped on it. Lighting another one, he looked at her. "Now that you've seen it, you don't want to stay here, do you? All you've got to cook on and heat with is that hearth, and you'll have to carry wood up that hill to do it," he pointed out. "And if it comes a hard winter, you'll have a hell of a time getting anywhere with a new baby—you know that, don't you? It's going to be cold and damned lonely, too."

"Yes."

"I don't see how you'll manage."

"I've got Dolly. If I have to, I'll ride down to camp."

"What are you going to do if a war party comes through?"

"I can make enough of a ruckus to get the folks down there up here. You can hear Jesse's Sharps for miles."

"As bad as it is, you're going to stay here?"

"I'm going to stay here."

"You know, Mrs. Taylor, there's a fine line between determination and folly."

"I'm not going back to North Carolina to be a charity case, Dr. Hardin. I'm going to get through the winter here, and come spring, maybe I'll have a better notion of what I can do. Right now, I'm just trying to fix it in my mind that Jesse's gone and he's never coming back."

"I'm sorry." The words seemed woefully inadequate when he considered what she faced, but he didn't have any others. "I'll take Clyde down and see if I can get some help moving your things in for you."

"Thank you."

She was in for a lot of backbreaking work before the place was fit to live in, but she was so determined to take care of herself that nothing he'd said had made any difference. He'd done what he'd said—he'd gotten her here—and he needed to move on. He had too many problems of his own to take on any more, he told himself as he untied his horse. He and Jesse were more than even now, anyway.

As he rode down the hill, she opened the door wider, letting in the chilly September wind to air out the place, then sat on the puncheon floor, making a list of what she'd need in her mind. Window glass. Kerosene. Whitewash. Lime. Cloth for curtains. Rags for a rug. Enough soap to last until she could make some. Two big washtubs. More rope for a clothesline. Wood for the winter. Pausing to stare into the empty room, she told herself if she kept busy enough, maybe the future wouldn't seem so bleak, maybe she wouldn't feel so terribly alone.

"You'll be careful, won't you?"

"Yeah." He grasped the saddle horn and stepped into the stirrup. Pulling himself up, he threw his leg over Clyde's back, then eased his body into the saddle before he looked down to her. "I wish I could say the same for you. I still think you're making a mistake, and you ought to go back to North Carolina while you still can."

"I don't know how many times I've told you I'll be all right—I may be a woman, but that doesn't make me a quivering coward," she declared firmly.

The wind whipped tendrils of hair loose, softening the effect of the bun that hugged the back of her head. Call it courage, or call it foolhardiness, she had a lot of grit—he had to give her that. Any woman he'd ever known would be scared to be in her shoes right now, and with good reason. With a wife like Laura, Jesse'd had everything to live for, but he hadn't. It didn't make much sense, but then nothing did anymore.

"I sure hope so, anyway," he said finally. "If anything happens to you, I'm going to feel responsible for leaving you alone out here."

"If you get back this way, stop in, and I'll fix supper," she offered. "I'll still be here come spring."

He nodded. "Maybe I'll have my boy with me. I'm hoping to find him once I get to San Francisco."

"I'd like to see him. Danny gave me a partiality for little boys."

"Yeah." Lifting his eyes to the sky, he frowned. "Looks like it could rain, so I'd better get on the road. I'd hoped to be in Laramie long before now."

"You should have gone on, but I can't say I'm sorry you stayed to drive my wagon over here. Jesse said you have a good heart, and you surely do."

Reaching under his coat, he pulled out the wad of banknotes, and peeled off fifty dollars. "Here—it's not much, but maybe it'll help you until you can get on your feet."

"I couldn't take your money, Dr. Hardin. I've got enough to get by."

"You're a bad liar, Mrs. Taylor. Go on—take it. If you don't need it, then save it for the baby."

She shook her head. "You don't know what you might run into between here and California, so you'd better keep it."

"No, I've got plenty. There's not many places after Laramie for me to spend it, anyway."

"You may find yourself wintering with the Mormons, you know."

"Look—count it as a loan," he coaxed, leaning down to hand her the money.

"I still can't take it."

"Why not?"

"It wouldn't be right."

"Damn it, woman!" he snapped. "I don't have time to sit here arguing with you!"

"Then don't. I'm not asking you to, you know."

He regarded her upturned face balefully for a moment, then dropped the money at her feet. When she didn't pick it up, he told her, "I'm leaving, so unless you want to watch it blow away, you'd better put it in your pocket."

"I guess it'll just have to blow, then."

He swore a string of epithets under his breath, cursing her soundly before he managed to grit out aloud, "Look, I figure I owe Jesse for helping me out back in Carolina. He'd want you to take it."

She shook her head. "No, Jesse wasn't one to take charity—ever. He earned everything he ever got. Besides, I can't repay you," she told him. "If I thought I could, maybe it'd be different, but I can't. And fifty dollars is a lot of money for you to be giving away, especially since you'll probably be needing it more than me. I haven't even touched his last railroad pay yet."

"How much was it?"

"Enough for me to get by on."

"That's not what I asked, Mrs. Taylor."

Sighing, she relented. "All right—not that it's any of your business, mind you, but Mr. Russell gave me the fifty-two dollars pay and the crew collected another nineteen, so that made it seventy-one dollars. And that doesn't include twenty I'd already saved up for when Jesse couldn't work this winter. Now that ought to tell you I don't need any charity yet."

"Ninety-one dollars," he said, shaking his head.

"Liddy spent more than that on one change of clothes."

"Well, I wasn't raised that way, and I'm not Lydia, so I don't have any right to take your money. I don't have any claim on you at all."

Confounded by her logic, he looked heavenward for patience, then tried again to reason with her. "Look—I don't have time to argue anymore. I've got to get to San Francisco, but I don't feel right leaving you to fend for yourself in this godforsaken place. That money's a salve to my conscience, because I know I should've hauled you back to Fort Kearny and made you get on that train."

"Oh, for—when you get a notion fixed in your mind, you just don't let go of it, do you?" Her eyes scanned his face, taking in those sober blue eyes, the set of his jaw, and she realized he was stubborn enough to mean it. "Well," she decided finally, "I guess you'd just sit up there all day to win, so I'm going to take your money to make you happy. But if you come back this way next spring, I don't want you to be too surprised if I've still got every penny of it waiting for you." Bending over awkwardly, she retrieved the bills. As she straightened up, she added, "I just want you to know I still don't think it's right for you to be giving me fifty dollars."

"It makes me feel better," he assured her.

"But you've got to let me do something for you— you wait here, and I'll be right back. Don't you go off until I give you something to take with you."

"I haven't got time—and I've got to travel light!" he called out. "I've got to go!"

She turned back to argue, "Well, you've got to eat, don't you? It'll just take me a minute."

With that, she ran into the house, leaving him to wait astride an impatient horse. "Easy now, Clyde," he muttered, pulling the animal up short. Resigned, he sat there, thinking he'd never known any two women as different from each other as Laura Taylor and Lydia Jamison. Like night and day. The only thing they had in common was contrariness, but he'd just about decided that peculiar quality afflicted the whole female sex.

His gaze strayed to the dilapidated trapper's shack for a moment. She'd be just plain lucky if it didn't fall down around her before he came back through. Or burn down when hot coals from the broken chimney hit that weather-beaten roof. As he looked at the place, he was angry with Jesse for dying and leaving a young wife in such straits. He'd had no business bringing her out here in the first place, exposing her to the lowest sort of men, leaving her to fend for herself while he'd gone off for weeks at a time. It had been a damned selfish thing to do.

She came out carrying two packages, a small one wrapped in a man's white handkerchief and a larger, bulkier bundle. Handing them up to him, she said, "There—at least you won't be having to make a fire between here and Laramie."

"What's this?" he asked curiously.

"The big one's some of Jesse's shirts and socks, and the little one's just jelly sandwiches, some pieces of buffalo jerky, and a chunk of cheese. It's not much for a man of your size to eat, but it'll at least keep body and soul together." Taking a step back, she added, "I know you want to travel light, but I didn't have anybody else to give the clothes to."

"Thanks."

"And I figured if it got cold up there, maybe you'd want to put on more than one shirt under your coat and two pair of socks in those boots."

"Yeah."

"Well, you'd better get started," she told him awkwardly. "And keep your eye out for Indians, because there's been trouble with the Cheyenne over by Laramie, and once you get past the fort there, there aren't any soldiers out patrolling the road this time of year. That's about all I've got to say," she said, stepping back. "Good-bye, Dr. Hardin."

She looked like a lost waif, standing there in that faded calico dress, resting her hands on that round belly. If he'd ever needed any proof that life wasn't fair, he could see it in her. Tipping his hat in farewell, he nudged Clyde with his knee, turning him down the rocky slope toward the road. As sorry as he felt for her, he knew there wasn't much more he could do to help her out. He had his own troubles to worry about.

Wyoming: October 5, 1865

So that was the Wind River Range of the Rocky Mountains. Slowing Clyde to a walk, Spence studied the majestic, snow-covered peaks towering in the northwest with unabashed awe. He'd thought when he went through the Laramie Plains, the mountains to the south were pretty impressive, but each successive spine of the Rockies he'd seen was grander than the last. These seemed to rise like giant, jagged shark's teeth above gray foothills, cutting across the high plains, a welcome change of scene after ten days spent crossing through a basin so dry that greasewood and salt sage seemed to be the only things growing there.

Claiming he'd trapped all the way from Lodgepole Creek in the south of the new Idaho Territory to the Powder and Yellowstone rivers in the north, from the North Platte to the Green, Salt, and Snake rivers in the west, an old sutler back at Laramie had pointed out the Overland Route on an army map of the territory, saying Spence was going to miss the best places by taking it. He'd told tales of peaks high enough to touch heaven, of bottomless canyons, of cliff walls descending into deep, sky blue lakes, of hot springs spewing steam and boiling water a hundred feet into the air. A man needed to spend years out here to see all of those things, the fellow said.

Right now, Spence didn't have weeks, let alone years to spare. Reaching behind him, he pulled out the map and unrolled it to study it. It was still one hell of a long way to California, and time was running out on him.

"From the middle of October on, you can start expecting bad weather," the sutler had said. "If you ain't got to the Mormon settlements before then, you'd better expect to stay there, 'cause there's not much chance you can get to the Sierras, let alone over 'em, before winter sets in. And you still got a big desert to cross before you run into the Sierras, anyway. I know the Mormons call it Deseret, which I guess is supposed to be the Promised Land to 'em, but I'll be damned if I saw anything but rattlesnakes and buzzards alive between the Salt Lake and Carson City. Everything else was just bones left from things that died of thirst. When you do find water, half the time it's got too much salt and soda in it to drink."

At the rate he was going, Spence wouldn't make it to the Mormons by then. He hadn't had anybody yet tell him he could get through to California now, he realized grimly. But he had to. He wanted his son, and there was no way to get him without going out there. And he'd be damned before he'd spend the winter as an outsider among an unfriendly religious sect he didn't understand. Lydia had been one wife too many for him.

No, if he waited until spring, Ross might move on, and his trail could be too cold to follow, even for the

Pinkertons, Spence reasoned. And there was a good
chance that Ross didn't want Josh, anyway. With
Lydia dead, he'd probably already offered the kid to
anybody who'd take him.

Or there was the other possibility, the one Spence
didn't want to think about, the one that woke him
up in a cold sweat at night. Maybe Ross and Josh
hadn't made it to California. They'd both had plenty
of exposure to cholera before Lydia and her Auntie
Fan died. The damned stuff took the young, the old,
and just about everything in between, and not too
many managed to survive it. Some, but not many.

Looking skyward, he saw several huge, redheaded
black birds circling overhead—turkey buzzards waiting for something to die. His hand went to his gun;
then he caught himself. No, he didn't want to fire
any shot he didn't have to. While he couldn't tell a
Crow from a Cheyenne or a Sioux, he could go a
lifetime without meeting any more of them. He'd already had two narrow escapes, and he sure didn't
want to push his luck again.

"Come on, Clyde," he murmured. "We're getting
nowhere sitting here." As he jerked on the little jenny's rope, the pack animal resisted, then fell in behind the horse.

By late afternoon, the going was rougher, and the
squat brush that had dotted the land for miles and
miles now mingled with a sparse sprinkling pine on
uneven, rock-littered ground. Nearly a month ago,
the last wagons of settlers had passed this way, and
now the route was pretty much deserted. He hadn't
seen another soul since the two railroad surveyors,

and they'd been less than fifty miles out of Fort Laramie. By now, they'd have already gone back.

The road was ascending into the foothills as they formed an uneven pass to the south of the Wind River. The vast emptiness, the red rock bluffs, buttes, and mesas dotting the landscape between mountains and canyons emphasized the insignificance of one man. It was beautiful and eerie at the same time.

The faint smell of distant smoke was in the air, he realized suddenly. Somebody had a campfire somewhere, and it wasn't likely he was a white man, so he had to be doubly careful. He couldn't afford to make a fire of his own tonight.

It was nearly dark before he stopped to make his camp. And once he'd fed and hobbled Clyde and Sally, he fixed himself a cold supper of hardtack, jerky, and water before putting down his bedroll in the shelter of a rock ledge. Rolling up in his blankets, he lay for a time, staring at the riffs of clouds drifting across the stars, feeling more alone now than at any other time in his life.

Somewhere out there in that wide expanse of night, a pack of wolves hunted, yipping and howling as they cornered something; then the world went almost silent, leaving only the sound of sagebrush rolling over rock. As he finally drifted off to sleep, Spence's last thought was how early he needed to get on the trail in the morning.

He awoke in pitch-black darkness, shivering from the cold of a strong north wind, and he realized a heavy bank of clouds had rolled in, obscuring the moon and stars. Adding another blanket, he turned on his side and pulled the covers closer, hoping to get back to sleep. As he crossed into that netherworld again, Lydia and Ross taunted him, and he promised himself revenge.

A cold rain ran down the overhanging ledge, spattering the rocky ground below, waking him again. This time, the dark had faded into a gray, dismal dawn. Groping for his saddlebag, he found his watch. It was almost seven, and the sky was pouring. For a moment, he lay there, thinking God had to be punishing him for some terrible, unremembered sin. Looking out across the scrub-dotted land, he noticed everything glistened. Ice. Nearby, the little jenny was huddled against Clyde, and the manes of both animals dripped icicles. A norther had blown in during the night, and he was facing a very different sort of nightmare.

He had to go on, he told himself. The stuff would melt in a few hours. Reluctantly rolling out of the blankets, he found the bundle of Jesse's clothes, and added two shirts to the one he already wore before he pulled on his coat. A rolled pair of socks crinkled as he pulled it apart, and several banknotes fell out.

Chagrined, he realized it was the fifty dollars he'd given Laura Taylor in what now seemed like an age ago, and he knew she'd outwitted him. The woman was just too damned stubborn for her own good, he muttered to himself as he tugged Jesse's socks over his own. Calling her everything from an idiot to a fool, he managed to get his boots on. Bundled in an oiled canvas overcoat, he rerolled his bedding and gathered his belongings, then quickly stuffed them under the tarp-covered packs on the jenny's back. Retrieving a rock-hard biscuit from his saddlebag, he tried to eat it while he tightened the saddle girth under Clyde's belly.

He broke camp cursing the miserable weather, then headed up the road again, hoping the storm wouldn't amount to much. It was still too early for snow to last, he reassured himself. By noon, the rain would have the last vestiges of ice washed away.

But as he rode hunched over the saddle horn, the wind whipped his face raw and cut through the canvas coat like a knife through butter. His hands hurt, then grew numb, as the north wind howled louder, pelting him with ice, and he knew it was folly to try to go on today. He'd have to wait it out.

He found a hollow place on the south side of a hill and made camp there, sheltering himself and the animals by tying a blanket to scrub pines growing out of crevices in the rocks above. Using a knife, he stripped small, scraggly boughs from the trunks and piled them up behind the blanket to keep himself off the cold ground. Spreading his bedroll over them, he wrapped himself in it and tried to get warm without a fire.

Shortly after noon, the sleet turned to snow as he watched in disbelief. He hadn't expected it to snow for at least another two or three weeks at the earliest. The flakes were big, wet, and heavy, and as soon as the wind shifted or died down, it would melt fast.

By three o'clock, the air was so white he couldn't even see the road through it, and the temperature was going down instead of up. The storm was turning into a blizzard before his eyes. To save the water in his canteen, he ate snow with his hands, then made another meal of jerky, while he faced his dwindling choices.

He was beginning to feel cursed, that everything conspired against him to keep him from reaching California this year. If he tried to go on, he risked getting lost as the storm worsened. If he turned back, it was a long way to Laramie now. And if he stayed put, the wind was apt to bury him in the drifting snow. But he had to go on, he argued. He had a son somewhere in San Francisco.

The conflict within slowly succumbed to reason. If it was already snowing here, there was no telling how bad it'd be farther west, and the passes in the Sierras would be worse by then. If he failed to get through them, he'd probably perish, and there'd be nobody left to search for Josh—nobody left to punish Ross. He'd been a damned stubborn fool for even thinking he could do it this late, he realized bitterly.

Staring into that snow-white sky, he fought an impotent anger. The comfortable life he'd expected medicine to give him had disintegrated, leaving him nothing but the ashes of dreams he'd once thought he and Liddy shared. Four years of war, her betrayal with the shallowest man of his acquaintance, and the loss of his son had left him with next to nothing, with no purpose except revenge. He wanted to shake his fist at the Almighty, demanding to know what terrible sin he had committed to warrant such punishment.

Thad Bingham had always preached that God had some grand plan for every creature in the world, and Spence had wanted to believe that, but he couldn't anymore. A God who could let Jesse Taylor die, leaving a destitute wife heavy with child, who could take everything Spence cared about from him, then keep him from finding the only flesh and blood he had left, wasn't the loving God Bingham had believed in. There could be no good reason to let him get this far, then force him to go back empty-handed. But right now, it looked like he'd be spending the winter at either Laramie or McPherson, whether he wanted to or not.

Nebraska Territory: October 16, 1865

Thank God for Indian summer. This last warm spell had made it possible for Laura to work outside instead of steaming up the cabin, and she wasn't about to let the opportunity pass. Perched on a stool, she pared soap into the big washtub, readying the water for the dirtiest batch of laundry she'd seen yet. To look at those clothes, a body'd think they came off coal miners instead of railroad men.

With more crews coming in every day, the camp was growing, and so was her business. Last week, she'd taken in fifteen dollars, and this week looked to be even better. Stopping to rub an itching nose, she reflected that while the work was hard, it kept her too busy to fret about much else. By the time she got to bed tonight, she'd be too tired to think, much less worry about life without Jesse.

As the last piece of soap hit the water, she laid aside the knife and went to the piles of clothes she'd already sorted. Scooping up a rank-smelling load of shirts, she carried them to the tub and dropped them into it, then stirred them vigorously with a pole. The water turned a dull brown almost immediately.

It was going to be a lot harder to do this after she

had the baby, but she'd manage. By then, the track work would slow down, and maybe she wouldn't have so much dirt to contend with. Pausing long enough to roll up her sleeves, she counted the batches of laundry. Eleven. When the weather turned cold, it'd be hard to get all those dirty clothes and the washtubs into a one-room cabin.

Her arms ached, and the small of her back hurt, but she returned to churning those clothes like butter, humming the tune of "My Darling Clementine" to take her mind off the backbreaking work. At least she was making enough to support herself, and for that she had to be thankful.

The path was steeper than Spence had remembered it, or maybe his tired horse just made it seem that way. As his eyes took in the still-green grass, the bright leaves on the scattered trees, he had to wonder if he could have gone on. It didn't matter now—he'd come too far back to even contemplate another try before May. No, he was just stuck for the winter in a godforsaken corner of Nebraska, where the only person he knew was Laura Taylor.

Yeah, there she was. She had her back to him while she hung wet clothes on a long laundry line. She had enough men's pants flapping in the mild breeze to outfit an army.

"What the hell . . . ?"

She turned around at the sound of the horse coming up the path, and she gaped at Spence Hardin for a moment before she found her voice. "What *on earth* are you doing back here, Dr. Hardin?" she asked, hurrying toward him. "I thought you'd be somewhere in Utah with the Mormons by now."

"I hit snow." Easing his leg over the saddle, he swung down to face her. She had her sleeves rolled to her elbows, her dress was wet in front where it clung to her big stomach, and her hair was a mass of wind-blown tangles, but after nearly three weeks in the saddle, she was a welcome sight. Looking away, he admitted, "I came back—I couldn't get through, so I guess you and just about everybody else was right."

"I'm sorry—I know how much you wanted to go," she said quietly.

"Yeah, well, it looks like I'm here for the winter."

"Here?" Momentarily nonplussed, she looked up at him with widening eyes.

"Yeah. I'll probably try to get room and board at the fort, if it's not against army regulations."

"Oh."

"So—what's all this?" he wondered, gesturing to the sagging clothesline.

"Washing." As his eyebrow lifted, she explained, "I've got myself a business now. Once a week, the men in camp send their dirty clothes up, and I wash, dry, and iron everything." Pushing back her hair, she added, "I'm making a living at it."

"It's a damned hard living, I'd say."

"At least I'm surviving."

"Why didn't you keep the money?" he asked abruptly.

"I guess you must've found it," she replied.

"That's not an answer."

"You already know why—it wasn't mine to keep." Stepping back, she looked toward the cabin. "I . . .

uh . . . I don't suppose you've got time for a cup of coffee, do you?"

"I've got about six months of it," he answered dryly.

"Well, then come on in. I've got real coffee now—and I've always got bread and jam."

"Anything sounds good—I haven't eaten since Laramie," he said, falling in beside her.

"If you came from Laramie today, you sure made good time."

"I left last night."

"And you haven't eaten anything in all that time? I didn't think a man could go that long without food." At the threshold of her door, she stopped to turn back to him. "Maybe you'd better stay for supper."

"I don't want to be any trouble."

"You won't be—I've got to eat, too." Holding the knob, she threw her shoulder into the door. "I don't know how many times I've planed this down, but it still sticks," she explained as it opened. "I'm afraid to take too much off—I don't want cold air coming in around it this winter."

The place didn't look much like it had when he'd left nearly a month before. "I see you've done some fixing up," he murmured.

"I had to. There's glass in the windows now, and I covered the walls with newspaper before I white-washed them, so maybe it'll be a little warmer in here when a norther's blowing outside."

"You make this rug yourself?"

"Well, it's just rags I braided together, but at least I can walk around with my shoes off without getting my feet full of splinters," she said, pleased he'd noticed. "Those curtains used to be my petticoat." As he looked around, she sighed. "I know—there's a little too much furniture, but I couldn't bring myself to throw anything out."

"No, it looks nice—real nice. I don't know how you managed to do all this."

Moving to the cupboard, she took out two heavy cups, the breadbox, and the jam pot. "I didn't want to sit around feeling sorry for myself, so I just kept busy." Turning around in the corner she called her kitchen, she asked, "Do you still want cream and sugar in your coffee?"

"Not if it's real coffee."

"It is, but I've got to go outside to fetch it. I didn't see any sense to making two fires, and I was boiling water for the wash out there."

While she stepped out, he continued to study the one room, thinking she'd made it pretty homey, considering what she'd had to work with. There was even a framed square of embroidered white cotton hanging on the wall. Looking closer, he could see the tiny stitches that proclaimed, "Laura Lane and Jesse Taylor, united in matrimony October 18, 1859." Exactly six years ago day after tomorrow.

She came in with the enamelware coffeepot and stopped when she noticed him reading the embroidered words. "It seems like that was a whole lifetime ago," she said softly. "I thought it'd be like that forever."

"I guess we all believe that way." He turned around, his face sober. "But some of us are just plain fools."

"I loved Jesse, Dr. Hardin. That was the happiest day of my life."

"I wasn't talking about you—I was thinking of me."

"It was a bad time to get married, right before the war like that, but we didn't know then Lincoln would win, and North Carolina would secede. The Jesse I knew back then was the best man I ever met."

"Yeah."

"I guess war changes men sometimes," she added sadly. "They seem to come back harder than they went in."

"Yeah."

Recovering, she carried the pot to the table and filled both cups before she sat down. "Your coffee's ready."

"Thanks," he murmured, taking a seat across from her. For a moment, he stared into the rich, brown liquid pensively, then recovered. "It wasn't me who changed."

"You sound like Jesse. He always said he came back to a different woman than the one he'd left behind. Maybe that was true, but I don't know. Maybe being alone all that time, sitting at home, waiting for both of them to come home, I got used to doing for myself like he said, but I don't think so. I mean, I'd always had to look after things as far back as I can remember. No, it was him that changed," she said positively. "Before the war, we'd always dreamed together."

"And after?"

"He'd been dreaming alone all that time he was gone, and he had it set in his mind what I wanted."

She took a sip from the steaming cup, then set it down. "And he was going to give it to me, no matter how many times I tried to set him straight."

There was a wistfulness in her voice that touched him more than her words. "Sometimes it's hard to know what's in someone else's mind."

"Yes." Her chin came up. "Yes, it is. I thought I could read Jesse's like it was a book. When he came back, I couldn't do that anymore, and it hurt. I liked what I had, Dr. Hardin—I didn't want to come out here."

"I sort of figured that out."

"But I *am* here, so I've got to make the best of what I've got. Otherwise, I'd just drive myself crazy wanting what I can't have."

"Which is?"

"My home back. Danny. Jesse the way he was before the war. They're all gone now. All that's left is me and this baby." Recovering, she leaned back in her chair. "I guess I sound pretty sorry for myself, but I'm not. Mama always used to say the Lord doesn't give us anything He knows we can't handle." Forcing a smile, she looked him in the eye. "She also liked to say life's what you make of it, not what you're given. If she was right about that, then I'm going to do all right. I never was one to complain about anything I thought I could change."

"I'd change a lot of things if I could."

"Maybe you just think you would," she murmured, sipping her coffee again.

"Well, I won't let another woman make a fool of me, that's for damned sure. Once burned, twice shy, as they say."

She eyed him curiously, wondering how a man like him had become so soured on his life. "Well, I wasn't exactly burned, but I don't think I'll ever want another husband. Not that anybody out here wants to believe that. They all seem to think that widowhood is an unnatural condition, you know."

"You've got admirers, I take it?"

"I've got a lot of idiots who ought to know better," she retorted. "I'd like to get a mirror for all of them, too. I don't know what there is about a man that makes him think a flea-bitten, louse-infested fellow who doesn't even know what a bathtub's for is a prime catch for a woman. And they aren't particular the other way, either—I could be cross-eyed, buck-toothed, stringy-haired, knock-kneed, and nigh to ninety, and it wouldn't make much difference to any of them, as long as I was interested in marrying. You've got no notion of how it is out here, Dr. Hardin," she declared with feeling. "I had to quit offering haircuts, because the money wasn't worth the importunity."

"You're a pretty woman."

"In this condition? I doubt that very much."

"You are."

"Well, I don't feel it, and I don't want to be, anyway. If I had two wishes in this world, it'd be a healthy baby and a chance to raise him in peace. If I had ten choices, none of them would be a man right now."

"I never met a woman who didn't want to live off a man."

"I'm not a leech."

"No, you're not. You're a remarkable woman."

"No." Leaning across the table, she refilled his cup, then stood up. "You're welcome to sit a while, but I've got washing to finish." For a moment, she allowed her expression to soften. "I must sound like a real harridan, I know, but I've let myself get behind. I *am* glad to see you, Dr. Hardin. I'm not too blind to know I owe you a lot."

"I'll make do with supper," he murmured.

"Well, to tide you over, you'd better eat some of that bread and jam you haven't touched yet."

When she came back nearly two hours later, he was asleep in her daddy's old rocker, his long legs stretched out in front of him, his head resting on the broad back of the chair. Tiptoeing closer, she reached to touch the thick black hair.

"Dr. Hardin . . . ?" she said softly.

Asleep, he'd lost his harshness, making him look years younger, more like the twenty-eight years he claimed. There was no question that he was a handsome man. This time, she shook him gently. "Dr. Hardin, you'll get a crick in your neck like that," she told him.

It was no use—he was dead to the world. Feeling sorry for him, she rolled up a towel and eased it beneath his head, then went to the kitchen corner to peel potatoes for supper.

He was just plain exhausted, she decided. It made her wonder how far he'd actually gotten before the snow stopped him. What a bitter pill that surely must have been for him to swallow. How terribly hard to turn back. He'd wanted to find that little boy so much, and now he had a long winter to wait before he could try again. It just wasn't right.

She still didn't know what his wife had done, but whatever it was, it'd left him a bitter, disillusioned man. As her knife circled the potato, making a ribbon of the peel, she knew his wounds were as deep as hers. And it was going to take more than a winter to heal them.

He awoke to find the room almost dark, and the smell of onions in the air. Sitting up, he twisted his head, trying to ease his stiff neck, and he saw that she had a fire going in the hearth. A big black kettle hung from a hook above the flames, and a heavy Dutch oven rested on a flat rock at the corner of the fire pit. Passing a hand over his eyes, he asked, "What time is it?"

"Good—you're awake. It's six-thirty, and I was beginning to be afraid the cornbread would burn waiting for you."

"I didn't mean to nod off."

"Well, if you hadn't needed to, you wouldn't have."

"You've got an answer for just about everything, don't you?"

"I thought you might wake up cranky," she murmured, taking the Dutch oven from the hearth.

"I'm not cranky," he muttered.

"No? Then I guess I'm just mistaken. Anyway, if you want to wash up before you eat, the water bucket's right outside the door."

"Thanks. I thought I smelled onions."

"I made potato soup."

"Potato soup and cornbread. I ate a lot of that back in Missouri, and I always liked it."

"Oh? I thought you were Georgia born and bred."

"No. We moved there when I was nine. My stepfather was the Georgian."

"And he was the preacher."

"Yeah." With an effort, he forced his tired body from the rocking chair and headed outside.

"The privy's around back," she told him from the door. "Mr. Hawthorne sent some Chinese up to dig it for me."

When he came back in, he looked as if he'd poured the bucket over his head, she decided as she dipped the soup from the kettle into the bowls. Carrying them, she met him at the table. "Go ahead—I forgot the butter."

"Do you mind if I crumble the cornbread into my soup?" he asked. "I know it's not mannerly, but I like it that way."

"Suit yourself," she said, setting the butter plate in front of him.

He ate with gusto, wolfing down three bowls of exceptionally good potato soup, while she toyed with hers, and he realized she was watching him. "Sorry," he apologized sheepishly. "I've been living on hard tack and jerky most of the month since I left."

"I figured you liked the food."

"Ummm—very much."

"I'm not going to clear the dishes yet. I've still got clothes to take down before the dew makes them damp again."

"Need any help?"

"Well, it'd be nice—I mean, I could use the company."

The whole sky was ablaze in hues of orange, pink, and a hazy purple as he looked across the rocky yard. It was the sort of sunset that took one's breath away just to look at it. Laura Taylor stopped walking to follow his rapt gaze. "Yes, it is beautiful, isn't it?" she said softly. "God's paintbrush, Mama used to call a sky like this."

"Yeah."

There was a crisp chill in the air now, and the smoke from the chimney wafted overhead, adding the warm smell of burning wood to the world. Down the hill, the white canvas tents took on a surreal look under that awesome sky. Spence took a deep breath, drawing in the autumn air, savoring it. A full stomach, a night like this—that was the way a man was supposed to live. Then he caught himself.

"Which end do you want to take?" he asked her, looking toward the long clothesline.

"You don't have to help—it's too pretty an evening to spend taking down laundry if you don't have to."

He spied the big woven baskets. "Tell you what—you just sit down, and I'll get the clothes. I need to work off some of that supper, or I'll be too full to sleep. Go on," he said, turning her back toward the house.

The sweet smell of cloth dried in the sun brought back memories of another time, when he'd lived in Missouri with his mother after his father died. It'd been a hard time for her until Bingham came along, but he could remember following her down that old gray clothesline, holding the basket while she put the clean clothes in it. It hadn't been the same in Georgia, where he'd watched the slaves do the task.

Hefting the heavy basket, he headed back toward the cabin. Laura'd brought two chairs from the house outside, and she sat facing the camp, looking out into the beautiful, darkening sky. Overhead, the moon gazed down benevolently, barely veiled by floating skiffs of clouds. Silhouetted against that sky, she was a picture to carry in the mind, her face mirroring the beauty of the place, her hands placidly resting on the mound that held her child. And he couldn't help admiring her, thinking she was truly an extraordinary woman.

"I thought you might want to sit out a spell."

"Yeah."

The night sounds of an Indian summer carried on the air like a lullaby, while the lanterns in the camp below glowed like lightning bugs in a Georgia swamp, gaining brightness as the sun sank deeper into night. Sitting there in silence, Spence realized it was the most peace he'd known in a long, long time.

"I come out here every night it's warm enough," Laura said, her voice low.

"I can see why."

"I expect I'd better go in," she said finally. "I've got all that ironing to do tomorrow." When he said nothing, she turned to him. "Did you find yourself a place to stay in camp?"

"No." In the moonlight, he could see her moon reflected in her widening eyes. "I've been sitting here, thinking some."

"Oh?" she asked cautiously.

"Yeah. A woman in your condition needs a man around, and . . ." He could sense her stiffening beside him, but he plunged ahead. "I'm not talking an impropriety, you understand, just an arrangement that'd benefit both of us."

"Oh, I don't . . . like how?" she managed to ask.

"I don't think Jesse'd like to see you taking in laundry, and—"

"Then he should've thought of that before he brought me out here," she cut in.

"I was just wondering how you'd feel about taking in a boarder for the winter," he went on. "I'd pay you for cooking and cleaning, and you wouldn't be out here hanging clothes in the dead of winter. And you wouldn't be alone if there was any trouble with the baby—you'd have someone here."

"I see."

He could tell she wasn't exactly enthusiastic. "Look—I'm not looking for another wife, and you say you don't want another husband. The next hardcase that comes up that hill to court you won't get past me. All I want is a place to stay, and I'll move on next May."

"There's only one room—and one bed, Dr. Hardin."

"I've got a bedroll—all I need is a place to put it. And we can figure out a way to divide the room."

"Well," she mused slowly, "I sure never expected anything like this to come up. I don't expect anybody'd think much about you staying here, but there'd sure be some talk about me."

"I'd be a boarder, nothing more."

"Nobody looking at you would think that—they just wouldn't."

"Why not?"

"You're a very handsome man. I'd be the widow trying to trap you."

"I'm not trappable. Hell will freeze solid before I go looking for another wife."

"Oh, I understand that. And if I learned one thing after Jesse came back, it was that I'd become too sure of myself to suit either of us. I don't want another husband, Dr. Hardin, and I probably never will. I loved Jesse, but I wanted my say-so, too, and he couldn't see why. A man and a woman have to pull together to get anywhere, and I don't aim to be the only ox in the yoke while my husband cracks the whip."

"I don't think I've ever heard matrimony put in those terms," he admitted.

"That's what I mean. None of you understand."

"But I suppose you've got a point about the talk," he conceded, heaving himself out of the chair. "Maybe we can make some arrangement for meals, and I'll see if I can get a place down there to sleep."

"I'm sorry if I hurt your feelings."

"No. It was a selfish, idiotic idea, anyway. I don't even know where it came from. I was just sitting there, thinking how peaceful it was up here, that's all. I just didn't think about the consequences for you, and I'm sorry."

He'd started for the cabin, probably to get his gun belt, and when he came out, she knew he'd be going. She sat very still, trying to figure out if it would work.

Sure enough, he came out strapping his gun to his hip. As he walked toward the place where Dolly grazed with the chestnut and the mule, she heard herself call out, "Wait . . ." As he turned around, the moon glittered in those blue eyes, making them look like steel. "That is . . . how much money are you talking about?—for room and board, I mean."

"How much do you make doing dirty laundry?"

"Oh—now, that'd be too much!"

"How much?"

"Well, it varies, but last week I took in fifteen dollars. That'd be sixty for the month, and I wouldn't pay that to stay with the queen of England," she declared flatly. "And all I've got is half a room, anyway."

He let out a low whistle. "You get fifteen dollars a week for doing laundry?"

"Well, I expect a decline in that now that you're here," she admitted frankly. "I think some of them just bring up their clothes so they can make eyes at me. I imagine your being here will discourage a lot of that."

"I could probably manage to pay twenty or twenty-five a month, considering the meals."

Now that she'd made up her mind, she couldn't help smiling at him. "I don't suppose you'd consider doing laundry, would you?"

"Only as the absolute last resort to keep from starving. But maybe with the board money, you could hire somebody." Coming over to pick up his chair, he studied her face through the darkness. "What made you change your mind?"

"With you around, I'll have somebody to talk to besides myself. I figure when a norther hits, and they say you can count on at least one every winter, we'll need the company."

Spence had seen slaves under the whip who couldn't work as hard as Laura Taylor. And it didn't seem to make any difference what she tackled. She could study something, then figure out a way to do it, whether it was patching the wall, evening the floor, or sending a bucket of wet laundry over a pulley next to the clothesline. In the week he'd been living in her cabin, his admiration of her had grown by the day.

And her Creator had certainly endowed her with an indomitable spirit. She was totally unwilling to give up on anything until she'd given it her all. He was beginning to think there wasn't anything she couldn't do, even though he knew it sounded ridiculous to say it. He'd thought he was doing her some sort of favor by staying there, but he was beginning to think she didn't need him.

She looked up from the table where she'd been counting her money. "Is something the matter?"

"No. I was thinking about getting a job with the railroad."

"They've got a doctor."

"I hear they might be hiring more men on the repair track."

"The rep track? It's hard, dirty work—a lot worse than washing clothes." Holding up the money jar, she said, "There's twenty dollars in here and another fourteen on the table." Stuffing the new money in with the rest, she added, "You've got too much education to work the rep track, Dr. Hardin."

"Hard work never hurt anyone. If it did, you'd be dead."

"But I'm used to it," she pointed out mildly. "I wasn't born to the purple like some folks I know. You don't need to be swinging a hammer—you've got a higher calling than that."

"I wasn't born to the purple, as you call it."

"What about that plantation you grew up on?"

"My stepfather inherited a share of it—he didn't own it all. Miss Clarissa had half."

"Well, all my daddy had was forty acres, and every time it looked like there'd be a good crop coming in, something would happen to it. It'd be too wet, or it'd be too dry, or the hail would beat it to pieces."

"Why did he stay on it?"

She rubbed the side of her nose pensively before answering. "He was a farmer, just like his father—he came from a long line of farmers. He didn't think he was poor as long as he had his land."

"Yeah, but if it didn't make a living for him—"

"Now, you're sounding just like Jesse. There are some things a lot more important than money. Like being honest, for instance. Or caring about your fellow man. Daddy never had a slave in his life."

"Bingham didn't want any. He didn't believe in slavery either."

"Then why didn't he free his and hire men to get his planting done?"

"It wasn't that easy."

"He wasn't forced to keep them, was he?" she countered.

"He didn't own them outright," he answered evenly. "His sister owned half of everything."

"Then he should have sold his half. You can't say you don't believe in something and keep on doing it, can you?"

"Look—I'm not Thad Bingham, so I can't answer that. I was a kid, so I didn't pay much attention at the time. I just know he preached against slavery."

"I see."

"No, you don't!" he snapped. "I don't know where you think you're going with this, but it must be somewhere, or we'd still be talking about your family's farm."

"I was talking about making amends."

"What?"

"Reverend Bingham put you through medical school, didn't he?"

"What's that got to do with slavery?"

"It was slaves that made all that money for him. You went to medical college on that money, Dr. Hardin."

"Go on."

"Don't you think you ought to atone for it by practicing what you learned?"

"I did my atoning in the Confederate Army. I sawed off legs while men screamed for me to stop— I held guts together with my bare hands, trying to stop the blood pouring through wounds that'd make a pig butcher sick—I watched boys too young to grow beards die on my table—I saw enough misery and death to last me a lifetime, Mrs. Taylor—and if I never see another capital saw or gaping gut, I'll still have the nightmares until I die."

"I'm sorry. I just thought—"

"Well, don't!"

"You did some good, too," she said softly. "Jesse wouldn't have had both his legs without you. And Danny—"

"That's another one," he cut in harshly. "I was the one who held Danny Lane down while he died. So don't talk to me about a calling, because I answered mine, and look what it got me—a thousand dead men—tens of thousands maimed! A wife who took off with another man because I couldn't go home! I answered that call once, Mrs. Taylor, and so help me God, I won't make that mistake again!" As she blanched, he realized he'd gone too far. "I'm sorry," he managed hoarsely. "I had no right to tell you that."

Rising awkwardly from the table, she crossed the room to lay her hand on his shoulder. "I don't know how you managed to live with that inside you," she said quietly. "At least I know now that Danny had somebody who cared about him there when he died." Moving behind him, she rubbed the back of his neck, feeling the tautness beneath her fingers. "As much as you blame yourself for what you couldn't do, you have to remember all the men who made it home because of what you did for them." Her fingers crept into the thick black hair that waved at his nape, stroking it. "You're every bit as much the hero as the majors, colonels, and generals who led them into battle. They lost the war, but you got men home alive."

He closed his eyes, feeling foolish for his outburst, as her hands eased the terrible tension in his neck. "Everybody at home reads the newspapers about how glorious the victory or about how devastating the defeat, and they think it's some sort of contest," he said softly. "It isn't—it's a blood-soaked hell. If people could see for themselves, there'd never be another war."

"Maybe there won't be—not for a long time, anyway."

"No. Politicians will trade insults and plot the destruction of a perceived enemy; then they'll sit back and watch somebody else's husband or son die for their mistakes. The world gets bloodier, not wiser."

"You have to think it'll get better, or you can't live."

"It won't."

"Bitterness eats a man's soul, Dr. Hardin. Sometimes, to live, you have to let go of it."

"Bingham used to say something like that."

"I'm sorry I said such things about him," she conceded. "I didn't even know him. I just think we paid too high a price for slavery, that's all."

"We did. For that, and a lot of things."

"I didn't mean to pick that sore when I said you should practice medicine, either. I didn't know about your wife—or any of those other things."

"I figured when you saw the grave, you knew she'd left me."

"No. I thought it a little strange that she was buried out here, and that you were going to San Francisco to look for your son," she admitted. "But I figured there was some explanation I hadn't thought of, and if you wanted me to know, you'd tell me— that it wasn't my place to ask."

"I guess she just got tired of waiting. I blame myself for sending a wounded friend home to her, asking her to welcome him. She welcomed him, all right," he added bitterly. "They took off together last March."

"He couldn't have been much of a friend, and she couldn't have been much of a wife. But I guess she paid a high price for her foolishness, seeing as she died on the way."

"I feel cheated about that, too. I wanted her there when I killed Ross. I wanted both of them to know they hadn't gotten away with it. Now he's out there somewhere, and I don't even know if he's still got my son."

"And you had to turn back," she said, her voice barely above a whisper. "That had to be hard to do."

"It was. I should've known better than to start out this late. I should've known when there were just two railroad surveyors on the road with me, there was a reason. Hell, they weren't even going through the pass."

Her hand stilled, then dropped. "I don't guess you heard, did you?"

"What?"

"They didn't get back. A cavalry patrol out of Fort Laramie found what was left of them. A rider came over to notify Mr. Hawthorne they'd been murdered by Indians."

He had to wonder if that was why he'd seen those

buzzards. "They were just a few hours ahead of me," he said, shaking his head. "If I hadn't been having trouble with a skittish mule, I'd have been with them."

"Then you were just plain lucky."

Yeah, for the first time in a long time, maybe. But he sure hadn't thought so then. Twisting his head to look up at her, he was struck by all that gold in those brown eyes. For a woman who'd had more than her share of grief in her young life, she'd managed to come through it with a dignity he had to admire. There was a calmness, a steadiness about her that went beyond any twenty-four years. As far apart as they'd been in character, it was hard to believe she and Lydia Jamison were close in age.

Moving away, she stood at the small window to peer outside. "I've been thinking about what you said last week," she said, breaking a short silence.

"About what?"

"Hiring somebody to help. There's a Chinese man Mr. Russell sent out to help me fix the door and some other things after you left. I didn't understand a word he said, but he did everything I showed him to do."

"Russell's not too impressed with the Chinese he's got working for him."

"So I gathered. I guess he gave up on this one, anyway. When I took the laundry down yesterday, one of the others who speaks better English told me he'd been let go, and he was taking it hard. I don't guess he's earned enough to get him home, and it's too late for him to go, anyway." Turning back to face him, she told Spence, "Since you think it's beneath you to wash clothes, I'm going down to see if I can find him. If I don't, he'll starve."

"I'd be damned careful about who came up here."

"You'll be here," she reminded him. "I figure the way business is going, I can afford to pay him enough to survive on. They seem to get by on next to nothing, you know. The rumor keeps going around that they eat bugs so they can send what they earn back to their families."

"It's your money."

"Yes, it is, but I wasn't worried about the money so much. Most of the white men around here have a lot of contempt for the 'heathen Chinee,' as they call them. Since your people owned slaves, I was wanting to know you'd tolerate Mr. Chen before I hired him. If I thought you'd treat him like a dog, I wasn't going to do it."

"Mrs. Taylor, I've never treated anybody like a dog in my life. Slaveholder or not, Bingham treated the Negroes on his place like family. Truth to tell, that was probably why he never sold or bought any."

"I didn't mean to get your dander up—I was just asking how you felt, that was all."

"You've got no business going down there yourself," Spence declared flatly. "Just give me the name, and I'll fetch him up here. Maybe if you see I haven't skinned and tarred him, you'll believe I don't give a damn what he is." Lurching to his feet, he reached for his coat. "His name is Chen—right?"

"Chen Li—or Li Chen. I'm never sure which name is supposed to come first. But you can't miss him."

"I suppose I ought to ask why," he muttered.

"He's only got the right eye—the other one is missing. He lost it in an accident last month."

As the door closed behind him, she sat down at the table again to close the money jar. If Chen came to work, there'd be two men up here during the day, and maybe some of the talk would stop. If he spoke better English, he could go back and tell the rest of them just how the living arrangements were before things got out of hand. Right now, nobody could seriously believe Spencer Hardin was sharing her bed, but after the baby came, talk could get a lot worse.

Western Nebraska: November 20, 1865

The wind howled, rattling the panes in the window frames, shaking the fragile rafters, while melting sleet dripped down the chimney to sizzle on the burning logs in the hearth. The last time Spence had been out to the privy, he'd strung a rope up to guide them to it if the norther brought heavy snow. Right now, it was just slicker than wet oilcloth outside, but the way that wind was blowing, it was going to get a lot worse.

There was so much ice on the windows it was difficult to see much from them, but he didn't guess it mattered, anyway. There wasn't much to see, just a gray sky pouring freezing rain. Expecting the worst, he'd already secured Dolly, Clyde, and Sally in the lean-to he and Chen Li had built next to the privy. They'd put it there so anybody going out could take care of everything in one trip.

Laura was quieter than usual. She was in the rocker with a blanket wrapped around her, reading one of her books. Restive in the silence, he rose to get himself some coffee, then stood at the window to drink it. It was as though the world had shrunk to this one small room, and he was trapped in it. It was going to be a long winter, he could see that now. Dispirited, he turned back to his prison, wondering how he could last until May.

His gaze shifted to the woman in the chair, and he wondered how she could stand being cooped up in here with him. She was a remarkable woman, no question about that. Honest. Forthright. Hardworking. Wise beyond her years. As lovely inside as out. In a lot of ways, she reminded him of Bingham. He had to wonder if Taylor'd had any idea how rare she was.

Not that she wasn't vexing. She had a stubborn streak nearly as wide as his own, and when she got something set in her head, she clung to it, turning it into a crusade. And she didn't always know when to stop, he reflected soberly. There wasn't a day he'd spent in this little cabin that she hadn't managed to find some way to talk about medicine, and it just plain made him feel pushed. And it was the same with their differences in class. He was supposed to feel some damned obligation to do good because Bingham had been rich enough to send him to medical school, because he hadn't been poor. He just didn't feel it anymore.

He didn't feel much of anything, except hatred for Ross, frustration with his own lot, and a yearning for a little boy he didn't even know. And there wasn't much he could do about any of those things right now. His whole life was in abeyance, held hostage by things he couldn't control. But the damned weather was the worst of it. It had kept him from going on. It had trapped him in this cabin. It had thrown him into the company of a woman with problems worse than his own. It had given him too many hours to brood on the emptiness of his life.

He didn't know how Laura could face the world with such determination to survive, how she could get up each morning and face the day ahead, knowing all she could truly depend on was herself. Indomitable spirit, he guessed—a will to survive.

She was looking a little peaked, even frail, he realized with a start. And the book in her lap was closed. Her hands were gripping the arms of that rocking chair so hard her knuckles were white. She was rigid with fear.

"Are you all right?" he asked her.

"I don't know," she gasped. "I'm going to be sick, I think."

He grabbed the washbasin and held it under her chin. "Maybe you shouldn't have eaten that sausage this morning."

"No."

He could see the beads of sweat on her forehand, the cornered look in her eyes—like an animal about to die. Alarmed, he gripped her shoulder. "What is it?" he demanded urgently.

She swallowed hard. "The pain . . . and it's too early . . . something's wrong." Closing her eyes against it, she cried, "Something's wrong . . . it's not my time!"

"My God—are you sure?"

"Yes—it's not something I could forget! The baby's coming early!"

"Just calm down now. There's such a thing as false labor," he reassured her. "Just lie down—I'll help you to bed."

"I can't lose this baby . . . I just can't . . . he's all I've got of Jess!"

"Hysteria won't help anything," he said, trying to sound calm. "Come on—you've got to lie down."

"I can't! I'll ruin the bed!"

"Breathe easy—don't get ahead of yourself. We'll put my bedroll under you—now, come on—everything's going to be all right." Bending over her, he got a hand under her arm and lifted her to stand. Bloody water gushed down her legs under her dress, soaking the rug at her feet. His first instinct was to go for the railroad doctor, but he didn't want to leave her alone like that. "Come on," he said again. "It's going to be all right. You're young and healthy."

"I was young and healthy the last time, Dr. Hardin," she managed.

"I'm going to help you." Even as he said it, the words seemed ludicrous. Putting his arm around her, he tried to walk her toward the bed. He could hear her gulping for air. Something was wrong, all right— the pains were coming too hard too fast. She grabbed her distended belly with both hands and held on. Afraid she would collapse on him, Spence swung her up into his arms, staggered awkwardly, then made his way to her bed. Easing her onto the side of the mattress, he put one of her hands on the bedpost. "Hold on," he ordered. "I'll get my bedroll."

When he came back, he could see the stain spreading along the hem of her dress. Dumping his blankets on the bed, he spread them out, doubling them in the middle. While she held onto the post, he knelt to unlace and remove her shoes. Rolling down the black cotton stockings over her garters down to her toes, he managed to get them off, too. Her plain white drawers were soaked clear to her knees.

"We've got to get you undressed."

"I can't," she whispered. "I can't move."

She was panicked, that was all, he told himself as he worked the drawers down to her ankles. Noticing for the first time the puffiness there, he asked quickly, "You haven't been having trouble passing water, have you?"

"Yes."

"Why didn't you say something? You should have told me!" Shouting at her served nothing, he told himself. "I'm sorry," he said, lowering his voice.

She closed her eyes again, this time to hide from him. "It didn't seem proper," she managed.

She was sweating, but her skin was warmer than his. "All right. Losing one baby doesn't mean you'll lose another. The last one was breech, that was all."

"It was early—this one's early, too."

"But the circumstances are different. You've got to get hold of yourself, Laura—I'm right here with you. We're going to do our best to help the baby. I'm going to help you, but you have to tell yourself this is going to turn out all right—you understand that, don't you?"

"Yes," she whispered.

He was surprised by his own calmness now. He'd trained as a surgeon, not as a practitioner, and if she'd needed a limb amputated, this would be easy. Instead, she was in labor and showing signs of kidney problems. "All right," he repeated matter-of-factly. "Let's get to work. I'm going to get you out of these clothes so I can see what's going on. Then you're going to lie down, and I'm going to get my bag in case I have to make this a little easier for you." Scanning her face, he could tell she was mortified. "Look—it's all right. I'm a trained physician."

Another contraction doubled her over, sending blood down her bare leg. He could see how hard it tightened her belly, and he knew it wasn't normal. It was as though her body was trying to rid itself of the baby in one painful contraction. Reaching up under her dress, he felt between her legs for the head. It wasn't down there, and she wasn't wide enough yet to deliver.

Silently cursing the excessive clothing women wore, he worked feverishly to undress her, then swung her legs onto the bed. She rolled onto her side and drew up her knees as he searched for his medical bag. He was out of nearly everything, but there was no sense in letting her know it. "Jesse didn't have any whiskey, did he?" he asked, coming back to her.

"He liked beer."

Beer. "Do you still have any of it?"

"No."

"Well, it's not that important," he lied. "Anything with alcohol in it?"

"Cough medicine. He . . . he . . ." Clutching her stomach, she held on until the pain eased. "He had a cough last summer . . . I made some."

"With what?"

"Honey . . . lemon . . . mash whiskey . . . I borrowed some—"

"Where is it?"

She hurt too bad to think. "Cupboard."

She had a lot of stuff on those narrow shelves, but

he found a bottle of something. Opening it, he took a whiff and smelled the whiskey in it. "There's half a bottle here, Laura—I want you to drink all of it down," he said, lifting her shoulders to keep her from choking.

She gagged as it went down. She felt her whole abdomen convulse, bearing down, but she could tell the baby wasn't going anywhere. "It's not moving, Dr. Hardin—it's not!" she cried.

"Then there's a reason. We'll just have to compensate for whatever it is." Moving to the kitchen again, he washed his hands in lye soap and cold water. "We've got time to fix it."

"How?"

"Close your eyes. I'm going to find the baby." Placing one hand on her abdomen, he palpated it, trying to feel the head. It wasn't in the birth canal. "This could be false labor," he lied again.

"Not with the water," she gasped.

"Maybe." It didn't seem possible that it could happen twice, but the baby was lying transversely. "We're going to give it a little longer to move down to where I can reach it, then I'll have to turn it into the canal," he told her frankly. "Don't worry—I'm not letting this go on for days." Reaching for her hand, he squeezed it reassuringly. "We'll make it."

"I hope so."

Sitting on the bed beside her, he reviewed his options silently. If he could turn it, he expected the labor to progress normally. If he couldn't, he was a surgeon, he told himself. He could get it out of her, but that wasn't anything he wanted to do. The baby would almost certainly die, and she'd never have another. No, he had to turn it, even if it came out breech again. If he didn't let her get too weak, she could deliver it. "I'm not going to let you get too tired," he told her again.

As the hours wore on, she lost all sense of modesty or dignity. It no longer mattered that she was naked, or that his hands touched the most intimate part of her body. Between contractions, his voice soothed her; during them, his hand gripped hers.

Every labor he'd seen in medical school had been without complication, but as he sat there in the waning hours of the afternoon, he called to memory the textbook cases that exceeded the norm, reviewing everything he could remember. His hands followed the progress of the child within her until he knew she'd done all she could without help.

Despite the risk of hemorrhage, he decided to attempt turning it into the birth canal manually. With one hand outside, pressing downward, and the other in the canal itself, he moved the baby. Blood gushed down his arm, forcing him to hurry. Finally, he felt the head tilt downward; then his hand touched the small cranium. Reaching behind him, he retrieved a scalpel and cut the tautly stretched perineum to give the child more room.

"The next hard one, bear down with everything you've got left, and we'll know if we're going to make it," he told Laura.

She took a deep breath, holding it against the coming pain, and when the gut-wrenching contraction hit, she pushed so hard she thought she'd split open. Somewhere a scream pierced the air, shattering it.

He could see the caul on the head now. Gripping

it, he told her, "One more, and it's over." As the pain intensified, the head slid into his hands, and he pulled the infant out. One glance told him it was too small. A second glance made his heart pause. Laura was bleeding profusely, and the afterbirth was coming. It slipped like a mass of dark red jelly onto the bed.

Laying the baby by her leg, he massaged its body, trying to bring life to it. Above him, Laura Taylor wept. She knew it wasn't breathing.

"It was just too early—I knew it was too early," she whispered brokenly.

"Maybe not."

With his clean hand, he opened the little mouth to poke a finger down its throat, clearing mucus. It was blue, but it was warm. He smacked the tiny feet, hoping the infant would respond, and he heard a choking sound, but no cry. Cradling the bloody infant's head with both hands, he bent his head to it and forced his breath into its mouth. At first he felt nothing; then the chest walls expanded. His forefinger pressed on the tiny breastbone, expelling the air before he tried again. He didn't know whether he just wished it to be so, or whether the blueness was receding. Stopping long enough to see if it breathed on its own, he waited, unsure if he saw anything. Finally, he turned it upside down across his knee, and there was a gasp, followed by a thin, reedy wail.

"Well, aren't you something?" he said softly. His face split into a full grin as he watched the baby girl turn pink, then red from the exertion of squalling. "Laura, you've got a daughter," he announced proudly. "She's little, but she's here to stay."

Exhausted, she closed her eyes. She had a daughter. Not a son, but a daughter. A moment of disappointment washed over her, followed by pure joy. Her daughter was alive.

"Thank you," she whispered as the tears streamed down her cheeks. "Spencer Hardin, you're wonderful."

He felt the intense emotion himself. "No—you were magnificent." Placing the shaking infant in her arms, he murmured, "We're not quite done, but almost. Now we've got to fix you up. I've got to sew together what I cut."

Overwhelmed by what he'd done, by the miracle he'd witnessed, he fought his own tears as he started stitching. Laura Taylor was crooning to the tiny daughter he'd brought into this world, and right now nothing else mattered.

"You'll freeze to death down there," he heard her tell him.

Shivering, he drew his knees up against his chest, seeking warmth from his own cold body. "I'm all right," he mumbled in the darkness.

"You can't be. You don't even have a blanket on."

Opening his eyes, he stared into the dying coals of last night's fire. He rolled over, touching the hem of Laura's nightdress, then came fully awake. "What's the matter?"

"Aren't you cold?"

"You shouldn't be up on your feet yet." Pulling his coat closer, he sat up. Every joint in his body felt as if it needed oiling. He was stiff, sore, and chilled to the bone. The rag rug hadn't made much of a mattress, he realized ruefully. "What time is it?"

"Two o'clock."

"In the morning?" It was a foolish question, considering it was pitch-black out. "Go back to sleep."

"I haven't slept a wink yet. For one thing, I'm afraid I'll take the covers off the baby in my sleep," she admitted. "For another, I'm afraid I'll smother her."

He could hear the wind still howling. If anything, it was eerier than the sound of a wolf pack cornering a hapless animal. Dragging himself up, he groped his way across the room to the wood box by the door. "Damned fire's about out," he muttered.

"I was thinking about sitting up for a while," she told him quietly. "If you get the fire going, I'll bring the baby over here, and you can have the bed. I'm too excited to sleep, anyway. I just want to look at her."

"Yeah." Yesterday, he would have thought the idea was just plain silly, but he felt it, too. "I did— twice."

"I know." Taking a match from the box she kept near the hearth, she lit the lantern, sending grotesque shadows up the wall. "She surely is something, isn't she? I just wish she was a little bigger, that's all. I'm afraid she's too small to get a proper start."

"Well, there's no way to put her back, so she'll just have to grow." Kneeling on the hearth, he blew on tinder, trying to get it to catch. He didn't want to tell her, but the baby's size still worried him also. "She'll grow," he said, reassuring himself as well as her.

"As little as she is, I'm almost afraid to pick her up, but I expect I'll get over that soon."

"Yeah." He watched the small flame spread up a dry twig. "If I put them together, she just about fits in the palms of my hands."

She sank into the rocking chair beside him. "You know, I was going to name a boy Jesse for his daddy—I didn't even think about a girl. I didn't have any girl's name picked out."

"Name her Jessica and call her Jessie," he suggested.

"I could do that," she allowed. "Jessica Taylor . . . I don't know," she mused slowly. "I'd have to think about it for a day or two before I make up my mind for sure. I always wished Mama had thought of something besides Laura, but I had to live with it."

"What's wrong with Laura? I think it's pretty myself."

"I always thought it rather old-fashioned."

"Well, it isn't. Old-fashioned would be something like Jane or Anne or Mary."

She was silent for a while, rocking while she watched him work on the fire. "I'd like for her to have your name, too, if you don't mind it," she said finally. "She wouldn't be here if it wasn't for you."

He rocked back on his heels as if he'd been hit. "What? Oh, no you don't—I didn't make a good husband the first time, and I'm not about to try that again," he declared flatly.

"You think that I—?" Taken aback by his reaction, she hastened to set him straight. "Well, I didn't mean anything like that, I hope to tell you. I was just wanting to ask if you minded being her *middle* name. Believe me, I'm not looking for another husband either. I already told you that, but I guess you just weren't listening."

Now he felt like a damned fool. "I guess I'm just too tired to think straight. It's been one hell of a night."

"Well—do you? Mind, I mean?"

"No, but neither Spencer nor Hardin is much of a name for a girl."

"Do you have a middle one?"

"David."

"Spencer David Hardin," she said softly. "It even sounds highfalutin."

"Well, it isn't," he retorted. "Spencer was my mother's maiden name, and my father's was David, so I came by all of it honestly."

"Jessica Spencer Taylor. Jessica Hardin Taylor."

"It'll sound like she's married before she's even out of the cradle. Why don't you give her a name that'll mean something to her later? Why not use your mother's?"

"Because I promised her I wouldn't. She was Nellie Mae Parrish before she was married, and hated being Nellie. And I'd never name anybody Mae, either."

"Oh. Well, I can't say as I blame you," he admitted. It looked as though the fire was spreading from the tinder to the logs. Standing, Spence brushed the soot from his clothes. "Look, I don't care if you use mine, but ten or fifteen years from now, she might."

"When she knows you brought her into the world, she'll think it's fitting. I'm going to tell her that if it wasn't for you, she wouldn't be here."

"Maybe."

"No, it's true. And I'll always be grateful for what you did for us." Looking up at him, she added, "Jesse said you were the best doctor he'd ever met, and I believe that, too. I don't know how you can even think of giving up medicine when you can do so much good with it."

"Well, I have, and I did. Hell will freeze solid before I saw off any more limbs—or deliver any more babies, either. I've had about all of the blood on my hands I can take," he declared emphatically. "I don't want any more."

She digested that for a moment, then shook her head. "If you kill him, that's what you'll get," she told him quietly.

"What?"

"You've still got it in your mind to kill that Ross fellow, don't you? You'll get more blood on your hands by taking a life than by saving one."

"Damn, but you never give up, do you?" Exasperated, he demanded, "Who appointed you my conscience, anyway?"

"Nobody. But it just goes against everything you stand for." Noting the set of his jaw, she decided to drop the matter for now. "I didn't get up to fuss at you, even if it sounds like it," she said, sighing. "I was just going to sit here by the fire and rock my baby, and I thought maybe you'd like to take the bed for a while. After all, it was me that ruined your bedroll," she reminded him.

"You belong in bed yourself."

"In a day or two, when she's squalling at all hours, maybe I'll get over feeling like this, but right now, I just want to look at her." When he didn't say anything, she added, "There's two feather beds on that bed, and it's real warm between them. Besides, if you get down sick, we're going to be in a real pickle. The way it's coming down, that snow's going to be three feet deep, and I sure can't dig myself out right now."

Tempted, he realized he was sore, tired, and cold. "All right," he said finally. "I guess if you need me, you'll wake me up. But you'd better get that rocker close to the fire and bundle up or you're both apt to catch pneumonia. As little as she is, she's got to be kept as warm as she was before she was born. She should've stayed in there another month," he reminded Laura.

"I know."

As soon as he was satisfied that the fire was putting out enough heat, he crawled gratefully between the feather beds, savoring the lingering warmth her body had left there. Too tired to think, he closed his eyes and slid into a deep, dreamless sleep. Neither the raging storm nor the steady creak of the rocker disturbed him.

"Dr. Hardin! Oh, my God—Dr. Hardin!" Laura cried. "My baby!"

He nearly tripped himself scrambling blindly from the bed. "What the . . . ? What is it?" he asked sleepily, groping for a lantern.

"I don't think she's breathing!"

"I thought a snake or something," he mumbled, not comprehending yet.

"She's not breathing, I'm telling you! Something's bad wrong!"

His mind snapped awake at that. Taking the infant from her, he said over his shoulder, "Bring the lantern to the table. I can't see anything in the dark." Positioning the tiny girl on the table, he ordered, "Hold it at my shoulder—yeah, that's right." Unwrapping her, he looked for signs of life. "When did this happen?"

"I must've dozed in the chair . . . I don't know . . . I just realized she was too quiet, that I couldn't hear her breathe. Before she was making a little chirp, but now there's nothing."

His hands ran over the little body, rubbing the fragile skin. It was warm. Repeating what he'd done earlier, he cleared her throat of mucus, and he heard her sigh. "She's all right," he said shortly. She hiccoughed, confirming that she breathed.

"Oh, thank God!"

He didn't know what had happened, but as the weak wail grew stronger, crescendoing in a howl that would have done a coyote proud, he thought maybe she'd sucked mucous down her trachea, maybe the chirp Laura'd heard had been the infant's attempt to expel it. But she was sure getting enough air now.

"You're sure she's all right?" Laura asked anxiously at his shoulder.

"I think so. But you could put just about everything I know about babies in a thimble, and you'd have plenty of room to spare," he admitted.

"You're a doctor," she reminded him.

"I was more interested in surgery." Lifting the infant, he held her close, stunned again by the seeming fragility of that little body, amazed by the life in it. "You go on to bed—I'll sit up with her."

"I couldn't—I just couldn't," Laura protested.

"Look, one of us needs to sleep, so it might as well be you. Come morning, she's going to want to eat, and I sure as hell can't help her there. Besides, whether you realize it or not, you've lost a lot of blood. You're weaker than you think."

"Yes, but—"

"Just try."

He looked so big, her daughter so very small. It

was as though his hands covered all but the soft down on the baby's head.

"Please, I'm asking you to do this," Spence said quietly. "I'm going to watch her sleep to see if anything seems out of the ordinary. Just give me that shawl so I can keep her warm."

"All right," she said finally. "But if anything happens, you'll wake me, won't you?"

"You're her mother—I'm just her doctor." Looking at the perfect little face, the tiny button nose, the miniature fists doubled up in the air, he felt an extraordinary tenderness for this baby, and at the same time, a profound sense of loss for missing his own son's birth.

As she went to bed, he held the infant to his shoulder and sank carefully into the rocker. Pulling the shawl close, he began rocking slowly, rhythmically beside the crackling fire, his ears alert to every sound she made. She was just so small, so terribly small, that he found himself praying she'd survive, repeating the plea over and over. She was so still, so quiet that he eased her from his shoulder to the crook of his arm to watch her. The tiny lips moved, and he realized suddenly that she sucked silently in her sleep. And the thought crossed his mind that when Laura's milk came in tomorrow, she probably wouldn't have much trouble getting her daughter to nurse.

"You are a wonder," he whispered, tracing the baby's soft cheek with his fingertip. "A little wonder."

Hours later, Laura stirred, painfully aware of her full breasts, then turned to look across the small room. The lantern was out, the fire was low, and the two windows were a solid white. Her gaze sought the rocking chair, and her question died on her lips. Spencer Hardin's black hair was rumpled, his head arched back to touch the wooden rail, unaware the baby girl nuzzled his neck eagerly, her little mouth hunting for food. It was a sight she was sure she'd never forget.

As she swung her feet over the side of the bed, she discovered she was almost too sore to sit. "I see you gave up watching," she said, waking him.

"Huh?" His blue eyes flew open, and he felt the baby rubbing her face in his neck again. "What the? Oh. I must've gone to sleep," he admitted sheepishly. "She didn't seem to have any more trouble breathing." His hand smoothed the soft, downy hair as he sat up. "If it's breakfast you're looking for, Jessie, you're in the wrong place," he murmured to the baby. "You want your mama for that." Looking down as he lifted her to his shoulder, he discovered the wet circle in the middle of his shirt. "Yes, ma'am, you sure do want your mama." Rising from the rocker, he carried her to Laura. "Her mouth's not the only thing that works," he noted ruefully, handing her over. "While you take care of business, I'd better find myself another shirt, then I'll throw some more wood on the fire," he added awkwardly. "I expect you're getting cold."

"No, but I think it'd be a good idea," she murmured, coloring.

After he placed two cottonwood logs on the coals, he spent a good ten minutes on his knees with his back to her, pretending he couldn't get the fire going, so she'd have some privacy. When he finally stood up, a quick glance reassured him that the baby instinctively knew what to do with a nipple. Then he realized Laura was in obvious pain.

"What's the matter?"

"It . . . it hurts," she managed. "I'm too sore for this."

"Let me see," he said without thinking. Moving to the bed, he leaned down to touch the swollen breast while he tried to remember everything he'd read in medical school on the subject. As small as she was, that baby would have to eat every couple of hours, and if Laura couldn't feed her, she'd be in real trouble fast. "I guess maybe if we'd tried this a little earlier, you might not be so tender there. I'd say you filled up a little fast."

Embarrassed, Laura turned her head and gritted her teeth as he rubbed her sore nipple between his thumb and forefinger, releasing a trickle of milk, while the thwarted baby cried shrilly. Closing her eyes, she managed to whisper, "It's not supposed to be like this, is it?"

"Maybe she's not strong enough yet to do much good for you," he guessed. "I'm going to see if getting rid of some of this will make it any easier on you." Straightening, he went to the cupboard and removed a ragged towel from the drawer. Returning to sit down beside her, he covered the breast with the towel and gently massaged the nipple while she sucked in her breath and bit her lip. "Feel any better?"

"I don't know. Maybe."

"If it does, she's not been sucking hard enough."

"She made enough noise at it."

"But she can't take very much." Transferring the towel to the other breast, he released more milk. "All right—let her try again."

Too mortified to meet his eyes, Laura nodded, then placed the infant against her nipple, and the squalling stopped.

"Any better?"

"Maybe."

The rosebud mouth was sure working at it. Touching the baby's lower lip with a fingertip, he could see the little tongue working, and Laura's milk bubbling around it. "She's going at it now," he murmured. "Just keep at it until she wants to quit, and I'll be back in a little while."

"Where are you going?" she asked, alarmed. "How do I know when she's had enough?"

"Outside—and she won't take anymore," he responded, answering both questions. "If I can get out, I need to make sure the animals are all right. With that wind still blowing, and the snow already up over the windows, I figure it's going to get even worse. I need to see if I can even find the rope I strung between the door and the privy, because I sure don't want to get lost out there."

"No."

"There's no two ways about it," he added soberly. "You'll have to use the chamberpot, so when I get back, I'll try to rig up a curtain of some kind for you to get behind."

Thinking she'd already lost most of her dignity, that he'd seen the most intimate parts of her body, she was nonetheless touched by his attempt to preserve that small corner of privacy for her.

"Thank you," she said sincerely. "I was getting worried."

"I know. I thought you had about all you could handle already. Besides, if it's as deep as I think it is out there, I may have to use it part of the time myself. We'll just have to get used to living real close for a while, but I'll do what I can to make it easier on you."

"You already have, just by being here."

"Well, we're both kind of stuck here, so we might as well accept it. Come May, I expect you'll be damned happy to see the last of me."

"Well, I wouldn't put it quite that way. I'll probably be a little sad to see you go, because I'll be used to your ways by then. I'll probably be lonesome for a little while, to tell the truth. But we'll do fine."

"You just can't stay here—there's no two ways about it—you can't winter out here again. I wouldn't send my worst enemy to Nebraska in the winter. And if you try to follow the railroad, you'll be in a worse place this time next year."

"I don't know—we'll see. When she's a little older, I'll have a better notion of what I need to do."

"Go back to North Carolina."

"I aim to think about it. I'm going to do what's best for her first, then worry about myself later."

"I'm telling you what you ought to do."

"But it isn't up to you to tell me," she reminded him. "I'm the one that has to live with what I decide, not you."

"You watch out—that stubborn streak you've got

just might take you to hell in a handbasket if you don't stomp on it."

Irritated because she never seemed to listen to good advice, he wrenched the door, trying to open it. It wouldn't budge, and looking down, he saw why. The earlier sleet had thawed enough to seep underneath; then the force of that arctic wind had refrozen it into a ridge of ice. Inwardly cursing the folly of living in such a place, he found a knife and started chiseling the ice away from the door. Standing again, he pulled the wooden slab inward, and as the rest of the ice broke, it opened. A wall of snow as high as his shoulders collapsed, sending an avalanche of the stuff into the cabin, making it impossible to shut the door again. The wind filled the whole room with a burst of bitterly cold air.

"Get the baby under the covers," he ordered tersely as he stared at the mound of snow. "It's going to take me a while to dig out."

Quickly bundling the infant, Laura tucked her under the edge of the top feather bed, then she rose to pull on a dress over her nightgown. "I'll get the broom and help."

"I'll do it," he muttered.

"Two work faster than one," she declared, putting an end to the discussion. "You take the ash pan and start shoveling."

They started digging and pushing with broom, shovel, and bare hands, fighting against that bitter, biting wind to get the snow outside. Finally, he broke through enough of the stuff to plunge into the icy maelstrom, while she finished clearing the threshold enough to force the door closed after him.

Afraid he'd lose his way in the blinding, swirling snow and freeze to death outside, she shouted, "Be careful!"

Shivering, Laura made her way back to the bed, where the baby lay squalling so hard she quivered. Sitting down, she moved gown and dress out of the way, then cradled her daughter against her breast. The crying ceased instantly, and within five minutes the baby was sucking in her sleep.

For a long moment, Laura gazed on the delicate little face, feeling an intense sadness that Jesse would never see this beautiful little girl they'd made. He would have been a proud daddy right now if it hadn't been for that terrible accident. As hard as he'd worked for the better life he'd wanted so desperately, he'd lost it all. Closing her eyes, she fought tears as she realized she didn't even have a photograph of him to show her daughter. His child would never know what her daddy looked like. From now until she was grown, it'd be just the two of them. It was a daunting thought.

Alone with the baby in this rough little cabin, with a blizzard raging around it, she felt terribly vulnerable. Before, as lonely and desperate as things were, she'd been able to delude herself into believing she could survive, but now, as she cradled her child, she was painfully aware she had more than her own destiny in her hands. She couldn't help wondering if she could give her daughter any kind of life at all, or if this little girl faced the same endless poverty she'd endured her whole life. It seemed now as though she'd worked as hard as she knew how for as long as she could remember, and she didn't have much of anything to show for it. Except this baby.

Jessie. Jessie Spencer Taylor. Jessie Hardin Taylor. No, *Jessica* Spencer Taylor. It did have an elegant sound to it. Highfalutin, as they'd say back in Salisbury, North Carolina. Her fingertip traced the tiny cheek, the little nose, feeling the soft breath there.

"Dear God," she whispered, "don't let me fail her. Give me the means to take care of her properly." And the wind seemed to answer, calming her fears. If the Lord wanted to test her mettle, He wouldn't find her wanting. No matter how hard she had to work, she'd see Jessie got what she needed.

Western Nebraska: March 8, 1866

The clothespins caught in Laura's mittens as she removed them from the laundry line. Holding them in her mouth, she pulled the stiff shirts down, letting them drop into the big wicker basket, sliding it along with her foot beneath the frozen clothes. Following behind her, Chen Li pinned up a load of long johns to the same line.

Even without that biting wind, it would be bitter cold out, but with it, her face felt raw. Since Chen Li never complained, she had to wonder if the winters were worse in China. They couldn't be, she decided. Picking up the full basket, she hurried inside.

There was one good thing about doing laundry on a day like this, she told herself. No matter how chilly it had seemed inside before, when she came in, it felt downright hot for a little while. As she kicked the door shut behind her, she instinctively looked to the cradle. Jessie still slept.

Laying the frozen shirts on the table to soften, she pulled off her mittens and poured herself a cup of coffee, savoring the smell of the steam curling in the air above it. Two more loads to wash and hang, then she'd be ready to start the ironing this afternoon.

Carrying her cup with her, she went to the hearth to peek under a cloth at the rising bread dough. It wasn't ready to punch down yet.

She still had to do the baking and start the ironing, and after Spence got back from camp with the cream, she'd be churning butter before she fixed supper. Fresh bread, butter, and potato soup were just the things for this cold weather.

Returning to the kitchen corner, she pulled out the potato bin, chose several, and was about to wash them, when Chen Li pounded on the door. As she opened it, the little Chinese man scurried past her to hold his ice-cold hands over the fire. His thin shoulders shook beneath that quilted cotton jacket he always wore.

"What you need is a good hot toddy," she told him, crossing her arms and shivering to indicate how cold he was.

"You velly cold?"

"No, you are. A toddy'd warm you right up."

"Li cold, too," he said, nodding.

Unable to communicate any better, she decided to give him coffee instead. She didn't know if he'd drink whiskey, anyway, she told herself as she filled his cup. She didn't know much about him at all, and it wouldn't do any good to ask where he came from or anything else. His English was so poor that she couldn't carry on a conversation with him. But once she showed him how to do something, he did it well, and that was what mattered. "Coffee," she said loudly, holding out the cup to him. "It's good and hot."

"Hot velly good," Chen Lii agreed.

Spence came in with his arms full, elbowed the door shut, then stamped his feet, trying to warm them. Looking across the room to her, he said, "You just said cream, but since I was already down there, I went ahead and bought some other things, too. There's sugar, a tin of arrowroot cookies, some hard candy, cooking chocolate, a bag of walnuts, and a bottle of cherry brandy in the gunnysack. Wagon came in just before I got there."

"If I eat all that, I'll be fat."

"Not the way you work," he answered, pulling off the heavy coat, mittens, and muffler, then bracing himself against the doorjamb to remove his boots. "Whooeeee, but it's damned cold out—I'll take Georgia any day over this." Moving to join Chen Li by the fire, he told her over his shoulder, "Hawthorne said they were short on the rep track."

"Oh?"

He wriggled his cold toes on the warm stones in front of the hearth, defrosting them as he added casually, "I told him I'd help out."

"Spence, you didn't—surely not!"

"Why not?"

Dismayed, she tried to keep her voice calm. "Well, if you think you're cold now, you don't even have a notion—you'll be toting and hammering on cold steel fourteen hours a day, then trying to sleep in a drafty tent with that old north wind blowing right through it. It's hard, dangerous work for a man not used to it—Jesse was killed doing it."

"I'm not Jesse, and I won't let them work me like that. Besides, I can use the extra money right now—

I don't know what'll happen between here and California."

"You know, I don't need the room and board you're paying. I mean, you do so much around here, helping out with the baby, carrying water, chopping wood—things like that—I don't feel right taking it, anyway. I just didn't want to insult your pride by refusing it, that's all."

"I need to do something. I just feel restless—it's hell knowing I've got to be somewhere else when there's no way I can't get there. I feel like a caged animal in this one room."

"Well, if it's work you're looking for, I could sure use help right here. There's so much laundry coming in now that it's almost too much for Chen Li and me to handle, and since word's spread to McPherson, I've had to turn away customers."

He could almost hear the panic in her voice. Sighing, he shook his head. "Doing laundry's no kind of life for you, Laura. Look at yourself—at those hands—at the circles under your eyes—you keep this up, and you'll be old before your time. You're part of the reason I'm doing this if you want the truth of it," he said.

"*Me?* Oh, now wait a minute, Spencer Hardin! I had a husband telling me that, in case you've forgotten, and I'm not about to bear that burden again! Jesse killed himself working for something he wanted me to have whether I wanted it or not—and now I'm a widow with a baby to raise by myself! No, sir—if you want to do something, you do it for yourself, because I don't aim to live with the blame if anything happens to you!"

Stung by the vehemence of her words, he caught her arm, forcing her to look up at him. "Will you listen before you go off half-cocked?" he demanded, his own voice rising. "I've got enough to get myself to San Francisco, but—"

"Then go!"

"Let me finish, for God's sake, before you start hollering in my face!" As her eyes widened, he strove to control his temper. "Look, I don't want to quarrel with you—I'm trying to help. I worry about you and Jessie, Laura. A couple of weeks' pay will leave me with enough extra money to send both of you back to North Carolina with a few dollars in your purse to tide you over until you get settled. It's where you belong, whether you want to admit it or not."

For a moment, she stared incredulously at him, then found her voice. "You know, Dr. Hardin, once you get something in your mind, you just hang on to it. I guess you think all that education you're not using entitles you to tell me you know what's good for me. It just doesn't seem to matter any to you that I've got a business out here, and there's nothing for me back there."

"You didn't want to leave it," he reminded her. "You told me that last May."

"I wanted to stay on my home place. It's different now—Jesse's dead, and I don't own the farm anymore. I'd be going back to nothing with nothing."

"Carolina's a better place to raise Jessie. What kind of life do you think you'll give her out here? There's bound to be better things for you to do back there than washing dirty underwear for a camp full of drunks and derelicts whose notion of a good time is spending a whole paycheck on cheap whiskey and cheaper whores," he declared emphatically. "You don't want to live like this—no woman would."

"I'm not a whore, Dr. Hardin," she said evenly. "I work with my hands and my heart—not my body."

Vexed to distraction, he ran his hands through his hair, trying to think of some way to convince her. "I didn't say you were, and you know it. All I was saying was there's lots of things you could do besides this."

"Oh, really? I'd like to have you name me one."

"Well, you can sew . . . or teach kids maybe. Hell, that's for you to decide, not me. But I do know a good Southern woman without a husband's got no business putting herself at the mercy of a bunch of dirty ruffians."

"Jesse wasn't dirty, drunk, or derelict," she retorted. "But even if he were any of those things, it wouldn't make much difference now. He's dead, and even if he wanted to, he couldn't help me now. As for teaching school, I've got no education—everybody back there knows I had to stay home to take care of Mama, and after that, it was Danny. When they got done laughing, they'd tell me their kids have already got more schooling than I had!" Pushing an errant strand of hair away from her eyes, she declared defiantly, "So you can put that in your pipe and smoke it, Mr. Rich Doctor Fellow, because I'm not going back there!"

"Because you're too damned bullheaded for your own good. What'll you do if you get sick?—if the baby needs a doctor? At least back in Carolina, you won't be packing up and dragging Jessie off someplace else every time damned camp moves. But have it your way—I'm going to salve my conscience by leaving you money in case you come to your senses, and then I'm getting out of here. I can't stand watching you work yourself to death."

"I'm not a charity case, and we're not yours to worry about," she declared flatly. Striding to the cupboard, she retrieved a big jar. "Look at this—I've got fifty dollars in here, and I earned every penny of it myself."

"And you work harder to get it than a slave in a Mississippi cotton patch ever worked under a whip. Just how long do you think you can keep this up?"

"Well, maybe I don't see it that way at all!" she snapped. "If I ever go back to North Carolina, I won't be draggin' my tail like some sorry dog. All my life, when I was trying to take care of Danny and growing up myself, I had people sayin' how sorry they were for me; then I'd overhear those same folks snickerin' behind my back because I was too poor to have a decent dress or anything else. Their notion of charity was givin' me something they wouldn't be caught dead in themselves!"

"Laura—"

"No, sir—they're not getting another chance to look down on me like I'm not good enough to step over. The next time I see any of 'em, I'll be holding my head high and showing 'em I've amounted to something. It sure won't be to ask 'em if I can sew or keep house for 'em, which is about all somebody like me can do!"

As she said it, her lip quivered, and Spence realized she was on the verge of tears. "I'm sorry—I guess I just didn't understand," he said quietly.

"No, you didn't!"

Pushing past him, she went outside and around the house to the privy. Slamming the door shut, she threw the bar inside, then sat down to cry. She hadn't meant to let anybody see the lingering hurt, least of all somebody who'd had enough money to go to medical college, who'd never known what it was like to eat nothing but potatoes and beans month after month because there was nothing else.

Spence was right behind her. Pounding on the out-house door, he shouted, "I said I was sorry! Come out before you freeze to death in there. It's too damned cold out for a woman with no coat on!"

"Go away, and leave me alone! I'm just dandy, so don't you worry yourself!"

"Look, I wanted to help you out, that's all."

"Well, don't! I don't need anybody's charity, not even yours!"

"Now, damn it, I've already apologized twice. I don't even know what started this, except I told you I was going to work a few days on the rep track. I figured you'd be glad to get rid of me for a while."

"It was the money—and I won't take a penny of it!"

"Laurie, for God's sake—"

That was what Jesse used to call her. She leaned her head against the wood wall and closed her eyes. For the first time in her life, she had to admit she was afraid of being alone, of never having anybody to hold but her daughter. She wasn't really any dif-ferent from every other woman in the world—she ached for someone to love her, someone she could love also. But more than anything, she didn't want him to go.

"Well, I guess you're not talking now," he said heavily. "I guess when you get cold enough, you'll come out. Since I don't have my boots on, my feet are freezing, and I've got to go inside."

As she heard him walking away, she swallowed back more tears. She'd always known he'd have to leave, she told herself, but she just hadn't expected it to happen before May. Maybe she hadn't wanted him here in the first place, but she'd grown so accustomed to having him around that it seemed like he just belonged here. She even liked that rumpled look he had when he came to the table in the morning, because it made him seem like a vulnerable little boy instead of the bitter man he was. And when he sat before the fire, rocking Jessie, it was like the baby belonged there.

She just wished she'd met him before he married that stupid jezebel. With that black, black hair and those sky blue eyes, he must've been the handsomest bachelor in the state of Georgia, and surely he'd deserved better than what he'd gotten. Nothing on earth could've made her do to him what Lydia had.

She sat very still for a moment, realizing she'd been lying to herself, believing she thought of him as Jessie's doctor, Jesse's friend, but he was far more than that to her. He was the man she should've met before Jesse. Catching herself before she could let that thought take hold, she knew he would've looked right past her. Men born and bred to privilege had no honorable interest in awkward country girls wearing flour sack dresses. And they never would.

Shivering cold, she unlocked the privy door, and with her arms crossed tightly across her breasts, she ducked into the icy wind, then ran for the house. Around the corner, Spencer Hardin stepped in front of her.

"You said you were going inside!" she cried.

Pulling off his coat, he threw it around her. "You can throw a hissy fit if you want to, but by God, you're going in with me," he told her. "I don't know why, but you're having some kind of nervous collapse."

"I'm not!" she shouted, trying to pull away.

"The hell you aren't! You're making yourself sick over nothing!" Out of all patience now, he swung her into his arms and headed for the front door. "You know it's a damned good thing Chen Li can't speak English, or he'd be going down the hill telling everybody you're a crazy woman."

"Put me down!"

Reaching around her, he managed to get the door open and stumble through it. He kicked it closed, crossed the little room, and dropped her on the bed. Standing over her, he needed a moment to catch his breath. When he looked down, she'd rolled into a tight ball, and she was shaking all over.

He sat down on the edge of the bed and touched her shoulder, feeling helpless. "Laurie . . . don't . . . you've got to get hold of yourself."

"I can't!"

Out of the corner of his eye, he could see Chen Li edging his way to the door. The odd little fellow obviously wanted out of there, and Spence wanted to be left alone with Laura. As the door closed, he began rubbing her back, her shoulders, her neck.

"Laurie—"

"Just go away! That's what you want to do, anyway!"

"I can't help if I don't know what ails you," he said gently. "Come on—you're making yourself sick."

"Why can't I be afraid like everybody else? Why do I have to be strong?" she wailed.

"Afraid of what?"

"I don't know! I just k-keep working . . . and . . . and nobody cares! I can't make myself try any harder!"

Lifting her, he turned her into his shoulder and wrapped his arms around her. "You won't let anybody help you," he murmured, stroking her soft hair.

She burrowed her face into his shirt and held onto him with both hands, sobbing hard. As warm and solid as he was, she didn't want to ever let go, but she knew she had to. Finally, she sat up, ashamed of herself for the inexplicable outburst. Gulping air, she managed to tell him, "I just can't get everything done—there's just no end to it—and if you go on the rep track, it's something more to worry about."

"I'll be all right."

"Jesse wasn't."

He thought he finally knew what was wrong. "It's Jesse—that's what this is all about, isn't it?"

"No." Trying to dry her eyes on a corner of the apron, she couldn't look up at him. "Jesse isn't even here anymore—he's just gone."

"Do you want to talk about it?"

"Not anymore. There was a time when I wanted to cry, but I couldn't—I was afraid I'd lose the baby, too, and there'd be nothing left. And, anyway, it wouldn't be for what you'd think—the Jesse Taylor who came home from the war was a stranger to me."

"I see."

"And after we got out here, it just got worse, because I hardly ever saw him." Looking up through wet lashes, she admitted, "It was like he'd been seduced by the money he was making, and all he wanted was more of it. If I said anything about him being gone all the time, he'd tell me I was holding him back, that I didn't want him to make anything of himself—but that wasn't true."

The catch in her voice touched him more than her words. "If he thought you were holding him back, he was wrong."

"No."

"Hey—whose money brought him out here, anyway?"

"It wasn't enough—there was never enough for what he wanted—he wanted things like rich folks had, and he died trying to get them, Spence. I couldn't make him see it wasn't what we had—that it was what we were that mattered."

"He was wrong."

"And now you've started talking about money, about Jessie needing a better life than I can give her, and I can't stand it anymore. I'm doing all I can to make it happen, but nobody thinks it's good enough."

"I'm sorry, Laurie, truly sorry."

Looking away, he stared bleakly across the room that held everything she owned. There wasn't anything there he'd give more than twenty dollars for. And he'd as much as told her all of her hard work didn't amount to anything either. He might as well have said she was worthless herself, he realized now.

"You just shouldn't have to work so hard—it's not right."

"What am I supposed to do?—just give up? Some days I just want to dig myself a hole so I can crawl in it and die, but I tell myself I can't—I'm all Jessie's got, and she deserves so much better."

"Laura, that's foolish talk. You don't know what you're saying."

"I don't want her to grow up like me." Wiping her wet cheeks with the back of her hand, she sniffed, trying to stop her runny nose. "I want her to know she's somebody."

As she dropped her hand, he caught it. Rubbing the rough, chapped skin with his fingers, he found hers small and almost frail. "God, Laura—"

Once again, those flecked brown eyes appeared almost gold as she looked up. Staring into them, he felt a dam of suppressed hunger break, releasing such a flood of desire that it overwhelmed rational thought. Every nerve in him was acutely aware of her woman's body, of the pleasure within it. Catching her shoulders, he bent his head to hers, brushing her lips with his. He could feel her cold flesh quiver as her lips parted to receive his kiss, telling him she wanted this as much as he did.

For one brief second, she told herself it was wrong; then her balled fists dug into his shoulders, holding on, while his tongue probed the depths of her mouth, shocking her. A feeble protest died in the fire of her own desire. Her arms twined around his neck as she returned his kiss with a passion that drove everything else from his mind.

His mouth left hers, and his lips traced lightly over the shell of her ear, while his warm breath sent shivers of anticipation coursing down her spine. It was as though the quick, feathery kisses he trailed along her jaw and down her neck brought her alive with the promise of ecstasy, and as he pressed his lips against the sensitive hollow of her throat, she felt the low moan rise within her throat. Her neck arched, offering more hot skin to his touch.

"Let me love you," he murmured against her flesh. "You need this as much as I—you want this as much as I."

Hiding behind her closed eyes, she whispered, "Yes, I want it, too."

Easing her down into the feather bed, he looked into her face, thinking she had to be the loveliest woman in the world. His gaze moved lower, taking in the promise of her slender body from the full breasts beneath the faded bodice, the narrow waist, the curve of her hip under her dress, and he wanted to see all of it. He wanted to feel her flesh under his. Fumbling at her bodice buttons with one hand, he worked those on his shirt with the other, tearing at them. Jerking his shirttail out of his pants, he managed to get his shirt and coat off together, then fling them to the floor. Easing his body down beside hers, he began stroking her hair, her cheek, the smooth skin above her bodice. She sucked in her breath as his fingers slipped under the cloth to touch the full-ness of her breasts.

"Don't—I'll leak," she protested weakly.

"I don't care, Laurie—all I care about is you. I want to be good for you."

His hand cupped her breast, and his thumb rubbed over her nipple, eliciting an intense, exquisite agony. As milk flowed into his palm, she felt the aching wetness between her thighs. "Don't," she whispered. "Please . . ."

"Please what?" he murmured against her breast. "Tell me what you want me to do."

"I don't know—I just don't want you to stop."

Feeling as if he'd burst, he kissed her lips again. "Are you sure?"

"It's been so long, Spence—love me now. I want it all."

Nuzzling her throat, he reached down to unbutton his pants. He could feel himself grow as the buttons gave way. Lifting his hips, he worked his pants down to his ankles, then kicked them off. "Touch me, Lau-rie," he said hoarsely.

"I . . . I can't . . . I've never done that before."

She had her eyes squeezed tightly shut, and her teeth held her lip. He could see the rise and fall of her breasts through her open bodice. Working fever-ishly, he pushed the dress and thin chemise down from her shoulders, tugging them past her waist, over her hips. Loosening the waist of her drawers, he got them and everything else to her ankles. His fingers caught the laces of her shoes, untying them, pulling them off.

Instead of parting her legs, he nuzzled the crevice

between her breasts, while his hands stroked the curve of her hip, moving over the nearly flat plain of her belly until his fingers found the soft fold below, then glided inside.

He felt her body tauten under his hand, her heels dig into the feather mattress. As he stroked the wet flesh, she began to move, opening and closing her legs as the pleasure intensified. More than ready to give her what she wanted, he eased his body over hers, and as her legs splayed to receive him, he guided himself inside.

"Oh, yes!" she gasped, clinging to him as he rocked within her. "Don't stop now!" Her legs came up, and her body joined his rhythm, bucking beneath him, demanding satisfaction. Grasping her hips, he rode hard, straining to reach that ultimate peak. Pounding blood roared in his ears, and her breath was coming in great gasps, drowning out the primordial cries of the woman beneath him. He felt the explosion, the intense pleasure of release. Wrapping his arms around her, he lay within her, floating back to earth.

For a time, she hugged him, catching her breath. She felt utterly, completely sated. Finally, he rolled off her, drew her into the crook of his arm, and stared at the cabin ceiling. He was so quiet she could hear his heartbeat under her ear. She lay there, thinking dreamily that she never wanted to move from the warmth of his body.

He hadn't meant to do this, it had just happened, he told himself. No, he was lying. He'd wanted her more than anything, but that still didn't make it right—nothing could. He'd wanted her, and he'd taken advantage of her loneliness, and when she came to her senses, she'd probably hate him for it. Or herself, and he couldn't stand that. The blame was his, not hers—he'd thought of little else these past few weeks, so much he'd tried to run away, but he hadn't made it. No, he was leaving with the railroad rep crew tomorrow, one day too late.

He looked down at the silky soft brown hair spilling across his bare shoulder, wondering what she was thinking, if he'd given her as much pleasure as she'd given him. If she had any idea how good her woman's body had felt, how much better than the others. The thought threatened to rekindle his desire, making him feel no better than an animal. If things had been different, if he'd met her before Jesse, before Lydia . . .

She was probably too mortified to face him, and he didn't want that. His hand crept to stroke her hair as his mind sought words. "I'm sorry," he said finally. "I didn't mean for this to happen."

The regret in his voice struck her like a slap, telling her she'd been a fool. It'd been lust, not love in his mind. She'd given her body wantonly, wanting to believe he could somehow love her. He probably thought her little better than a whore now. Somehow, she managed to whisper, "It's all right—the blame is as much mine as yours."

Nothing was worth the shame he heard in that whisper. "I guess you're as sorry as I am, aren't you?"

What was she supposed to say to that? Not wanting to lower his opinion of her any further, she swallowed the lump in her throat. "Yes."

"It's not your fault, you know. At least I knew where I was headed."

"I was married—I had a notion." Pulling away from him, she sat up with her back to him, acutely conscious of her nakedness now. "You didn't exactly have to ravish me."

"Laura—"

"Please don't." Her hands gripped the edge of the bed. "Since I'm still nursing Jessie, I won't be having another baby, so you don't have to worry about that."

"God, Laura—it wasn't like that at all."

Leaning down, she retrieved her clothes from the floor, grateful he couldn't see her face. "Mama told me that, you know. I wasn't old enough to be thinking about such things, but she knew she wouldn't be there to tell me later."

He took a deep breath, then expelled it slowly, knowing he was about to pay the piper for the dance. "If you want to, we'll get married. While you get yourself cleaned up, I'll go down and make arrangements with the preacher in camp."

Humiliated, she could barely whisper, "I want better than that."

Mistaking her meaning, he said, "There's not time for anything else. I told Hawthorne I'd be ready to leave tomorrow, and I don't know for sure when I'll be back—probably in a couple of weeks—so it's got to be today. When I head for San Francisco in May, you can either go with me, or I can come back through to get you after I find Josh." When she didn't respond, he told her, "Look, it may not be what either of us wanted, but I don't mind. It's probably the best thing, anyway—Jessie will get a father, and Josh a mother, so it's not a bad bargain. At least you'll have somebody to take care of you this way."

Fighting tears, she pulled her dress over her head, thrust her arms into the sleeves, and yanked the bodice down to cover her breasts. Standing up, she dropped the skirt down over her hips. "Those aren't exactly the things a woman wants to hear, Spence. I married for Danny the last time, and if there's a next time, it'll be for myself. And it'll be to somebody who loves me, not somebody who thinks he's doing something honorable." Turning away so he couldn't see her face, she added, "I've got to want to be your wife, Spence, and right now, I don't."

"I thought you and I had a pretty good time, but I guess I was mistaken."

She swung around at that and looked him in the eye. "I had a real good time, all right," she said evenly, "but that's not enough for me to promise my life away. If it's a good time you're after, go to the hog ranch—the whores down there can probably give you a better one than I can."

"I didn't say that's what I was looking for. I said I thought you—"

"I'm looking for somebody who wants to spend his whole life with me, who won't mind growing old with me. I want to be everything to somebody, Spence. Any man that asks me had better be ready to convince me he's got his heart set on me and nobody else. Otherwise, I'm going to be a widow for the rest of my life. That's all I've got to say about it."

"Well, that was quite a speech."

"It came from my heart," she said simply. Her eyes

took in his tousled black hair, his strong, masculine shoulders, and she condemned herself for being a fool. A man like that could never love her. Looking down to button the front of her dress, she told him, "Since you're leaving in the morning, you can stay tonight, but when you get back, I think you'd better figure on staying somewhere else. Jessie and I'll miss you, but what we did just now wasn't right. And since I don't think I'll be likely to forget it happened, having you around would be just plain awkward."

The look on her face would haunt him a long time. "I see," he said heavily. "I don't think I've been sorrier for anything in my life."

"Yes—well, I've got to get busy, or I won't get the laundry finished up and ironed by tomorrow. I'll try to have your shirts ready before I go to bed, but if I can't, I'll get up early."

"Is there anything I can do to help out?"

"I guess if you get your packing done, you could chop wood. I'll probably be needing a lot more before warm weather gets here."

As she walked away from him, he felt drained, utterly empty. "I'll chop what I can, then leave you money in case you have to buy some. It's the least I can do."

She whirled to face him furiously. "Don't make me feel any worse than I already do, Dr. Hardin!" she snapped. "I may be a sinner, but I'm not a whore! I don't want to hear any more talk about money—now or ever!"

He finished dressing in silence, telling himself he'd tried, that there wasn't much more he could do to help her. When he sat down to pull on his pants, he saw she was punching down the bread dough with a vengeance. And he felt as though he'd just lost his best friend.

Light from the three-quarter moon overhead shone on the murky waters of the Platte, revealing the flat plates of ice churning by, breaking the other-worldly stillness of the deserted road as Spence gathered dead sticks into the burlap sack. The air was so cold his breath formed ice crystals on the bandana over his nose, telling him Nebraska wasn't any place anybody from Georgia ought to be. Down home, it'd be starting to feel like spring about now.

The other members of his railroad crew, most of whom had wintered on the plains before, claimed that as long as it didn't snow, they didn't mind being out in weather like this. A body got used to it, they said, but so far he hadn't. And if he ever got out of Nebraska, he damned sure wasn't coming back to give the place another try.

Every night since he'd left Laura's cabin, he'd rolled himself up in four heavy blankets and shivered himself to sleep so he could wake up before dawn, gulp a cup of scalding coffee to wash down his share of hardtack, then head out to tear up pieces of broken track for twelve or thirteen hours. She'd been right about that, like just about everything else.

It wasn't the hard work that bothered him. At night he was almost grateful to fall into bed too tired to even think. No, it was the damned, unrelenting wind—and Laura Taylor. That wailing, otherworldly wind swept the bitter cold down from the mountains and bore it across the plains, driving everything but wolves and railroad men into dens and lairs. It made him long for the warmth of that tiny cabin. It made him miss her.

But tonight he was going to be warm, he promised himself. He'd already cut a small vent hole in the roof of his tent to draw the smoke, and as soon as he had enough wood and tinder to make one, his water bucket was going to hold a fire instead of ice. He was going to show these Yankees some good old Rebel engineering he'd seen in the Tennessee campaign. Once he got a bucket full of red-hot coals, the metal'd give off at least enough heat to keep him from freezing, maybe enough that four wool blankets could keep him warm. And if he could keep the fire going until morning, he'd throw an extra buffalo chip on it, put some holes in an old rusty pan he'd found, and cover the bucket with it to make himself a cookstove. Instead of hardtack for breakfast, he was going to have soda biscuits and fried potatoes with his coffee.

As he twisted dead twigs from a limb, he couldn't help wondering how she was. By now, she'd have Jessie asleep, and she'd have that rocker pulled up close to the hearth. She'd probably be reading one of her books again, wearing her eyes out in that yellow light, or if she was trying to save on kerosene, she'd be knitting in the dark. He just hoped she wasn't running low on wood or anything else. He didn't want her trying to split logs or walking down to camp by herself.

He had to wonder if she missed him, or if she was doing just fine without him. She'd say she was, anyway, and she'd try her damnedest to believe it. She was the stubbornest woman of his memory, determined to take care of herself, refusing to go back home poor. He guessed he understood that—if he hadn't had to wait for Pinkerton to answer, he sure as hell wouldn't have spent those last months in Georgia, pretending not to notice conversations turned to furtive whispers whenever he entered a room. Pity wasn't anything either of them could stand.

He hadn't thought much about Lydia lately, or Ross either, for that matter. It was Joshua who occupied his thoughts. And Laura. Lydia didn't matter anymore. The speculative gossip that had probably found him wanting as a husband was a distant memory that no longer stung. It was the here and now that plagued him.

He just didn't know what to do about Laura, and he knew she wouldn't help him any. She wouldn't go home, she couldn't stay where she was, and she'd refused to go to California, too, which was going to make it damned difficult for him to leave when the time came. As if he didn't have enough on his plate, she was haunting his waking thoughts, seducing him in his dreams.

He'd go to bed telling himself he'd already been deceived by one pretty face, that women were all more or less faithless creatures, and he would vow he'd never make a fool of himself over a woman again. Then, before he could get across that hazy netherworld leading to sleep, rational thought would slip away, and he'd relive every word, every movement, every touch that had passed between them in that bed, and he'd ache for her—not just lust, ache.

Her response to him had been a revelation, showing him yet another way Lydia had cheated him. He'd mistaken lying words for passion, accepted it as fact that a decent woman wasn't supposed to pant and writhe under him like a whore pretending to enjoy it, that she'd be shocked and repelled by what a man really wanted. Lydia had done her best to plant and nurture that notion. Looking back, he could see now that there hadn't been much about marriage she'd liked except the Mrs. in front of her name. It made him wonder why she'd turned to Ross—or Ross to her, for that matter. They must've made quite a pair, two beautiful people intent on deceiving each other.

He could close his eyes and feel Laura's warm skin, taste her mouth, and he could hear her whisper, "Yes, I want it, too." And her body had proven her words. The only thing she'd been unwilling to do was touch his manhood. *I can't—I've never done that before.* It made him wonder if Jesse had cheated her as Lydia had cheated him. He didn't guess he'd ever know that answer either.

Well, he'd offered to marry her, and she'd turned him down, freeing his conscience if he wanted to go. And go he would, because he had to. Somewhere there was a four-year-old motherless little boy who needed him, who had no other relatives closer than distant cousins left, and Spence could not fail him. They'd be strangers, but the love would come later. No, Laura had made her choice to stay, and he had chosen to go. And sooner or later, she'd leave his mind. It had to happen that way.

He'd taken this job to escape from her, to avoid falling into a trap he'd regret, and it hadn't helped him much. He'd just forsaken a warm cabin, good food, and clean clothes for nothing. Now he was wandering around picking up sticks so he could build a fire in a bucket, feast on buffalo jerky and rock-hard biscuits, then try to sleep with that howling wind slashing through canvas walls. And the memory of another woman who did not want him was driving him mad.

Forcing his thoughts from her to the task at hand, he reached for a hollow branch and stopped dead, nearly paralyzed by shadowy figures riding behind the black, skeletal branches of leafless trees so silently he had to blink to make sure his eyes weren't playing tricks on him. Spence edged back into the cottonwood grove, thinking he had to alert the rest of the camp without giving himself away. His stiff fingers sought and closed around the Navy Colt, drawing it soundlessly from his holster as he watched the Cheyenne war party skirt the small cluster of tents. They were after the picketed horses, and a big buck had his eye on Clyde.

Spence put two fingers in his mouth and gave a long, shrill whistle, and the big chestnut gelding's head came up. The second time, the animal kicked over a barrel anchoring the rope picket and broke out, heading for him with mane and tail flying, and the commotion stampeded the others, alerting the men in camp. Rolling away from a blazing campfire, most of the crew scrambled to get behind a pile of ties while a man who had a repeating rifle handy covered them. Within seconds, the thundering booms of buffalo guns had picked off two Indians trying to round up the horses, and after a mad dash back for the bodies, the rest of the war party took off.

Matt Hadley yelled, "Where's Hardin? Did the sons of bitches get Hardin?"

"There he is!" somebody answered, seeing Spence running toward them. "Damned if he ain't got that big horse of his chasin' him! Must've been him that sounded the alarm!"

"That's some eyes you got, Mr. Hardin," Hadley told him as he caught up to them. "Don't know how you seed 'em at night, but if you hadn't, I reckon as soon as they got the animals, they'd been back for scalps."

"Yeah."

"Reckon at least some of us owe you for that whistle. I'd say you're damned lucky them injuns didn't come right at you soon as they heard it," the crew boss went on.

"I thought they'd be too busy chasing horses."

"Well, you got guts and a cool head to go with 'em, I'll say that for you."

"Thanks."

"Looks like they'll be looking for easier pickin's on up the road—guess I'd better send somebody to warn the main camp."

"Aw, they ain't going there," Billy Watson argued.

" 'Sides, ain't no way any of us could get ahead of 'em the way they was hightailin' it out of here."

"Better warn Hawthorne, anyway," somebody else countered. "Hell, Bill, they been bold enough to run off government horses over at McPherson right under the cavalry's noses. Looks like they're headed that way again, and a bunch of railroad men's bound to look better to 'em than the U.S. Army."

"Humph!" Billy snorted. "If we put 'em on the run, they ain't got no stomach for a real fight, Ben. No, sir, they'll be lookin' for easy pickin's, all right, so I'd say it's folks they can catch alone that's in for trouble. Like last summer when they killed that old German farmer right outside Fort Kearny. Hell, you know he thought he was safe settlin' in less than a mile from an army post, but by the time anybody heard the commotion and the soldiers got mounted up, the damned savages had scalped the old gent and got clean away."

"Yeah, I remember that," Hadley murmured, nodding. "Snuck up on him right at sunup, and if anybody'd been looking, they'd seen it from the fort."

"I'll go," Spence offered.

"I dunno—don't seem like you been out here long enough to be trailin' injuns."

"I've got the strongest horse."

"Something to be said for that, Mr. Hadley, 'cause you know they'll be switchin' off to rest those ponies, which is how they keep the cavalry from catchin' 'em," Billy observed.

The older man considered Spence for a moment, then sighed. "Think you can find your way without taking the road? There's not much cover anywhere, but you're out in plain sight if you stay on it."

"Yeah, but if I don't get going, I won't catch up to them between here and McPherson."

"They might make camp for the night somewhere. Seems like the times you got to watch out for the sneaky bastards is right before sunup or right after sundown." Without turning around, Hadley called over his shoulder, "Frank, you lend Hardin that Spencer—you got a Quick Loader for it, ain't you? He don't need to be trying to reload in a fight."

As Spence swung into the saddle, Frank Davidson ran up to hand him the rifle and a cartridge loader for it. "There's thirteen seven-round loads in there," he said as Spence stuffed it into his coat. "All you got to do is open the butt-trap, pull out the magazine spring, and drop the load in. Soon as the spring's back in, you're ready to go again—whole thing takes about five seconds."

"Beats my Colt," Spence admitted. "Thanks."

"Just don't forget where you got it, 'cause I'm lookin' to get it back—you hear?"

"I will."

Pulling wide on the reins and nudging the big chestnut with his knee, Spence turned Clyde toward the road, then leaned forward as he applied his spurs, and the horse took off like a bullet from a full charge of powder. It took almost a furlong for him to ease off a gallop into a canter. At a wide bend, Spence left the road to skirt along the row of trees following the river.

It took him close to an hour to get his first glimpse of the war party. Relieved that he hadn't missed it entirely, he dropped back to trail the Indians at a distance until he could find enough cover to pass them. Slowing to a trot, then to a steady walk, Spence told himself they'd probably turn off somewhere before McPherson, and he was probably making a long ride in a miserably cold night for nothing. But he wasn't taking any chances as long as they could be headed anywhere near Laura and Jessie. The thought had already crossed his mind that if they scouted the perimeter of the main camp, they stood a good chance of stumbling onto her cabin, and tomorrow morning was wash day. It'd be damned easy for them to catch her and Chen Li outside hanging the laundry.

Hell, he didn't even know where they were going yet, he reminded himself again. Nebraska Territory was a big place, and it was damned unlikely that out of thousands of square miles of empty land, a small band of Cheyenne would find one very small cabin perched on the side of a hill. But at least he had an excuse for coming home, one they both could believe.

Forcing his straying mind back to the Indians ahead, Spence realized that while he'd been lost in thought, they'd gotten away. Or they'd seen him and were lying in wait up ahead. The thought was enough to make his scalp crawl. Spurring Clyde into a lope, he took the river side of the road, where the moonlight on the ice made it easier for him to see. As he came around a wide bend, he gave a sigh of relief.

Yeah, there were five of them riding right up the middle of the road, and he was close enough to hear them talking to one another. Slowing again, he widened the distance. If they fell silent, he didn't want the sound of Clyde's hoofbeats alerting them. With McPherson still more than thirty miles away, it was hard to guess where they were going. Maybe he was green when it came to Indians, but it didn't seem reasonable that a war party of five would want to go anywhere near a fort.

They were stopping. Moving Clyde into the trees, Spence watched them, wondering what the hell they were doing, until he heard more riders. A larger party was joining them. The whole group dismounted and stood around while someone made a small fire. It looked as though they might camp for the night.

Spence dropped from his saddle to the ground, then crept closer. They were chattering like magpies, joshing each other, posturing. As the tinder flared, there was no mistaking the yellow streaks on their faces—it was a war party all right. More riders joined them, and their leader waved a war lance, dipping it close to the fire for the others to see. Long blond hair rippled in the flickering light. He'd taken a woman's scalp, and he was bragging about it.

Moccasins crunched on dead leaves and sticks about twenty feet from Spence. He held his breath, thinking he'd been a fool to leave his horse. They'd posted a sentry, making it almost impossible for him to leave unnoticed.

Spence lay on his stomach in the frosted grass, fighting sleep, telling himself it was too cold, that he'd freeze if he didn't stay awake. As tired as he was, it seemed like yesterday's dawn had been in another lifetime. Now that he had time to think about it, he realized every muscle in his arms, shoulders, and back ached from a full day of digging up broken track and hammering down new rails. A nine-pound hammer, they'd called the one he'd swung, but by the end of the day, it had felt like ten times that heavy.

They weren't picketing the ponies, so they weren't planning on staying the rest of the night, after all. They were just gathering a large party before they went on—and swapping tall tales while they ate, by the sound of it. Spence kept his eyes open by counting them. Sixteen full-grown warriors and two young boys, one of whom looked white, even with that war paint on his face.

It seemed as though they were there for hours while Spence shivered in the sharp-bladed, icy grass. Finally, they buried the fire, chose fresh ponies, and mounted up. The sentry dropped from his perch on a rock to follow them. The whole war party took the road west toward McPherson again. If he had to guess, Spence thought they'd get there just before dawn. So sore he groaned when he pulled himself to his feet, he found Clyde and mounted up again.

Sometime later, he dozed, then caught himself as his chin dropped to his chest. Rallying, he looked over his shoulder. It was still dark overhead, but a layer of red hugged the horizon, fading to a pink haze before it met the sky. He'd been up almost twenty-four hours. And McPherson was just a couple of miles up the road.

It looked as if they were going to skirt the fort, surprising him, but then the two boys split away from the rest of the party, dropped to the ground, and snaked through the grass on their bellies, right past two soldiers on guard duty. Spence considered sounding an alarm, but the rest of the party stood a good chance of getting away before a troop of cavalry could mount up to chase them. Besides, it was the others who worried him—there wasn't much of anything else out here except the railroad camp. And Laura's cabin. The cavalry couldn't get there in time to warn anybody, and Spence couldn't get past the Cheyenne himself.

In the graying light, the boys emerged again with a pair of government horses. As bold as you please, they swung up onto the animals' bare backs and rode off, leading their ponies. They'd tweaked the U.S. Army and gotten away with it.

They were going for the railroad camp, all right. Alert now, Spence realized if they raided it, there was a good chance some of them would ride up that hill. Digging in his coat pocket for the Quick Loader, he checked it, then reached for the Spencer rifle. Five seconds to reload, Frank Davidson had said, but he doubted that. Between the Colt and the Spencer, he had twelve bullets, and after that, it'd be hell reloading under fire. But as long as he had a breath in his body, that war party wouldn't get Laura and Jessie.

He could see them clearly now, and he could see a faint curl of smoke rising above the cluster of white tents. At least someone was up to raise the alarm if he didn't get there. The damned Indians were intent on surprise, and he intended to give them one. He cocked the Spencer's side hammer, jerked on the reins, and dug his spurs into Clyde's flank, praying the big horse still had enough left to make a run for it. The chestnut took off across the road to the left side, then shot down it, and headed straight for the Cheyenne.

Bending down against Clyde's neck, Spence pulled the rifle's trigger, and an Indian pony went down. His second shot hit one of the kids bringing up the rear. The boy pitched forward, then fell under the horse. The Indians wheeled to defend themselves and rode hell-for-leather toward Spence. Knotting the reins over his saddle horn, he reached across to draw the Colt with his left hand as he urged Clyde to go right through the middle of the war party.

He hit them firing both guns, and for a few seconds he was surrounded by yelling, yipping Cheyenne warriors. He felt a hot sting in his ribs, and then he was past them. Clyde staggered, and for a moment, Spence figured he was done for, but the big animal's front legs regained their footing, widening the gap as the war party wheeled to pursue.

He hit the camp at full gallop, shouting, "Indian raid! Indian raid!" before he saw men already scrambling from tents. They'd heard the gunfire. Two of the grimiest fellows he'd ever seen were dragging out the wagon, while someone else had climbed onto it to load the Gatling.

"Hold your fire! Let 'em get close!" Spence yelled. Dismounting, he reloaded the Spencer, crawled behind a supply wagon, and drew a bead on the closest Indian. Still thinking they had a chance of overrunning the defenders, they charged. "Now!" A volley of rifle fire, followed by the steady spitting of the Gatling, shattered the dawn, and as half the Cheyenne dropped, the rest fell back, trying to get out of range, while men with Sharps took over, picking them off. Within minutes, the battle was over. As Spence stood up, he was surrounded by railroaders wanting to shake his hand.

"Mister Hardin, I been in four years of war, and I ain't never seen anything like what you just did—you got to be either the nerviest or the stupidest son-ofabitch I seen yet," a grinning man told him.

But all he could think of was getting to Laura. Pushing through them, he pulled himself into his saddle, turned Clyde toward the path, and shouted, "I've got family to look after—cover me up the hill!" As the horse climbed, he could hear men running behind him.

Laura came awake with a start, sitting up in bed. For a moment, she thought maybe the baby had made a sound, but when she lit the lantern and crept to look into the cradle, Jessie was asleep, her little rosebud mouth working as though she nursed in her dreams. It must've been something stirring outside in the dawn.

Turning to the window, she froze, and the hair at the nape of her neck prickled, sending a shiver down her spine. The face pressed against the pane was painted, the black eyes watching her. Trying not to panic, she turned away as though she hadn't seen the Indian, and she knelt over the cradle to tuck the shawl around Jessie while her mind raced. She knew every move she made could be seen from that window, and as soon as she got to a gun, she'd better be prepared to shoot.

She began humming, then started singing "Dixie"

as she picked up Jessie. The startled baby blinked blankly; then her eyes focused, and she let go with an indignant cry that gained volume and intensity while Laura carried her into the kitchen area. Rummaging in the cupboard drawer, she eased Jesse's old Colt into a fold of her skirt before she turned around. For a moment, she stood there, trying to figure out how she could make a stand, what she could get behind that could stop a bullet.

There were two sources of light—the lantern and the fire. And when she doused one, they'd probably attack—in fact, it was a wonder they hadn't tried to break in already. The hopeful thought crossed her mind that maybe there was just one and he wasn't hostile; then it died. Out here there wasn't any such thing as a friendly Indian, and if there were, he wouldn't have yellow paint on his face. He was just taking his time getting down to the business, she decided. Or he was waiting for others to catch up.

Stalling for more time, she carried Jessie to the fire and unhooked the kettle of hot water. If worse came to worst, the first one inside was going to get his face scalded. She'd heard too many gruesome tales to go to her fate tamely. As she carried the kettle close to the bed, she counted her bullets. Six in the Colt, not counting the double load in the shotgun, and the heavy slug in the Sharps. But those guns were on the other side of the room.

Laying Jessie under the bed, she hesitated, then blew out the lantern. Dropping to the floor, she crawled in the near darkness with one hand clutching the gun, the other reaching for the shotgun. Now she could hear a horse, and it was coming at a full gallop.

Gunfire burst like popcorn over a fire, and when she looked up, there was no one at the window. Not knowing if he was creeping toward the door or he'd been joined by others, she tensed her finger on one of the shotgun's triggers, ready to fire the first barrel. It sounded like men were running and shouting. Then the door shook as someone pounded on it.

"Open up—it's Spence!"

She sagged in relief, then started to cry, overwhelmed by the fullness of her heart.

When she didn't answer, he pounded harder. "Laurie, are you all right?—for God's sake, answer me!"

"Yes—yes, I'm fine!" she called out, scrambling for the door. "Spence . . . oh, Spence . . . thank God you're here!" she cried through her tears.

As she slid back the bolt, he shouted over his shoulder, "She's all right!" before he stumbled across the threshold into her arms. In the light of the doorway, she could see he was half frozen and utterly exhausted. Wrapping her arms tightly around him, she walked him toward the rocker. "You look like death warmed over," she managed, "but you sure are a sight for sore eyes. You'd better sit down before you drop."

"No—I just want to hold you." Weaving, he held onto her as though she were his life. "If I lost you, I think I'd want to die," he murmured into her hair. Unable to speak, she turned her face into his and found it as wet as her own. His hands moved over her back and shoulders; then he buried his face in her tangled hair, and she heard him whisper huskily, "Oh, God, I love you, Laurie—more than anything."

She held his shirt tightly as she looked up at him through tears. "What did you just say?"

"I've chased a war party nearly sixty miles in the dark to tell you I love you. I want you to know that before I ask you again to marry me." His palm smoothed her hair back from her face. "Laurie, I want to take you to San Francisco as my wife. I'm not asking because I feel obligated to—I'm asking because I want to spend the rest of my life with you." He could see her lip quivering. "Hey, I don't want you to cry."

"I can't help it—I just want you to mean it."

"I do. I should've never gone off and left you like that. All I could think of all the way home was how much you and Jessie mean to me. It was the longest sixty miles of my life—and the coldest."

He'd said *home*. Feeling as though her heart would burst with happiness, she smiled through her tears. "I love you, too, Spence, and I guess I have for a long time now—ever since Jessie was born. I'd be proud to be your wife, but I want you to be sure yourself. I don't want you to be ashamed of me later."

"Ashamed of you? What on earth are you talking about?"

"I'm not like your people, Spence. I was raised poor, and I don't know much about being a lady."

As tired as he was, he had to gape for a moment before he shook his head. "I was raised by a man I wish you could've met, Laurie," he said quietly. "He used to say class isn't what you have—it's what you do. He was probably the smartest man I'll ever know. Last night as I was riding back, I couldn't help thinking how much he would've liked you."

"He sounds like somebody I would've liked, too," she said softly. Leaning into him, she rubbed her cheek against his shoulder, wishing she could hold him forever. As cold as he was, it took a moment for her to realize her nightgown was being soaked by something warm. Steeping back for a look, she saw the wet place on his coat. "You're hurt!"

He let her go reluctantly. "It looks worse than it is—a bullet grazed a rib, that's all."

"You've got to take off your coat and shirt and sit down so I can look at that. You can't know how bad it is without looking."

"I'm a doctor," he reminded her. "I'm just going to wash it off with a little turpentine before I turn in. Right now, all I want to do is find a warm place and go to sleep. And say hello to Jessie," he remembered. "She's squalling someplace."

"Jessie!" she gasped guiltily. "Oh, Spence—I left her under the bed! It was the only place I could think of where she'd be safe if bullets started flying."

"I'll get her." He crossed the room and leaned down to pick up the baby. Her indignant wail ended in a hiccough as she moved her head back to look at him owlishly. Her chubby little fists waved, and her mouth blew bubbles. He held her close, nuzzling the soft, silky hair on her head with his cheek, feeling an intense tenderness for the tiny little girl. "Yes, Miss Jessie, you are a wonder," he murmured. "And one of these days, you're going to be as pretty as your mother."

"And the apple of your daddy's eye," Laura said, taking the baby. As she carried the baby to a chair, Jessie's eyes stayed on Spence. "I guess you're as glad to see him as I am." Sitting down, Laura pulled the shawl over her shoulder, then unbuttoned her bodice. "As soon as I get her fed, washed, and into dry clothes, I'll take a look at that wound," she told Spence.

"Just tell me where to find the turpentine."

"I poured it into the bottle in your bag. I figured if you weren't going to use those things, I might as well. I've been reading your formulary, too, just in case I want to make my own medicine."

He didn't answer, but Laura heard him rummaging in it. Her gaze dropped to her daughter, and watching the baby suck, she couldn't help thinking how much she owed Spence, how much she loved him. Happy beyond belief, she began singing softly as Jessie closed her eyes, but that little mouth just kept working.

When she finally decided the baby had to be full, she eased her to her shoulder and stood up. "It won't take long to wash her, and then I'll fix you some eggs before you go to bed. I know you're bound to be hungry." Looking to his chair, she saw the open bottle of turpentine, the rag in the washbasin at his feet. His bloody shirt was hanging open, revealing a shallow gash over his rib cage where the bullet had grazed it. He was sleeping soundly.

Moving closer, she studied the well-chiseled face, the tousled black hair, thinking he had to be the handsomest man she'd ever met. And the best. He'd ridden all that way because he loved her. Looking lower to his bare chest, she couldn't help remembering the feel of his skin against hers, and she felt weak all over. She'd never been loved like that before. But she would be again, she reminded herself. As hard as it was to believe yet, he was hers.

"Spence . . ." When he didn't respond, she shook him. "Spence, you need lie down. It's been a long day and night for you."

"Huh?" He sat up and rubbed his face. "Yeah." Pulling himself up, he stumbled over to the bed, fell in face first, then rolled onto his side, still fully clothed. His eyes closed again as soon as his head touched the pillow.

Leaning over, Laura pulled the heavy covers over him, then tiptoed away. As soon as she got Jessie down for her morning nap, she was going to get in bed with him and hold him. She wanted to be there when he woke up. She wanted to see him open those bright blue eyes.

There was a dusting of white already on the ground, and the hazy clouds were spitting snow. Holding the heavily bundled baby close, Spence hurried to the wagon. Behind him, Laura closed the cabin door, then ran across the yard. "I think I shall never see a March day that it does not snow," he muttered, giving her a hand up.

"What?"

"Nothing. I'm ready for spring, that's all." He waited for her to settle onto the wagon seat before he passed Jessie to her. Grasping the cold iron ring, he pulled himself up beside them and took the reins. "By now, everything's green in Crawford County."

"Spring's day after tomorrow," she reminded him placidly.

"Yeah—a couple of hundred miles south of here."

"You don't like cold weather, do you?"

"Does anybody?" he countered.

"I don't mind it." Pulling a blanket from under the seat, she wrapped it around her and the baby, then leaned against him. "I feel pretty lucky myself."

Glancing down at the melting flakes in her hair, he was struck again by the beauty of the woman

beside him. In less than an hour, she'd be his wife,
the baby in her arms his daughter by choice, not
birth. Yeah, he felt it, too. "You've got your mother's Bible?"

"Yes."

"Then I guess we're ready," he decided, slapping
the reins over the same mismatched team that had
brought them here.

"You're sure you want to go through with this?"
she dared to ask. "I don't want you to think you
have to."

"I want to." As the wagon creaked into motion,
he added soberly, "I just hope you never think marrying me was a mistake."

"I won't."

He couldn't help thinking how different this was
from the day he'd married Lydia. Everything Laura
owned wouldn't fetch what Cullen Jamison had paid
for one of his daughter's dresses. The ring Spence
had put on that slender white finger had cost a pretty
penny, too—he'd paid three hundred dollars for that
pigeon blood ruby. He wondered if Ross had it now,
or if Lydia had sold that with everything else. Surprisingly, it didn't matter to him anymore.

It was Laura who deserved things like that. Instead, she was wearing the least faded of the only
three dresses she had, and if he had to guess, he'd
say she'd made all of them out of calico flour sacks
like the ones Bingham used to give to his slaves. But
worst of all, he hadn't had time to get her any kind
of ring, not even a dollar gold band. Maybe he
should've waited until he could do this right, maybe
he was just plain selfish for not even giving her time

to think this marriage over, but he wanted her now. He wanted the right to wake up next to her tomorrow morning.

"You're awfully quiet."

"Am I?" He forced a smile. "I guess I was just thinking you deserved a whole lot better than you're getting."

"Oh, I don't know about that," she told him, smiling herself. "I'd say a doctor's a pretty good catch."

He let that pass.

She sighed. "That's not what you wanted to hear, is it? You're still being pigheaded about going back to doctoring, aren't you?"

"I don't want to—I don't know if I ever will. Right now, I don't think so, anyway."

"The war's over, Spence. You'd be healing folks instead of cutting off their legs and holding their guts in."

"You don't forget anything, do you?"

"Not much," she admitted. "Daddy always said to put everything I read or heard into my mind and keep it, because it's hard to tell what's important and what's not until it's needed. In a lot of ways, he was like your Reverend Bingham, but he didn't have the money for an education. If he'd had the chance, he would've made a good preacher."

Thinking to change the subject away from himself, he asked, "And your mother—what was she like?"

"Mama?" She considered for a moment, then spoke slowly. "Well, everybody said I got my looks from her, and my mind from him, but it's hard to tell. In her own way, she was a pretty smart woman when it came to things that mattered. She took sick a long time before she died, so she tried to prepare me for losing her. Galloping consumption, they called it, but it didn't gallop—it was more like it crawled—she just got sicker slowly," Laura recalled. "So she was able to teach me to do things a little bit at a time. I was nine when she first started coughing, and she didn't die until I was eleven. She started showing me how to cook, because she was afraid we'd catch it from the food she fixed; then it was the washing and the cleaning, and in the last year it was how to take care of Danny if he got sick, what it'd be like when I was growing up, becoming a woman, getting married."

"She sounds like she was a remarkable woman."

"She was. She was afraid I wouldn't remember everything, so she wrote it all down until she was too weak to write anymore. There were pages and pages of it—she filled three housekeeping journals for me."

"I would've liked to have read them."

"Well, I've still got all of them packed away in a box. I used to get those journals out and read them when things were bad, and I'd know if she could take the time to write all that down as sick as she was, I could do it. When we left North Carolina, Jesse wanted me to burn them—he said we didn't have any room for anything we didn't have to have—but I sneaked them into a box with the towels, anyway. They just meant too much to me to let them go. It was the same way with Mama's Bible. He said we didn't have any use for more than one, but she'd written down all the births, marriages, and deaths in hers and Daddy's families in it, and I'd kept it going, so I wasn't about to part with that either. That's why I wanted to bring it today. It's like having them with me."

He reached for her hand, covering it with his, thinking how small it was. "Laura, I'm going to do my damnedest to take care of you and Jessie—as long as I've got breath in my body, it's not going to be like that anymore. I don't want you scrimping and saving and doing without, and it's my job to see you don't have to. You're going to have what you deserve."

"Just don't treat me like Jesse—please," she said, looking up at him. "He said he wanted me to have a big, fine house, a fancy carriage, things like that, but it was him that wanted them, and whenever things went wrong between us, he'd always throw it up to me that he was working himself to death for me. I don't want to live like that, Spence—I've got nothing against having things if they're what *we* want, but I want us to work together for them—I want us to be partners, Spence. In everything. I don't want to be left out, then blamed for something I didn't do. I don't want to be left by myself on some pedestal, and just get dusted off when you happen to think about it."

"I want to take care of you, Laura."

"I've got to think that what I do means something, too—even if it's just cooking and sewing and keeping the house clean. I spent too many years alone, and then I got myself a husband who didn't want to talk to me—he and Danny'd get together and make plans for me, thinking they were *my* plans, too, but they weren't. I'm not saying I didn't love Jesse, or he didn't love me—it'd be a lie to say that—I'm saying I wish he'd just listened to me sometimes." Taking in a deep breath, she exhaled heavily. "I don't guess that makes much sense to a man, does it?"

"Yeah."

"I've got to be respected, Spence. Nobody ever loved anybody more than Mama and Daddy loved each other. Maybe they went through hell on this earth and everything was a struggle for them, but they did it together. I saw it, and that's what I want."

"You've got yourself a deal. I've always appreciated honesty, Laura."

"No, I've got myself half a deal. I didn't mean to make a speech just now, but since I did, you've got a turn coming, too. I'd like to know what you want from me."

"I'm a man—the things I want are pretty simple."

"Food on the table, clean clothes, and a clean house?"

"Well, I'd like that, too," he admitted. Sobering, he looked into the depths of those beautiful eyes for a long moment. "What I want most is a woman who loves me, who wants me to touch her, who wants to wake up beside me. I want you to want me as much as I want you, Laura."

She felt the lump rise in her throat. "Heart, body, and soul," she answered huskily. "You won't ever have to ask for that. You've got yourself a deal, Spencer Hardin."

"Anything else you feel like settling here and now?"

"Children. If you're thinking because I had a hard time twice before, I won't want anymore—well, you're wrong. We'll have Josh and Jessie, I know, but we've got to have at least one more to tie them together and make them feel they belong to both of us. Then they'd each have blood in common with a little brother or sister. And two would be even better, because from what I've seen, an even number of kids makes for less quarreling."

"You don't plan on leaving much to chance, do you?" he teased her, grinning.

"Well, it's up to God to decide whether they're girls or boys. All I can do is tell him I'd like one of each."

He reined up in front of the half-finished company store and tied the traces to a rusty nail at his feet. "You probably won't want to wake up Jessie yet, so I'll just go in and ask where we can find the preacher."

"His name is Farrell, and he's got the last tent before you're out of camp."

"Yeah, but they're starting to build now, so he could've moved."

"I don't think that's likely."

"Just the same, I'd like to check."

As he disappeared into the store, she leaned back against the board behind her. The snow was coming down steadily now, filling the air with huge white flakes, but in the absence of the usual wind, it made for a lovely, peaceful scene. By tonight, the country-side would be blanketed, making the little cabin seem isolated in a world all its own. As soon as she got home, she would put on supper, then play with Jessie before she fed her. She hoped the baby would be tired enough to go to sleep early.

She had two big white candles she'd been saving for years, waiting for something special to happen before she used them, and tonight she'd place them on the tables by the bed. When Spence came in from tending the animals, she'd have herself washed with that sliver of lavender-scented soap she kept in her underwear drawer, and she'd be wearing her tucked lawn nightdress with nothing underneath. It'd be a little cold this time of year, and it might shock Spence, but he'd probably appreciate not having to help her out of any extra clothes.

Closing her eyes, she relived every sensuous moment of that night almost two weeks ago, and she felt weak with the wanting again. He'd find her more than willing to keep her half of the bargain tonight and every night thereafter, whenever he wished. She wouldn't have to lie awake, staring at the ceiling, wondering if there was anything left in this life for her anymore. She'd be Mrs. Spencer Hardin, his wife, the mother of the rest of his children.

"Well, you were right," she heard him say. When she opened her eyes, he was climbing up beside her, then stowing a sack under his seat. "His name's Farrell, and he's right up the street."

"What's that?"

"Not enough, but it'll have to do until we can get something better."

"That's not much of an answer."

"You'll see soon enough."

Smoke curled from a firepot at the side of the last tent, and Spence took it for a hopeful sign. "Looks like he's home," he observed, pulling up in front. Retrieving the sack, he braced a boot on the wooden block he'd nailed to the side of the wagon, and he dropped to the ground. "Hand me the baby, and I'll help you down." Taking Jessie, he balanced her against his hip, then reached for Laura. She missed the step and slid the length of him before she gained her feet. "Are you all right?" he asked quickly.

"Well, if you weren't marrying me, I'd be pretty embarrassed, but otherwise I'm fine. Here—I'll hold her."

"No sense in passing her back and forth, is there? We're getting along all right." Shifting Jessie to his shoulder, he took Laura's arm. Squinting into the falling snow, he exhaled fully. "Well, I guess this is it."

"Right now, you look like a man about to be hanged," she chided.

"No. I just wish it was a church, that's all, but I guess the words will be the same."

"I expect so." Pausing to look up at him, she added, "You can still escape, you know."

"Not on your life. I went through hell getting here last night, wondering if you were all right, and I'm not leaving again without you."

"Then I guess we'd better go in."

As they ducked under the tent flap, a man stood up. To Spence, he looked more like a gambler down on his luck than like any man of God he'd ever seen. Seedy was the word that came to mind. And the way the fellow was looking at Laura irritated him.

"Are you the Reverend Farrell?" he asked finally.

"I might be. Depends on what you've got in mind."

Feeling Spence's arm tense under her hand, Laura stepped forward quickly. "This is Dr. Spencer Har-

din, and I'm Laura Taylor. We were hoping you
could marry us."

Farrell's gaze shifted to the baby on Spence's
shoulder, and his mouth curved knowingly. "Little
late now for that, I'd say."

"She's a widow," Spence snapped. "I was a friend
of her husband. Come on, Laura—let's go. You don't
have to put up with this."

"No. A shifty-eyed messenger doesn't make the
message wrong," she declared, holding onto his arm.
"Are you licensed to perform marriages, Mr.
Farrell?"

"I am."

"Of what persuasion?"

"Baptist."

"If he is, you can bet he's been defrocked,"
Spence muttered.

"There's all different kinds of Baptists," she said
mildly. "You can either go ahead with this, or you
can tell me you don't want to marry me."

"Damn it, Laura, Thad Bingham would turn over
in his grave if he could see the fellow."

"Yes, well, he's not here, and there's not another
preacher around, unless you want to go over to Mc-
Pherson tomorrow."

"It's about time for supper," Farrell told them, "so
you'd better make up your minds. It's a dollar-fifty
if you just want the words, nine if you want a fancy
Bible to go with 'em."

"I have my own Bible, sir, but I'd be obliged if
you'd sign the wedding page for us."

"I can do that."

"Thank you."

"You *want* him to marry us?" Spence asked incredulously.

"I don't want to wait for tomorrow," she said softly. "I've already got a big supper planned."

The way she said it made his mouth go dry, and the pressure of her small hand on his sleeve told him he hadn't gotten the message wrong. "It's your wedding," he managed finally. "If you're satisfied, I am."

The words were brief, the vows amounting to little more than two "I do's" apiece, and then Farrell was signing the territorial certificate and Laura's Bible. As he handed over the money, Spence asked the man, "You in a hurry to get someplace?"

"As a matter of fact, I am—there's some boys getting up a poker game over at the hog ranch, and I told 'em to count me in."

Handing her into the wagon again, Spence told her, "I've half a mind to drive over to the fort, anyway. You can't even feel married after that."

Settling onto the seat, she took Jessie before she retrieved the folded certificate from the Bible. "Well, it's got our names spelled right, and the seal makes it legal. And to tell you the truth, I'd rather go home than anywhere right now. But if it'd make you feel better, once we're out of sight, you're welcome to kiss your bride."

As he forked hay for the two horses and the mule, Spence knew he ought to be bone-tired after an all-night ride followed by less than five hours of sleep, but he wasn't. And he wasn't hungry either. He'd sat across the table, watching how her hair shone in the lantern light, the way her smile lit up those beautiful eyes, thinking he had to be the luckiest man alive. Right now, he couldn't even remember what he'd had for supper.

Today, he'd made himself responsible for a wife and daughter, and tonight he'd make himself a husband, sealing those few words he'd said earlier with his body. And, God willing, it'd be right this time, and this union would heal her pain and his anger with the balm of love and give him a measure of peace.

Maybe it already had. He didn't hate Lydia anymore—he could think of her now without feeling much of anything. But he didn't know how he felt about Ross yet, whether he still wanted to kill him, and he probably wouldn't know until he found Josh. And he had the gnawing fear that might never happen. Come May, the trail would be cold, and if Ross wasn't still in San Francisco when he got there, he might never know if Josh had gotten there alive, if Ross still had him, or for that matter, if both of them had died of cholera somewhere along the way. There might not even be a marked grave.

His thoughts turned to the woman inside, and he realized in his anger with Farrell, he'd forgotten to give her his gift. Laying the pitchfork aside, he checked the place where an Indian lance had glanced off Clyde's flank, then rubbed some of Laura's goose grease and turpentine salve on it. The snow crunched under his boots as he walked back, but for the first time all winter, he didn't mind it. Tonight, he had a roaring fire, a soft feather bed, and the prettiest woman on earth waiting for him.

Inside the door, he pulled off his boots, hung his coat on the peg, and headed for the fire before Laura caught his eye, and he stopped dead in his tracks. Two candles burned by the bed, casting her shadow on the wall. Her bare arms were pale in the soft light as she brushed her shining hair. He felt his mouth go dry with desire as his hungry gaze took in her bare legs, the outline of her body under the thin nightdress.

"You're going to freeze to death in that," he heard himself warn her.

She turned around, and her mouth curved into a smile. "I'm expecting you to keep me warm, Spence," she answered softly. "I've been saving these candles for years, but if you want, I'll blow them out."

"No. I'd like to see all of you." His pulse pounding in his ears, he walked toward the bed, unbuttoning his shirt. His fingers felt too big, too clumsy for the little holes. As she slid off the side of the bed to face him, he smiled crookedly. "I guess I could use a little help."

He closed his eyes and stood as still as stone while she finished taking off his shirt. It was as though every inch of his body was acutely aware of hers. He could smell lavender on her skin, feel the heat of her hands on his bare chest, on the buttons of his pants, and he could hear her sharp intake of breath as he grew beneath her fingers. Instead of backing away, she touched him lightly, running her fingertips the length of him, sending an exquisite ripple of desire through his whole being.

"I never thought a man's body could be beautiful,

Spence," she said, her voice barely above a whisper, "but you are."

As her hands slipped under his waistband, he caught his fingers in her silken hair, imprisoning her face for his kiss. He tasted her warm lips eagerly until she parted them, giving him access to her mouth. While his tongue explored its depths, his pants loosened, then slipped down his legs, followed by his drawers.

There was no other time, no other place than this, no other woman beyond the one in his arms. His hot mouth devoured every part of her he could reach, while his hands moved over the thin lawn, smoothing it against her back and hips, molding her body into his. His blood coursed through his veins as though it were liquid fire, igniting every sense with total desire.

She pulled away to whisper breathlessly, "Tell me what you want, Spence, and I'll want it, too."

"I want to know every inch of you."

He could see her throat move as she swallowed, the rise and fall of her chest beneath the thin cotton lawn, and his own breath caught as she untied the satin ribbon over her breasts, then quickly released the row of tiny buttons, revealing the white skin, the pink nipples. Her arms came up, her hands grasped the crocheted neckline, and she pulled the nightgown over her head slowly, letting the hem linger at her knees, her thighs, her waist, before her gleaming body emerged whole. For one brief moment, her composure wavered under his gaze; then she managed a smile.

"Here I am."

"God, you're beautiful," he whispered hoarsely.

Stepping out of the trousers and drawers at his ankles, he followed her as she backed toward the bed. The naked desire in his eyes fueled her own. As the back of her leg touched the edge of the bedstead, he caught her and they sank into the depths of the feather mattress. Her last rational thought was that he was hers, that she didn't have to hold anything back now. There'd be no shame in giving him anything he wanted.

As his mouth explored her ear, her throat, her breasts, her hands opened and closed restlessly in his hair. Turning her away from him, he nuzzled the nape of her neck, her shoulder, while his arms circled her, his palms brushed her nipples, his fingers stroked her belly to the thatch below. Parting her legs, she gave herself over to his probing fingers until her breath came in great panting gasps, her low moans rising into a crescendo of cries. As his hand left her, he rolled her over him, and her whimpered protest died as she took him inside.

"I'm all yours now," he panted. "Do what you want."

She moved tentatively at first, savoring the feel of him. When she looked down, his eyes were closed, his expression intense as his body anticipated every twist, every rock. "Ride," he urged her. "Ride hard! *Now!*" Grasping her hips with both hands, he bucked beneath her, pounding into her as she ground her body against his, seeking ecstasy. Biting her lip, she worked harder, until she felt it build, until the flood sated her. Drawing her knees tight against his sides, she curled forward into his embrace, exhausted.

Despite her weight on him, he felt as though his mind floated, buoyed by the languorous peace of utter physical fulfillment. He didn't want to leave her. He didn't want to move. He just held her, listening to her ragged breath, feeling her heart pound above his chest. Finally, he reached to stroke her damp hair back from her temple.

"I love you, heart, body, and soul," he whispered, giving her own words back to her. "I swear it." The back of his hand brushed her cheek. "Laurie, are you crying?"

"Yes, but I can't help it—I just love you so much I can't stand it." Turning her face into his shoulder, she confessed, "I'm a crier, Spence—sometimes, I cry when I'm too happy to laugh."

"I guess you had a good time," he murmured.

Her fingers crept to caress his bare shoulder. "What makes you think that?" she managed to ask.

"Well, for one thing, you were howling your head off," he teased her. "I thought Jessie'd wake up and think I was killing you."

"I did not."

"Oh, yes, you did. I never heard such caterwauling in my life before tonight."

She could feel her cheeks redden, and she was grateful he couldn't see her face right now. "Well, it was probably from shock—I . . . uh . . . well, I never . . ." Her face was so hot she couldn't go on.

"Never what?"

"Well, Jesse wasn't . . . I mean, I was never on top before. But I liked it . . . I just didn't know anybody did this quite that way. I guess he just wasn't one to spend much time courting—he . . ." Her voice trailed off guiltily. "One man doesn't want to hear about another, does he?"

"Only if he's better."

"Much, much better."

"Then it's all right."

"There wasn't anything *wrong* with him, but he wasn't much for hugging and kissing." She felt his arms tighten around her, holding her even closer. "Most nights, I didn't know he was interested until he pulled up my nightgown and put his knee between my legs."

"He probably would've suited Lydia better than I did. I don't know what Ross thought he was getting with Liddy, because she wasn't exactly a passionate woman—she liked being admired by men, and she enjoyed flirting with them, but she was pretty repelled by where it led."

"But she was so beautiful."

"No more than you—no more than you," he said softly. "And you've got a hundred times more heart than she did. But unless you've got an overwhelming interest in her, I've said about all I want to on the subject. I just want to lie here with you."

"Yes." She felt him slip from her as she eased off him. "But I almost feel sorry for her, because she didn't know what she could've had with you. That's the last thing I'm going to say about her—she cheated herself as much as she cheated you."

"That's two things," he reminded her, turning against her. "Did anybody ever tell you, Mrs. Hardin, that you have the most incredible eyes?" he murmured.

"No, but I always wished they were darker."

"Now that would be a pity. There's nothing I'd change about you but your hands, and that won't take long."

"They've always been pretty rough. And hanging wet clothes out in this weather doesn't help them any."

"Wait here—I'll be right back." Picking up his shirt, he covered himself before he walked over to the table. When he returned, he had the mysterious sack, and he had a smug grin on his face. "I've got the real wedding present on order from Omaha, but this will have to do for now," he said, climbing back into bed.

"But I didn't give you anything."

"You just did."

"Yes, but that's not—"

"Go ahead—take a look inside."

"Well, one's a jar of something," she observed curiously. Holding one to the light, she read, " 'Mrs. Holland's Recipe for Soft Skin.' I sure need that."

"Go on."

She took out a flat, tissue-wrapped package. As she unfolded the paper, she gasped, "It's beautiful!"

"It's just a comb."

"But it's silver—and it's got little roses on it."

"There's one more."

It was a stoppered bottle. Holding it gingerly, she removed the glass top and sniffed the contents. "It smells a little like lilacs—Spence, this is French perfume! Real French perfume!"

"I thought it smelled pretty good," he admitted.

"Good! It's lovely, that's what it is. I've never had *any* perfume in my life—ever."

"Then it's about time."

"But you must've spent a fortune!"

"No."

"I'll bet it was close to ten dollars."

"It was a tad more than that."

"Then I didn't need it."

"Well, since I won't be buying you a ticket east, I could afford a lot more than this. I would've, too, but the sutler didn't have much to choose from."

"But these are women's things, so I wonder who he thought he could sell them to." She wet the stopper, then dabbed the perfume behind her ears. "How do I smell?"

"Good enough to kiss," he answered, taking the bottle from her. If he lived to be a hundred, he'd never tell her it had been ordered by someone at the hog ranch. Reaching past her, he set the bottle next to one of the burning candles. "You know," he murmured, nuzzling the nape of her neck, "there are more than two ways, if you're interested."

As his warm breath caressed the sensitive skin there, she felt a shiver of excitement, and she knew exactly what he was talking about. "How many?" she asked weakly.

"Probably dozens."

Turning over to face him, she slid her arms around his neck. "Oh, then, I want to learn all of them," she whispered huskily.

"It'll take a little time."

"We've got the rest of our lives, don't we?" With the scent of French lilacs rising from her skin and the flickering light of a candle reflected in her eyes,

Laura settled deeper into the feather bed. "But I expect we'll need some practice."

As he lowered his head, Laura's lips parted, inviting him to love her again, and he felt whole in heart, body, and soul.

Perched on the seat of the wagon, Laura wrote in her journal, despite the roughness of the road. At her feet, Jessie lay snugly wrapped in the wooden box Chen Li had made for them. A gift, he'd called it when he'd come to take possession of the cabin. It'd taken some doing, but Laura had finally managed to persuade the railroad officials to let him have it, using the argument that it was ideally suited to the laundry business she'd just sold to him. In her last memory of the odd little Chinese man, he'd shown up in red silk padded pajamas to bid them good-bye, then stood in the cabin doorway to wave them out of sight.

To mark her new life with Spence, she'd started this journal the day after her wedding, and she intended to keep writing in it until she died or went blind. Someday, it would belong to Jessie, so she filled her account of each day with descriptions of what she'd done and seen, observations of people she met, the little joys and hardships of travel in the prairie schooner Spence had bought for this journey, daily recipes, and whatever advice struck her mind. While Spence teased her, saying she was writing so

much she'd need a whole library just to store her
journals by the time she was done, she wrote in the
hope Jessie would cherish them as much as she'd
cherished those her own mother had kept for her.

One thing she wouldn't recommend was traveling
so far in a wagon. Even with a new team of six mules
pulling it, the cumbersome Conestoga was slow,
grinding out the miles at a rate of three to the hour
on flat road, less than two where it was rocky, and
hours to the mile on the steep, winding grades of
mountain passes. By the time she got to California,
she was sure her behind would be made considerably
wider by sitting all these days on the hard wooden
seat.

Not that the trip so far was without interest. She
and Spence had fallen in with a military wagon train
headed west from Fort Kearny in Nebraska to establish a new fort of the same name in northern Wyoming, journeying with them between McPherson and
the place where the Bozeman Trail left the Platte
Road to head toward Montana. The army wagons
had been accompanied by the remarkable old mountain man Jim Bridger, who'd had nothing good to
say about Mormons, but was considerably more phil-
osophical when it came to Indians, possibly because
he was reported to have married more than one of
them in the course of his colorful life. She'd duly
recorded his observation, "Whar you don't see no
Injuns thar, they're sartin to be the thickest." Not a
comforting thought given the ever-increasing hostility of the Sioux and the Cheyenne to the hordes of
whites settlers, even though most of them were crossing the land, not moving in for good.

Indian troubles seemed to be on everybody's mind as war parties shadowed the Platte and Bozeman routes, harassing wagon trains, running off horses and cattle brought along for milk and meat, and cutting off anyone who lagged behind. Well-armed men had to go out in groups to get firewood, and only fools strayed from night camps. A headstrong Miss Peake, declaring, "I refuse to be intimidated by the rumor of heathens," had walked over a hill and disappeared two days out of Fort Casper, Laura had noted in the journal.

Unlike the military train, which had had seven hundred soldiers, more than two hundred wagons, and ambulances carrying officers' wives and children, the group they were with now was terribly small—forty-two people in ten Conestogas, four supply wagons, sixty-four oxen, nine mules, and twenty-three cows, all guided by a former army scout and a half-breed Crow, who only spoke to the scout.

Several disputes had broken out since Fort Casper over Matthew Daniels beating his pregnant wife so badly she now walked with a cane. After a brawl between Daniels and the other men resulted in his being exiled, his wife and five children had refused to go with him, and the desperate family was now trying to survive on handouts and by living in one of the supply wagons. Every time Laura saw Abigail Daniels, she tried to give her something. She remembered too well what it was like to be dirt poor.

"You'll be down to nubs and out of paper long before we reach California," Spence commented.

"I don't want to forget anything—since she's too

young to remember her journey, I want Jessie to know everything about it."

"Everything?" he teased, raising an eyebrow. "How much have you put about me in there?"

"Not *quite* everything," she admitted. "I try to keep it decent enough for her to read. Maybe someday she'll have children who'll want to know what life was like in 1866. As much as things have changed in the twenty-five years I've been living, there's no telling what's going to happen before I die. They might want to know about goose grease salve and willowbark tea someday. Or about what was in a Conestoga, for that matter. Once the railroad gets clear across the country, not too many folks are going to travel like this."

"Is that the sort of thing your mother wrote for you?"

"Well, we didn't go anywhere to write about, so hers was mostly how to take care of things, what to use, how to tell what ailments we had, how to make up her home remedies and special concoctions, things like that."

"I'd still like to read it. I'd like to know what you were like as a little girl."

"Daddy used to say I was 'yaller-haired and skinny'—my hair didn't start turning brown until I was thirteen or fourteen. And Mama didn't write much about how I was—it was more about what I ought to do. Only thing she said much about me was I used to get sick a lot, and she was afraid my lungs were weak, and I'd get her consumption. She used to grease my chest up every night it was cold out with stuff she made out of turpentine, camphor, clove oil, and lard; then she'd wrap a long piece of flannel around me until I looked like one of those Egyptian mummies when I went to bed. I don't know what it did for my lungs, but my nose never got stuffed up. She put that recipe in one of those journals, along with a lot of others. She had concoctions for everything from cleaning soot out of chimneys to making hair shine."

"Did you use all of them?"

"If I had the ingredients handy. And whether you believe it or not, they all worked. And some of her medicines were a lot like ones in your formulary—when she dosed a body up, he knew he was dosed. She just couldn't do anything with consumption, though, and she sure tried. Mama wanted to live to see me and Danny grow up more than anything."

"Yeah. She would've been proud of you, Laura."

"I hope so—I'd like to think so, anyway."

"She would."

"I still miss her. I'd give anything if she could be here now, if you could know her."

"I'll get to know her through those journals."

"You really want to read them?"

"Very much. I don't know too many remarkable people—most of them just think they are."

"Well, you are."

"No. I don't even know who I am anymore. I spent years learning to do something I came to hate, so it was pretty much a waste of my time and Thad Bingham's money. When I showed up at your tent over by Kearny, I was going to San Francisco to kill Ross—maybe Lydia, too—then I was planning to take Josh up to Canada and hide out someplace the law wouldn't find me. I didn't even know what I was going to do after that."

"And now?"

"I don't know what I'll do to Ross when I see him. A lot depends on what he's done with Josh."

"But you're not going to kill him."

"No, but I may horsewhip him within an inch of his life. Since I've got a wife and family to look after, I'm not going to do anything that'll get me hanged."

"It still hurts, doesn't it?" she asked quietly.

"I haven't thought about it in a while, if that's what you're asking."

"Not even about Lydia?"

"Just as Josh's mother. She's not part of me like you are, and she never was. If I'd had the time to get to know her, I'd have spared myself a lot of grief. She wasn't anything like I thought she was, and she obviously thought I was somebody else. I don't even know why she wanted to marry me—maybe because we both had black hair and she thought we'd look like a matched pair."

"You're a handsome man, Spencer Hardin."

"I don't know. I just know if she hadn't left me, living with her would've been hell for both of us. I had all those dreams about coming home to her loving arms, and that's all they were—dreams, delusions. Separation made it easier to pretend we had something—I could look at the picture of her and Josh, and it would take my mind off the hell I was in then without having to give much thought about what she was really like."

"You're still bitter, Spence."

"No, the bitter part's over—life's downright sweet

now. I've got you and Jessie to love, and the only thing that's missing is Josh."

"We're going to find him. He's been in my prayers every night, and I know we're going to find him."

"If he's not dead. If he and Ross both came down with cholera, there wouldn't have been anyone to put up markers for them. A year later, anybody coming through would never find the graves, even if they'd been buried. Hell, for all I know, the wolves could've eaten the bodies, and left nothing but a few bones."

Laying aside the journal, she turned to him. "I don't want to hear you talking like that—it's faith that carries a person through, not pessimism. You've got to believe, or you can't make it happen."

"I'm in this wagon, Laurie. If I didn't think there was a chance, I'd be going east, not west. Unless we have a child, he's the last of my blood, and that means everything to a man. He may be the only one to carry on my name. As much as I love Jessie, she can't do that for me—she'll have her husband's name, not mine. And until then, she'll grow up a Taylor, not a Hardin."

"I don't guess she has to," Laura murmured.

"It wouldn't be right to take that away from Jesse. He wanted that baby."

"Like every other man, he wanted a *son*, Spence. When we lost the other baby, it was the first time I'd ever seen him cry. He wanted that boy so bad."

"He nearly lost you, Laura."

"That made him mad—it was his son he wept over."

"It's the name I'd feel bad about—it's all he had to leave her. I'll have the joy of raising her, of watching her grow up. I'll be the one some totally unworthy boy asks for her hand in marriage. I'll be the one not wanting to give her away to him. Jesse won't be here to see it, but I will. Besides, her middle name's Spencer, so she'll know I wanted her to have it. I just don't want to take Jesse from her."

"I have to believe he knows we're in good hands," she said softly. "I have to believe he'd be pleased."

"You don't think about him much, do you?"

"I do when I look at her—she'll hold her head in just such a way sometimes that I can see him in her. And there's an emptiness, a sadness that doesn't completely go away. But it's tempered with happiness, because I've got you. We've got something that he and I never had—we talk, we share, we show our love to each other. Maybe he wanted to, but he couldn't do those things. I know he loved me, and I know I loved him, but in a lot of ways, the depth just wasn't there. He made up his mind about things, and that's the way they were. He never asked, he just told me what I wanted, Spence. I had to follow him to Nebraska because he wanted to go."

"You're following me to California."

"Maybe that's the difference—I don't want to be without you. I got used to being without Jesse."

The late afternoon sun haloed her brown hair with gold and lit those light brown eyes, filling him with pride, not only in her beauty, but her artlessness. Everything about her was the genuine article.

"You're always honest, aren't you?" he said softly.

She cocked her head at that, and the corners of her mouth lifted into a elfin smile. "Well, not quite always," she murmured. "I told you to go when I didn't want you to leave. When I told you to pack your clothes and take them with you on the rep track, I had to figure out some way to make you come back."

"Oh?"

"The morning you left, I told you I couldn't get all your clothes ready, that you'd need to stop back by for them, but since I'd already ironed the shirts, I had to stick them in the washtub so they wouldn't be done. I wasn't going to chance never seeing you again."

"But you weren't going to let me live there. You'd already told me I'd have to find another place to stay."

"That part of it wasn't a lie. I just wanted you to have to come by for a visit. I thought maybe if you'd had time to clear your head some, you might rethink your proposal."

"As I recall it, it was you who turned me down," he reminded her.

"Well, there wasn't any enthusiasm in it. You thought you were obliged to marry me, but you didn't want to do it. If I didn't mean anything to you, that proposal wasn't worth anything to me either. I may be practical, but I've got my pride, Spence."

"I know. I must've heard the charity speech a dozen times."

"Some people take a while to learn." Changing the subject abruptly, she noted, "We ought to be stopping before long, so I've got to figure out what I can fix that will have enough leftovers to feed Abby and her family."

"Food for six people isn't leftovers, Laurie. It's the whole meal."

"I know, but she's got her pride, too. If she thought I'd made something up just for them, she wouldn't want to take it, and those boys of hers are beginning to look kind of scrawny. Here she's got a baby teething, another one on the way, and four more under the age of six. If I ever cross Matt Daniels's path again, I'll horsewhip him. Spence, that's a baby a year!"

"So much for your mother's theory about nursing."

Ignoring that, she went on. "And day before yesterday, Jimmy tore a hole in his leg when he fell out of the wagon. He caught it on an old nail sticking out the side."

"Which one's Jimmy?"

"He's four. I think you ought to take a look at it, Spence. She says it's beginning to fester." As he took on a pained expression, she shook her head. "I'm not asking you to practice medicine—I'm asking you to look. Maybe you can tell her what to do for it."

"That *is* practicing medicine."

"You're a surgeon. I'm not asking you to cut it off. Besides, I told her you'd give her some advice when they come to supper."

He suppressed a groan. "I don't mind feeding them, Laurie, but I'd rather not eat with six little heathens. I'm tired, and they'll be crawling over everything,"

"It'd be better if they weren't all boys," she conceded. "But there's only five—it'll be a couple of months before there's six."

"They're like a litter of mongrel puppies, fighting and yipping all the time."

"You don't even know them. All you see is them running around when we make camp."

"Everywhere. If they were mine, I'd tie 'em down."

"There's no room in that supply wagon. How does ham and greens with bread and jam sound?"

"Meager for nine people."

"Nine?"

"I can eat at least enough for two."

"Well, there's enough ham for that," she said. "I'll have to boil it before I fry it to get some of the salt out, and that'll make it swell up some. You don't mind, do you, Spence?"

"I guess not. I just hope they don't get Jessie tuned up for the night."

"They're more apt to tucker her out. After I feed her, she'll probably sleep like the dead until morning. And as cozy as it is back there, that's not exactly a bad thing, is it?" A slow, seductive smile curved her mouth as she added huskily, "I'll make the inconvenience of company up to you later."

"You're shameless—you know that, don't you?"

"But you love me."

"Very much. Heart, body, and soul."

"She's definitely going to sleep tonight," Laurie said. "Even if I have to wool her around a little myself."

As Spence washed up after tending to the mules for the night, he heard the shrieks and laughter that told him the Daniels' brood had found his wagon, and he wondered why the woman couldn't make them behave. Every night, two of them ran wild in camp while their mother hid out in a supply wagon with no thought to anybody else, and the collective sympathy was shrinking daily.

"Spence, you haven't actually met Abby, have you?" Laura said as he came around the side of the Conestoga. "Mrs. Daniels, this is my husband, Spencer Hardin."

"Right pleased," the woman murmured.

He was stunned. While he'd seen her around, he hadn't paid much attention, but she looked worse up close. The only real curve in her body was her big belly. Everything else just hung from her bony frame. And the thin, stringy hair didn't help the overall gauntness at all. Her nose had obviously been broken more than once, and when she smiled, two front teeth were missing. She walked slowly, obviously with pain. She was a young woman made old by poverty, too many children, and a brutal, loutish husband.

"Mrs. Daniels."

"She didn't bring Jimmy, Spence."

"He wasn't feelin' up to it, bless his soul—said he wasn't hungry," the woman explained apologetically.

"Maybe you ought to go take a look," Laura told Spence.

"Oh, no—he'll be all right. He ain't felt really good since his pa left. Maybe he's missin' him—I don't know. But you know how kids is, always under the weather with something."

"Laura says he hurt his leg."

"He did. Fell out o' the wagon day before yesterday mornin'. Got hisself cut up on a nail stickin' out."

"What did you treat it with? Turpentine?"

"Didn't have nuthin'—we just tied it up t' stop the bleedin', that's all. It ain't the first time he's hurt hisself, and it ain't going t' be the last. You get boys, you expect 'em to get all scarred up, you know. If it ain't him, it's one of the others—always something."

"But you washed it?" Laura asked quickly.

"I was goin' to, but I wanted to keep the blood from gettin' over ever'thing in the wagon, since most of it ain't mine, so I just covered the hole. Washed it this mornin', though, in the river, and it was festerin' some, so I put a piece of pork over it. That'll draw it out, you know."

"My husband's a doctor, Abby."

"That so? Then I reckon he knows that's about all t' do for something like that."

"Spence—"

The warning tone of his wife's voice kept him from saying what he really thought. "It depends on how deep the wound is," he explained diplomatically. "If he starts running a fever, or if the area feels hot and has red streaks, it could be serious. If it's swollen or discolored, I'd be worried, too. There are several things that can happen to a puncture wound—tetanus, blood poisoning, gangrene, cholera, to name a few—and they're all serious. You can wash with river water if you boil it, but otherwise with the dirt and animal dung in it, you'll run the risk of introducing infectious material into the body."

"He ain't drinkin' it," Abigail Daniels hastened to assure him. "We just been washin' with it."

"Spence will look at Jimmy's leg," Laura volunteered.

"Ain't no need—it's just a hole. And I ain't got no money for a doctor, anyways."

"There's no charge, Mrs. Daniels," Spence found himself telling her. "When you go back after supper, I'll send you some medicine to put on the wound, but it's a little late now—there's already been close to sixty hours for anything to incubate."

"It ain't got that—it's just a little pussy, that's all."

"Anyway, I want you to wash the area thoroughly with boiled water as hot as he can stand it, then put two teaspoons of salt into a cup of hot water and make a compress with it. Keep it hot, and keep it on the wound at least half an hour, and it'll help draw the pus out better than pork. And burn that piece of meat before you throw it out, or somebody's dog's apt to get sick from eating it."

"That hole's just got to bust open, then it'll heal," the woman insisted.

"Not if a deep infection is present. When you get back, I want you to light a lantern and hold it close enough to get a good look at the wound. If any of those conditions I mentioned—in dry gangrene, the area will be dark and without feeling, and the skin above it will be red; in the wet form, it will look the same, but there will be blisters on it, and it'll stink to high heaven; in blood poisoning, there'll be red streaks down the limb, and it will feel hot."

"What about the other two—cholera and that other thing you mentioned?"

"Tetanus—you probably call it lockjaw. It's too early to tell yet. I'd say if he develops a bad stomach ache with a fever within the next week, he'll be coming down with typhoid or cholera. Lockjaw takes a little longer to manifest itself—usually about two weeks, sometimes more. He'll have a stiff neck and jaw, fever, and joint pain, followed by an inability to talk, a drawing of the body backwards, and light will cause convulsions."

"Spence, you're scaring her," Laura protested.

"I'm just telling her what she needs to look out for."

"Where did you learn all this stuff?" the woman asked, awed.

"Medical school and the army."

"He graduated from one of the finest institutions in the country, Abby—and he was the best surgeon in the whole Confederate Army," Laura told her proudly.

"You don't say," Mrs. Daniels murmured, looking at him with new interest. "And we was all thinkin' he was just a plain mister. I'll have to tell it around."

"I'd rather you didn't. I'm not practicing right now," Spence declared flatly. "I'm giving myself time to discover if I want to do it anymore."

"He cut off thousands of legs, Abby, and he had one of the highest recovery rates recorded. He just got a little sick of it." But as Laura explained the situation, she realized that he'd cracked the door a smidgeon. "Four years of seeing nothing but dead or broken bodies was hard for a man who cared. He sees all those dead men, but he forgets the thousands who went home alive because of him."

"Laura—"

"Well, it's the truth."

"Anyway," he said, returning to the matter at hand, "if any of those conditions I mentioned exist, you'll need to bring him over here so I can take a look at him. Do you want me to repeat the symptoms again?"

"I understand what you said."

"Good."

"Jimmy's going to be all right. He's my sweet boy—makes me wish I had a dozen of him. Nate and Frankie's the wild ones, you know. Jack's too little to be much trouble, and the baby's teething right now. I guess you could say I got my hands full. But I'm better off without Matt, I keep tellin' myself. I just wish he hadn't took hisself off with all the money, that's all. It's gettin' hard to feed my boys."

"Mmm—you smell good," he murmured, nuzzling Laura's neck while his hands explored her body beneath the covers.

"It's that French perfume—when we're doing this, I close my eyes and think I'm somewhere else instead of in a wagon."

"As long as you don't think you're with anyone else." He found the hem of her nightgown and began easing it up. "Someday, Mrs. Hardin, we're going to be enjoying ourselves in the finest hotel in San Francisco."

"I wouldn't have anybody else, Spence." Twining her arms around his neck, she pulled his head down for her kiss.

"I's got to find the doc! I's got to find the doc! Ma says he's over here somewheres, but I ain't findin' 'im!"

A child's high-pitched, agitated voice penetrated the cocoon of intimacy, breaking its spell. "What the hell—?" Spence muttered. "It's too late for a kid to be out."

Pulling her nightgown down, Laura sat up. "You're the only doc around, Spence. He's got to be screaming for you."

"The hell he is."

Somebody stuck a head out of another wagon, cursing. "Get out of here, you goddammed little varmint—we ain't got no doc!"

"I gotta fetch 'im! I just gotta! It's Jimmy, and he's taken bad!"

"I'll find your bag," Laura murmured, rolling from the feather mattress. Calling through the hole in the gathered canvas, she shouted, "He's in here! He'll be right out!"

Spence sat still for a moment, taking several deep breaths. He didn't want to do this, he told himself. If the wound was making the boy sick, it was going to be bad, all right. He just didn't want to face any more sickness and death.

Holding his bag in one hand, Laura laid the other on his shoulder. "Spence, you've got to—you said you would."

"I don't have to do anything, Laura! If it's the wound, the stupid woman's already killed him! What am I supposed to do?—sit there and watch a kid die?"

"You told her—"

"I know, but the way she was talking, it was nothing—she didn't even care enough to clean it up! Now she wants me to make it right—and I'll bet she never even put the carbolic acid I sent with her on it!"

"It could be something else. You don't know what she's thinking now."

"She's thinking I'll fix him up!"

"Spence—"

The small boy crawled through the hole, sobbing. "My ma's skeered, mister! Jimmy's out of his head, and he ain't feelin' nuthin'! She's a-cryin', sayin' he's a-dyin'!"

"Did she put the medicine my husband gave her on his leg?" Laura asked the child.

"She couldn't right away, 'cause—"

"I told you she didn't," Spence muttered.

" 'Cause Billy was a-crying, mister! He's yallerin' his head off, too, 'cause his teeth ain't wantin' to come in, an' that sugar titty ain't doin' 'im no good. Ma's got to keep 'im quiet, else folks is gonna turn 'er out. But she just got around to gettin' everything quiet, so's she could help Jimmy."

"You're Nate, aren't you?" Laura asked gently. Pulling the scruffy kid onto her lap, she wrapped her arms around him. "It's got to be hard bein' the man of the family," she added softly, soothing him. "Spence, where's the horehound candy? Nate needs a piece to calm him down."

He felt as though the walls of a prison were closing in on him, that he was trapped. "I don't know— under the seat, I think." Heaving himself to his feet reluctantly, he reached for the leather bag. It seemed as though it had the weight of the world in it.

"Ma ain't got nobody else," the child whispered,

resting his head on Laura's breast. "I gotta be strong, she says, 'cause I's the oldest one."

"How old are you, Nate?" she asked, leaning as far as she could to reach under the seat. Holding him with one arm, she managed to open the sack with the other. "I've got something little boys like right here. If you suck on it, it'll make you feel better."

"I's five." As he popped a piece into his mouth, he looked up at her. "Kin I take some to m' brothers?"

"It'll make it easier for her to keep them quiet, Spence."

"Yeah. Well, come on, Nate—you'll have to show me where we're going. And don't give any candy to the baby, or he's apt to choke."

As he walked across the dark and silent camp with Nate Daniels's small hand in his, Spence almost wanted to cry himself. Five was too young for a kid to be bearing such a burden. Hell, he didn't want to bear it himself.

"What seems to be the matter with Jimmy?" he asked finally.

"He cain't feel nuthin' in his leg—when Ma took the hot water to it, he didn't cry or nuthin'. And the stuff you give 'er for 'im—she said it was supposed to burn, but it didn't do nuthin' to 'im neither."

"I see."

"That's bad, ain't it?"

"Well, it might be."

"He gets well, I'm givin' 'im this whole bag of candy," Nate decided. "He's always been a mite sickly long as I 'member, but he ain't a bad brother, mister."

"How old is he?"

"He ain't but four."

Laura had told him that, Spence recalled now. "Four," he repeated.

"You got any boys?"

"One. He's four, too."

"Oh."

He sounded downcast, forcing Spence to ask, "Why'd you say that?"

"Ma says she cain't feed all of us. I guess she's fixin' to give us away."

"She won't do that."

"I was thinkin' if you wasn't havin' no boys, you might could take Jimmy, seein' as he's the one that's gettin' sick mostly, and you bein' a doctor man. I'd miss 'im, but Ma cain't take care of him proper, and ain't nobody gonna want 'im like he is."

"She's not going to give any of you away," Spence consoled the boy. "Mas don't do things like that."

"She cain't help it. We ain't eatin' most times. And it ain't gettin' no better, 'cause Pa ain't comin' home. He done busted her up for the last time, and he ain't comin' crawlin' back, even if she's got to starve, she says."

To Spence's way of thinking, that was a damned sordid situation for Abby Daniels to be discussing with a child. As hard as things had been for his own mother before she married Bingham, she'd never let on to him. It had taken him years to realize it for himself.

"I ain't goin' to no orphan place," the kid went on. "And when I get growed up big enough to work, I'm gettin' back any of us that does." Nate stopped in his tracks. "We been talkin' till I went plumb past it—that's Ma's wagon over there. Well, it ain't ours," he conceded. "But we got to live in it."

"It's easy to miss in the dark."

"She ain't lightin' the lantern agin till I get you here, 'cause we ain't got enough kerosene neither. I got 'im, Ma!" he yelled, climbing onto one of the supply wagons.

"Let me get the light on, or he's liable to fall. There—you kin bring 'im in now."

The wagon was a mess. Boxes of supplies came up above the canvas, leaving little room for six people to live, but the Daniels woman had covered the flattest area with a ragged blanket and called it bed for the entire brood. The only things he saw that could pass for her belongings were two gunnysacks stuffed with what looked to be clothes. An Indian in a teepee was a lot better off than this.

Her haggard face looked up at him as Spence climbed over the boxes barring the entrance. "Well, you was right, Dr. Hardin, and I was just dead wrong," were her first words to him. "It ain't just a hole anymore. His whole laig's swelled up, clear above his knee bone—I had to take a knife to his pants just to get a look at it. Guess I ain't paid enough attention to know how bad it was gettin'."

"I'll have to have some room."

"Nate, you and Frankie take Jack outside."

"Ma, I hain't got no britches on," a small boy protested.

"You hush that, Frankie. I'll be comin' out with the blanket when I bring Billy out. He's last, 'cause I don't want 'im catchin' cold while he's teethin', or ain't nobody gettin' no sleep. We'll wrap up together, and nobody's goin' to know if you're nekked or not."

Spence waited until they were all outside before he opened his bag. He was probably going to need help, but there wasn't room for all those kids, and the last thing he wanted was a cranky baby screaming in his ear. He had to crawl to reach the sick child, and even then, he couldn't stand up.

"Jimmy?" he said gently, touching the boy's face. It was hot enough to burn him. "Jimmy, it's Dr. Hardin. Your mama wanted me to look at that leg."

The little boy's fever-dulled eyes fluttered open. "It ain't there."

A chill ran down Spence's spine. "Yes, it is," he said, touching it, finding the skin hot and tight. "See?"

"It ain't hurtin' no more."

Holding the lantern closer, Spence looked down, and his gorge rose in his throat. The boy was so thin his eyes looked huge in a small, pinched face, but his injured leg was as big as Spence's forearm. From the knee down, there were about two inches of hot, red flesh, but below the zone of demarcation, the skin ranged from slate gray to black. The wound itself stunk like something rotten. The June warmth had helped the infection along.

"How bad is it?" Abigail Daniels asked from outside.

"Damned bad." Closing his eyes for a minute, he summoned the strength to break the news to her. "It's gangrene."

"I was afeard of that once I seen it tonight. I guess he's goin' to die, ain't he?" There was a fatalistic sadness in her voice—no anger, just acceptance. "It's my fault," she added, sighing. "I wish t' God, I'da paid more attention, but I didn't."

He wasn't going to disagree with her. "Send Nate for my wife," was all he could say. "Have him tell her to ask Mrs. Wilson to look after Jessie."

"I kin look after her."

Nearly too angry for words, he wasn't about to let her touch his daughter. "You've got enough to take care of," he answered curtly. "I just want Mrs. Hardin here right now."

The wait seemed like an eternity, but he knew it wasn't. She had to dress, get Jessie up, and wake Mrs. Wilson before she could come. But he wanted to talk to her before he decided what he'd do, and that made the minutes pass slowly.

Finally, he heard her tell Nate, "You're such a good young man," and he wanted to cry. A boy of five needed to be a child.

"Spence, what's the matter?" she asked, climbing into the wagon. "Nate said you wanted me, and Abby isn't saying anything."

"Because she knows she killed her son."

"*What?*" she fairly screeched. "He's dead?"

"Not yet."

Crawling over crates and boxes, she managed to get to him. Her eyes found the child's face first. "Oh, Jimmy—how you must hurt," she whispered, smoothing dirty hair back from his forehead. Kneeling beside the little boy, she murmured soothingly, "It's going to be all right, honey—you don't listen to anybody who says it isn't. Spence is going to do his best to make you better." Looking up at her husband, she said, "He's burning up."

"I don't know that Spence can make him better," he said wearily. "Laura, it's gangrene. You can see the demarcation clearly. He can't feel anything below it because the tissue's died. And by now, he's probably got blood poisoning to go with it."

"You can't say that in front of him—he's got to fight." Tears welled in her eyes, and her throat was so tight she could scarce breathe. She had to force herself to look at the child's leg. "Good God!" she gasped before she gagged. When she finally managed to swallow, she whispered, "But how could this happen so quickly?"

"There are a lot of reasons, but two are pretty obvious—the wound was dirty, and it's summer."

"Yes, but—" She had to bite her lip to keep from crying. "He's just four, Spence."

"Yeah." His palm caressed the boy's forehead, absorbing the burning heat. "I'll need chloroform." As she looked up, he took another deep breath, then nodded. "I'm going to amputate, Laura—it's the only chance he's got, and even then it may not be enough. If the poison's in his blood, everything's going to fail. She lied to you, Laura—I don't know why, but she lied to you."

"What?"

"This wound's more than sixty hours old. Maybe she didn't want anybody to know she hadn't done anything for it. I'd say this leg started swelling up day before yesterday instead of today. It's got to come off."

"Oh, Spence—I'm so sorry—so very sorry."

"I need chloroform, Laura, and I don't have any. If I have to do it without putting him out, as bad as he is, the shock's going to kill him."

"I don't want him to hear that."

"He's too sick for it to sink in. He told me the leg was gone."

"I don't know where to find any chloroform—it's not anything a body'd be carrying with him."

"Ask around. If we can't get that, we'll have to use something, and whiskey's not much of an answer. As small as he is, enough to put him out will give him alcohol poisoning."

"I'll see what I can find. You want his mother in here, don't you?"

"No. I want you here to help me. I want you to see what it's like, and maybe you'll understand why I can't do it anymore."

The very thought made her sick, but she nodded. "I'll do what I can for you. But Abby—"

"I don't want to look at that woman again in this life."

"You've got to tell her."

"I'm going to let you do it. I already told her it was gangrene, and I don't think she cared. All she could say was she probably should've paid more attention when it happened."

"I don't know what to say to her."

"I had to say it a thousand times to somebody— you can say it once."

"All right. I'll be back as soon as I can. Do you need anything else?"

"Not for this. Ask her to boil water, if it's not too much trouble."

"You're being hard on her, Spence."

"Any woman who tells her kids she's giving them away doesn't deserve to have any. I don't care how poor she is, she had no right to say something like that to Nate. And don't get started on that, Laura, because I don't want to even talk about it. I'm just damned mad."

Leaning his head against the cold metal canopy frame, he closed his eyes, thinking God had led him to the promised land, only to show him hell again. He could hear Laura outside, explaining, "If the leg doesn't come off, he's going to die, Abby. He may, anyway. Why didn't you say something sooner, when Spence could have done something else?"

"It happened like I told it," the woman maintained stubbornly. "Just like I told it."

"But not when you said it did."

"To tell the truth, I didn't know when it happened. I'd been feeling bad, and Nate was looking after the kids. It was him that tied it up, I guess."

"Oh, no, you don't, Abigail Daniels! You're not shifting responsibility to a five-year-old child!" Laura told her hotly. "It's just not right, and you know it. I don't care how bad things are for you; God gave you those kids to raise, and you're supposed to do it."

"It ain't like that. You just don't know what it's like bein' poor like me."

"I've probably been poorer than you," Laura snapped. "But rather than dispute over that, I've got to find some chloroform so that man in there can do something he despises, and it's because you didn't take care of that child! You're going to have a boy hobbling around on one leg, Abby—and if you don't want him, I do!"

It took a few moments for the words to sink into Spence's consciousness. What the hell was she talking about? He had enough on his plate without adding to it.

"I want my boy, Mrs. Hardin! I want all of 'em—but you tell me how I'm supposed to feed 'em!" Abigail shouted after Laura. "Does God want me to watch 'em starve?"

He couldn't hear his wife's answer. He straightened up and shrugged his shoulders, trying to ease the tension in them, before he crawled closer to Jimmy Daniels. Unable to do anything else at the moment, he lay down next to the boy and held the hot little body, offering what comfort he could.

He must've dozed, because the next thing he knew, Laura was telling him, "Aside from whiskey, all I could find was some peyote."

"Peyote?" he mumbled, rousing.

Behind her, the half-breed Crow guide hovered. "Cheyenne get peyote from Comanche. Peyote heap good medicine."

"He can talk, Spence. He says it comes from a cactus."

"I know what it is."

"Peyote make dream."

"I don't think he had much contact with the white side of his family," Laura offered. "But he can speak, and he thinks the stuff will help."

"You don't make much of an interpreter." Opening his formulary, Spence thumbed through the index. He probably wouldn't find it under peyote. If it was in here anywhere, it'd be listed in Latin. "Well, I'll be damned," he said softly. " '*Mescal. A potent intoxicant, capable of producing inebriation and hallucinations.*' I don't have any idea of a dosage, but I'm willing to give it a try. God knows I don't have much else to use. I'll have to have a medium for delivery, and I'll have to give a little at a time until I know what its effect is."

In the end, he used a mixture of medicinal alcohol and water, steeping the crushed buttons in it, reasoning it was better than using mineral oil. He didn't want any oil getting into the kid's lungs if he vomited the peyote up.

Since the kid was almost unconscious anyway, he used the mixture sparingly. When he finally took his surgical kit from the bag and unrolled it, Laura flinched. Closing his eyes briefly, Spence prayed silently, then turned his attention to the boy's leg. "I want you to get his arms," he told her. "I'm going to tourniquet the leg, and then I'll hold my end down. If he jerks, hold on. I want a clean incision before I start sawing."

Jimmy Daniels didn't respond when the catlin knife cut through his skin. White-faced, Laura watched from above the child as Spence pulled back the skin just above the knee, then sliced open the muscle to expose the bone, to scrape it clean where he intended to saw. The sound of the surgical saw cutting through bone made her almost sick, but at least it didn't last long. It seemed as if he'd just gotten started when he was tying off blood vessels with silk thread. He filed the bone stump nearly smooth, then pulled the skin flap over it and closed it with neat stitches. When he finally sat back on his heels, she realized her dress was wet with her own sweat.

"That's it," he said. "I'll need to dispose of the severed limb and clean up some of the mess, but whether he pulls through or not, it's not going to be gangrene that kills him. I got all of it off."

"Then he'll make it."

"Not necessarily. There's still the danger of blood poisoning, but I'd say his chances are considerably improved right now." Looking across the still little body, he met her eyes for a moment. They were brimming with tears. "It's all right," he said quietly. "You need to go on and get Jessie. She doesn't need to be up all night."

"What about you?"

"I'm going to stay here for a while and see what I can do about his fever. It'll be a couple of hours before I can expect any kind of improvement, anyway, but I'll feel better if I can get his temperature down."

"Thank you," she said quietly.

"You're welcome. I'll try not to wake you when I climb into bed."

He sat with Jimmy Daniels most of the night, and it wasn't until the gray light of dawn crept through the open canvas that he decided it was safe to leave. While the boy hadn't regained consciousness, his fever had come down enough for him to rest peacefully, and the bleeding was now minimal.

Bone-tired, he crawled into the back of the Conestoga and crept on his hands and knees, trying to keep from waking Laura or the baby. They were asleep together, Laura's body curved around Jessie's. He didn't move for a moment; he just stared at their faces, thinking they had to be the two most beautiful females in the world. Rather than disturb them, he decided to sit up a while longer. She'd have to drive while he slept later.

As he was about to crawl back out, he felt something crackle under one knee, and he realized he was crushing her journal. Taking it with him to smooth the pages out, he tried to make out the words of her last entry, but it was still too dark. Curious as to what she'd written in all those pages, he found the lantern and lit it.

June 19, 1866. Beneath the date, she'd chronicled the usual things, all the way down to a description of supper. But it was the last paragraph that caught his attention.

> Tonight, my husband did the most remarkable thing I've ever seen. He saved the life of a four-year-old boy by removing a gangrenous leg with such precision that I felt as if I were watching a great artist at work. He has as much God-given talent for surgery as Michelangelo for art. While he believes heroes are made on the battlefields of this life, he does not realize he is one himself. Great generals send men into battle to die; Spencer Hardin repairs broken and diseased bodies, giving many of the fallen a chance to go home. Surely God did not give him this gift if He did not mean for him to use it as he did tonight.

Somehow all of her spoken words on the subject had not moved him, but there was no denying the effect of the lines she'd written on this page. They'd never been meant for his eyes, something that made them even more powerful, because he knew they'd been written from her heart.

As the stars faded into the grayness above the rich, warm hues of dawn, he closed the book and crept to bed, where he eased his body onto the mattress behind hers and reached his arm around her to hold her close. "I love you," he whispered.

She stirred, then turned over to face him. "Are you all right?"

"Yes. I just read your journal."

"Oh. I wasn't writing it for you to find, but it's the truth, anyway. I wanted Jessie and Josh to know the kind of man you are." She yawned sleepily, then asked, "What time is it, anyway?"

"Sun's coming up."

"How is Jimmy?"

"It's too soon to tell, but I'm hoping he'll make it. I cut it high enough to get all of the gangrene, and his fever was down some by the time I left. Not normal, but down." Brushing her tangled hair with his fingertips, he murmured, "Where did you learn to write like that?"

"Mama. But she was better at it. She didn't have much education either, but she had a way with words."

Rolling onto his back, he stared up at the metal supporting the canvas. "I feel pretty good about his chances. I liked what you said to his mother, too."

"I was just plain mad at her, Spence. It's one thing to make a mistake, but when it's made worse by not admitting it, that's something I can't excuse. When I saw that leg, I was sick to my stomach. I don't know how you did it—I honestly don't."

"It was a pretty clean cut," he admitted. "But I ought to be good at it—God knows, I've had enough practice."

"It's more than practice. Whether you want to admit it or not, it's a gift."

"That's what you wrote in your journal."

"Well, it is."

"Michelangelo, huh?"

"Well, he was the first painter who came to my mind. I could just as easily have said da Vinci."

"Now *that* would have been the ultimate compliment," he murmured.

"If my words impressed you so much, what are you going to do about them?"

"I don't know—maybe read your mother's journals. I'd like to know where you come up with some of the things you say. I figure maybe there's something in them that'll tell me."

"I don't think like her, Spence—Mama was more practical than I am."

"Now that's impossible. You don't have a foolish notion in that steel-trap mind of yours."

"But you're going to think it over, aren't you? You know I wrote the truth."

"I'm going to think it over, but I can't promise anything. All I know is I'm glad I knew what to do. I looked at him, and I thought he could've been Josh."

"They're both four."

"If I didn't think I'd be biting off a lot of trouble, I'd take them, you know."

"Who?"

"Nate and Jimmy."

"Then who'd take care of Frankie?"

"Laura, I'm not opening an orphanage. You know, you're just like Bingham—every stray dog that came to Willowood wound up staying."

"Well, maybe if Abby had some money, she'd do better."

"Maybe. If I've got anything left by the time we get to Sacramento, I'm giving it to her," he decided. "God, I'm tired."

"I'm not—not since you woke me up." Turning to face him, she ran a fingertip along the dark shadow on his jaw. "There's something real masculine about a man right before he shaves," she murmured.

"The baby's going to wake up."

Her fingertip moved to tickle his ear. "Mrs. Wilson couldn't get her settled down, so I just finished feeding her less than an hour ago, and she took a lot of milk. But—I guess if you're tired, I might as well get up."

"Not on your life—you know where all that teasing leads, don't you?" he whispered, rolling her onto her back. "I don't like teases who don't pay up, Mrs. Hardin."

Her arms reached for his neck. "Well, you don't have to worry," she assured him softly. "I'm a woman who likes to settle things right."

San Francisco: July 10, 1866

"Well, it's really something, isn't it? I think the water's even prettier out here than at home," Laura observed.

Standing on the observation hill, Spence followed her gaze, taking in the wide expanse of the bay, then the city below. "It's about as pretty a place as I've seen," he agreed. As he hoisted Jessie to sit on his shoulders, she grabbed his hair and chortled. "What do you think from up there, Jess? Do you want to settle in for a while?"

"She wants to be anywhere up high. But I thought you'd want to go back to Georgia."

"I don't know as I'd want to spend another day in a damned wagon, let alone cross the country again. But if you've got your heart set on someplace else, I'm willing to listen."

"We just got here," she pointed out. "We don't know anything about San Francisco except that it's big and the bay's beautiful. What are you going to do if Josh isn't here?"

"I don't know," he answered, sobering. "Keep looking, I guess. If he's not here, I'm at a dead end, unless I want to hire Pinkerton again." Looking out over the water to where the azure sky met the bay, he felt almost at peace. All he needed to complete his life was his son. "Come on," he said, putting an arm around Laura's shoulders. "We've got to find a place to stay for the night. When we get up tomorrow, we'll start looking for Ross."

"All right."

"You know, you're looking a little peaked these days," he noted. "I don't think living in that wagon suited you."

She realized he'd given her the opportunity if she wanted to take it. Drawing a deep breath, she let it go. "It's not the wagon—it's the baby."

"She'll get over teething soon enough, and then—" He stopped. "That's not what you meant, is it?"

"No."

"How long have you known?"

"You could sound happier about it, you know," she murmured wryly.

"That's not what I asked."

"About a month. I guess you just didn't notice I haven't come around twice now."

He sucked in his breath and held it for a moment. Looking up at the bright blue sky, he sighed heavily. "I'd be a lot happier if I weren't afraid, Laura. I don't think I could stand losing you."

"I'll be all right."

"That's your answer to everything," he said almost angrily. "Ever since I met you, you've been telling me you'll be all right."

"Well, I have been. Being a doctor, you ought to have expected this, anyway. It's not like we haven't been enjoying ourselves every night."

"I just didn't think it'd be this soon, that's all. It's not been that long since Jessie's birth." He frowned, then sighed. "You're happy about it, aren't you?"

"Yes."

"Then I guess I am, too."

"There's not much we can do about it now, Spence. You know, I didn't exactly expect this quite so soon either. Dr. Burton told me after what happened that first time, it'd take some work for me to conceive again. And I kind of believed him, because Jesse was home four months before it happened again."

"God, Laura . . . I just wish—"

"I'm a lot healthier now—I've been taking care of myself, mostly because you're taking anything that looks like work away from me. Look at these hands," she said, holding them out to him. "There's hardly a callus on them anymore. Pretty soon, you'll have 'em looking like they belong to a rich lady instead of a North Carolina country girl."

"Maybe they will, but—"

"Now don't you go sounding like Jesse. I wouldn't know what to do if I had a lot of time to waste. And if you've got any notion of working yourself to death for me, Spencer Hardin, I'll throw you a fit that'd put the likes of Lydia to shame. But I just wish you were wanting this baby," she told him, returning to the matter at hand. "It's not right not to."

She said it so wistfully that he realized he wasn't being fair to her. She obviously wanted him to be pleased, but it had just hit him like a bucket of cold water. "I want it very much, Laura—I'm just worried about you."

"I'm not about to leave you and Jessie alone. You're my life, Spence."

He couldn't talk about it anymore. Shoving his hands in his coat pockets, he stared at the tiny white-caps on the water. "The thing with Jimmy Daniels keeps coming back to me, Laura. I'm thinking about practicing medicine again, but if I do, we'll have to throw down roots somewhere. I'll have to affiliate with a hospital."

She stood very still. "I want that very much, but I want you to be sure you're doing it for you and not me. It's a calling like preaching—you've got to have your heart in it."

"I'm giving it a lot of thought. The war taught me I can't fix everything, and it was a hard lesson. But now that it's over, I won't have to be picking shrapnel out of shredded guts, and I won't have to be cutting off limbs I know I can save. I'm a man with a lot of pride, Laura. I felt like a hog butcher could've done what I was doing those last two years, and he could've probably done it easier, because he got to kill the hogs first. After every battle, I had to have three men holding down boys, a lot of them no older than Danny, and almost every one of them was screaming for me to stop while my saw was cutting through their bones."

"I couldn't have done it—I'd have cried myself to sleep every night," she said quietly.

"I felt helpless. It wasn't what I'd hoped to do, but I couldn't leave. It's hard to lose your belief in what you do."

"You didn't lose it in what you could do, Spence. You lost in what you had to do."

"Between the war and Lydia, I thought I was pretty much a failure. I want you to know I don't feel that way anymore. I wasn't a bad husband to her—I wasn't a husband at all. It took you to show me I'd never loved her, that she hadn't fallen out of love with me. As silly and sentimental as it is to say it, I had to find you to know what it was supposed to be like on both sides. You've taught me a lot about love and what it means to give of yourself."

"Oh, Spence," she whispered, swallowing hard.

"Please don't cry—I haven't quite learned to deal with that yet. I just wanted to tell you I've got my pride back. I didn't want to cut that little boy's leg off—hell, I didn't even want to look at it, and I probably would've turned my back on him if it hadn't been for you."

"Never. Once you saw it, you'd have done exactly what you did."

"I wouldn't have gone to that wagon. But when you started asking that woman questions, I didn't like her answers. And when I did see the leg, I knew Jimmy Daniels couldn't keep it and live. I still didn't want to do it. That's why I had to come to help. I figured if you saw what it was I do best, you'd be about as sick of it as I was."

"Spence, I nearly threw up my supper."

"But that didn't stop you from doing what you could. That's what counts, Laura. Seeing that kid on crutches, hopping around with that one leg, made me pretty proud of what I'd done. He was alive, and if that woman will just take care of him the rest of the way, he's going to grow up."

"I can't help it, Spence—I'm going to cry again."

Sniffing hard, she tried to control the flow of tears. Finally, she was able to look up at him through her brimming eyes. "I'm sorry, but you're going to have to get used to it, because that's just the way I am. Whenever my heart's full, I'm going to cry. Whether I'm happy, sad, or mad, I'm going to cry."

Before he could say anything, Jessie started to bounce on his shoulders, kicking him and waving her chubby arms, while she chattered excitedly. "Chee—chee—Da—che!"

"Ouch, Jess! Watch it, or you'll fall off!" Reaching up, he caught both her legs. Instead of stopping, she grabbed his hair, then his eyes. "Jess, if you don't stop that, you'll have to come down, and I'll be handing you to Mama."

"It's the birds, Spence—one just flew past her. Here—let me take her before she kicks you to death."

"No, she's all right now." Adjusting the hand over his eye, he tried to look up at the blond, pink-faced baby. "You like the seabirds, huh? Well, the next time we're up here, we'll do some serious watching. We'll bring some bread, and maybe they'll get close enough to feed. But I'm not a horse, Jess—little girls aren't suppose to kick their daddy."

"You're going to be blind as well as black and blue," Laura said, reaching up to take her. Lifting her down, she nuzzled her daughter's face. "You're a little dickens—you know that, don't you? But Mama loves you, anyway," she added, settling the baby on her hip. "Actually, you're as good as gold," she conceded. "All you do is sleep and eat and play."

"She doesn't get a chance to do much else. She's

spoiled rotten. All she's got to do is open her mouth, and you're ready to feed her."

"And who is it who's always walking around with her on his shoulders? Who's always tossing her up into the air, making her giggle? And whose lap does she go to sleep on at night?" Laura asked archly. "Last night, I was reading, and when I looked over to see why it was so quiet, you were lying down with her on your chest, and both of you were asleep. If there's any spoiling done, you're as much to blame as I am."

"It's hard not to," he admitted. "I don't think I've ever seen a prettier baby."

"Neither have I, but I expect it's because she's ours." Shifting Jessie to the other hip, she murmured, "You go on and watch the birds all you want. Daddy and I'll just stand here and talk. Now, where were we, Spence."

"Talking about Jimmy Daniels, I think, and you were getting ready to blubber some more."

"Oh. I was going to say I was glad you've changed your mind," she recalled. "I've been telling my journal I wanted you to."

"I know. The entry I read probably helped tip the scale. And seeing the city from up here made me think about those roots. But it doesn't have to be here if you don't want it to be. Once we get Josh, we can go anywhere."

"I know of a little cabin in Nebraska," she said, teasing him.

"No, it's got to be somewhere where there's a good doctor to deliver the baby."

"You did all right—Jessie and I are both alive and kicking."

"Childbirth's too bloody to suit me."

"What a thing for a surgeon to say."

"Listen, when I'm cutting something, I know what I'm doing—I know what to tie off to stop the bleeding. That was one of the things that appeals to me about a big city like this, not to mention the fact it'd be fairly easy to establish a practice here."

"I don't have my heart set on anywhere else. I've already told you I'm not going back to North Carolina, unless I'm going back to flaunt my money, and so far I don't have any to flaunt."

"That reminds me of something else. I want you to consult with a publisher about your mother's journals."

"*What?*"

"There's a quality to them that transcends the writing, Laura. It may be a voice from the grave, but it's good advice for any woman. I don't think you'd have any trouble finding enough in them to make a damned good book. If you made any money, it'd be yours to use for anything you'd want. If you wanted to fill a library in the house, you could."

"Mama never thought about anything like that, you know," she said slowly. "I just cherished them because she wrote them to me. I could hear her voice when I read her words."

"I know. So could I. I just thought she deserved to be heard by a lot of women. She managed to raise a daughter with good values with it, and she wasn't even there. You could call it something like *Mrs. Lane's Advice to a Young Woman.* Or *A Guide for the*

Modern Woman—hell, I don't know. I just think there's some damned good points in it."

"There sure are. All those things that country woman knew . . . well, I almost couldn't believe everything myself, but there wasn't a recipe for anything that didn't work. I don't guess it would hurt to talk to somebody about it before I made up my mind."

"I think it's a good idea. Spence, she's getting fidgety, so I expect she'll be wanting to eat before long. Besides, I'm about ready for that fancy hotel you've been promising me all the way from Nebraska," she added, taking his arm. "It'll be real nice soaking in a bathtub tonight. I'm going to stay in there a solid hour; then I'm going to dab some of that French perfume where it counts, and I'm going to put that lawn nightgown on."

"It won't stay on long."

"I sure hope not, anyway."

As he walked beside her down the road from the observation hill, he took a deep breath of the sea breeze blowing in. Now that he'd made up his mind, it felt as though a heavy weight had been lifted from his shoulders. He almost had everything he'd ever wanted, and with Josh, the circle would be complete. San Francisco was a beautiful place, and if he found the right spot, he was going to build his wife the house she didn't think she wanted. Jesse just hadn't realized it was easier to convince a woman of something if she thought the idea was hers.

She came out of the water closet, pea green from losing her breakfast, to announce, "I'm going with you, Spence. I'm not about to let you face Ross Donnelly alone."

"I'm not looking for him today—I'm just going to the bank and a couple of other places. Since I don't know my way around the city yet, I don't know when I'll be in. I don't want to be dragging you around as sick as you are."

"I'm not sick—I'm having a baby. My stomach's going to settle in a little while, and I'll be fine."

He shook his head. "Besides, you need to stay with Jessie."

"Spence, I'm not a fool. I know why you're going to the bank, and it's because that's where you think you can find out about Donnelly."

"Laura—"

"You just don't want me there when you confront him, and I don't want you to go without me. I don't want you getting that temper of yours up enough to kill him."

"If there's any trouble, he'll be the one making it. All I want from him now is Josh."

"I don't want him killing you either. And according to this folder that came with the key, I can hire someone through the hotel to watch Jessie."

"Yeah, and I'd like to see somebody else try to feed her. And I'm going to be gone all day."

"If you're going to be civilized when you talk to him, it's not going to take all that long to ask him where the boy is," she argued reasonably. "For one thing, I don't want anybody to start anything. For another, if the news is bad, I want to hear it, too."

"Laura, I don't *want* you there. This is something between him and me, and even if I get an address, I'm not going there today, I told you. I've got something else to do first."

"A man doesn't spend a year coming thousands of miles to wait another day. It's not going to take me long to get ready," she promised.

"You can hardly stand up. You've had your head in the commode, puking up your guts, not ten minutes ago."

Exasperated, she snapped, "You don't listen to me! It's over for today—I'm not going to be sick again today! I said I wanted to go, and all you want to give me is some mumbo jumbo about why I can't! And I'm not having it, Spence! I've got an interest in this, too, and his name is Spencer Hardin!"

"Damn. Do you think I'm lying to you? Is that it? Well, I'm not. I've got some other business to attend to; then I'm going to visit this uncle of Ross's. He might not even tell me anything, but if he does, you'll be the first to know."

"I'm not sick, Spence."

"You could use a rest. We've spent damned near two months bumping around in that wagon, and we just got here day before yesterday. Look—put your feet up on the bed and get some rest this afternoon, order dinner up when the boy comes by, and have a nice quiet evening."

"Will you promise me you'll take me with you when you call on Mr. Donnelly? I don't want you going alone," she maintained stubbornly.

"Laura, I'm twenty-nine years old—I don't need a nursemaid. I managed to live twenty-eight of those years on my own."

"When I married you, I told you I wanted to be a partner, that I didn't want to be left out of anything. Well, I'm holding you to that now."

"I don't know what the hell you think you could do that I can't!" he snapped, his patience at an end. "Tell me that, will you? What are you going to do if he *does throw down on me?* Get in front of me?"

"I just don't feel right about this—I feel like something bad's going to happen."

"You're the one who's been telling me all along I'm going to find my son."

"I just don't feel right."

"You're damned right you don't—you're tired, and you're sick. We can discuss this later if you wish, but I'm telling you for the last time I don't intend to look Ross up today! I don't intend to kill or be killed, and I'll be damned if I know what's gotten into you!"

"Don't you raise your voice to me, Spencer Hardin. Screaming at me is about as bad as hitting me!"

"I've never hit you in my life, and I never will, but if you start screaming at me, then I'm damned sure going to yell back!" Stopping, he ran his fingers through his hair, trying to make some order of his mind. "Look—you don't have to stay here in this room if you don't want to. Take the baby and go shopping. Buy yourself something pretty. If you don't want to take her out, go ahead and hire someone to watch her. I don't care if you have yourself a little outing, as long as you can take care of Jessie."

"I never had the money to shop, Spence. I wouldn't know how," she said evenly.

"If that's all that's stopping you, here's some money." Opening his wallet, he pulled out several banknotes. "There's fifty dollars there, Laura—that ought to buy you something nice. Spend it on your-

self, or on Jessie if you want. I don't want to see a
dime of it back."

"I couldn't spend fifty dollars if my life depended
on it."

"Well, try!" he snapped. Shoving his wallet into
his pocket, he headed for the door. "I'll be back
sometime tonight."

She sat on the bed, shaking, as he slammed the
door. She hadn't wanted to argue with him. She'd
just wanted to go, and she couldn't see anything un-
reasonable in that. Fighting tears, she slid off the bed
and walked to the washstand to pour water into the
fancy porcelain bowl. Using the pretty lilac soap, she
washed her face, then stared in the mirror. Now that
he'd got her to someplace where she didn't show to
advantage, he was probably ashamed of her. He
didn't want Ross Donnelly seeing how he'd lowered
himself by marrying somebody who couldn't hold a
candle to the rich, beautiful Lydia. She was all right
for bed, but not good enough to be seen on his arm.

She caught herself. He just wasn't that kind of
man. Still, as she looked at her face, she could see a
catalog of faults. Her hair was brown. Her eyes were
brown. If anybody looked close enough, they'd see
that fine smattering of freckles on the bridge of her
nose. And her hair was a fright—there hadn't been
any other woman in the hotel lobby who had her
hair wadded up in the back like hers. A style like
that required a perfect face, and she didn't have one.

She didn't talk right, she didn't look right, and she
just felt plain. She wouldn't even get her milk dried
up from Jessie before the next baby came. And her
cotton dress looked like what it had been—a calico

flour sack. The only crinoline she owned was as limp as a dead chicken's neck, and everyone else had skirts as wide as the door. It was a wonder they'd let her into a place like this.

But that wasn't what ailed Spence. She looked the same way when he'd met her and when he'd married her. He just didn't want her to hear what he said to Ross Donnelly. It was a private matter between them, and he'd made it plain that it didn't have anything to do with her. No, she might be a frump, but he loved his frump just fine.

Somewhat relieved, she pulled the pins from her hair and let the knot at her neck tumble over her shoulders. It wasn't bad-looking hair—it was just not fashionable.

A knock sounded at the door, and for a moment, she dared to think he'd come back. Opening it hastily, she faced a uniformed young man, who looked more like a hussar than someone who worked in a hotel.

"Oh . . . I'm sorry. I thought you were my husband."

A lopsided grin spread across his face as he looked at her streaming hair. "Makes me kinda wish I was, but I'm just supposed to find out if you wanted supper sent up." Producing a blue leather folder stamped in gold, he handed it to her. "You can order anything on the menu, ma'am."

The cheapest thing on it cost enough to feed a whole family in North Carolina for a week, but she didn't want to seem any more countrified than she looked. "Yes, of course. I'm not much for duck or pheasant," she murmured to herself, reading down the column. "What would you recommend?"

"They don't let me eat any of it, but the crab in cream seems pretty popular."

"I'll take it."

"And the wine?" he asked, pencil poised.

"My husband usually takes care of such things," she fibbed. "I'll take whatever's being ordered with the crab."

"There are several choices being picked."

"All right, then. I'm not all that choosy about what I drink, so just pick one for me."

"And after dinner?"

"Dessert."

"Which one?" Sensing that she wasn't familiar with most of the names, he offered, "The ices are quite popular this time of year. There's a peach with raspberry sauce."

"That sounds appealing."

"Very good, ma'am. Supper will be up promptly at thirty minutes after eight."

She'd starve by then. "I'll be looking for it." As he turned to leave, she dared to say, "I was planning to shop a little this afternoon, but I hate to take the baby out while she's teething."

"I'll tell them at the desk to send someone up whenever you wish."

"How much?"

"It will be billed with the room."

"One-thirty," she decided. "I don't suppose there's any place that does hair around here, is there?"

"There's a desk off the lobby where arrangements can be made for just about everything you'd want—

theater, ballet, a carriage to take you anywhere from a shop to the park on the hill. Just tell them where you want to go, and they'll fix you right up. If you don't know the city, they can direct you to which stores carry what."

"And they'll know where I can get my hair fixed?"

"Yes."

"I believe I'll go down and visit with them."

It proved to be even easier than he'd said. While she sat in a little padded chair, the hotel sent messengers out to confirm appointments with a hairdresser nearby and a dressmaker several blocks away. Within the hour, she was in a handsome conveyance, making her way around the city, gawking at everything until it was time to go to the dressmaker. While there were places selling ready-to-wear clothing, the woman at the hotel had insisted the garments were of the poorest quality "suitable only for menials." Surely, a dressmaker would have a variety of prices as well as styles.

She felt like a fish out of water, but if Spence did set up practice here, she needed to learn where things were. And while it seemed like an extravagance, he *had* said he didn't want any of that fifty dollars back, she reminded herself. And if she went to the proper places, she was fairly certain she wouldn't be tricked out like a freak.

Feeling quite elegant, she ate her supper in her new wrapper with her feet propped up on a footstool, and she couldn't complain about a thing except the cost of the wine, which was more expensive than the whole meal. Having paid for it, she intended to drink it, whether she liked the taste or not.

She was on her fourth glass when Spence let himself in the door. Feeling somewhat sheepish for his earlier outburst, he'd brought her a gold locket on his way back from the bank. Depositing the key in his coat pocket, he turned around.

"Good God—what happened to your hair?"

"You don't like it."

She looked crestfallen. Recovering, he told her, "I didn't say that at all—I just wasn't prepared for the change, that's all. Actually, once the shock passes, it's quite becoming," he said. "I'm just not used to you with all those curls."

"But you're sure you like it?"

"You look like a fashion plate," he assured her.

"Good, because it took two hours for her to get it this way. I didn't think she was ever going to be done with all the curling and crimping."

"Can you do that yourself?"

"I don't know, but I'm sure going to try. I'm not about to spend two dollars getting somebody else to put it up for me."

"Actually, that doesn't sound too bad."

"Spence, do you have money I don't know about?" she asked suspiciously. "You gave me fifty dollars to spend on myself, and everything in this place comes dear. We must be paying a fortune to stay here. And it doesn't make sense, considering you worked the rep track in Nebraska because you needed money."

"I had a bank draft on me that I couldn't cash anywhere out there. I took it in with me today."

"And I suppose we're rich, and you forgot to tell me?"

"We've got some money, Laurie. Bingham and his spinster sister inherited equal shares of the plantation, and since he didn't have any children of his own, I came into his share when he died. Unlike my stepfather, Aunt Claire wasn't much of a patriot, and when she saw the war coming, she managed to convert her money to gold and bury it under a privy, pretty certain that nobody would want to dig it up. She bought Bingham's half from me and paid cash for it."

"But you've been watching your money ever since I've known you."

"I didn't want to carry all of it on me. I put some of it in the bank at Macon, and had the banker give me the rest in a demand draft and cash. We've been living on the cash."

"You still should've told me. A husband and wife shouldn't have secrets from each other."

"Would it have made any difference? I figured if you'd marry a poor man, you wouldn't mind discovering he had a little stash of money somewhere. And to tell the truth, I hadn't thought much about it myself until we had to store everything yesterday. Besides, what if I'd said I had a draft, and then when I went to the bank out here, they wouldn't honor it. The way things are down home now, there's no telling what shape the bank there is in. You'd have felt pretty damned cheated if you thought we had money when we didn't."

"Well, I spent the fifty dollars today, so I guess it's good they honored it."

"Good—it's about time you spent something on yourself. I spent something on you, too—I brought you a little present."

"Oh now, Spence—"

"Well, I knew we'd both said some things we didn't mean, and I thought maybe I ought to make up for my part. I knew you didn't feel well, and I should've just gone on." Reaching inside his coat, he drew out the jeweler's packet. "It was going to be a nice wedding ring, but I got to thinking you might want to pick that out yourself."

"You didn't need to. I actually spent a little more than what you left me," she confessed. "When I had it put on the hotel bill, I didn't know this wine was going to cost ten dollars a bottle. I could've drunk water just fine."

"Ten dollars isn't much, Laura. I'd have been pretty peevish if you'd said you'd run up hundreds of dollars on me without talking about it, but a bottle of wine isn't going to break us."

"I don't suppose you'd care to tell me what we've got in the bank? I don't want any of it, but I'd like to know."

"That's fair. I intended to tell you as soon as I knew for sure we had it."

"It's hundreds of dollars, isn't it?"

"I deposited close to five thousand today. And I've got about that much left in Georgia. If we decide to stay for sure, the bank here will make arrangements for the transfer."

"Five *thousand*? In dollars?" she choked out.

"It wasn't what the place was worth. But I probably won't see it again until Bingham's sister dies, and the whole thing goes to probate. And since I'm her heir, too, it didn't make much sense to fight over the money with her. I just wanted out of there."

"But we've got five thousand dollars?"

"Ten. It'll keep us comfortable for a while—at least until I can build up my practice."

"Comfortable. Yes, I'd say so," she managed, still trying to believe it.

"Well, don't you want to see what this is?" he asked, directing her attention to the package in his hand. "Or are you holding out for diamonds?" he teased her.

"A diamond is just a rock, Spence." Unwrapping the gilded tissue, she gasped. "It's beautiful! I wanted a locket all my life, but I never had one—" Her voice dropped to a husky whisper. "Thank you."

"I can't take tears tonight, Laura." Moving behind her, he asked, "Do you want me to put it on for you?"

"I'm never taking it off." Noticing he hadn't said anything about Ross, she asked casually, "I don't suppose you found Mr. Donnelly's uncle, did you?"

Straightening out the fine gold chain, he dropped it over her head, then fumbled with the clasp. "As a matter of fact, I did."

"And?"

"He gave me the only address he had, so I reckon we'll be going to look Ross up in the morning."

"He's still got Josh, hasn't he?"

"Ross's uncle is a real nice fellow, which probably explains why he and Ross are estranged. He said Ross didn't want to learn the banking business enough to work at it."

"You didn't answer me."

"Both of them got here."

"Oh, I'm so glad—so very glad."

"He said Ross found somebody to take Josh right after they arrived."

"Oh . . . no!"

"Yeah. I'll tell you about it on the way there tomorrow. There's nothing we can do tonight."

She swallowed the lump in her throat. "I'm sorry." Reaching up to cover his hand, she sought words to comfort him and found none.

"I'm going to kiss Jessie and turn in. I just don't feel like much of anything tonight. I'll be taking you along to keep me from killing the bastard, Laurie."

"I don't know, Spence. This doesn't look like much of a place for a fine southern gentleman to be living. Are you sure you were given the right address?"

"The uncle said he'd taken to drinking heavily, that he was pretty down on his luck."

Laura eyed the ramshackle boardinghouse skeptically. "I'd say so."

He sucked in a deep breath, then expelled it before he started up the steps. The faded sign above the door bore the pretentious name of Hathaway House. He rapped several times, and when no one answered, he opened the door into a dark, narrow foyer backed up against a steep set of steps.

The only illumination was a row of smoking candles set in chimney sconces following the stairs upward to the landing above. The walls had once been painted a lovely shade of green, but now they were streaked with soot and rusty rain. The pattern on the carpet snaking up the steps had disappeared, exposing the frayed strings of jute underneath. As his eyes grew accustomed to the dimness, Spence saw the bank of small wooden cubicles along the front wall.

Moving closer to them, Laura read the names until she found a yellowed piece of paper with the name R. Donnelly on it. "Well, I guess he's here, all right." Squinting, she tried to make out the faded number penciled above it. "I think it says eight, but it could be a three," she said.

"We'll try the three first." Moving down the dark, dank hall, he found the number on a door, and he knocked. He could hear a stirring of sorts within, then a lumbered gait approached the door, and somebody threw an iron bolt, opening it a crack. A fat, toothless crone looked him up and down before asking, "Hep yeh, dearie?"

"I'm looking for Ross Donnelly—his name's on one of the mailboxes, but we couldn't make out the number."

"I don't know any—what was the name again?"

"Donnelly—Ross Donnelly."

"No McDonalds here—less'n it's Mr. Ross upstairs—that's all anybody knows him by—Ross. I got no notion what he's callin' hisself but that."

"Where is he?"

"Upstairs—second door right of the top."

"Thanks." Taking Laura's elbow, he propelled her toward the staircase.

"He ain't fit comp'ny!" the woman called after them. "He ain't nuthin' but a sot!"

"Well, I guess this is where we find out," he said, hesitating. "It's been a long, hard old journey to get to this."

Stepping past him, Laura banged as hard as she could on the warped slab of wood. "Mr. Donnelly, are you in there?" she shouted.

"I could've done that," Spence muttered.

"Yes, but he might not answer you. You said he was a ladies' man, so I thought I might have the better chance."

"Who's there?" a slurred voice demanded from the other side.

"Laura—Laura Taylor!"

He slipped three bolts before the door swung in. Her eyes took in the disheveled blond hair, the pale stubble on his cheeks, and his rumpled clothes. Seeing her first, he passed a hand over bloodshot eyes. "Who're you? Don't know—"

"Hello, Ross," Spence murmured. "She's my wife." Before the other man could shove the door closed, Spence blocked it with his boot and shoulder. "Now is that any way to treat an old friend?" he asked silkily. "I've come a helluva long way for this visit."

"Jesus."

"That's just plain blasphemy coming from you," Laura declared. Looking him up and down again, she shook her head. "You sure don't look like much of a ladies' man to me," she said.

"I was good enough for Liddy. She—"

His words died on his lips as Spence shoved the door into his face. "Now, wait jus' a minute, Spen—"

His head snapped back from the blow to his chin, and he fell to the floor.

"You want to live, don't you, Ross? Well, I'm going to give you one chance, and one chance only."

"Spence!" Laura shouted.

Ignoring her, he advanced on Donnelly as the man

tried to pull himself up by a faded settee. "Where's my son, Ross?"

"I don't know—dammit, Spence, but you got no right—"

"Oh, I've got every right—I could kill you right here and now, but I'll let you live if I get my boy."

His low voice was much more menacing than any shout. Catching his right arm, Laura cried, "Spence, you can't!—he's too drunk to defend himself!"

"I don't know what you're talking about—I never had your boy."

"You ran off with him and Liddy, Ross. Now, I'm not fooling around—either you tell me where he is, or this is your last day on earth." Shaking free of Laura, Spence doubled up his fist again, and when Donnelly didn't answer, he delivered a hard body blow, sending Ross backward into the settee. "Answer me! Damn you, answer me!"

"She's dead, but I didn't kill her—I swear it! It was cholera—she and the old nigra both got it, and both of 'em didn't make it." Looking up sullenly, he shook his head. "She wasn't worth killing me for. I wasn't the only one—she was usin' me, just like she was usin' you."

"I don't give a damn about Liddy! You hear that, Ross? I don't give a damn about her!" Yanking the man up by the banded collar of a dirty shirt, Spence pulled him within inches. *"Where is he?"*

"I don't rightly know now—"

Laura winced as his head hit the wall. "For the love of God, Spence!"

"You stay out of this—it's between me and him."

Grasping Ross's head by his hair, he banged it into

the wall again, cracking the plaster. "You've got a choice, Ross—your brains or my boy. How many times you want me to crack your head? Five? Ten? More than that? Because I'm going to keep doing it until I know where he is—either that, or you'll die without telling me."

"I'm tellin' you I don't know!" As the wall met his face again, he cried, "Jesus God, Spence—I don't know!"

"He was with you when you got here. Your uncle saw him, and he described him to a T, so don't you lie to me."

"I'm not lying!"

"Then I guess it'll be number four."

"No! I haven't seen him in a year—I swear it."

"What did you do with him?"

"Nothing—he was fine—"

"Where, Ross? Pretty soon that skull of yours is going to crack wide open, but I guess you must figure you've got it coming."

"Turn me loose, Spence!"

Instead, he threw him into the cracked plaster, then watched as the man slid to the floor. Standing over him, his fists still clenched, Spence told him low, "I don't care what I have to do—I'll stomp you—I'll knock your brains out—I'll beat you to a bloody pulp. I promised Laura I wouldn't shoot you, but by God, that's about all I won't do."

Donnelly leaned over to spit blood on the floor. "You've got it all wrong, Spence. It wasn't even my idea—it was Liddy's. I wasn't there two weeks before she was beggin' me to bring her out here. She wasn't

waitin' for you—we were just tools to get what she
wanted— She—"

"I don't care about her, I told you—I don't care
about her."

"But you got to hear it." Pausing to wipe blood
from his mouth, Ross looked up at him through
swelling eyes. "She was like a black widow spider.
She'd spin that web of hers around a man and just
pull him in, and when she was done with him, she'd
spit out his bones. She did it with you, with me, and
with a dozen other fools just like us."

"She's dead, Ross. You hauled her dead body into
McPherson and dumped it; then you took off with
Josh, with him crying all the way out of the fort. You
don't have to tell me anything else, because I *know*.
I saw that grave out there."

"I'm telling you she was using both of us!"

"It doesn't matter now. If you want to tell me
something, you'd better make it something I want
to know."

"It wasn't me she wanted—she just wanted a way
out here. She had somebody else waiting for her."

"Don't tell me lies. I saw the hotel registers in St.
Louis, St. Joseph, and Omaha with my own eyes."

"Oh, I'm not denying I had her—that's not what
I'm saying. I'm saying she played both of us false.
She didn't want me, and she didn't want you. I
should've known what she was when I saw what she
did to her father, and if that wasn't enough to open
my eyes, I sure should've known the day we left
Sally Jamison with the Richardson woman. She
sucked her own folks dry, Spence. She thought she
had Charlie out here waiting, but he was smarter

than we were—he told her he was coming to California, then went somewhere else."

"I don't want to hear any of this—just tell me what you did with Josh."

"I'm gettin' to it. She was bringin' the boy to join him. I didn't find out until she was babblin' mad with fever, but that's how it was. She was cozyin' up to me, lettin' me do what I wanted with her, and I thought it was me she wanted. I should've known it wasn't, because she was the coldest woman I ever had. She opened those legs to get me, but it was like laying a block of ice by the time we got to Missouri. She didn't care about the boy either, you know. She was just using him to get Charlie, but I guess maybe Charlie wasn't buyin' this time. Maybe he knew he wasn't the only one she'd been going down for."

"I don't even know any Charlie, so he's got nothing to do with me."

"He's the boy's daddy, Spence. Cullen caught 'em in the peach orchard one night, threatened to kill 'im if he came around again, told her he was going to lock her up. A day or two later, he brought you home, and she must've thought you'd get her out of there."

"She knew I'd already joined up."

"Maybe she thought she could make you come back, or maybe she liked having you gone—married woman belongs to her husband, not her father. But I don't have to know, anyway. When she was wanting me to bring her out here, she said she was afraid when you came home, you'd find out the boy wasn't yours. She said she was afraid you'd kill her. That's how she started working on me. You ever notice how she'd demand impossible things, then use 'em as an excuse for something else? Until things got bad from the war, she had everything the way she wanted it."

"You're a lying bastard, Ross—a damned lying bastard."

"The kid's daddy is Charlie Madsen, Spence. Big strapping, good-looking fellow who used to train horses for Cullen. At least you came from the gentry, so even if he didn't like the notion, he could stomach you a whole lot better than a horse trainer. But in the end, it was Madsen that got even for both of us. He didn't want her, and he didn't want the kid either."

Afraid Spence's temper was about to explode, Laura moved closer to Ross. "Lying's apt to get you killed right where you sit, Mr. Donnelly. You've got no business ruining lives by saying despicable things you can't prove. We've come over mountains and deserts and fought off Indians to get here, and all we want to know is where we can find Joshua Hardin. The rest of this stuff is just pig slop."

"Well, if it's proof you want, ma'am, I've sure as hell got it. After I heard all that ravin', I went through her things, tellin' myself it wasn't true, that she was just out of her mind, but it was probably the only time she told the truth. She had a letter from him, answering one of hers. And you want the worst of it? I found the lying little bitch's half-finished letter she was writing him after she took sick, telling him the old woman was dead, and she was afraid she was dying, too. She asked him to take care of the kid."

"I'd like to see it."

"And you want the real hell of it all? As mad as I was at her, I brought that kid out here, thinking Madsen would want him. Hell, he wasn't even here! I was stuck with the boy, havin' to look at him every day, when he was the spittin' image of her!"

"Where's the letter, Mr. Donnelly?"

"Over there," he answered with a sweep of his hand.

"Over where?"

"Leave it be—I don't have to see it." His eyes on Ross's battered face, Spence muttered, "You're not worth killing."

"Over where?" Laura asked again.

"I've got a box—over back of the chair. But he won't want to read 'em any more than I did."

"I said I don't want to see it!"

"Well, I do. I don't believe it even exists." Walking across the little room to a worn wing chair, she bent down to find the box. As she opened it, she saw several envelopes.

"It's the one that stinks like a whorehouse," Ross said tiredly. "She even perfumed it up for the son of a bitch."

"It must be the one on top," she said.

"Yeah. Every now and then I take it out and read it to remind myself I was a damned fool. I wanted to believe in her as much as Spence did, and I knew what she was." He laughed mirthlessly, then winced. "I even made myself believe I loved her."

Opening the folded paper, she started to read before she heard the door slam. "Spence! Spence!" Running after him, she watched as he hit the boardinghouse door with his fist, then walked out.

By the time she reached the street, he was nowhere in sight. The only thing there was the horse-drawn cab that had brought them. "Spence, don't listen to him! Come back!"

He was just gone. Standing in the street, she finished the letter, thinking what an idiot Lydia must've been. When she got back up the steep stairs, Ross Donnelly was still sitting in the same place.

"If you want this back, you'll have to tell me where you left Josh."

He looked up morosely. "I guess Spence was the lucky one, wasn't he? Looks like he got over her."

"Yes. We're expecting a baby next winter."

"Yeah."

She could almost feel sorry for him. "You shouldn't have told him. It was a cruel, vicious thing to do to somebody who believed you were once his friend."

"Maybe I wanted to share the misery."

"I'd like to see Josh, Mr. Donnelly. Whether he wants to be or not, Spence may be all that little boy's got left."

"I took him to the Catholic orphanage. I just couldn't look at him anymore."

"Do you have an address for it?"

"In the box." As she lifted the lid again, he sighed. "Damned if Spence doesn't have all the luck. I figured you'd be the one dragging him out the door, glad to wash your hands of the kid."

"I just hope he's still there. We've made a lot of plans for that little boy, and I hope I can see them happen."

When she left, she handed the driver the scrap of

paper with the orphanage's address. "Do you know where this is?"

"Yes, ma'am."

"I'd like to go there before you take me back to the hotel."

Closing her eyes, she leaned back against the padded seat, wondering how on earth a woman like Lydia had managed to pull the wool over so many men's eyes, when she didn't know how to love with her heart or her body. She'd just cheated herself while she was cheating them.

He'd walked for miles, trying to ease his anger and the worst disappointment of his life, until he was too exhausted to go any farther. With the old Presidio behind him, he sat staring across the gray water to the barren island rising from the bay, telling himself he had no son, that he'd chased the breadth of the continent for something that didn't exist. All those days and nights spent in searing heat and bitter cold, crossing plains, mountains, and desert had just gotten him more pain.

Tossing a rock into the water, he watched it disappear, leaving rippling circles on the surface. The boy had been a stranger, he told himself—his love for the child had been based on his blood, not Josh himself. He ought to have known Liddy would lie, he ought to have suspected the early birth of the baby, but even Sally Jamison had said he was small. At barely five pounds and only a few days premature, Josh's arrival hadn't seemed all that unusual. And with the war going on, he hadn't been able to get home for months afterward. It hadn't meant anything to him that everyone kept pointing out how much Josh looked like Lydia. With both parents having dark

hair and with the mother having almost black eyes,
it was to be expected that the boy would favor her
more than Spence.

The irony wasn't lost on him. Lydia had fooled
him into marrying her even before she knew she carried the other man's child; out of spite and perver-
sity, she'd lied to him for four long years, begging
him to come home, knowing she didn't want him,
knowing he couldn't come. She'd toyed with his
mind, whipsawed his emotions, and she hadn't even
cared a snap for him. She'd been giving herself to
other men while he'd lain awake nights, wanting desperately to go home to her. And even now, she'd
been able to reach out from her grave to deliver her
final blow.

A seagull skimmed the water, then dove to fish,
and the quick little splash drew his notice to the re-
flection of a pink haze spreading over the bay. Lifting
his eyes to the dawn, he sighed. "Lord," he said
softly, "Thad Bingham believed with all his heart
that everything has a purpose, so I'd like to think
You brought me out here for some reason. All I know
for sure is I've wasted a year of my life chasing a
dream through hell."

A boat's horn blew in the distance, breaking the
early morning peace, as he realized the pursuit of
one futile purpose had given him more than it had
taken from him. He might not have a son to call his
own, but he had Laura and Jessie and a baby on the
way. Lydia had done him some terrible wrongs, but
without them he'd still be with her, and he would
never have known the warmth, the complete love,

of Laura. He would never have felt the complete, unquestioning trust of her baby.

The war had done about as much damage to him as Lydia, leaving him with a sense of emptiness, of futility, causing him to doubt his calling. All the senseless death, the carnage too terrible for memory, the agony he could not ease, had nearly destroyed him. It had disillusioned him, and it had made him think he'd failed all those men by sending them home less than whole. It had made him think he'd lost the battle.

But unbeknownst to him at the time, Jessie's birth had replanted the seed in his mind that he still had something to give, and then little Jimmy Daniels's badly infected leg and Laura's steadfast belief he'd been ordained to practice medicine had made it grow until he couldn't ignore it. No, despite the sadness and disappointment he felt now, the trip west had been worth the price. He might have followed a false hope, but it had led him to Laura Taylor, and through her, it had redeemed him.

Standing up, he dusted off his pants and took one last look at the rising sun in the water. By now, she was probably frantic with worry, and he had to get back to her. He wanted her to know she and Jessie were enough for him.

Laura heard him unlock the door, but rather than confront him, she lay still, wondering if he'd let her tell him about Joshua, or if he'd be too hurt and angry to listen. He crossed the room silently to look into the cradle at her sleeping daughter. Watching through a veil of lashes, she saw him reach down to pull the little blanket up and tuck it in before he went into the water closet.

Not wanting to wake either of them, Spence undressed before he came out, then crept into bed. Turning over to lie against Laura's back, he lay quietly, drawing warmth from her body. The scent of the French perfume he'd bought her the day they'd married lingered on her smooth skin and in her hair.

He realized suddenly she was too quiet, that he didn't hear the deep, even breathing of sleep. "You're awake, aren't you?" he whispered.

"Yes."

"Did you get any sleep at all?"

"Yes," she said, turning over to face him. "I waited up until past midnight, then decided you were a grown man, and there wasn't anything I could do for you until you came back. I figured you needed to do some thinking."

"I did. I don't know how far I walked, but I wound up clear down by the bay. I kept thinking how bad I felt over Josh, how much time I'd wasted looking for someone who wasn't anything to me."

"He still could be, Spence."

"No. I've accepted it, and I'm ready to go on with my life. I've got you and Jessie, and if the baby gets here and you're both fine, that's about all that matters to me. Maybe the baby will be a boy, but if it's not, I've discovered a partiality for girls, anyway. I may not have a son, but I've got a daughter I'm damned proud of. You don't have to say anything or start crying—I just want you to know I'm all right."

"Did you stop to think Ross could have been lying to you?"

"He wasn't. I didn't have to read any letter to know it. It just sort of added up, anyway."

"I hate to think of a child out there with nobody to love him. He's probably hurting a lot worse than you are."

"Did you read Lydia's letter?"

"Yes."

"It just confirmed what he said, didn't it?"

"Yes." Snuggling against him, she added, "But she could've been lying about that, too, you know. While I hate to speak ill of the dead, I wouldn't put anything past her."

"No. As pretty as she was, it was all on the surface. But I'll say this about her; then I don't want to talk about it any more—she sure knew how to use her looks to her advantage."

Tracing his bare arm with her fingers, she said, "You know, strange as it seems, I almost feel sorry for him."

"You would—you've got a soft heart. Look, I'd rather not waste any more time on either of them." Responding to her touch, he wrapped his arms around her, drawing her into his embrace. "I just want to forget them and think about you."

"As despicable as he is, he loved her, you know."

Rather than repeat himself, he kissed her, stifling conversation. "When did you feed Jessie?" he murmured as his hands found the ribbon at the neck of her gown.

"Midnight."

"Think if we're quiet about it, she'll sleep a little longer?"

"Probably. Spence—?"

"If it's about anything but us, I don't want to think about it. I just want to lose myself in you, and stay there forever."

"As much as I'd like that, it's pretty impossible," she murmured, helping him with the buttons. "I just wonder—"

"You're pretty talky this morning, aren't you?"

"I've just got something on my mind, that's all." As his hand worked her gown up, her breath caught, and she felt that familiar wave of desire flood her body. "But it can wait a while," she managed to whisper. "Right now, there's nothing I'd rather do than this."

"Just don't wake the baby," he reminded her. "I don't want her thinking we're killing each other."

Settling under him, she reached for his neck and parted her lips for his kiss. "Mrs. Hardin, do you have any idea how good you are?" he asked huskily.

Smiling seductively, she said softly, "I'd rather you showed instead of told me. I won't need a lot of time this morning, Spence. I'm downright ready."

As he began kissing her in earnest, her last rational thought was that the other matter wasn't going to be easy. Then he found the dampness between her thighs, and she tried to remember not to moan as she gave herself over to him.

If he hadn't loved her, he would've put up more of a fight about going to church on a weekday. It was a quaint old church she'd discovered, she told him, one where the old Spanish dons had worshipped, and he ought to see it. It didn't make much sense to his Baptist mind for him to sit through a

Catholic Mass neither of them understood, but she'd asked him to humor her, and he would.

"It looks pretty deserted to me," he observed as the driver halted the pair of horses. "They must turn out more on Sunday."

"We're early. I thought we could walk around the grounds first. There's a lovely garden, a school, a convent—things like that—it's really quite remarkable. There's a goodly number of Catholics in California because the Spanish brought missionaries with them."

"You sound like a damned guidebook—I hope you know that."

"I just want you to see it, that's all."

"Thad Bingham would turn over in his grave if he knew I was here," he muttered.

"I thought he was a man of God."

"He was."

"Then he surely wouldn't feel like that. If it hadn't been for monks copying scripture back in the Dark Ages, none of us would have the Bible, including us Baptists. Besides, whether I accept the religion or not, I know the nuns do a lot of good in this world."

"I'm not disputing it. I just never knew you were quite so broadminded, but I guess there's probably some other things about you I don't know yet either."

"Probably a lot of them." She'd always disliked devious people, and she hated being one. No matter how she did this, she had a pretty fair notion he was going to be angry. "That's the convent over there," she told him, pointing. "And that other building is where the nuns work with the children."

Following her direction, he could see the black-robed woman standing before several rows of dark-skinned kids, lining them up to march them somewhere. "They don't look old enough to be in school. That looks more like some sort of nursery."

She drew a deep breath, then looked up at him. "It's an orphanage, Spence. Ross Donnelly brought Joshua here and left him. The only truth he told the nun in charge was that Josh wasn't an orphan. He said the child had been abandoned and had nobody to care for him. He told her that no one wanted him, but that is a lie." She could see his face darken, and she knew she was in for a fight. "I want him, Spence."

"No! I'll do a lot of things for you, but not that!" Shoving his hands in his pockets, he turned and walked away, his anger evident in every step.

"Spence, listen to me!" she cried, hurrying to catch up with him. "He's already lost his mother! Do you want him to grow up without a father, too?"

"He's not mine!" he shouted at her.

"He could be! You don't know that she didn't lie about that just to get herself another man!"

"He had to have slept with her, Laura!"

"So? Does that make it a certainty that that little boy in there is his? She gave herself to you, too!" Lowering her voice, she tried to reason with him. "But whether he has one drop of your blood or not, he's got your name. They've got him listed as Joshua Hardin in their records here."

"Laura," he said hoarsely, "don't ask me to do this, because I can't."

"If you could just see him, it'd touch your heart.

Please, Spence—that's all I'm asking. You don't even have to tell him who you are."

"I'm nothing to him! Don't you understand?—I'm nothing to that kid!"

"All right, maybe you aren't. In that case, I'd like to adopt him."

"*What?* Have you lost your mind?"

"I think he's yours, but if he isn't, we can make him yours, anyway. Spence, he's got black hair like yours. Anybody who looked at him would think he belonged to you."

"Lydia had dark hair."

"And so do you. So what if it's not quite as black as yours—it's real dark. You've just got to see him—you've just got to."

"No!"

"Looking can't hurt anything," she persisted.

"The hell it won't! It'd be just like looking at her, and I'm damned if I want to! A man doesn't want to be reminded he was a fool—can't you understand that?"

"No, I can't. I know you were married to her, and I know you must've wanted her, and I know she was a beautiful woman who had you first, Spence. And I know everybody says he looks just like her. If I used your logic, I wouldn't want to look at him either, just because I'd be reminded she'd lain in your arms first, she'd been the one you whispered all those passionate words to first, but—"

"Then you ought to understand. I don't ever want to see her again."

"She's in the ground back at McPherson. You're not looking at her—you're looking at Joshua Hardin.

You're looking at a little boy who's got your name. If I can stand to do it, you can, too." When he turned away again, she caught his arm, holding him there. "Every morning, you hold Jessie and hug and kiss her, Spence. Doesn't it bother you that she looks like my first husband? When you look at her, do you see me lying underneath him, doing to him what I do to you? If you do, you sure are good at keeping it to yourself, because I could swear you love her as much as if you'd planted her in my body."

"Laura—"

"I can't help it, Spence. He's a handsome little boy, and he's going to grow up in this orphanage. He's going to grow up with black-robed nuns taking care of him instead of a mother. But worst of all, he's going to know his name's Hardin and he isn't an orphan. Don't you think he's going to wonder what he did that was so awful his daddy didn't want him?"

"You're not being fair!"

"If I can love him, you can, too," she said evenly. "Adopt him in your heart, and he'll be yours."

"I don't think I can."

"I haven't asked for anything of you but your love in the months we've been married. I've been as good a wife to you as I know how, and you wouldn't deny it. Well, I'm asking for something now."

He stood there, looking into her upturned face, seeing the tears spilling down her cheeks. "If I look at him, then walk away, he's going to feel worse," he said finally.

"I don't think you'll walk away. I don't think you can."

"If I do, will you still be satisfied to leave it at that—or are you going to pester me to keep coming back?"

"If you can't stand to look at him more than once, I guess I'll have to accept it. But I want you to understand, I'll be coming to visit him. You don't have to come with me, but he's going to know somebody cares about him."

"But you won't mention him to me again?"

Afraid he could see the elation in her face, she had to force herself to meet his eyes. "I won't mention him to you again, Spence. You'll have to ask me to find out how he's doing."

"All right. You've made sure that she's still got a hold on me—I hope you realize that."

"She's dead. She can't do anything to or for anybody anymore, including herself. But you'd better come on—I told the sister in charge we'd be here at four, and we're late."

As they entered the building, there was a waiting area in front of the office door. Sitting ramrod straight, a stern-looking couple waited in chairs by the entrance. As he passed them to take a seat across the room, Spence thought the woman looked as sour as if she'd been drinking vinegar. A young nun sat in the corner, watching several children, trying to keep them quiet.

"If you'll wait here," Laura told him, "I'll see if we can still arrange to see him."

When she entered the office, he could see her talking to someone behind a desk. He wanted to pray the sister wouldn't let them see the child, but he knew Laura would just drag him back tomorrow. No, he might as well get it over and done with. When he looked up again, the door was closed, and he realized he'd been left to fidget while she told the head nun only God knew what.

He didn't notice the child come in and sit down next to him until the kid began swinging his legs, kicking the wooden rung of his seat restlessly.

"I hope I'm not in trouble again," boy said wistfully.

"You get in trouble often?" Spence asked, his eyes on that closed door.

"Some."

Turning to look at him, Spence froze. "Oh, God."

"You in trouble, too, mister?"

It was hard to say anything. "I don't know."

"Well, you put your hand on the table 'stead of holdin' it up, and it don't hurt near as bad when she hits it."

"I'll try to remember that." It had been like looking into Lydia's eyes again. "What did you do?"

"I dunno."

"You must have an idea."

"No. It's always somethin' I didn't know I did."

"Like what?"

The kid gave his chair several kicks before he answered. "Bad words. You're not s'posed t' say hell or things like that, but I must've."

"You don't remember?"

"I get mad."

"Oh."

"You cuss, mister?" the kid asked curiously.

"Some."

"Then you can't let sister hear it, or she'll smack your hand real good."

Casting a sidewise glance at the child, Spence was struck by how sober he was. "So—have you been here a long time?"

"Yeah." Leaning close, the kid confided, "I hope them folk's not comin' to 'dopt me. Don't she look mean?"

"Well, she doesn't look like she'd be much fun to live with," Spence conceded.

"That's what I was thinkin'."

"Do you want to be adopted?"

"I dunno."

"I'd think you'd have to be an orphan to be adopted."

"I dunno." The boy's dark eyes looked at nothing for a moment before he turned them on Spence. "My mama's dead."

"That's too bad."

"I guess so. I'd druther have m' mammy, but she's dead, too."

"Auntie Fan."

"How'd you know that? You got one, too?"

"No. I just knew her, that's all."

"She was a big ole fat mammy, and she didn't 'llow no sassin'. She got mad, even Mama was skeered of her. I liked that ole woman."

"Yeah, so did I."

The office door creaked as it started to open, and the boy jumped down from the chair. "Bye. I gotta go see her."

He looked sturdier than Spence had pictured him, and he had that all-boy look to him, like he could be

handful. And there was no question about it—
Laura hadn't lied when she'd said he was a handsome child. He watched Joshua Hardin cross the
room, trying to see something of himself in that little body.

"Well, Josh, if you're not a sight for sore eyes! You
look even bigger than you did yesterday!" Laura was
in the doorway, bent over, greeting the kid. "You
remember me, don't you?"

"Yes'm. You was comin' back to visit me."

With an elderly nun hovering behind her, she took
the boy's hand. "I've got somebody over here who
wants to meet you, Josh. He'll be real excited," she
added, pointing to Spence.

"No, he won't. I done seen 'im."

"Did you tell him your name?"

"No, 'cause he didn't ask me."

"Well, maybe you'd better."

The kid wasn't looking sober at all now. "I'm not
in trouble?"

"Of course not. I asked if you could come down
to see me."

A sigh of relief escaped him. "I was 'fraid I was
gettin' 'dopted, and she just don't look like a mama."

Stopping in front of Spence, she urged the child,
"Tell him your name."

"Joshua Hardin."

"We've met," Spence managed.

"No, we ain't—not 'xactly. Not till you tell me
yours, we ain't. We just been jawin' some."

"Spence?"

Her eyes were swimming as she looked at him,
and he knew he couldn't disappoint her or the kid.

Bending down close to eye level with the dark-haired, dark-eyed boy, he tried to smile. "My name's Hardin, too—Spencer Hardin. I'm your daddy, and I've been looking for you for a long time. Last time I saw you, you weren't much bigger than a minute, so I don't expect you to remember me."

The kid's eyes grew big like saucers; then an excited grin lit his face. "I been waitin', that's for sure." Wheeling, he ran to the office. "You hear that, Sister 'Lotta? I ain't got to stay!"

The tears spilled over, streaking her face, as Laura whispered, "Thank you."

"He cusses."

"Surely not—he's too little."

"He told me himself."

"Well, we're going to change that." She hesitated long enough to take a quick look at Joshua before she turned back to Spence. "You do want him, don't you? No matter what I told you outside, it's going to take both of us to raise him." Before he could answer, she added quickly, "I know I can love him. I'm halfway there already, because there's just something about him that reminds me of you."

Just then, Josh emerged from the office to make a dashing sweep of the room, whopping, "My daddy's come to get me!" As he passed the other couple, he shouted, "You ain't takin' me home—you got to get you another little boy now!"

"Since he's got the Hardin name, he might as well have the Hardins to go with it," Spence said finally. "But with three children by this time next year, we'll damned sure need to build a house."

As the boy ran past her, Laura scooped him up to

hug him. "I'm your new mama, Josh, but we're going to get along just fine, 'cause we've both got brown eyes. And you know what?—you've even got a little sister, and her name's Jessie."

Setting him down, she looked to Spence. "You can build me a fancy house if you want to, but it's the people in it that'll count to me."

"As long as I've got the money to pay for it, you can have anything you want, Laurie."

"Well, then I want you to give up cussing. All those damns and hells will have to go, or he'll just keep repeating them."

"I'll try." Afraid she'd start crying again, he put his arm around her shoulders. "Well, I guess we round him up and take him home."

"Yes—just as we planned on all the way out here. Sister Carlotta says if you're his natural father, you don't have to sign but one paper. Actually, I think she's more than a little glad to see him go."

"I was afraid of that. I don't know why, but he's not quite what I'd imagined."

"Oh?"

"He may be the spitting image of Lydia, but aside from that, there's nothing about him that reminds me of her. I just hope he's not too much for you."

Under the disapproving eyes of the two nuns and the sour-faced couple, she pulled his head down close enough to kiss him. "Now that I'm not ironing and scrubbing, he'll give me something to work on."

His arms closed around her, holding her tight, as he fought the lump in his own throat. "We've got everything now, Laurie," he told her. "And it's just going to keep getting better. I'll get my practice built up, we'll have a fine house up on the hill, and you'll be the belle of San Francisco."

"As long as you never forget all I really need is you." Leaning back in his arms, she wiped his wet face with her hand. "I think we'd better get him and go before we scandalize these folks so much they won't let us have him. I mean, after all this, we don't want to leave empty-handed now." For a moment, her chin quivered again. "Spence, I'm about as happy as I've ever been," she said, her voice dropping huskily. "I don't ever want to forget how I feel right now."

And neither did he. "Come on," he said gently, "let's go home. It's time he met Jessie."

San Francisco: November, 1871

"Ladies and gentlemen, it is with a great deal of pleasure that I give you a truly remarkable woman who must surely be an inspiration to all of us," the formidable-looking society matron announced. Holding up two leather-bound books, she added dramatically, "By sharing her mother's gift to her, she has enriched the lives of thousands of other women, young and old."

"Who's that, Daddy?" Jessie whispered.

"Shhh—it's Mama," Josh answered for Spence.

Shaking her head, the little girl pointed. "No, it isn't—Mama's over there."

"Ladies and gentlemen, please welcome Mrs. Lane's generous daughter!"

There was a soft rustle of petticoats beneath the skirt of her green silk dress as Laura stood up, smiling, and the polite clapping erupted into a thunderous burst of applause. In the front row, Spence rose to pay his own homage to her, and the chairs emptied behind him. As he watched her move gracefully to the podium, he was too proud of her for words.

"Thank you." Discovering she'd only encouraged them, she smiled and waited a minute before she held out her hands to quiet all those people. "Thank you," she said more loudly. "And now that I have everyone's attention, I'd really appreciate your ears." Pausing, she looked out over the cream of San Francisco society, then her gaze dropped to Spence, Josh, and Jessie, and she waved happily at them.

There was no trace of her earlier nervousness. In fact, she looked like a cat about to dive into the cream pot, Spence decided.

"That's my mama," Jessie told everyone around her.

As the applause tapered off, Laura acknowledged it again. "Thank you so much for your kind welcome. I find myself quite overwhelmed by such generosity of spirit." Clearing her throat discreetly, she began her speech. "While some of you already know me through an acquaintance with my husband, Dr. Spencer Hardin, I suspect those of you who've read *Practical Advice to a Young Woman* or *The Household Companion* have come to meet my mother's daughter, as Mrs. Kendall so aptly introduced me. Yes, I was and am the grateful recipient of all the wisdom in these two books.

"For those of you who've never met me before, my name is Laura Lane Taylor Hardin, and I was born twenty-nine years ago on a small farm near Salisbury, North Carolina. The publisher has kindly described my family as less than prosperous, but the truth is we were downright poor." As a murmur of disbelief rippled through the audience, she nodded. "My daddy dreamed of preaching instead of farming, but he had a family to feed, so he kept plowing the poorest piece of land in Rowan County, hoping the crops would be better the next year.

"My mother was the truly extraordinary one. Born Nellie Mae Parrish nearly twenty years before me in that same little house, she was most certainly poor in material things, but she had her dreams, too— she'd grown up wanting to be a schoolteacher. Unfortunately, my grandfather saw little purpose in educating his sons, and absolutely none in teaching his daughters to do anything but cook, clean, sew, and raise babies. It made no difference to him that she'd taught herself to read, write, and work arithmetic— she still had to stay home to help her mother tend eight younger brothers and sisters.

"She was two months short of her sixteenth birthday when a virulent fever wiped out most of her family—both parents and five of the nine children. An uncle she'd never met came to bury the dead, then took the three younger children back to Tennessee with him. She felt that loss as long as she lived.

"When she married, she wanted a big family of her own, but it never happened. I was born when she was eighteen, then she lost several babies before my brother came along six years after me. When I was eleven, she died of consumption, and the next year, my father passed on also, leaving Danny and me alone.

"Because of what had happened to her own family, Mama made me promise I wouldn't let anybody have Danny, and if you don't think I was scared half to death, then you're sadly mistaken. I was a skinny little girl trying to manage a wild little boy by myself, and I couldn't ask anybody to help me with him. I was afraid if I did, there'd be somebody coming out to take him away from me.

"Now, I'm not going to tell you any hair-raising tales of what it was like for us back then, because unless you're not nearly as smart as I think you are, you've got a pretty good notion. I worked hard, and we got by. Thanks to Mama and God, Danny turned out to be a fine young man, one any of you would have been proud to call yours. When my first husband enlisted in the Confederate Army, Danny joined up, too, and since he was too young to fight, he drove an ambulance until he died in a cholera epidemic.

"Today, whenever I hold my two daughters, Jessie and Nell, or my sons, Joshua and David, I think of Danny and Mama. When she knew she was going to die, my mother filled three journals with everything she wanted me to know. While she never got a chance to see me or Danny grow up, she was there for us in her words. Her wisdom and her foresight guided us through the terrible times, and they guide me still."

Spence looked around him, noting she had her audience spellbound. Several women quietly dabbed at their eyes with handkerchiefs, while more than one man *harrumphed* to clear his throat. As many times as he'd heard her speech himself, it still had the ability to form that lump in his throat. As in just about everything else, she had a gift for this, too.

For more than five years now, she'd shared his bed and enriched his life immeasurably, and yet as well as he knew every inch of her body, she still fascinated him. All of the wealth he'd gained from his practice and she'd gotten from the books hadn't really changed her. She had a grand house on the hill, expensive clothes, a fancy carriage, and social position now, but her anchor was still him and their children.

And while she'd let him hire a maid and a housekeeper, she'd refused to have a nursemaid for the children, insisting on taking care of them herself. Most days when he came home, she'd either be chasing six-year-old Jessie and four-and-a-half-year-old David barefoot across the lawn, or she'd be sitting in her old rocker, singing baby Nell to sleep. Whenever she had to travel to promote the books, she took her family with her, saying she didn't mind letting the hotels provide someone to watch them for a few hours, but strangers weren't going to raise her children.

His gaze strayed to Josh, and he couldn't help thinking what he'd have missed if she hadn't dragged him to the orphanage that day. Nearly ten now, the boy didn't even remind him of Lydia anymore. Laura's patience and love had made him her son.

It was funny how things had turned out. The once-boisterous Josh had developed a passion for books, while Jessie had become a real tomboy with David trotting into mischief right behind her. Elinor, whom he'd nicknamed Nell after Laura's mother, wasn't two yet, but if he had to guess, he'd say she was going to take after Jessie.

"Five years ago, I let my husband read Mama's journals, and he thought it rather selfish of me to keep them to myself. He said her advice was as valu-

able now as it was when she wrote it, and he thought
there'd be hundreds of young women who would
find it useful. Well, he was right about everything
but the numbers."

"Daddy, she's tellin' 'em about you," Jessie
whispered.

He looked up as Laura paused to look out over
her audience. "Mama's first journal, published as
Practical Advice to a Young Woman three years ago,
has been read by thousands, not hundreds, and judging by the letters sent to the publisher, the words of
an incredibly honest woman from backwoods North
Carolina have reached out to touch girls and women
of all stations. And it looks as though *The Household
Companion* will be an equal success. I am so very,
very proud of my mother, and so grateful for the
love and wisdom she left me. Thank you so very
much for appreciating her."

As she turned away from the podium, Spence
watched the crowd erupt in deafening applause.
Standing, he clapped as hard as anyone, while Jessie
tugged on his coat.

"Daddy, I can't see anything!"

"Stand on the chair, Jess," Josh advised her.

Instead, Spence lifted her, then reached for his
son's hand, holding it tightly.

"Ladies and gentlemen—please, may I have your
attention?" Pounding the gavel, the woman who'd
introduced Laura waited for the crowd to hush.
"Please—I have an announcement to make!" she finally all but shouted. As the applause began to sub-
side, she hammered the podium again. "For those of
you who'd enjoyed hearing Mrs. Hardin—" Holding

up the books, she noted loudly, "For those of you who have not yet had the privilege of reading these remarkable works, they are available for purchase in the lobby. And for those of you who aren't aware of it, Mrs. Hardin donates half of the income from both books to a local orphanage."

As the crowd filed out, Spence made his way to the stage. "That's my mama," Jessie told everyone they passed.

"Dr. Hardin!"

"Huh?" Spence swung around impatiently to face a stranger.

"I just wanted to say your wife's quite a woman to have overcome such a dreadful beginning," the man told him. "I admire her very much."

"So do I."

"She's my mama," Jessie said again.

"And who's this fine young man?" the fellow asked, noticing Josh.

"I'm her oldest son."

When they finally got to the stage, Laura was waiting. "You were magnificent," Spence declared before she could ask.

"You don't have to tell me that."

"I meant it. Judging by the way everybody was stampeding for the lobby, I'd say Sister Carlotta ought to be very happy."

"She prays for me, you know." Turning to Josh, she asked, "Would you like to go with me to visit her tomorrow? She always asks about you."

"She probably wants to know if I'm still cussing," he muttered.

"Well, you aren't, are you?"

"No."

"He still says hell sometimes," Jessie spoke up.

"Jess—"

"But not very often," the little girl added quickly.

"Come on—it's getting pretty late," Spence murmured. "I know two kids who belong in bed right now."

"If you want to avoid the crowd, there's a door behind the stage that goes outside," Laura said. Looking up at him, she added huskily, "I wouldn't mind retiring early myself, Spence."

And as he looked into those gold-flecked eyes, he felt his pulse race, his mouth go dry. "Neither would I."

In the carriage on the way home, she rested her head on his shoulder while she listened to Josh tell her about a woman in a big hat. Spence closed his eyes, thinking what a lucky man he was. His arm tightened around her, pulling her closer. Turning his face into her fragrant hair, he whispered for her ears alone, "I love you heart, soul, and body, Laura Hardin."

Snuggled against him, she felt no need for words. He knew what he meant to her, and when they got home, she was going to show him. Again.